Lucifer's Game

LUCIFER'S GAME

CRISTINA LOGGIA

LUME BOOKS

LUME BOOKS

Published in 2021 by Lume Books
30 Great Guildford Street,
Borough, SE1 0HS

ISBN 978-1-83901-284-6

Typeset using Atomik ePublisher from Easypress Technologies

www.lumebooks.co.uk

ABOUT THE AUTHOR

Cristina started her career as a newspaper reporter for *L'Eco di Biella* and *La Provincia di Biella*, in Piedmont, Italy. After a spell running the press office of an MP, she moved to London, where she worked for several years as a public affairs and media relations professional, advising major multinational corporations on communications campaigns. Cristina read English Literature and Foreign Languages at the Catholic University of Milan, Italy. Writing and reading have always been her greatest passion. *Lucifer's Game* is her first fiction novel. She currently lives with her husband in Berkshire, United Kingdom.

For my mother and my husband

PROLOGUE

Gazala, North Africa, June 1942

Erwin Rommel removed the goggles that had been sheltering his eyes from the desert sand, stepped out of his Horch armoured cabriolet and walked to the edge of the cliff perched over the East Mediterranean Sea. He was a sober man, of medium height. His sharp, inquisitive eyes scanned the horizon as if his next military target were due north, rather than west. His gaze remained fixed across the water.

In a day that was coming to an end, the General inhaled a deep breath of the fresh and humid air blowing from the sea, a sudden relief from the heat of a scorching and unforgiving North African sun. His lungs felt an immediate balsamic cooling. The evening dew was starting to appear on the few blades of surviving grass. He could hear the soft backwash of the waves crashing on the narrow beach at the bottom, foamy and shining in the glow of the last rays of light.

Von Mellenthin, his intelligence officer, had travelled with him up there, just outside Gazala, after a twenty-minute car trip on the road along the rugged east coast of town. He handed the General a cup of mint tea that Rudolf Schneider, Rommel's driver, had rushed to pour from a field thermos as soon as they stopped. The Desert Fox, as he came to be known for his daring manoeuvres that routinely outwitted an enemy in far greater number, had adopted this habit from the Berber tribes that had been roaming over those lands for centuries. He found the drink quite refreshing, despite the heat of the liquid.

Von Mellenthin lit a cigarette, observed the spiral of smoke that came out from his lips, then looked at Rommel. He wondered if a Roman General, or a Persian, or even a Carthaginian Commander before him, had stood in that same vantage point to admire the vastness of the sea, while plotting his next move. Time and time again, Libya had been a land of conquest by the powerful empires of the ancient past, and now it was the turn of the mighty Third Reich.

Rommel turned around and began to observe the hauntingly beautiful dunes of the desert. A hawk was screaming, high in the silent, clear sky, which was rapidly turning to a deeper blue now. What a stark contrast with its earlier blinding whiteness, the clouds of dust and the infernal noise of the heavy artillery in the battle that had raged until a few hours before.

The Panzers of the German Afrika Korps and the Italian Ariete Division tanks had defeated the Eighth Army of the British Forces, which was left flying in disorder. In a relentless attack, his men, fighting like devils, had conquered the all-important Gazala line, west of Tobruk, taking a substantial number of enemy prisoners. A landslide, an overwhelming victory, achieved despite the desperate situation of his supply lines: Rommel had been receiving a third of what was necessary.

That's what was on his mind right now.

And he was furious.

If the Axis forces were to conquer Egypt, establishing there the solid stronghold necessary to capture the strategic oil fields of the Middle East, that vital flow had to reach full capacity.

Instead, the convoys arriving from Italy had been sunk by the attacks of the Royal Air Force with astonishing regularity. Troops, guns, ammunition, vehicles, medical supplies, food, and above all, petrol, were all sent to the bottom of the sea, slowing down the ability to push forward at the speed the General was capable of.

The situation was nothing short of disastrous.

'I should be well on my way to Cairo by now,' Rommel said sourly to Von Mellenthin. 'Instead, we are forced into a stop, stuck here, waiting for the next shipment to Tripoli. If only we had adequate, uninterrupted and secure supplies, I would probably be there already, looking at the Pyramids from General Auchinleck's felucca on the Nile.'

He felt frustrated that the thrust of his action was curbed by shortcomings beyond his control.

'There's something very wrong going on in Rome and I am determined to get to the bottom of it. I want quick and decisive action to sort it out, once and for all,' he said sharply.

Or quite frankly run the risk of having to get out of North Africa altogether, he reckoned, but kept that thought to himself.

Von Mellenthin was well aware of the problem. Based on a number of reports he had received over the past weeks, he had conveyed to the General his suspicions of leaks in the Italian security, which meant that the route of the convoys had been passed onto the British, enabling them to be so precise in targeting and sinking the ships.

'Mein General, I have been assured that renewed efforts have been made to narrow down the list of possible suspects, whose identification could be imminent.' But he knew that Rommel wasn't going to be satisfied with that.

'I do not have the luxury of time for the culprits to be found,' he snapped. 'Arresting those responsible might take too long. In the meantime, we need to make sure we get those supplies right now! I don't want another ship to get sunk, for God's sake. We can't afford it.'

Rommel had a hard, practical streak, almost businesslike. Being a man of rapid decisions, he preferred swift solutions.

He continued. 'I have discussed a plan with the Fuehrer; he agrees that's the best course of action. And I have spoken with Kesselring this afternoon.'

Field Marshal Albert Kesselring, the Wehrmacht Commander-in-Chief South, was stationed in Rome, Italy's capital, and responsible for all operations in the region.

'He reassured me that Goering would give full air cover. I've made plans for a meeting with them both. I need to see them personally to seal the deal.'

The support of Hermann Goering, Commander-in-Chief of the Luftwaffe, the German Air Force, was equally crucial.

That must have cost both men quite something, Von Mellenthin thought, for Rommel had gone straight to Adolf Hitler to demand that his high officers, of a rank superior to the General of the Afrika Korps, would give him full backup.

Rommel had such direct access to the Fuehrer. Hitler adored Rommel. The Desert Fox was cunning, daring, brave and possessed an untiring will: he incarnated the perfect fighting animal, proving to be as such since his very first battle, standing out for his great grasp of strategy, his ruthless execution of orders, his indomitable spirit. But what counted for Hitler most of all, was that Rommel seemed to be unstoppable: he was winning, winning and winning again. The Fuehrer felt ecstatic every time news was announced to be arriving from the North African front: he knew they would not disappoint.

Hitler had promoted Rommel from Colonel to General in a matter of months. The man had become his favourite General.

That did not go down well for a few in Hitler's General Staff, including Kesselring and Goering, although nobody ever questioned the decisions of the leader of the Nazi Third Reich. But they secretly snubbed Rommel.

'I will go to Rome with my personal aircraft tomorrow. I've already given the order that my Junker be ready to leave,' Rommel said. 'Colonel Friedrich Schaeffer will go with me. You will brief him as soon as we get back to camp. I do not want anyone else to know the reason for my sudden departure; that's why I wanted to speak to you in private.'

Von Mellenthin nodded to the General and they started discussing all the details of the mission. The intelligence officer dared to ask, 'Sir, do you believe that Mussolini will accept handing over control of such an operation so easily?'

Von Mellenthin knew the sensitivity of that matter, for his secret reports told him how enraged the Italian Prime Minister had been at the prospect. It was an issue of pride, and losing control meant admitting that once again, he might need to step back and let a German do the job, due to the failures on his side.

Rommel replied, 'Benito Mussolini was convinced by our Fuehrer in less than half an hour of discussion.'

The Duce, too, in the end, could not say no to his powerful Axis ally, Adolf Hitler.

A light breeze started to pick up. Von Mellenthin noticed a file of camels in the distance: they were the Meharians, part of the colonial troops that supported the Italians in Cyrenaica and Tripolitania, their colonies in Libya. The Italians had been so demoralised before General Rommel was sent to their aid, after their ruinous defeat by

13

the Commonwealth forces. The Italians once more were proving to be the weak link in the critically important task of ensuring that supplies arrived timely and intact across the Mediterranean. The fortunes of the war in North Africa were depending on that.

'The Gestapo is waiting for your visit at the Embassy. They will be joining forces with the Fascist police to find out who and where the intelligence is leaking from,' he commented, adding, 'They intend to establish how it is then passed on to the enemy. They have reasons to believe the Vatican might be involved.'

'Well, let's hope that the devil is on our side then,' Rommel said, in a half serious, half funny tone.

Both men walked towards the car and got in. 'Drive on, Rudolf,' ordered the General.

Schneider started the engine of the Horch to take Rommel and Von Mellenthin back to base.

PART I

ALL HELL BREAKS LOOSE

'Now this is not the end. It is not even the beginning of the end. But it is, perhaps, the end of the beginning'.

Winston Churchill

CHAPTER 1

Rome, July 1942

At this point, Cordelia was certain that nobody was following her. And now, with the spires of Castel Sant'Angelo in sight, the Vatican was just a few minutes away. I am almost there, she thought, reassured, but still slightly lengthening her stride. Cordelia was heading to a secret appointment in the Holy City with Father Colombo, an old friend of the family, who had promised to help her escape from Rome under a false identity. Although desperate to get there, she resisted the temptation of taking her car. It might have been quicker, but as not many women drove an automobile in Rome, she was afraid to run into a military patrol, be stopped and perhaps even taken to the Fascist command for questions. The last thing she needed was for them to start enquiring about her whereabouts and log her name to an official document at the station.

That morning, Cordelia had woken up quite early, quickly put on her robe and had left her home in the dépendance of the hotel, Palazzo Roveri. Cosier and more private, it was originally the former dwelling of the chief mistress of Cardinal Roveri, who could visit his mistress in total secrecy through a passage that connected it with the main building.

Looking at the palace's glorious stone façade, she marvelled again at how successful it had become in a matter of a few years.

I have to leave all this, possibly forever, Cordelia thought with regret.

She crossed the scented, manicured garden and went straight into the kitchen through the back door. Alma, the cook, a dark-haired stocky lady in her late fifties, had already arrived, and the kettle on the stove was spreading a fragrant smell of freshly brewed black coffee. Flaminia, the waitress and hotel maid, was late as usual, but today Cordelia didn't mind; in fact, it was better that way.

'I have to go out this morning and might not be back for a couple of hours, Alma,' she said.

Although the tone of her voice was calm, Alma knew her too well and could read a trace of tension on Cordelia's face, but being a person of few words, she said nothing, and poured her an abundant cup of the aromatic liquid. Thanking Alma, Cordelia sat down and sipped it slowly, while enjoying the cool breeze coming in from an open window. It had been quite hot over the past week, and despite the storm of the night before, the weather was already warming up again.

Romans were already out in good numbers in the streets. It looked all so normal, with people going about their business, despite the war. But it wasn't normal, not at all. Everyone needed to have ration cards to go shopping now, a system put in place by the regime, right after Mussolini made the ill-fated decision to enter the war in 1940. Finding certain types of food and other goods was becoming more difficult and, therefore, wives were rushing out of the door as early as possible to make sure they got at least the basics for the day. Cordelia could easily melt into the crowd.

She finished her coffee, got up and returned to her dwelling to get dressed.

Choosing to appear as ordinary as possible, Cordelia picked a light blue cotton skirt and a white blouse.

She looked at her image in the mirror: a bit taller than the average, with an hourglass figure and long voluptuous legs, she didn't want to attract the usual attention from men. She was twenty-three years old now, but since she had reached her late teens, she had noticed heads turned when she went by. She hid her long, golden-brown hair under a silk headscarf, crossed it under her chin and tied it behind her neck. She grabbed her bag and slipped out of the side door of the walled garden.

Instead of taking a more direct route, which would have brought her to Father Colombo's house inside the Vatican in less than thirty minutes, Cordelia decided to go a different way. It would take longer to get there, but if somebody was following her, she would have the chance to spot her pursuer. She had had the sensation she was being watched of late, although Cordelia never really saw anyone to justify that suspicion. It was real yet immaterial at the same time, as if a shadow was behind her every now and then.

Perhaps I am becoming paranoid, she thought, shivering.

At the corner of Via dei Tigli, she looked furtively over her shoulder, crossed the road and stopped in front of a shop. She glanced at the images reflected in the window, but saw no one suspicious. Cordelia became aware of the sound of her footsteps on the stone pavement as she walked on. A couple of Fascists in their black uniforms were stationed at the corner of Piazza Abate so she chose to go around the opposite side, keeping an eye on them. They continued to chat between each other, not seeming to notice her. As she was halfway round, they entered the café on the corner, disappearing into its dimly lit interior.

She walked for about an hour, avoiding the main squares, doubling up a couple of times, only to retrace her steps as soon as she was sure she didn't have anyone tailing her. She finally arrived on the bank of the river Tiber and crossed it on the Ponte Vittorio Emanuele II. Instead of taking Via della Conciliazione, which led directly to St Peter's Square, she headed for the side entrance of Porta Sant'Anna, guarded by the Lansquenets, the Papal Swiss Guards, in their glorious medieval striped uniforms. Entering the Vatican, she felt her shoulders relax a bit – she was in neutral territory.

The Holy See and the Republic of Italy had agreed the incorporation of Vatican City as an independent state under the religious and political sovereignty of the Pope with the Lateran Pacts in 1929. Since then, the current head of the Roman Catholic church, Pope Pius IX, with the agreement of Mussolini, had declared the city completely neutral in the matter of all international relations.

At the oratory of Sant'Egidio a Borgo, Cordelia turned right in Via dei Pellegrini and knocked on the heavily carved wooden portal just beside a small stone fountain used for centuries by the pilgrims visiting the Holy City.

Brother Filippo, the taciturn assistant of Father Colombo, an old bald friar, wearing the long dark habit of the Franciscan Order, was quick to open it. He gave her a warm smile and with his gentle, soft voice said, 'Come in. Come in, child.' Smiling back, she swiftly entered, closing the door behind her. Once inside, the tension almost instantly abandoned Cordelia. It was as if the imposing oil portrait of a Mary Magdalen with open arms, gracing the simple entrance hall, whispered to her: *Welcome. You're safe here. You can rest now.*

'Father Colombo is waiting for you, Miss Olivieri,' he said.

They climbed the stone staircase and reached the first floor. Father Colombo was working in his smaller and more private study. The room looked Spartan, with its white walls, an oak desk by the window, and two old armchairs that faced each other in front of a fireplace. A large number of books in various languages and of different subjects were lined up on the shelves arranged across the study. Many were quite old tomes, some ancient. Works varied from *The Confessions of Saint Augustine*, to *Homer's Odyssey*, Shakespeare's *Othello*, a couple of editions of the Kabbalah, and then Stendhal, Dickens, Leonardo Da Vinci, the Coran. Father Colombo was an avid reader. The only sign of luxury was a thick oriental wool rug that a parishioner returning from his pilgrimage in the Holy Land insisted he accepted as a gift.

The whole room smelled of the freshly picked lavender flowers Brother Filippo had placed in a vase sitting on the windowsill the day before.

'Come here, Cordelia. I am glad you have arrived without delay. Sit down,' Father Colombo said. 'I've asked Brother Filippo to prepare us one of his miraculously relaxing herbal teas.'

Brother Filippo, an expert in medicinal herbs, smiled, secretly pleased by Father Colombo's appreciation of his knowledge. He left them and silently hurried to the kitchen to prepare his potion.

Father Colombo was an imposing man, over six feet tall, with a thick white mane and a flowing beard, which he had grown since he was a young man to cover a bad scar on the right side of his cheek. With piercing blue eyes surmounted by bushy eyebrows, the Franciscan friar was reminiscent of a Biblical, almost Messianic figure, a Moses perhaps, or even the Almighty God himself. At least that was the impression that Cordelia had been given from the very first time she saw him. Sometimes she wondered how old Father Colombo was, as his looks had hardly changed over the years.

He glanced outside the window, then drew the curtains and sat in front of her. Father Colombo was well aware of how dangerous it was for Cordelia to stay in Rome any longer, especially in light of what had happened in the last few days. But the main menace for Cordelia had been growing far more serious for some time now: her mother was a Jew, and by definition of the Racial Laws declared by Benito Mussolini in 1938, although her father was not Jewish, she would be considered a Jew as well. If the regime discovered her descent, it could have critical, if not mortal, consequences.

Father Colombo was acutely aware of what the Nazi regime had been perpetrating against the Jews, of the beatings, of their properties and businesses destroyed or confiscated, of the humiliating treatments, incarcerations and murders. Some sinister rumours about concentration camps had started to emerge. Initially, this sporadic news trickled out of Germany, Austria and Poland, but then some local priests travelling from there had made full accounts to the Vatican of what was going on in those countries. Mussolini bowed to that atrocious policy by declaring the Racial Laws, and although nothing to that scale had happened in the Kingdom of Italy thus far, measures were put in place to marginalise Jews from public life.

Was it just a matter of time before this country saw that tragedy materialise here, on its own streets?

Father Colombo reckoned it could be imminent. Cordelia's departure was a matter of urgency now.

'The documents I have been promised for you are going to be delivered very shortly. You will travel under the name of Sister Lilia Maria of the Order of the Clarisses,' Father Colombo said. 'A letter signed by the Abbess of the monastery of Jesus Sacred Heart here in Rome will say you are a missionary travelling to Angola to join the convent down there, to replace a nun who recently died of yellow fever. The Abbess is an old acquaintance of mine and she has already been briefed to back the story, should she be asked to confirm your authorisation papers. You will board a Portuguese mercantile ship docking in the port of Anzio. It's less busy than Ostia and has a lower level of controls. The vessel will stay in port just for one day and then set sail for Angola.'

Angola was a Portuguese colony, part of a neutral empire, so it would not raise any question as a destination as far as the Fascist regime was concerned. Nor would anyone boarding a ship under that flag be closely scrutinised.

'In reality, the vessel will be heading back to Lisbon, where you will be safe. And from there you can embark for the Americas,' Father Colombo went on explaining.

Cordelia, hearing of her new identity and the escape plan for the first time, felt both elated and saddened: it was all becoming very real now. Since that day back in late April, when she had asked Father Colombo for help to find a safe passage, Cordelia had been waiting for weeks to know. She knew she was asking for a miracle, for only desperate cases were considered for help.

Father Colombo continued. 'Here's what you will have to do. The day before the arrival of the mercantile, which is every other Monday, you will go to the Church of the Holy Spirit at the corner of Via dei Penitenzieri and Via Borgo Santo Spirito to attend the morning mass: it's a stone's throw from the Vatican and a lot of nuns stop there to confess before going to the Angelus, the Sunday's prayer of the Pope in St Peter's Square,' he said. 'I will be waiting for you in one of the confessionals with a small case containing your Clarissa habit, the cap, a big rosary to be arranged around your waist, a pair of sandals – Poor Clare nuns do not wear shoes – and your documents, which you will hide under the long skirt. Get changed and leave your old clothes in the confessional booth. Brother Filippo will take care of their disposal.'

They were briefly interrupted when Brother Filippo arrived with his tisane; he poured two cups and left the room again.

Father Colombo went on explaining that Cordelia would then join the many congregants gathering for the Pope's mass, and once it was over, she would board a coach to Anzio. There she would spend the night in Nino Conti's home, a fisherman and trustworthy friend who was living near the harbour; Nino would take her to the port in the morning the day after, where she would board the ship and sail to a safe haven.

Everything had been planned in meticulous detail to make sure there was no room for error, that everything would go smoothly, so that it was a sure thing. It was a familiar route that had been tested before. His contact was a master of such matters; so far he had never failed to deliver. And in fact he had already proved a determinant on something of crucial importance for Cordelia.

The Gestapo, the secret state military police of the Nazi Third Reich, had set up office in the German Embassy of Via Tasso in Rome. And with their arrival, a magnifying lens was being applied to all citizens with renewed energy. The net was widening fast: the Italian Ministry of Race was now looking at people who might have a Jewish lineage to add to the lists. They were making sure that no Son of Israel could go unaccounted for, stepping up the pace of this work.

But despite this imminent danger, Cordelia's name hadn't come up to be investigated, as a dark and powerful hand sheltered her descent from those prying eyes.

For now.

Thank God, Father Colombo thought.

But it was Lucifer that Father Colombo had to thank.

CHAPTER 2

Rome, June 1942 – a month earlier

Lucifer was in a foul mood.

He had been the victim of such a mood for days now, from the very moment he had heard the news. He was furious when his boss told him, but of course he gave no hint of his emotions.

Could he continue his mission now? He strongly doubted it, and in any case, it might prove very difficult.

And perhaps sticking around might pose a threat to all he had achieved so far. He couldn't risk being discovered, nor risk revealing what he was, and did, for that matter.

Ironically, Lucifer had become the victim of his own accomplishments. He had been quite successful at his job and was getting better at it. He had proved to be a cool, smooth operator. He also knew that his was a dangerous game to play, and even though gambling was one of his greatest pleasures – he thrived on the rush of adrenaline that extreme peril unleashed in his veins – this cat and mouse exercise could suddenly take a turn for the worse.

In a way, Lucifer was startled he had got away with it so far. It was probably time to call it a day, and move on to his next victim, so to speak. He was sure he'd be sent after one, when this mission came to an end.

Lucifer was sitting at his desk on the first floor of the Fascist command in Piazza Alberini, his black-booted feet firmly planted on the windowsill. He was a member of the Blackshirts, the violent militia of Benito Mussolini: a paramilitary wing of the Fascist Party. Formed in imitation of the Roman Army, the *squadristi* were staunch, loyal supporters of their creator, the Duce himself. This voluntary corp was in charge of leading the fight against all enemies of the State.

The State being Mussolini, of course.

Lucifer found the notion of having been assigned to that organisation almost ludicrous, as he was working precisely against the regime of the Italian Dictator. But as the master of deception that he was, nobody remotely suspected him, at least until now. He had been careful; his existence depended on it.

Lucifer had blended in perfectly since joining the Blackshirts, quickly climbing the ladder to be appointed as the right hand of an arrogant and influential officer, in charge of the supply operations for Libya and North Africa. He had learned to become a skilled adulator, quite adroit at ingratiating himself to people whose vanity fed on the flattery and sycophancy of those around them.

Lucifer had been chosen for that job after a careful selection. His superiors had to be sure he wouldn't fail.

Lucifer was a British spy.

His real name was Peter Lord.

He was recruited after Scotland Yard released him from prison almost fifteen months ago now. The release was subject to his acceptance to work for Cecil De Clerc, a high commander of the SOE, the

Special Operations Executive. This was a secret organisation created in 1940 by Winston Churchill to operate in Axis territories, whose operatives had the task to infiltrate, gather intelligence, disrupt and deceive the enemy.

Lucifer, the code name he had been given since becoming an agent, was the son of an affluent Yorkshire merchant, whose family fortunes dated back to Victorian times. His grandfather was a captain of the East India Company, whom, upon leaving the army, started a lucrative pursuit. Using the relationships built as an officer, facilitated by his fluency in the local native languages and dialects he had a natural inclination to learn, he started trading spices, silk, cotton and tea, as well as a variety of other goods, from India to England. The business grew exponentially over the years, turning him into one of the richest merchants of the Kingdom. So much so that he built a marvellous, grand mansion back home, a crowning sign of his new social and financial status, granting him a place among the great and the good of English society. Although he sent his son and daughters there to get an education and eventually live, he was never able to make the permanent transition to a colder climate again. The truth was that his grandfather loved the ease of colonial life, with its pleasures, lascivious women and the freedoms that money could buy, far from the rules that Victorian morality dictated back home. It was a place where people, without necessarily having a noble background, could become a new breed of rulers, not only aspiring to be rich, but in the spirit of the true self-made man, could actually turn that dream into reality.

His grandson inherited his taste for an easy life as well as his ability to master languages, build fruitful relationships and, in some way, his entrepreneurial spirit. But sadly, not his business work ethics. Peter preferred to spend time betting his family fortunes in the casinos of

Monte Carlo and the nearby Italian Riviera, in Sanremo, and then heading all the way to the West Indies, to sample the gambling houses on that side of the pond.

He loved the thrill of the games, the crowd, the days without end, the drinking and the women. His father warned him he was turning into a Sybarite. And he believed him.

Peter won a lot, lost a lot, won a lot again. It was a constant up and down, with no sign of it coming to an end. But with this uncertainty, he often asked for loans from his father. When his desperate old man finally decided to turn off the tap, Peter had no choice but to return home, only to come to the conclusion that the only way to continue this lifestyle was to take a permanent advance of his future inheritance. So, one day, he decided to pay a visit to his father's study. It was such a beautiful room, with dark oak panels on all walls, and a gigantic oil portrait of his grandfather towering above the fireplace. He slipped behind the desk and opened the cupboard on the right side. There was the safe he'd known about since he was a child.

He picked the lock, grabbed a huge sum of money, his father's precious watches, a few of his mother's jewels, and then disappeared. He travelled back to Italy, choosing to settle in Venice – there was a casino there, of course – where he changed his name to Count Montefiore, pretending to be the heir of a wealthy Argentinian family with Italian ancestors.

He impersonated this new character with gusto. Actually, he was surprised at how easy it was to play an act, and a convincing one too. People, he quickly discovered, were happy to offer credit to such a high-level member of society. Eventually though, he ran out of luck and money again, and, to escape his creditors, he fled back to England, unaware that his father had reported his burglary to the police. When he was finally caught, Peter tried to plead for his father's forgiveness. But his father preferred the law to teach him a lesson this time: he was thrown in jail for theft.

And that's where Cecil De Clerc found him. Peter hadn't gone unnoticed during his years on the casino circuit. One of De Clerc's friends, Sir Charles Arbuthnot, who had heavily lost to Peter a number of times, was with Cecil when he read the news of his arrest in *The Times*. Sir Charles talked extensively about Peter, and Cecil learned of his coolness, of his ability to put up the most convincing poker face, and how he could mingle with the rich and famous. He learned of his ability to manipulate people who could potentially be in a position to lend him money or hide him from creditors or women who became too attached. Cecil made further investigations, discovering how resourceful Peter was, and how he never seemed afraid to go for the next challenge. Peter was a cunning and smooth operator. And he had a charming playfulness about him that fascinated both men and women.

For Cecil, Peter was perfect material. He could use such qualities, for SOE operatives were mostly unusual people with all sorts of talents. People with strong nerves, willing to take incredible, often life or death risks, make impossible bets, and dare against the odds.

Peter fitted that profile marvellously well, almost like a glove. Cecil was sure that playing a high-octane game would be quite appealing for such an individual, while remaining calm under pressure. Panic often resulted in fatal mistakes.

After all, winning the war was the greatest gamble of all.

Britain was not winning and the country was being pushed to the brink of an abyss. Cecil needed to play all the cards he was dealt to avoid the frightening prospect of seeing the British Empire falling over that edge.

So he made a bet and went to see Peter Lord at the prison one morning of a very cold February in 1941. By the evening of that same day, Peter was on his way to one of the SOE training camps in Hertfordshire. Cecil had been delighted with the reports he was regularly getting from the trainers; his instincts had proved right. Peter was a fast learner and graduated top of his class. He was now ready to be sent beyond enemy lines, infiltrate, blend in and disappear. He had done that before; he would do it now for King and Country.

It was a Monday in May when Peter was sent back to Cecil's office in London. He was going there for his first briefing. He approached a grey building not far from Green Park, reached the third floor and found Cecil in a corner room, at the end of the corridor. They greeted each other; then Cecil dived straight into his instructions. Peter was to become operative with immediate effect and sent into the field, into enemy territory.

'Your code name will be Lucifer, Peter,' Cecil told him. 'The Lord becomes the Devil – I thought you'd appreciate the irony of the antithesis.'

Peter stared at him and grinned. 'I find it very appropriate, Sir.'

Looking at Peter, Cecil couldn't agree more. He found it funny that war had given that young man the opportunity to do something good with his ability and skill set developed on the gambling table, especially in service of King and Country.

De Clerc went on to explain his mission. 'You are being sent to Italy tomorrow, to its capital to be precise. You will be parachuted on the hills near Castel Gandolfo,' he said, showing the location on a map.

'From there, get the train to the capital. Once you arrive in Rome, you will go to the church of Santa Chiara, at the junction of Via della Rotonda and Via di Torre Argentina, and ask to confess.'

'I haven't been a devil for a day and you already want me to ask for redemption,' Peter said wryly.

'Not at all, in fact, we hope that in the face of the enemy you would be considered to have committed the greatest sins. We want you to cause a lot of damage to the forces of the Axis,' Cecil replied.

'Every Friday afternoon, Father Pietro Colombo, a Franciscan friar, is at that church to hear the confessions of worshippers before the evening mass. You will be among them. Once you enter the confessional, you will tell him these words: *May the Black Virgin with three golden crowns bless you*, to which you should get this answer: *Thanks to the Madonna of Oropa*. That's the confirmation you are talking to the right person. Only then will you tell him your code name. He knows you are coming. Father Colombo will have your instructions.'

Lucifer was supplied with an Italian identity, a fake past and a letter of recommendation with which he was accepted into the Blackshirts. Assigned to the central office of operations for all supplies to North Africa, Lucifer was able to access all classified information about dates, routes, number of ships, troops and goods that the Italian command was sending to Tripoli in Libya. A regular flow of this valuable intelligence was transmitted to Cecil De Clerc, who in turn informed the RAF, and precise attacks were able to be planned and executed to sink the convoys. Bombings of those vessels had been crucial in slowing down the advance of the Afrika Korps of General Rommel, who had been heavily and successfully fighting the Allied forces in that part of the world.

But now, his direct superior officer, Fascist Major Marino Severi, had informed Lucifer that the whole supply chain operation would be taken over directly by the German command. An officer was on his way to Rome as they spoke, he said.

'The Germans think that the British might have a mole,' Severi whispered angrily to the man who had become his right hand and confidant. 'They questioned how they could be so successful in ambushing our convoys so frequently in the open sea otherwise.'

'It was not just a matter of luck,' Severi added, confessing that it seemed that the Gestapo had also intercepted a wireless message that proved such a theory. 'Benito Mussolini himself asked us to take a step back for now and collaborate with our ally. But he also demanded that we find that mole, if he exists, find out how he managed to get our plans to the enemy undetected and arrest him. Us, not the damn Germans! The Duce has been quite adamant that he won't accept anything short of a resounding success on this front. He wants to regain Hitler's full confidence, restore his status of equal partner, and more than anything else, regain total control. He will hold us responsible if this doesn't happen.'

Marino Severi was fuming for having been stripped of his command: that demotion represented such a bad blow to his position, his career, his future ambitions. And a massive scar on his vain, self-centred ego. He greatly resented looking like a fool in front of his superiors; that's what he hated most, really. He also hated the prospect of having to work with the Gestapo: if the spy was to be captured, he did not want to be overshadowed nor share the praise and success of his arrest with anyone. He wanted that glory all for himself. It would have a big payback.

Lucifer didn't mind seeing him squirming for once, but he was certainly enraged about that setback, as it would deeply affect him and his mission; that was crystal clear.

Lucifer learned that the officer in charge would be Lieutenant Colonel Friedrich Schaeffer, a key member of General Erwin Rommel's staff. And because the Fascist command was deemed unsafe, to keep a water-tight control, Schaeffer's operation headquarters would be moved to a new location in the centre of Rome, Severi confirmed, although there was no way to tell where the Germans would choose to go. Everything had already been arranged. Only the men under Colonel Schaeffer's direct command would be allowed to have access.

Lucifer would now be completely cut off.

What a damn, bloody disaster, he thought, while pacing up and down his office. He needed to inform the British command of this dramatic new development.

Fast.

It was time for a confession.

CHAPTER 3

Rome, September 1938 – 3 years and 10 months earlier

In late 1938, Fascist Dictator, Benito Mussolini, who took over state power in Italy in 1922, announced the introduction of Racial Laws by a Royal Decree, passed by his government in November of that same year.

Cordelia heard the news when the Duce announced it in a speech during a visit to the northern town of Trieste in late September.

It was a Sunday.

She remembered it particularly well, for that day, her friend Lea Segre, a plump Jewish girl with short, curly black hair, an infectious laugh and a great sense of humour, came to visit her, to tell of her engagement to violinist Giacomo Bruni. As soon as Cordelia opened the door, Lea entered like a storm, enthusiastically announcing, 'I am going to be married. I am going to be married! Giacomo proposed yesterday evening!'

Lea was over the moon and couldn't contain her excitement. Cordelia burst into laughter.

'How wonderful, congratulations.'

Lea hugged her friend, then dashed towards the radio.

'Let's turn it on. Giacomo is playing in the quartet broadcasting from Palazzo Corrini.'

She had always been exuberant, cheerful, full of life, and Cordelia loved her for that. They couldn't have been more different. Their families couldn't have been more different.

Cordelia and Lea met in primary school. The two girls had been best friends ever since.

Cordelia was an only child. Her mother died when she was just eight months old. She could not remember her at all, and the only way she knew what she looked like was from the few pictures that his father jealously kept in a beautiful wooden box, placed on the top shelf at one side of the fireplace in the main drawing room of the house. He took it down every now and then, opened it and looked at the photographs with his daughter. Her mother was gorgeous, Cordelia thought.

She had her mother's eyes, for they were green, like hers; both had quite thick, dark eyebrows, and very full lips. Her father once said to her, 'You have a way of pouting just like your mother used to do.' He wept when he said that. Whenever her mother was mentioned, tears would appear in his eyes. He would remain silent for hours afterwards.

My father is a very sad man, Cordelia thought as a little girl. She hardly remembered seeing him smile during her childhood. She knew he had been very happy when Mum was alive, for he was always smiling in the pictures. At the time, Cordelia had been afraid that it might be her fault.

'Am I to blame? Have I done something wrong?' she asked her nanny, Alma, one day. Alma tried to comfort her as much as she could. She knew Cordelia's father was a good man, but he was unable to show the affection that a child needed. It was tragic that he couldn't see his daughter was suffering. He couldn't help it, though.

At the time, Cordelia couldn't understand that her father had fallen into a deep depression, following the dreadful accident that had killed her mother.

He had been testing a car for the Targa Florio race, a prestigious competition, and was so excited about its new prototype engine. He asked his wife to sit beside him and go for a test drive. He wanted her to experience the powerful, custom-built new machine he'd so passionately designed. The car was travelling at a very high speed when, unfortunately, one of the tyres burst. Unable to control it, they crashed ruinously against a tree at the side of the road. His wife died instantly, while he was fortunate to survive. He blamed himself all his life for that and was never able to overcome the sense of guilt, especially towards his child, who was to grow up without a mother, his beloved, beautiful wife. And all that for his stupid ambition to show off. He was never the same again.

From that moment, her father threw himself into his work, becoming incredibly successful, one of the best in his field – he was a mechanical engineer and sports car designer – but he delegated the parental duties almost entirely to Alma. Money was never a problem, as his was one of the richest families in Rome, and he would generously provide for his daughter. But he withdrew from her emotionally. The only conversation father and daughter had was around the business, which Cordelia, with age, took an increased interest in, becoming quite involved.

Cordelia would have grown up quite lonely if it hadn't been for Lea. The girls spent a lot of time together, as Cordelia was often asked to go to her home after school. Lea's family lived in a flat full of light on the fourth floor of a building in the Ghetto. The Segre household had a very lively atmosphere. Cordelia experienced what family life was like through Lea's. Lea had two brothers. Her mother was always cooking something in the kitchen, and all the children gave her a hand in turns, while endlessly chatting. 'Would you like a slice of pie, Cordelia?' she used to ask her as soon as she arrived. Lea's mum often baked the most wonderful cakes. Lea's father traded in all sorts of spices from the Middle East, and had established a flourishing import business, with offices and a warehouse occupying the ground floor of the building where they lived.

I want to have a family like this one day, Cordelia thought. She loved the warmth of their mutual affection, the laughter, the banter, even the endless noise. They talked and discussed everything, all the time. The Segres often gathered in the living room, where Teo, the oldest of Lea's brothers, would play the violin, while Vittorio, the youngest, accompanied him at the piano. Cordelia and Lea would dance to the tune. They were fond of music and took great pleasure in sitting around the radio to listen to a broadcast.

That Sunday in the September of 1938, the radio broadcast, which had always been a harbinger of pleasurable, light-hearted moments and fun, would be the bearer of the worst news Lea's family, and many Jews like them, would ever expect.

'Let's turn on the radio,' Lea repeated that day, while Cordelia went to sit in an armchair. The radio was switched to life. Lea was fumbling to adjust the frequency to get a clear signal, when the transmission was interrupted.

'*And now, live from Trieste, the Duce is going to speak to all Italians,*' the croaky voice of a commentator announced.

Lea and Cordelia looked at each other, almost amused, for neither ever really took him that seriously. The speakers conveyed the background noise of the mass of people in the square, who were impatient to listen to their leader. Cordelia could picture him speaking from a balcony right above them. The Duce loved to lecture his people from high up, so that everyone could see and hear him very well.

Benito Mussolini came on. He started his speech in a solemn tone. *'Blackshirts, Italian men, Italian women!'*

Pause.

With a higher pitch, his voice rhythmic, he continued. *'A problem of utmost urgency is regarding the issue of race.'*

Pause again.

Then, resolutely, he said, *'And we will adopt all the necessary measures to address it!'*

The sound of a roaring crowd came from the speakers.

Mussolini went on to explicitly name the Jews as an incontestable enemy of Fascism, and with a vehement, almost sermonic tone, he declared that a policy of separation would follow.

'A clear and strict racial conscience will establish not only the difference, but also the decisive superiority of the Aryan race.'

Cordelia and Lea listened to the vigorous clapping of an approving crowd, which started to repeat in perfect unison, *'Duce! Duce! Duce!'* A familiar chant that always accompanied his eloquent performances.

On hearing this, Cordelia was speechless, incredulous. It was like being in a bad dream. Was everybody just going insane?

She turned, moving her gaze from the radio to Lea, who, after a moment of eerie silence, whispered, 'Oh my God.' In one of the rarest moments of her life, Lea was lost for words. With her eyes still fixed on the radio, she stepped back, as if that physical instrument was to blame for delivering the most bizarre, horrible, frightful news, and she wanted to put some distance between them: a sort of physical rejection. She reached out for a chair and slowly sat, her legs suddenly weak, unable to hold her weight.

Cordelia jumped up from the armchair, as if the energy that had animated Lea when she'd arrived, had transferred to her. She switched the radio off. Lea was clearly petrified, not a word was coming out of her mouth.

'This cannot be happening. It's ridiculous. I cannot believe it. There must be a terrible mistake!' said Cordelia, with unconcealed anger.

'Has Mussolini gone completely mad?'

It felt like an atrocious, absurd joke.

But it wasn't. And worse was to come.

Rome, September 1938

On 18th September 1938, Father Colombo listened to the whole broadcast of Mussolini's speech from Trieste with increasing dismay. He was in his study with Brother Filippo that day. By the end of it, Brother Filippo was holding his head in his hands, his eyes clearly showing the despair he was unable to express verbally, while still gaping in the direction of the radio that had just delivered those terrible words.

Father Colombo switched the radio off. He was appalled and saddened. The whole thing seemed grotesque.

'What have we become…' he whispered.

'This can't be true. The King wouldn't allow this, would he, Father Colombo?'

'I'm afraid he already has,' responded the Franciscan friar, 'otherwise Mussolini wouldn't have announced it as he did today.'

Father Colombo looked out of the window. Lost in his thoughts, he remained silent for a moment.

The sun was slowly disappearing behind the menacing grey clouds which were gathering in the Vatican sky. A storm was on its way.

To Father Colombo, it felt like a dark, ominous curtain was closing above their heads. A flock of starlings seemed to chase away the pigeons from the roof of the opposite building, perhaps hunting the last prey of the day.

Another much more sinister hunt was looming, like the one that was in full swing in Nazi controlled territories now, Father Colombo pondered with horror.

He thought of the many Jewish families in the Ghetto of Rome and across Italy for that matter, and the fear Mussolini's speech would cause.

'I must do something – there must be a way to combat this,' he mumbled.

He went to his desk, pulled out a sheet of paper, wrote a short letter and put it in an envelope. Then, addressing his faithful assistant, he said, 'Filippo, I need you to deliver this letter personally to the British Embassy first thing tomorrow morning.'

Father Colombo sought to see Lord D'Arcy, the British Ambassador to the Vatican.

It was time for him to accept his request for help.

Lord Francis D'Arcy, a member of the British aristocracy, was actively involved in organising the escape of those people who needed to flee the Fascists, the Nazis, or both, and get them out of the country. For this task he needed all the help he could get, especially from those able to freely go in and out of the Vatican, a neutral territory, without causing any obvious suspicion, or being questioned by the Italian police or the Gestapo. This was an essential part to play in order to organise the movements of fugitives, who often had to be moved from place to place before reaching safety. And who better than priests or nuns, friars or monks to do that? After all, Italians were very reverent, even in awe in some cases, of the religious orders;

despite everything, their figures still commanded respect and authority, carrying by proxy the weight that the Pope projected on the population and its representatives.

Father Colombo and Lord D'Arcy had met for the first time during a reception for the nomination of the new cardinals earlier that year. The Franciscan still remembered well, how, at the time, the British man had reminded him of an English country gentleman of the past century, with his white moustache, and his elegant and poised manners – quite formal and yet, oddly, Father Colombo admitted, so warm. Lord D'Arcy possessed an unflappable diplomacy combined with a down-to-earth attitude that made people feel at ease. Father Colombo subsequently met him again on a couple of more private occasions, and it was during one of these that Lord D'Arcy approached him about his secret group and what they were planning to do.

'After all, salvation comes in many facets, don't you agree, Father Colombo? Everyone can be an instrument of God in these difficult times,' Lord D'Arcy said to him, suggesting he could become involved in that operation.

'I cannot deny the rationale of your argument, Lord D'Arcy. There's a time and a place for each of us to play our part, and I will give due consideration to your proposal,' Father Colombo replied.

Initially, in fact, Father Colombo was taken aback by such a prospect, as he never participated in secret operations of any sort, especially the kind that would be breaking the law.

But what was the law to break now?

If it meant opposing the ominous discrimination of men created equal, the persecutions and the violent regime behind it, the time to do that had finally arrived.

He had been tolerant for too long. Turning a blind eye to what was happening in his country, had meant silently accepting the government's dictatorial prevarications. Not after Mussolini's speech that afternoon, for sure.

It was in this spirit that Father Colombo wrote a note to Lord D'Arcy, and shortly after, Brother Filippo delivered it; an invitation to go over to the British Embassy was issued. The official motif was very different to the real purpose, and sufficient to deflect unnecessary attention. Many in the Vatican wanted to maintain the face of neutrality to avoid retaliations by the Fascist regime, but behind closed doors discussions were happening, and in the case of Lord D'Arcy, actions were being planned.

Father Colombo headed to D'Arcy's office late one afternoon. He was shown in by his assistant. The British Ambassador was standing next to the French doors which opened onto the internal garden of the Embassy building. He had a cup of tea in his hands. His private secretary, Rufus Bridge, was finishing some notes.

'That'll be all, Mr Bridge.'

The secretary folded his diary, nodded and glided out of the room, softly closing the door behind him.

'You just missed our afternoon tea, Father Colombo.'

'Perhaps I'm in time for something that is going to taste of a much more appealing prospect for both of us. I am here to offer my help and support for your salvation plan,' Father Colombo said, getting straight to the point.

A subtle smile appeared under Lord D'Arcy's moustache. He was clearly pleased with himself, as if he knew that sooner or later the Franciscan would come and knock at his door.

He invited the Franciscan to take a seat.

'My secretary, Rufus Bridge, will be in touch,' Lord D'Arcy said. 'He will call on you tomorrow.'

They continued to talk for a while, and after an hour of conversation, both men were ready to take their leave.

'I hope you don't feel as if you have signed a pact with the Devil,' said the Englishman with a half-smile.

'Sometimes desperate times call for desperate measures, as my fellow countryman Machiavelli stated once.' And with those words, the Franciscan left.

A new mission was waiting for him.

Rome, 1939

The house was quiet when Cordelia arrived. Apart from her friend, Lea, no other member of the Segre family was at home. They had gone to the synagogue for a wedding. Going to a wedding ceremony was the last thing Lea wanted to do.

Since the declaration of the Racial Laws, Lea had slowly descended into a spiral of depression. Her fiancé, Giacomo Bruni, had called off their engagement, under huge pressure from his family, just a week after his proposal during that infamous Sunday. He was a promising rising star of the Royal Italian Orchestra and an association with a Jew, let alone being married to one, would certainly damage his career, and possibly have meant the end of it.

Lea was devastated. It would later become clear that Giacomo wouldn't be able to marry her anyway, though, since in November 1938, a *Regio Decreto* – a law of the State – prevented any citizen from marrying Jews. The theory behind it was that mix-race marriages would alter the traits of Aryan Italians, both physically and psychologically and, therefore, to maintain the purity of the race, they were totally banned. Italians had racial characteristics completely different from those people of Oriental origin, and, in particular, Jews represented a part of the population that, despite having settled in Italy for centuries, had never been assimilated and absorbed into their host country. A net distinction and stark separation had to be made, according to the new law.

Even if this later escalation would help her find closure, Lea never really got over the break-up, and became almost a recluse, leaving home just to go to work at the hospital obstetric clinic. Cordelia knew that didn't help either, as, seeing pregnant women on a daily basis, constantly reminded Lea of whom she would never be. She became convinced she had no future as a wife and a mother, and deep down she anguished about it. And she wasn't the only one who suffered emotionally from that. In fact, the practical, hard truth of the effects these new laws had on the Jewish community were starting to emerge.

On her way to Lea's home in the Ghetto of Rome, Cordelia saw a sign on the office door of Lepora & Sons Accountants, saying that they had closed their activity for good. That Jewish family had been there for at least three generations. One of the most renowned and esteemed professionals in that part of the city, their firm had an enviable list of wealthy clients. But the new law had imposed tight restrictions on their business operations, causing a severe loss of clients in a short space of time, to the point that it had become no longer sustainable for them to continue. Mr Lepora, together with his four sons, had decided to cut their losses and emigrate while they still could, and rebuild a new life elsewhere.

'They are selling the office premises and their home well below market price,' Lea told Cordelia. 'Some shark will make a huge profit out of their misfortunes.'

'Do you know where they are going to go?' asked Cordelia.

'To Palestine. Mr Lepora still has some family there, a distant relative of some sort, apparently. He said he doesn't want to end up like Eugenio Franconi.'

Mr Franconi, a lawyer, committed suicide the month before, by throwing himself down the stairwell of the building where he lived, just a couple of blocks down the road from Lea's house. He had been a widower since the December before. He was heartbroken by his loss and missing his wife dearly, but nobody believed entirely that that was what drove his tragic act.

'Mr Lepora told my father that Mr Franconi was a close friend of his. He knew he had grown more and more disconsolate well before the death of his wife, already since Mussolini's declaration of the Racial Laws. Mr Lepora fears that the restrictions imposed on his practice might awaken in him the same demons that killed Mr Franconi. Or bring other demons in black shirts to his door to do the job. He doesn't want to be a sitting duck,' said Lea despondently.

Cordelia was aware of a new legislative act that stated the obligation of citizens belonging to the Hebraic race to declare they were Jews, which meant their automatic inclusion in a register called the Special List of Professionals. It gathered names of all Jews working as pharmacists, lawyers, accountants, university professors, architects, bookkeepers, veterinarians, doctors and surgeons, engineers, obstetricians: the list went on.

The law sanctioned strict limits in which Jews could practice those professions. In addition, some jobs were forbidden altogether to Jews. They couldn't be notaries for instance, or journalists. Breaking the law meant incarceration, heavy fines, cancellation from the register – a legal obligation if you wanted to work – up to the loss of citizenship.

Cordelia tried to change the subject.

'Lea, let's go for a walk. It's such a pleasant evening, and a bit of fresh air will benefit your spirit,' she said, hoping to distract her friend from her brooding mood.

'Come on, put on that purple dress your mother bought you for your birthday. You really look lovely when you wear it.' But Lea was not up for it. She started to cry.

'What's wrong, Lea? You are worrying me now. Did something happen at work that you want to tell me about?'

'No, no, it's not work,' said a teary-eyed Lea in a broken voice.

'What is it then?'

'Dad has decided we are all to leave Rome. For good. We had a discussion last night. Mum is distraught and doesn't want to go. But Dad is afraid that the regime will try to find a reason to accuse the Jews when anything bad happens. Blaming the Jews was exactly what the Russians did. They blamed them for the assassination of Czar Alexander II in 1881, Teo said, sanctioning pogroms and passing anti-Jewish laws. He is siding with Dad, and Vittorio is the same. It's only me and Mum who are resisting the idea.'

Cordelia was taken aback by the news.

'Oh, Lea, I am so sorry to hear that, and I wonder if it is not too premature for your father to make such a drastic decision. After all, Mussolini is not Adolf Hitler.' But she knew those words were only meant to console Lea. Cordelia reckoned that, with a total lack of opposition, the government could potentially become more extreme in its views and actions. And the new Racial Laws were starting to reveal the truth about its dark side, pointing exactly in that direction. Perhaps leaving could be the safest thing to do for Lea and her family.

'Father has already spoken at length with the Rabbi, who said he can help us settle in New York, in a place called Brooklyn. We can move our business to America and continue trading with the Middle East for supplies from there,' said Lea, brusquely.

To America! So far away. Cordelia felt a cramp in her stomach when she heard that. Her life had been dotted with abandonments. First her mother, who she never knew, then her father, and now her most affectionate, best childhood friend. She would be alone again.

'But I won't go,' said Lea.

'But Lea, why don't you want to go with them? I will miss you terribly, but they will miss you even more.'

'No, my life is here, among these streets, shops, among the things I know and love. Among my people that don't speak in an alien language and won't look at me as if I was a stranger. My grandmother is still here and she won't move. Who will look after her if all of us go? And once the regime is over, perhaps Giacomo will come back to me.'

That was the real reason then. Despite it all, Lea still hoped.

Cordelia deeply felt for her.

'Besides, who will be your best woman for your wedding?'

Lea tried to cheer up, showing a glimpse of her old self, and almost smiled.

Cordelia hugged her, noticing how much thinner Lea had become. She could feel the ribs of her back and see a few white hairs lurking here and there in her dark, curly mane.

'Ah, but Augusto and I have only just met, and I don't want an important decision in your life to be affected by a marriage that might never happen,' Cordelia joked.

'Oh, but it will. And you will be the most wonderful bride Rome has ever seen – I won't miss it for the world.'

'That's a pathetic excuse, Lea. You know it is.'

But in the end, Lea did not go with her family, who travelled to Genoa and embarked on a transatlantic crossing heading for the

States a few months later. Her mother tried everything to convince her, but Lea had shown an exceptional stubbornness, resisting all calls for reason.

Her father sold off all his stock to a competitor, dismissed his staff and boarded up his business premises, perhaps wishing to find them again sometime in the future.

It was hard to let go and knowing of the mere existence of his store and warehouse there, waiting to be occupied again, meant a glimmer of hope to come back one day. Having a past was as important as the promise of the future they would find in their new adventure. They took as much as they could with them, but left everything Lea needed for her to continue to be comfortable in their home.

Cordelia went with Lea to Stazione Termini train station to see them off, one cold day in November 1939.

And not even a month later, Lea was gone as well.

She died of pneumonia that December 1939.

It was as hard as the day when her father had died.

CHAPTER 4

Rome, June 1942

That evening, Lucifer headed out of the Fascist command and went back home. He lived in a three-storey building. His flat, occupying all of the top floor, had a beautiful terrace with views over the river. He could easily see all three roads leading to it from above, so should a patrol come for him, he'd see it from afar and could make an escape via one of the routes he had already planned. He had no neighbours, apart from those below him, an elderly couple he hardly ever saw. He passed the porter's office on the left side of the iron gate leading to the internal courtyard. Although there was a lift, he climbed up the stairs as usual to reach his refuge. He needed to swap his uniform for civilian clothes. It took him less than ten minutes to be in and out again.

He had a protocol to inform Cecil De Clerc back in London. He took a bus to the Quartiere Pigna, in the historical centre of Rome. He needed to reach the Pantheon, the imposing ancient Roman temple built by the Emperor Hadrian, with a beautiful circular structure graced by Corinthian columns at the front entrance, dominating the square bearing its name. After the conversion of the Roman Empire to Christianity, it was turned into a basilica, which was its current status. It took the best part of half an hour to get there. He preferred to travel by bus as it allowed him to observe the surroundings without the need to think about his final destination, while at the same time checking out if he had a tail.

He got off the bus not far from the square, and then he took the Via della Minerva. Even if he was under surveillance, which he was pretty sure he wasn't, he would not raise any suspicion by being in that part of town. If anyone was observing his movements, he would simply appear to be going to buy some fresh bread from the renowned bakery of Cosimo Farina, famous for his special range of focaccias, right at the bottom of the street.

Situated on the ground floor of a four-storey building, the shop of Cosimo Farina was one of the oldest bakeries in Rome, tracing back to medieval times. It had always belonged to the same family, which, generation after generation, continued in the tradition of making bread. The family surname probably originated from the trade undertaken. Cosimo's great-uncle, Quirino, kept repeating an old story that even the Knights Templars had been customers, but that was likely to be more of a legend than the truth. Certainly, the bakery had been very popular, and it was still well loved by its Roman customers.

The business had survived throughout the various battles, wars and invaders that the Eternal City had witnessed over hundreds of years. The family members exported their craft beyond the national borders, and a successful branch was opened in New York at the beginning of the decade by Cosimo's brother, Fabio. When war broke, Fabio didn't respond to the request to enlist in the Italian Army to serve the Duce. Writing to Cosimo, he asked him to join him in America. But Cosimo refused and replied to his letter saying that if the bakery had survived the Spaniards and the French of Napoleon Bonaparte, it would survive the regime of Benito Mussolini and the German Third Reich as well. He was not going to abandon the fruit of the sweat of his ancestors' brows for any reason at all, despite his contempt for what the Fascist regime had turned into. Cosimo had the Solomonic certainty that, as many before them, they would go when the time was right.

The baker could help speed up that process though. That's why he became a sort of post office for the British to pass on messages delivered by their agents on the ground.

Lucifer had been using it regularly for months now.

He stopped in front of Cosimo's shop. He glanced at its interior through the window. It seemed empty. At that hour of the day it was almost time to close, and everyone was rushing home before the blackout came into force.

Lucifer approached the entrance, climbed the two stone steps and went inside. The apprentice, a young boy who looked no older than twelve, popped his head round the back door.

'Mr Farina will be with you in a moment,' he said cheerfully.

'Thank you, Renzino.'

The boy smiled and rushed back to fetch his master.

Cosimo Farina appeared a moment later, and in seeing who the customer was, made a slight nod, signalling that there were still a few of his employees working in the laboratory. Then he put on his white apron and went behind the counter. A few bags of white flour were lined up just beside the scale. One was open.

'May I have a loaf of wholemeal bread, please?' Lucifer asked.

'Of course, here it is,' said Farina.

But instead of getting the bread just behind him, he reached inside the open bag of flour, grabbed a handful and, with a rapid movement of the hand, scattered it on the top of the glass counter.

Lucifer quickly wrote a day and a time on the white powdered surface. The recipient knew the place already, so there was no need to provide that information.

Cosimo read the message, swiftly erased it, cleaning everything up with a damp cloth.

The exchange took less than ten seconds, leaving no tangible trace it had ever happened.

Cosimo grabbed a loaf.

'How much is it, Mr Farina?' Lucifer asked smiling, while the baker was putting the bread onto the scale to weight it.

'Let me see… One lira and fifteen centesimi, please.'

Cosimo wrapped the bread in a piece of brown paper and handed it over. Lucifer paid, took the parcel and exited the shop.

All that Cosimo Farina had to do now was to place three long baguettes in the window, the signal for his contact that he had a message to deliver.

The baker did that immediately after Lucifer left, then closed the shop and went home.

The interior of the small chapel of St Francis of Assisi, in a narrow side street of the old centre, was barely lit during the week, just a few candles at both sides of the altar. Perfect for somebody who preferred a private moment of prayer. It was an ancient medieval Romanesque building, with a central nave separated from two smaller ones by stone arches on each side. It had a very simple décor, typical of that period, the only fresco representing the Saint with the wolf at the centre of the semi-circular apse behind the altar. And it was always very quiet, especially during weekdays. Today there were not many people left inside after the daily morning mass; all would be gone in a few minutes.

Lucifer arrived just moments before the end of the service. He slipped inside the church and, avoiding the central aisle, turned right towards the side nave. There was a smell of incense. He took a seat in the last row of wooden chairs and pulled out a candle from under his jacket.

He had a good view from there, and could see two old ladies, each wearing a black lace veil, still standing in front of the statue of St Francis, just beside one of the stone columns. A third, who had lit a candle, came back to join them, and they all started to say the rosary.

A couple, sitting three rows in front of him, probably man and wife, stood up, genuflected and went straight out.

Nothing seemed unusual.

A nun was coming in his direction, her gaze towards the ceiling. She slowly walked past him. He was about to stand up when he heard the sound of light steps coming from behind. A hand tapped on his shoulder. Lucifer froze for a moment.

'Is this yours, sir?'

It was the nun. She had picked up a handkerchief that must have dropped out of somebody's pocket.

'It isn't, Sister,' Lucifer said.

He noticed she was quite young and wondered how anybody could choose that life of physical and mental constriction.

She smiled at him.

'Then I will hand it to the reverend, in case someone claims it.'

'God bless you,' he said, while she approached the door of the sacristy and disappeared inside.

Lucifer waited a few moments, then moved in the direction of the confessional booth at the top of the nave. He approached the wooden step on one side and kneeled. A small window at the same level of his face, screened by an iron grate with an intricate and fine pattern, designed to partially conceal the identity of the confessor, opened. Father Colombo was on the other side.

'Hello, Lucifer,' he said to the secret agent.

He and Lucifer were not new to this way of getting in touch; they had been following this same script since they came into contact the very first time the British spy landed in Rome.

Earlier that week, during his morning errands, Brother Filippo had passed in front of Cosimo Farina's shop and noticed the three baguettes displayed in it, the signal the baker had a request for contact. So he went inside, got the message, and immediately delivered it to Father Colombo.

As usual, the meeting was to take place two days later, in a place they had agreed during their last encounter. It was different every time, and only the two of them knew it. Even under torture, Cosimo wouldn't be able to relay that information.

'There has been a new development,' Lucifer said. 'Marino Severi will no longer be in charge of managing the supplies to Tripoli, which means that I will no longer have direct access to the shipping schedule documents.'

The friar immediately understood the implication of this.

'That's really bad news. Why, though? What happened? Has he been sidelined?'

Father Colombo's thoughts were faster than his ability to ask questions.

'The Germans are convinced there's been a leak of information, and that crucial intelligence has reached the RAF. They seem to be adamant that our aerial attacks were not just a matter of ability or luck,' Lucifer whispered. 'But there's more. The Gestapo has evidence through an intercepted wireless transmission, confirming that's the case, although they have not been able to locate exactly where that wireless might be just yet. All they know, Severi tells me, is that it's near the Vatican; potentially, it could be inside the Vatican. Severi has started an investigation himself. He wants to find the mole before the Gestapo does.'

'The Gestapo is involved? That's very serious, and extremely dangerous for you. The Fascists are one thing, but the Gestapo is a whole different kettle of fish to face. They are as tenacious and aggressive as those terrible Doberman dogs they have, and will not give up until they find what they're looking for.'

'I agree. I think I will have to abort my mission sooner rather than later. But I cannot vanish into thin air all of a sudden. If I disappear now, it may well just confirm their suspicions that there is a spy at the very heart of their ranks. Besides, I would no longer be able to bring your own personal project to a conclusion, Father Colombo; I need a little more time for that.'

Lucifer had been helping the Franciscan to hide Cordelia's name from those listed to be investigated for their potential Jewish ancestors. Since her mother was not born in Italy, there were some who wanted to make sure that the certainty of her race was established. And tragically enough, the demand came from her fiancé Augusto's circle. His snobbish, wicked cousin, Anna Maria, had always disliked Cordelia, not only for her lower-class origin, but because Augusto dumped her fellow aristocrat and best friend, Giulia, for her. She challenged him to find out who he was dating exactly. And by who, she meant race. Purity of the race was such an important social requirement for a member of a well-known noble family quite close to Benito Mussolini.

He wouldn't want his ancestors' name to get an infamous stain for associating himself with the wrong person, would he? Reluctantly, Augusto gave in, and the process was set in motion. Although Cordelia did not have a Jewish surname, an inquiry was made at the Ministry of Race, which in turn would send a request to her town of birth to check her records.

As soon as Cordelia was made aware of what was happening, she went to see Father Colombo, telling him that her mother was of Jewish descent. The friar asked for Lucifer's help. As a Blackshirt and right hand of Marino Severi, Lucifer had access to many public offices, including that of the Ministry of Race. With the excuse of a background check for one of the members, who had recently joined his garrison, he befriended a very pretty – although married to an army officer stationed in Libya – secretary, one Maura Boni. And she made it quite clear she wasn't immune to his charm. They soon started a sexual affair. Mostly happening in her office after everyone was gone for the day, their encounters were brief and torrid, both enjoying their voracious appetite with great energy. Usually, after they had finished, she went to the bathroom next door to be presentable again, before going out of the ministerial building.

Lucifer worked out how much time he had before she came back: approximately seven minutes. Enough to search a different set of cabinet files each time. He needed to find where the requests to be sent to the Podestà – the city mayor – were kept.

Luck was on his side: success came quite early on only his fourth attempt – not that he disliked the preceding activity by any means – but hearing the sound of her steps closer and closer, sooner than expected, the only thing he managed to do was to place Cordelia's request at the bottom of the pile. He was only just in time when she returned, in a rush. He would get it next time.

'I almost got caught by my colleague, Luigi. I hope he did not see me at this time of the night. What the hell is he doing here anyway?'

She was really upset. She did not want anyone to suspect and, above all, risk her betrayal being reported to her husband, who would kill her for sure, she said. Unfortunately, after that episode, she became very resistant to meeting him there.

'And also, my husband is coming back from Tripoli, so we will have to take a break for a little while, darling,' she said to Lucifer.

His attempt to grab and destroy Cordelia's request was to be put on hold.

'I will go back to the Ministry soon and finish the job, rest assured about that,' Lucifer said to Father Colombo.

'But I will stop shadowing Cordelia, as I did every now and then, to see if she was under any kind of surveillance,' he added.

The church was completely deserted by now, but even so, Lucifer knew that he hadn't very long to talk; short and sweet had always been his rule for the drops. It had kept him safe all this time. 'Esculapio Temple, in the gardens of Villa Borghese is where I will meet you next time,' he said to the Franciscan friar.

'I have prepared a report for the Ambassador,' he continued. 'It is inside this candle.' And in saying that, he quickly passed it through one of the largest holes in the grate.

Lucifer had written a cyphered message the night before. He had carefully rolled up the minuscule piece of paper and inserted it in the interior of a candle, where he had previously drilled a small hole in the white beeswax. Going into a church to pray carrying a candle to light was perfectly plausible.

Father Colombo grabbed the candle, bent to reach the brown leather bag at his feet and put it inside.

When he turned to face the window, Lucifer was gone.

CHAPTER 5

General Erwin Rommel's camp, near Gazala, Libya, June 1942

The Junker was ready to depart at exactly five o'clock in the morning. Rommel's green and black camouflaged personal aircraft had been on the airfield, just outside the camp, for the previous two hours, on stand-by. The mechanics had performed all the necessary checks on its three BMW engines and filled up the tanks with enough petrol for the seven-and-a-half hour journey to Rome. The two pilots were sitting in the cabin, performing the last instrument checks before departure. The aircraft propellers, kept at the minimum until a few minutes earlier, were picking up speed. They started to whirl faster and faster, producing an increasingly louder, rumbling sound.

It was a nice day to fly, with no wind and the clear blue sky of a sweltering African midsummer.

The plane would soon be skimming above the waves of the Mediterranean with two passengers on board.

Friedrich Schaeffer, Lieutenant Colonel of the Afrika Korps, had arrived a few minutes before the General that morning. He was wearing his desert uniform and carried a small brown leather briefcase. Taking his hat off for a moment, he ran his hand through his dark blond hair, still wet from the shower. It would dry soon. He closed his eyes, rubbed his eyelids, massaging them with a gentle movement, still indulging in a brief moment of darkness, before facing again the brightness of the morning. The African sun had given his fair complexion a glowing and healthy honey-coloured tan, which made his blue eyes stand out even more. At twenty-seven, he was a tall, muscular, well-built man. If Hitler ever had a specimen in mind for the Aryan race, Friedrich Schaeffer's athletic figure fitted it perfectly.

In that moment, Erwin Rommel's car arrived. The vehicle stopped at the side of the aircraft and the General stepped out, walking in his direction.

'Good morning, Schaeffer,' he said, with rare joviality. Perhaps the prospect of going back to a civilised place even for a few days had cheered him up a bit, Schaeffer thought.

'Before I left my tent this morning, Von Mellenthin told me that he briefed you in detail with the crucial elements necessary for our mission.'

The Desert Fox didn't care for small talk and got straight to the point.

'Yes, he has been quite thorough, Mein General.'

Rommel had summoned Schaeffer days ago, outlining his strategy and the key role the Lieutenant Colonel had to play in bringing this mission to a successful conclusion. Von Mellenthin added insights about the other actors, namely the Italian Fascist command and Himmler's Gestapo in Rome.

'Sir, what I still don't quite fully understand is why the Gestapo has got involved. They are an unnecessary hindrance to the plan, and quite frankly I want to keep a water-tight control on the number of men in the know, even those supposedly on our side.'

'Himmler has reason to believe that the intelligence leaked is the work of a traitor. He wants to find him, while making sure no eyes and ears other than ours are privy to the operation. That logic does not leave us too much of an alternative – at least for the time being. Besides, Kesselring has agreed a restricted number of Gestapo officers will be an integral part of it, for this reason. But also because he prefers to avoid an open confrontation with Himmler in particular, who, for some time now, has had the firm belief that the Vatican is a nest of spies, providing shelter for them and other traitors.'

'Well, General, let's hope their meddling doesn't become an intolerable interference, like these damn black flies we have over here,' Schaeffer said, not hiding his dislike for the Gestapo.

'I am not sure if it's an excuse for that devious little man to eventually portray himself as the real kingpin of the whole thing in the end, to gain Hitler's praise and more power.'

The Desert Fox wasn't a fan of Himmler either.

'But I'd rather look at the bigger picture. Have you heard of the Saxon proverb, *an eagle hunts no flies*? Let's pick our battles, Schaeffer.'

Rommel's tone was that of a man resolute to make the most of what the battlefield offered. He didn't want to, or chose not to pay too much attention to the politics of Hitler's General Staff. They could do what they wanted, as long as they contributed to the outcome he needed.

'If we can manage to secure the men and the tanks we need to get to Cairo, victory will speak for itself. And with you there, we will. I fully count on you,' said Rommel.

Schaeffer knew when he had to rest his case. As a civilian, he had been a brilliant lawyer after all.

Rommel nodded, raised his gaze and made his way to the Junker. At that moment, one of the pilots peered out of the plane's main door, signalling that they were ready for take-off. The BMW engines increased their vigorous noise, running almost at full power.

Rommel clambered the short staircase followed by his travelling companion. They took their seats, and the pilot closed the door with a loud bang, taking his place in the cockpit.

The Junker taxied onto the landing strip; its propellers kicked in full power. The aircraft accelerated at a speed of seventy-five miles per hour and was airborne within less than twenty seconds, leaving that barren, dry, rocky land behind.

Schaeffer watched the coast of Africa recede until it became a line thinner and thinner on the horizon, and then he saw nothing but the blue waves of the Mediterranean Sea just below them.

The second pilot walked into the passenger cabin as soon as the Junker reached cruising speed.

'There are a couple of sandwiches made with white bread and ham, courtesy of the Allied troops we captured recently – fresh coffee, canned fruit and some dates if you like, gentlemen,' he offered, indicating a basket where the provisions had been stored.

Dates were the only fresh fruit they had in abundance; the rest was a welcome departure from the usual rations of tinned meat, black bread and cheese, which even the commanding officers had to get used to, given the shortages.

It was ironic to think that the food provided to British troops – and the British were certainly not famed for their cuisine, like the Italians for instance – was now considered a rare delicacy. The war had changed the order, as well as the perspective of things, in so many ways that previously would have been difficult to imagine.

Strangely, Schaeffer wasn't hungry just yet. Instead, he opened his briefcase, reaching for one of the photographs which he had put in the inside pocket the night before.

It was a picture of an attractive young woman, bent on the marble balustrade of a terrace overlooking the street down below. She wore a beautiful dress and had a glass of champagne in her hand. With her head slightly tilted, she was smiling at the camera. A warm, generous smile.

He looked at the image, as he had done many times before, then slipped it back in the briefcase. He closed his eyes, trying to imagine what her voice might sound like.

After a while, lulled by the regular vibrations of the aircraft and the constant, repetitive sound of the engines, a sense of torpor came upon him, and he fell asleep.

Berlin, 1933

Friedrich Schaeffer had always wanted to be a lawyer. He loved the law, and this was probably the fault of his uncle, Otto, a bachelor, who had a very successful practice in the German capital city. Uncle Otto often engaged him in discussions about the law and its principles, and was certainly instrumental in instilling in his nephew, since an early age, a great sense of justice. Friedrich enjoyed accompanying his mother's older brother to trials and watching him in action, perorating his cause with great eloquence. More than anything else, he enjoyed seeing him prevail on his opponents.

Young Friedrich came to admire how the application of jurisprudence could solve conflicts, without the need of resorting to violence.

Uncle Otto used to cite the quote, *Law is order, and good law is good order,* by the great Greek philosopher Aristotle. Friedrich believed those words outlined one of the fundamental concepts of a great civilised society.

His father, a Wilhelminian, an aristocratic man of Junker Prussian landowner's stock, had different ideas. Brutal force was the cultural currency of his profession and a presence in the military had been a constant in his family history. More than that, it was a given.

A career officer, Field Marshall Rudolf Schaeffer wanted his son to follow in his footsteps and become a career soldier himself, in keeping with the proud tradition of his ancestors. After all, Friedrich showed he had great talent in the use of the sword and the pistol, and he excelled in sports, as well as at maths and geography. The Field Marshall was sure his son had the potential to become a great strategist and commander, as his great-grandfather had been.

Friedrich had known of his father's ambitions since childhood, and he thought he wanted the same thing as well, except Uncle Otto made him discover a new passion. He knew that choosing a different career wouldn't stand a chance with his father, though.

Rudolf Schaeffer was adamant that Friedrich was to enter the Academy and forget about jurisprudence, totally immersing himself in a military environment that would forge his discipline and strengthen his spirit, and turn him into a warrior dedicated to serve and defend his country.

Especially now that Germany had a new Chancellor, himself the embodiment of a new order. He had started a rearmament programme, resurrecting grandiose military parades in a reorganised and re-energised army: the Wehrmacht, now a unified force that included the army – the *Heer,* the navy – the *Kriegsmarine,* and the air force – the *Luftwaffe.* He was a leader who loved to refer to the Third Reich as a prominent force for progress and modernity, with the new Teutonic race at its helm, celebrating the young, physically fit new Germans, powerful in the body and, by default, in the mind. He was a man who provided the hope of a clean break from the past to his fellow citizens, and to that end he was shaking the country from the misery and drastic weakness that the Great War had left it in. This was thanks to what he considered the most appalling, despicable agreement that a weak and corrupt ruling class could have signed, in a cowardly move to end that conflict: the Treaty of Versailles, which had thrown Germany into a state of economic bankruptcy, catastrophic inflation, unemployment and social unrest. This man had restored confidence in the nation by embarking in huge and highly symbolic reconstruction projects, like the new Autobahn, making Germans believe in themselves again as the central protagonists of a new era that they would be able to build. This man was the Fuehrer and Nazi Party supremo, Adolf Hitler.

Like many in Germany during 1933, the year in which Hitler rose to power, Rudolf Schaeffer shared his fellow citizens' enthusiasm for the new ruling party direction. At least at the beginning, Nazism seemed the right cure for a sick patient. And the robust cure it was imparting showed it could work. He wanted Friedrich to be part of what he thought to be the next glorious chapter of his country's history.

Friedrich did not mind the thought of joining the army, although he wasn't as enthusiastic as his father expected. He would have obeyed his father's wishes without discussion if it hadn't been for his mother, Birgit, a Baroness, daughter of a high-ranking member of the diplomatic service, who had inherited his father's art in so many ways.

Although politics was of almost no interest to her, she did not particularly like what she considered an angry, arrogant little man with a dark moustache, who seemed to have a perpetually brooding facial expression. And a bit of a lunatic, really. Respect didn't come to mind when she thought of the Fuehrer, although she admitted he was a skilled orator who had proved able to command and galvanise huge crowds. She remained suspicious of his concept of the New Order.

A woman of great intelligence, charm and tact, Baroness Schaeffer wasn't completely against the idea of her only son continuing the family military tradition, but seeing Friedrich's intellectual ability and how keen he was on jurisprudence, she proposed to her husband a compromise: let Friedrich study law at university and practice with Otto for a while, and then he would join the army as a cadet, as he had planned for him.

Rudolf initially went berserk at the prospect. How could she envisage that sort of detour?

'I don't want Friedrich to become one of those weak, liberal intellectuals that universities are full of!' he affirmed with a degree of irritation. 'I don't want to see his mind poisoned with socialist, or even worse, communist ideas that could destroy his future.'

Rather than the idea of his son going to university, it was this very fear that made him so annoyed, as he had had to quell a number of riots that had erupted during the years, organised by revolutionaries linked with the communist party.

Then, with sarcasm, he added, 'Besides, I don't see what's wrong with going straight to the academy: I didn't turn out too bad, did I?'

Birgit Schaeffer saw that her husband was getting upset. She moved towards him, taking his hands in hers, and with a velvety voice aimed at defusing his disappointment, she said, 'Rudolf, Friedrich has too much respect for you to disobey your orders.'

The Baroness knew that trying to go head to head with her husband wouldn't work. He was too skilled on any type of battlefield, and this was his terrain. His mood did not improve her chances either. He was cross, and in that state there was no way he would easily change his mind. Logic was her only weapon. So, she continued.

'But you mentioned more than once how Ludwig, the son of our dear friend, Herr Kleiber, was fast-tracked through military ranks because of his law degree: isn't he now the Senior General Staff lawyer? A position of great prestige and influence, even among the other officers of his same rank. I would have thought that you'd be pleased if Friedrich had that head start in his career.'

Baroness Schaeffer's last comment caught her husband off guard. He had to admit his wife had outflanked him by referring to his own words as a counter argument, leaving him without ammunition to respond. He couldn't fault her line of reasoning either.

'The final decision will be yours, my dear, but please give it a bit of consideration,' she added.

In the end, he conceded temporary defeat and, reluctantly, accepted.

Birgit Schaeffer had triumphed. Her son was ecstatic at the news. And he didn't waste that window of opportunity either.

Friedrich graduated *summa cum laude* two years in advance, and soon after he joined his uncle's famous practice in Berlin. Tragically, his father died of a heart attack a few months later, just when Friedrich had won his first big case.

He never joined the military academy afterwards, but eventually he would be called and drafted in the army, soon after the invasion of Poland in September 1939.

Nobody knew it then, but the Second World War had begun.

Rome, June 1942

The Roman airport of Ciampino lies at approximately seven miles south-east of the Italian capital city. Originally built in a large area of countryside, it served as a base for the Italian Royal Marine airships from its opening in 1916. Ten years later, it was from that airport that Italian General Umberto Nobile undertook the first European attempt to reach the North Pole with his Zeppelin,

'Norge', successfully crossing the ice cap to get to Alaska in the United States. In the summer of 1942, there was no longer any sign of those majestic, balloon-equipped dirigibles, substituted for a plethora of more modern aeroplanes.

The Junker approached the airfield at around midday, after a pretty uneventful trip. Looking down, Friedrich Schaeffer saw the rows of military aircrafts lining up on the ground, mostly Caproni and Fiat Cicogna bombers, and the much smaller Breda fighter planes. He noticed a train station just beside the main terminal building, probably linking the airport to the Eternal City, he reckoned. All roads lead to Rome, and now the railways were no exception. There was farmland all around but little else, just a few isolated houses, probably farms. Some crops he could recognise, like the cornfield next to the vineyard they circled above before landing. At a lower altitude, some people were tending to the grapes, while in the distance there was a flock of sheep grazing in a pasture bordered by woodland, minded by a couple of teenage boys. A girl with a large straw hat and a red skirt was trotting on a donkey along a path leading to a wooden bridge over a brook. This verdant view was dramatically different from the burned, arid, dusty North African landscape. It was an uplifting sight to see the lushness of the trees and the cultivations below, and animals that not only were familiar, but that didn't seem on the brink of starvation all the time, like those cadaverously thin flocks of Libya.

'It seems such a bucolic scene down there compared to the desert we just left behind. One almost forgets what the civilised world looks like, doesn't one?' General Rommel said, guessing his thoughts.

'I didn't know how much I missed it until now,' Schaeffer responded.

'Don't get too used to it, Lieutenant Colonel. I want you back at my side as soon as your mission is concluded. Have you been to Rome before? It's a fascinating old city.'

'Once, prior to the war, but it was a short visit. I was on a business trip.'

'On business?'

'I had to interrogate a witness for a trial. It seems ages ago now.'

'A battle in a court of law. Well, be prepared to fight again this time, Lieutenant Colonel. We will have to defend our ground, and I don't intend to lose.'

The General stretched his legs, stiffened from the hours spent sitting down.

Schaeffer admired the Desert Fox's will of steel, but noticed he seemed tired, and not just from the effect of the war. He wondered if the politics of the Oberkommando der Wehrmacht – the German High Command of the Armed Forces – was starting to have an impact on this extremely talented high officer, who had turned fifty just a few months ago. Schaeffer was glad he didn't have to worry too much about juggling and negotiating with those personalities. Wasn't it enough to fight the enemies outside?

The aircraft approached the runway from the west, pointing its nose slightly skywards. Progressively, the pilot reduced its speed and, gliding slowly through the air, they touched down.

The Junker rolled smoothly towards the left of the terminal, only to park a few metres away from a car, a magnificent Lancia Astura with Fascist flags, similar to the one that Mussolini used to host Hitler during his visit to the Italian capital. It was clearly awaiting their arrival. Four soldiers of the Fascist guard in their black military shirts, trousers and boots, on Moto Guzzi motorbikes, were stationed right beside the vehicle. An officer emerged from the back seat, stepping out of the car as soon as the silhouette of the pilot appeared in the frame of the plane's open door. Right behind him, Rommel and Schaeffer made their way out of the aircraft.

There was a smell of freshly cut grass, and although there wasn't a breath of air and the sun was at its peak, it was not stifling hot. The car, a cabriolet, had its top down.

The officer, a dark-haired man, probably in his early thirties Schaeffer reckoned, snapped to attention and raising his arm upward in the Roman salute, in a clipped tone said, 'Heil Hitler! I am Captain Schmidt, military attaché to the Quirinale. Welcome to Rome, Mein General.'

'Heil Hitler!' responded the Afrika Korps officers.

'I hope you had a good trip. I have orders to accompany you to your quarters at the Albergo Flora hotel, on the Via Veneto. Field Marshall Kesselring has ordered me to make your reservations. It's a very good establishment.'

'Very well, Captain, I don't doubt Field Marshall Kesselring's excellent taste. I am certain we will be very comfortable there.'

'This evening, I will take you to Field Marshall Hermann Goering. He arrived just a couple of days ago with his train from Berlin. He is staying in a private villa, courtesy of the Duce. He is hosting a dinner tonight.'

The three men made their way to the car, Schmidt getting into the front seat beside the driver, while Schaeffer and Rommel took their seat at the back.

The motorcade set in motion. Two of the motorcyclists led at the front, the other two in tow at the back. In exiting the airport, they took the Appian Way, an ancient Roman road built by Consul Appius Claudius Caecus some three hundred years BC. Lined with maritime trees, some tracts still had the old pavement made of stone, which caused the car to bump up and down a bit.

They regularly passed groups of women carrying baskets of fruit and vegetables, and male workers coming back from the fields with hoes and shovels on their shoulders. Two friars on their bicycles moved aside, staring at them as they drove by. In the distance, Schaeffer admired a couple of ancient Roman ruins standing out against the green surroundings, not far from the road. After some twenty minutes, the rolling countryside started to be dotted with houses, a few initially, then more and more.

'We have reached the outskirts of the capital, General, as you may have guessed,' Schmidt said, half turning to face his two passengers.

The General asked, 'Tell me, Captain, where is Goering staying exactly? You mentioned a villa.'

'The Field Marshall has taken residence in a house close to Villa Borghese, a very fine building. He preferred it to the quarters in Via Tasso, Sir, and didn't want to stay in a hotel.'

'Who could blame him,' Rommel whispered to Schaeffer. 'I am sure he wasn't very pleased to hear the screams of prisoners over dinner.'

Via Tasso was the headquarters of the Gestapo and of the Sicherheitsdienst, or SD, the counter-intelligence unit of the SS that Himmler had set up back in 1931. And their methods of interrogation weren't short of torture.

Schaeffer nodded, knowing all too well what the SS and the Gestapo were capable of, and especially the notorious SD's infamous *modus operandi*, made of intimidation and beatings at best. Like Rommel, he secretly held them in contempt, and did not approve of such a dishonourable way of operating for German officers. The army had quite different standards, but those men were far from being soldiers.

The car slowed down its pace once they reached the centre of the Eternal City, with its narrow, winding, cobbled streets teeming with life. Romans seemed to be out in force; roads were crowded with people. They turned into a boulevard and stopped in front of an imposing Liberty style, seven-storey high, white and pink building, sitting at the top corner of Via Veneto, overlooking ancient walls and arches. With its two beautiful giant statues at both sides of its roof top, the Albergo Flora had stood proud in that part of town since 1907, and the years that followed saw a cohort of sophisticated guests, which made it one of the places to be, and be seen, in Rome.

As soon as Captain Schmidt opened the door of the car, a doorman in elegant livery reached out to them while signalling to the bellboy to take care of the baggage.

'Good day, gentlemen, welcome to the Albergo Flora,' he said with a smile.

The three German officers entered through the revolving glass door.

'I will leave you here to get accommodated. I took the liberty to order lunch delivered to your bedrooms. I will pick you up later and drive you to dinner,' Schmidt said.

'Thank you, Captain, see you later.'

'This way, please.' The concierge showed them to a lift and to their rooms.

A warm, long bath in a proper bathtub, when was the last time he had enjoyed that? It must have been at least a year ago now. Schaeffer couldn't really remember exactly. And white, soft cotton towels, crisp bed linen, a vase of fresh flowers on the table where the concierge had left a basket of fruit, a bottle of Frascati white wine, and some elegantly arranged food on a porcelain plate. He sat down and ate slowly, enjoying every bite, sipping his drink with great pleasure, feeling the freshness in his mouth and throat, and the light inebriating sensation it gave.

It felt like heaven. Schaeffer felt human again.

Then he put on the Wehrmacht uniform, ready to face Goering.

* * *

Villa Portia had seen many occupants over its seven hundred years' existence. Originally built on the ruins of the dwelling of a Tribune of the First Republic of Ancient Rome, what was already an imposing house went through an iteration of styles, until it was acquired by Count Francesco Doriacci, a rich banker from the Tuscan town of Siena, in the late Renaissance. The nobleman had extended it considerably to make room for his wife, twelve children, two junior brothers and his extensive number of servants, employing a plethora of sculptors, painters, masons and carpenters to turn it into the palatial mansion it was today.

Since then, it pretty much remained untouched in this stately appearance.

Now the property of a Fascist hierarch, the villa was officially leased to the regime to host high-ranking national and international guests. People could enjoy its multiple, generous rooms and lounges inundated with light coming from their large French-style windows; its high-vaulted ceilings; exquisite frescos; rare paintings from different historical periods; magnificent marble floors and delicate *boiserie*. All this in the privacy, seclusion and quiet granted by its vast, shaded garden, with mature trees and immaculate lawns surrounding the property.

Schaeffer and Rommel, driven by the obsequious Captain Schmidt, had been picked up in the same car at the Albergo Flora just before sunset. Although the address was no more than a few miles away, when they crossed the grand iron gates, it almost felt as if they were somewhere out of town.

The car slowed down past the gates, following a gravel road leading to the main entrance of the house. Parked in front of it were several other automobiles.

'The red vehicle over there is the Alfa Romeo 8C, the sports car of Count Galeazzo Ciano, the Italian Foreign Minister,' Schmidt said.

'That saves me the time to go and see him,' Rommel replied. For diplomatic reasons, he had to pay him a visit, according to the protocol.

'Himmler must be here as well, General; that man there, in the open-top green Mercedes, is Gunther Klein, his personal driver. We met before. I remember him well,' Schaeffer added, pointing at a blond giant that was about to climb out.

Klein was the first surprise meeting of that day, and Schaeffer looked at him with disgust, noticing he had been promoted. Clearly his abilities had impressed his superiors.

He and Klein had crossed paths only once, in Poland during the blitzkrieg of 1939.

Schaeffer had just arrived with his unit in the outskirts of a village near Warsaw, when he saw him relentlessly kicking a woman on the ground. Schaeffer, observing how cruel his expression was, extracted his Luger pistol and, aiming at a point just above his head, shot at him to make him stop. But it was too late: the attack had been so savage that she died of her injuries. Schaeffer punched him as hard as he could, leaving that vile bastard lying unconscious in the mud.

When Klein saw Schaeffer approaching with General Rommel, his mouth twisted into a grotesque grimace, revealing that his face had suffered nerve damage, with two upper right teeth missing since that day in Poland.

'He doesn't seem pleased to see you, Schaeffer. A close encounter with your fist, I've been told.'

'That's correct. How do you know that, if I may ask, Sir?'

'I have my sources, Lieutenant Colonel, and I make a point of choosing my men carefully,' said Rommel.

Although the Afrika Korps officers exchanged salutes with the SS, Schaeffer ignored Klein's hateful gaze and Rommel didn't dignify him with the slightest glance when the two men passed by him.

They proceeded to climb the stone steps and reached the heavily ornate wooden front door. All lights were on in the house and music could be heard coming from an open window.

They knocked and soon after, heard steps on the other side.

The door opened.

A hulking figure appeared in front of them.

In disbelief, Rommel stared at him, as he almost did not realise who he was.

Schaeffer, taken by surprise by the improbable character that had materialised in front of him, was equally bewildered by the vision and just about managed to avoid his jaw dropping.

Dressed in a white and richly-draped Roman toga, a lush laurel crown around his temples and several golden rings on both hands, Field Marshall Hermann Goering stood in all his puissance and with a jovial smile on his face.

A big, all powerful, overweight man, his florid physical features were accentuated even more by his bizarre outfit.

A pair of brown leather sandals were strapped around his feet leaving them almost bare, and for reasons beyond anything Rommel and Schaeffer could remotely comprehend, the *Reichsmarschall* had decided to varnish all his toenails bright red.

The man has gone mad, the Desert Fox thought.

Although he knew all too well Goering's larger than life personality and his flamboyant taste in clothes, nothing prepared him for this incredible, eccentric transformation.

Schaeffer noticed Goering also had make-up on: his cheeks were slightly rouged, and his eyelids had a dark line at the top.

Goering greeted them with a raised arm: 'Heil Hitler! Welcome to this magnificent mansion! Isn't the Roman salute the sign and symbol of a true empire?'

'You are certainly paying a tribute to Emperor Caesar today, too, I can see,' Rommel said, retaining his composure in front of Goering's caricatural impersonation.

The Head of the Luftwaffe's pale blue eyes darted back and forth interrogatively between him and Schaeffer, whom he clearly didn't seem to know.

'Lieutenant Colonel Schaeffer, Reichsmarschall!' Schaeffer was quick to say to avoid further embarrassment, addressing Hitler's most powerful acolyte.

'Come this way. All the others are already here.'

They followed the bedizened figure inside.

The music sounded a bit louder now, and somebody had started playing a piano.

'Aren't these paintings just splendid,' Goering commented, gesticulating right and left to point at the pictures hanging on both sides of the long corridor.

'There's a Piero della Francesca, and here is an exquisite pastoral scene by Tintoretto.'

His love of art and sculpture was not a secret, and Schaeffer heard he had a huge collection at his hunting lodge, Carinhall, in Germany, and he was always looking for new additions. This much he knew about him.

A waiter in a white jacket, standing just at the entrance of the room, offered the three men a glass of champagne when they reached the large hall where the reception was taking place. The guests were all dressed in military high uniforms, except for Goering, who had elected to wear the unconventional uniform from a different era.

'That over there is Count Galeazzo Ciano, Foreign Minister,' Goering said, indicating a dashing man with dark, slicked hair standing by the fireplace, who was clearly enjoying puffing a cigar.

'I was invited to lunch with him earlier today, at Palazzo Chigi, on the Via del Corso, and he was telling me that his wife, Edda Mussolini, is a fantastic cook. I will sample her cuisine tomorrow.'

Edda Mussolini, the eldest daughter of the Duce, married Ciano in an ostentatious public ceremony back in 1930, transforming the wedding into a state event attended by the Fascist elite, and with Blackshirts marching and saluting the couple as if they were royalty.

'And after that, he will show us his remarkable automobile collection.'

Goering had a lust for all pleasures in life, and a particularly voracious appetite and passion for sports cars.

'I thought we had a meeting with Mussolini tomorrow,' Rommel said drily, sipping his drink.

Goering had already finished his in two single large draughts, and cleaning his lips with the back of his hand, he responded, 'Well, yes ... but later in the afternoon, so we have some time. Italy is so full of splendid treasures. It will be an unforgivable sin to miss a single one while we are here, don't you agree?'

This is not looking good, Schaeffer thought, seeing how Rommel was barely containing his irritation at that remark. He, himself, was quite annoyed. The Field Marshall seemed to underestimate the urgency of the task ahead. His attitude was far from serious and his focus appeared to be elsewhere.

The Afrika Korps General did not really trust his fellow officers to take the necessary, swift action that was a must if they were to win on the North African front. He feared they had miscalculated the imminent danger of giving the Allied forces the time to reorganise their defences and strategies in that theatre of war. The reasons why Rommel had asked him to come to Rome and the critical impact of his mission started to become completely clear to Schaeffer.

From across the room, Heinrich Himmler, the head of the SS and the Gestapo, was observing the scene. The *Reichsfuehrer*, in his black coat despite the hot weather, reminded Schaeffer of a gigantic black crow and looked as sinister as his notorious reputation. Behind the gold-rimmed glasses, he appeared permanently and nervously attentive, suspicious, almost defensive, as if he was about to deliver an arrest warrant. His perfidious, cold eyes regularly scrutinised the other guests, while he kept chatting with two Fascist officers.

But it was a third man in a dark suit, now standing close to Himmler, that captured Schaeffer's attention. He noticed him out of the corner of his eye initially, as the bony figure had his back to Schaeffer. Then his head slightly turned, and for a fraction of a second his profile silhouetted against the background.

In that instant, Schaeffer thought something was vaguely familiar about his distinctive aquiline nose. At first, he struggled to recall where he had seen him before. But then Himmler bent slightly towards him and said something.

The man turned to look at Schaeffer and met the Afrika Korps officer's gaze.

Schaeffer stiffened, the hair at the back of his neck bristling.

Instinctively, he reached for his gun and his fingers slowly closed around the grip of the pistol.

CHAPTER 6

Karl Blasius turned to look over his right shoulder. After a moment of uncertainty as he saw the officer, his gaze became vitriolic. He was surprised by how strong his hatred for that man still was, after all those years. Schaeffer had ruined him, and not only did he not forget, Karl would never forgive.

The Afrika Korps officer was a bit older and was tanned, but there was no doubt about his identity. As soon as he recognised him, it all came back in a millisecond, like it was yesterday.

Blasius never expected to see him again, today and here, of all places. They were on such different trajectories back then, perhaps even more now. It felt like a strange twist of fate to come across him.

Well, well, he thought, finally God has given me the opportunity to settle my account with you. I prayed so much to find a way to pay you back – perhaps my wish is finally going to be granted.

That notion secretly gave him an unexpected, pleasurable excitement on which he dwelled for a moment, letting the feeling pervade his senses. Karl always experienced elation when he knew he could take revenge and was sure to succeed.

Last time all his allies had abandoned him, one by one. Weak, fearful traitors, ready to profit from his position when they were sure he could give them all they asked for, but quick to betray him as soon as he was no longer in power.

He would not let that happen again.

He had more than just God on his side this time.

He had the Gestapo.

'You seem to know Lieutenant Colonel Schaeffer, Karl,' said Himmler, who had noticed his sudden change of expression at the sight of the Afrika Korps officer.

'Yes, you are right. We met before – a long time ago,' Blasius said, but didn't elaborate any further. He didn't need to. He was pretty sure Himmler knew. His deputy Heydrich would have informed him thoroughly about every detail of his past. He would not have been transferred from Palestine to Rome without any questions asked.

'And he clearly seems to know you,' Himmler added in a tone that suggested he relished every word, while at the same time taking Blasius under an arm to walk over to Schaeffer.

'Let's have a word with him, shall we, Karl?' Himmler suggested.

But it sounded more like an order to Blasius.

'I have been waiting for this moment for some time now, Reichsfuehrer,' said Blasius, realising that Himmler might have had that in mind from the moment he was summoned to the meeting.

Himmler must have a plan, Blasius reckoned, and perhaps that could be a stroke of luck for me: a double luck in fact.

On the other side of the room, Schaeffer saw them approach.

In a perverse way, it was a formidable-looking duo, a perfect image of evil: the powerful SS and Gestapo chief, beyond all laws of man, and the Benedictine monk, who somehow had defeated all the divine laws of his order that condemned him to exile in Palestine in perpetuity. Making a miraculous comeback, it was as if God had performed a moral resuscitation, all his past sins written off, and restored him to his old life in the Holy City, the centre of Christianity.

Karl Blasius had had a gangly figure when Schaeffer first met him, he remembered. He was looking even thinner now. The angular tracts of his face were sharper, which made his lips look disproportionately big under the hook-shaped nose that dominated those hollow cheeks. His pale complexion was accentuated by his dark hair, still long, but not the rebellious curly mane Schaeffer recollected: now it was evenly cut and neatly combed back behind the nape.

Karl Blasius certainly had a striking appearance that didn't go unnoticed: you could not forget him once you met him. His mean expression had always reminded Schaeffer of a medieval painting of a Holy Inquisition priest, possessed by the sacred duty to administer judgment by fire, convinced that condemnation to death was the only purifying solution for any sort of heresy.

Schaeffer was sure that, given the opportunity, despite his religious vows, Karl Blasius had in him the ability to kill.

He let his fingers relax over the grip of the pistol, but kept his hand there.

'You are not going to shoot us, are you, Lieutenant Colonel?' said Himmler, gesturing at Schaeffer's hand on the Luger.

'Heil Hitler, Reichsfuehrer! No, you have to excuse me. It's a habit of all of us soldiers in the desert to stay alert the whole time. The enemy is always ready to attack at any moment, from any direction,' Schaeffer said, realising how unwillingly he was letting his arm drop to his side.

'Ah, but you are among friends now, aren't you?' said Himmler.

Schaeffer did not believe him for a moment.

'May I introduce you to Father Karl Blasius, Chief Archivist of the Pontifical Biblical Institute here in the capital. Karl isn't wearing his classic black habit today, but he is a Benedictine monk, and a very good friend of the Third Reich. He has been helping us quite a lot in Rome so far.'

Schaeffer saw Blasius gloating at that remark. The monk kept his eyes fixed on Schaeffer while displaying a most duplicitous grin.

So, that was the reason Himmler had Karl Blasius be a party to today's gathering.

He was surely an informer for the Gestapo. Who was he spying on for them, though, exactly?

'Please tell me, in what way? I can't imagine how somebody in such a position would be of help to the Gestapo,' asked Schaeffer, casually.

'Everyone is of help to the Gestapo,' said Himmler. 'Collecting information is always a matter of priority for the Third Reich, especially if it can be sourced from places we do not necessarily have access to.'

'Like the Holy See, I suppose.'

'I knew you were very good at maths, Lieutenant Colonel. You have put two and two together quickly and correctly.'

So Von Mellenthin was right: the Gestapo had strong suspicions about the Vatican's role in channelling intelligence to the enemy.

'And what sort of information have you gathered, Father Blasius? To my knowledge, the Vatican is a neutral state and has a pact, as well as good relations, with the Italian Regime. They are not enemies, rather the contrary. I struggle to understand what the Holy See could hold that might be of such value to the Gestapo. Unless you are all thinking of a mass conversion, of course,' Schaeffer said.

Himmler laughed nervously at the joke, but was clearly not amused.

'You have a sense of humour, I see, Lieutenant Colonel! Be careful though. The Fuehrer does not want us to wait for any state, even the neutral ones, to become our enemy before we know it. So we are keeping an eye on them, just in case we need a preventative action.'

'And do you think we will need one, Reichsfuehrer?' asked Schaeffer.

'As you know, there are enemies within the Italian Regime who will take advantage of every opportunity to harm us. Liberals, socialists, communists, Jews, all will be too happy to see us fail. They are looking for safe haven and allies, and we have reason to believe that somebody in the Vatican might be listening to them, perhaps helping them already.'

'So are we preparing to invade the Vatican this time?' Schaeffer said, ironically.

Blasius, who had kept silent during the exchange between Himmler and Schaeffer, intervened.

'Well, well, let's not be so drastic in jumping to conclusions, Lieutenant Colonel. I reckon the Reichsfuehrer meant that it is better to thwart a rebellious crowd at the outset. After all, as a member of a religious order, I am the first to condemn those who could drag the Vatican on a dangerous collision path with the Italian Regime and his Axis ally. Eradicating those elements represents a mutual gain.'

'I see you have the best interest of the Pope at heart, Father Blasius.'

'And I am sure you have the best interest of the Reich at heart, Lieutenant Colonel Schaeffer.' Blasius was quick to sharply comment. 'On that point, perhaps you want to tell us what your role is going to be here in Rome?'

Schaeffer was about to answer when Rommel, who had been watching the trio while Goering was distracted by all the food arriving, joined the conversation.

'He will be taking over the direct command of the supply chain to Libya. We are all here today to discuss the details of this operation, but the decision has been made.'

So, Schaeffer is going to be stationed in Rome for a while, Blasius gathered.

And he has a mission to accomplish. If he fails, though... Could he? Blasius pondered.

A wild idea started to form in his mind. His thoughts were interrupted by Heinrich Himmler.

'And the Gestapo will be making sure that Lieutenant Colonel Schaeffer brings his mission to a successful conclusion, General. For too long, now, intelligence has been clearly passed onto our enemies. I am sure you will agree with me on that. They managed to sink so many ships with their aerial attacks. An initial investigation has indicated that the Vatican might have been used as a channel, and Father Blasius' presence here today is aimed at helping us to monitor that such information does not filter through, once the new plan is put in place. He will be our official gatekeeper at the Holy See, so to speak.'

'I am grateful for your concerns, Reichsfuehrer,' said Schaeffer, 'but I believe that moving the operation to new headquarters will avoid that danger.'

'We can't run any risk, I'm afraid,' Himmler said, and his comment sounded final.

Schaeffer and Rommel did not argue further. Whether they liked it or not, the Gestapo would have oversight.

'I will hold you to that, Reichsfuehrer,' said the Desert Fox, 'and the Fuehrer too. The oilfields of Persia are in clear sight. We need that petrol, and this operation is crucial to the success of the North African war effort, and beyond.' With that, he signalled to his fellow high-ranking officer that if something went wrong, he would have to take responsibility too.

'Gentlemen, gentlemen! Let's sit down now! Look at the sumptuous meal that has been prepared for us.' A glutton, Goering, who was looking at the richly laden buffet with hungry eyes and couldn't wait to start sampling that marvellous looking food which smelled delicious, invited all guests to assemble around the table. People could talk while they ate. Wasn't that the overall purpose of having this meeting over dinner?

'You Italians pull out all the stops when it comes to food. Well done, Count Ciano!' he whispered to the Fascist Foreign Minister, who was about to sit down.

'Hospitality is due and most necessary for our biggest ally, Field Marshall. It's an honour,' he replied obsequiously, and then, addressing Schaeffer he asked, 'You still haven't told us where you would base your headquarters, Lieutenant Colonel Schaeffer. I have been told that you intend to move your operation to a different location and want to make sure you get all the support from our Fascist supply chain office in transitioning the responsibilities of the handover.'

'When I was in Tripoli, my good friend, Major Count Nuvoli, told me that his fiancée runs a magnificent hotel: it's the perfect place. I will take residence there from tomorrow morning.'

'Excellent, I will send a note to comrade Major Marino Severi to transfer all the documentation there upon your arrival.' In saying that, Galeazzo Ciano signalled to his attendant to make a note of the address.

'Where is…' but the Italian Foreign Minister couldn't finish his question as Blasius was quick to ask Schaeffer, 'And what's the name of that hotel?'

He wanted to make sure he knew exactly where the Afrika Korps officer would be.

Schaeffer knew he couldn't hide that information, whether he wanted to or not. There was no point in delaying it either.

Reluctantly, he answered: 'Palazzo Roveri.'

Beuron, Germany, 1919

Karl Blasius had often dreamed of living in that castle above the hill since the moment he had arrived in the village. It was huge and magnificent, with a beautiful façade and an infinite number of windows.

At five years old, he didn't know that building was the Benedictine Archabbey of Beuron, a German town in the Swabian mountains of the Baden-Wurttenberg region.

When his mother died of pneumonia, Karl became an orphan and went to live with his aunt, Leni, there in the upper Danube valley. They were poor people, but they didn't go hungry. Aunt Leni had a small farm that she ran with her husband, Uncle Heinz.

Certainly, their wooden alpine house didn't compare with the imposing building that proudly dominated the town.

I will live in a place like that one day, little Karl thought, looking up at that hill.

The young Blasius soon made the decision that he didn't want to be a farmer. It was hard work. He knew it first hand, as he had to wake up in the early hours of the morning to milk the cows and then take them out to pasture.

'Everyone has to do his duty to earn his fair share of bread,' Uncle Heinz kept repeating to him.

Karl preferred to use his brain though, rather than his hands.

He was a clever boy, cleverer than the boys of the village, who were in the same class at school. Karl had learned to read well before everyone else, had a beautiful calligraphy, and could name all the capitals of Europe by the end of the first year.

He learned quickly and had an almost prodigious memory for his age, which won him the praise of Herr Braun, his teacher, who was constantly pointing him out as an example to his schoolmates. Karl interpreted the remarks by his teacher as a sign of disdain for his fellow students, and soon came to regard them as inferiors: stupid, dumb peasants. They were hopeless and would turn out just like Uncle Heinz, he thought.

His mother had once taken his little face in her hands and told him he was intelligent, far more intelligent than everyone else.

And Mother never lied.

Even Herr Braun concurred he was better than them.

Physically, he was different too; while almost all the other children were blonde with fair eyes and a rosy, healthy-looking complexion, he was quite pale with very dark, rebellious hair and pitch-black eyes.

He definitely didn't fit into that group, and it was clear to see.

Karl never made any real friends among them. He thought that he was way too good to keep company with those retarded idiots. As a result, the boy increasingly displayed a superb, hubristic attitude and kept to himself all the time, becoming a loner.

The other boys came to see in that stringy, bony fellow, who always outclassed them, an arrogant and mean little man. Karl preferred not to talk, never helped, never wanted to play. In their eyes, he was odd.

Children can be very cruel, but they also have the ability to see through their fellows, despite their innate ingenuity, with a clarity that somehow is lost in adulthood.

So, quite soon, they avoided him altogether or played nasty tricks on him.

Karl didn't like that at all. He suffered from it tremendously. It was an insult to his ego though, more than anything else.

Once, a well-built, older boy, who was an obtuse, aggressive student in his class, beat him so hard on his way back home that he passed out. The reason? Karl refused to do homework for him.

He made his return home hours later. Aunt Leni had been really worried, as he was so late and it was beginning to get dark. When she saw the state he was in, she demanded to know what had happened. The day after, she went straight to school to talk to Herr Braun.

The teacher discussed at length with Aunt Leni. He expressed his concerns about Karl's inability to socialise, but he also told her that he was quite special, as his results were well above the average.

'The Arch Abbott is a good friend of mine. Perhaps it would be best for Karl to enter the monastery,' Herr Braun suggested. 'He will get a better education and certainly better company at the Abbey. It is the best solution for Karl. I will write a letter of recommendation,' his teacher said to her.

Aunt Leni agreed with his judgement, and although she felt affection for the boy, it also occurred to her that she would have one less mouth to feed in those hard times.

On hearing the news, the young Blasius couldn't believe his luck, and accepted with enthusiasm the new arrangement. He would live at the castle and live like a prince. He couldn't have felt happier to leave all that mediocrity behind.

And so Karl's destiny was sealed.

He entered the monastery of the Archabbey of Beuron to become a Benedictine monk.

Rome, 1937

'You have to believe me, Your Grace, Karl Blasius has framed me! I am innocent!' he protested with a vigour mixed with desperation. He was a broken man, and he flopped back on his seat as if life had abandoned him.

The Arch Abbott of Beuron Abbey, Petrus De Borg, was in tears in front of the Primate of Saint Benedict, Fidelis Von Stotzingen. The Supreme Head of the Congregation of the Benedictines was his last hope, and he had travelled all the way to the official seat of the Order, at the College of Sant'Anselmo in Rome, to seek his help to dismantle this absurd accusation.

The Primate had known him for years and never had he seen him in that state before. In all previous encounters, he always found Petrus De Borg a calm, measured man of steady character, and now the person in front of him was a wreck, in great distress, clearly very upset and quite desperate. But through that desperation, Von Stotzingen couldn't help but notice that De Borg appeared to have a deep resolve to clear his name. He reckoned that, quite frankly, De Borg's account and logic made more sense than the official version of events that had discredited him, causing his removal from office. At the same time, Karl Blasius appeared to have uncovered a corrupt practice that had been going on for years.

De Borg was determined to prove he was wrong, and for the past two days, despite all the questions that had been fired at him, his account of all the facts hadn't changed: his story was consistent. And that was coming either from an honest man or an exceptionally good actor. Von Stotzingen was inclined to believe the first option.

The senior black monk, as Benedictines were also referred to, removed his spectacles and confronted his dilemma.

'I believe you, Petrus,' he finally said, 'but we will have to prove that Blasius' accusations are not true, which will be tricky as he has three key witnesses, and, apparently, solid evidence. Moreover, he has now been appointed as interim Prior of Beuron, so the whole matter has to be handled carefully and with great tact to avoid further discombobulation at the Abbey, and beyond. Nevertheless, I want to get to the bottom of this very serious matter once and for all.'

'I am ready to confront my accusers. I am truly grateful to have your confidence; you cannot imagine the hell I've been in. The last thing that I would want is to create embarrassment for you or for our sacred Order, to which I so proudly belong. The truth must come out, as otherwise the damage will be worse and long-lasting. I cannot bear the thought that a devious fellow monk, as, in my eyes, Karl Blasius is, will lead my brothers astray. I don't know how I didn't figure him out earlier. He has fooled me for years! The Devil has been at work here and has struck at the very heart of our congregation.'

'With God's help, truth always triumphs, Petrus. The plan is to uncover all facts beyond any doubt. So, here's what I have set out to do. I have a very good friend in Berlin, Baroness Schaeffer, whose son, Friedrich, is one of the finest and most successful lawyers in the country. He is known in forensic circles for his indisputable integrity and he is highly regarded for his ability to thoroughly investigate and uncover the truth. He will help us to unravel this mystification, Petrus. You will go and see him and tell him everything that happened to you.'

'I will make arrangements to travel back to Germany at the earliest then. I will book my ticket for Tuesday morning.'

'Excellent, I will write Friedrich a note of presentation and a letter to carry directly with you. Have faith. Go in peace, Petrus.'

And so, the Arch Abbott left Rome on the first train from Stazione Termini a few days later.

Once in Berlin, he called on the law practice of Friedrich Schaeffer. His office was in an elegant street overlooking the beautiful chestnut trees and peaceful ponds of Tiergarten. At that time of the year, the main park in the centre of town was in full bloom, and many Berliners were enjoying its winding paths inundated with the light and warmth of an early spring sun.

Frau Raeder, his white-haired secretary, showed him in as soon as she was handed the envelope containing the note of presentation and the letter that Fidelis Von Stotzingen had written for the disgraced Arch Abbott, who was in his traditional black habit and wore a crucifix around his neck.

'Kindly wait a moment, Sir,' she said politely, and disappeared behind a polished wooden door. A moment later, it was Friedrich Schaeffer in person that opened the door again.

'Father De Borg, welcome, please come in!' he said cheerfully, inviting the Arch Abbott to join him in his study, while Frau Raeder went back to her desk.

The room had a splendid view and its walls were lined with dozens of juristic treaties and law codes, all neatly arranged and leather bound. On his large desk was a sheaf of documents with the letter sitting open on top.

'Thank you for seeing me without a previous appointment, Herr Schaeffer,' De Borg said, sounding genuinely obliged.

'Do not mention it,' the lawyer said in a soothing tone that always put his clients at ease. 'Fidelis Von Stotzingen is a very good friend of the family. We go back a long way and he would never call on me to ask for a professional opinion unless it was a matter of great importance to him. And from what I can see, this definitely is. So, perhaps it's worth starting from the very beginning. But before you do that, let me bring in my secretary again. She will take some notes for us.'

In saying that, he pressed the intercom button on his desk.

'Frau Raeder, please could you come here immediately, and bring a notebook with you, thanks.'

Petrus De Borg relaxed a bit, believing he was in good hands. If it wasn't for the presence of Frau Raeder, the experience could almost be compared to a confession. Only, this time, it was him that sought to be pardoned.

'Tell me all you know and remember, Father De Borg,' said Schaeffer, 'and don't leave any detail out, even if it might seem trivial or irrelevant.'

The Arch Abbott started his narration.

'Karl Blasius, my fellow Benedictine brother, the chief accountant and administrator of the Abbey of Beuron, my right-hand man really, accused me of falsifying the monastery's entries and embezzling thousands of Reichsmarks for personal gain. And with that money, he said, I indulged a lavish secret lifestyle and even paid for the sexual favours of prostitutes.'

Schaeffer sensed Petrus De Borg's deep shame at proffering those last words.

'I have never done such things. I am an honest man and I have always regarded chastity as the greatest gift to the Lord.'

He seemed to be worried more about this last accusation as it represented a moral stain on his principles, beliefs and rule of his Order.

As he continued, the voice of the religious man was full of emotion and started to tremble.

'I loved all my brothers, and all the people in my community, equally. Nevertheless, the person I probably trusted most, that I favoured most, has been the Brutus that has stabbed me in the back, without thinking twice, and with the utmost heinous, indecent accusations.'

He went on to explain that it was he who took young Karl in, guided him, nurtured his talent and gave him more and more responsibilities, up to the nomination of Chief Accountant of the Abbey.

Petrus watched young Blasius' blossoming intelligence with the eye of a pious father and took him under his wing. The poor orphan deserved a second chance in life. He interpreted his determination to learn and achieve great results as God's response to choose the finest to serve him. And Karl had a fine brain indeed.

'But I should not have ignored his increasingly erratic behaviour. And clear signs that, in fact, all he did was in service of his ambition to reach a higher status, the highest in the Abbey, and perhaps beyond. I cannot explain otherwise the reason for his infamous betrayal.'

Schaeffer heard how Karl Blasius, in cahoots with a banker in Tuttlingen, a vicious tenant of a farm on the Abbey's land who was angry at the Abbott, and a prostitute, had built up a story. Then they further corroborated it with false proofs which framed the Arch Abbott. Behind his back, Blasius reported his alleged crimes to his superiors, and asked for his removal. He was successful and was nominated as the interim Prior of the Abbey, pending further investigation. Karl knew full well that with those three witnesses, his accusation would be as solid as a rock, especially because it was Karl himself who had falsified all the records in the books. He intended to make De Borg appear as a fraudster who had funnelled money from the monastery income into a personal bank account, which he then used for his own pleasures.

Schaeffer was startled that Blasius had managed to paint such a crucifying picture.

A distraught Arch Abbott kept talking, with Frau Raeder furiously writing down dates, times, people, places. After almost three hours, a visibly shaken, but equally reassured De Borg left Schaeffer's office.

Schaeffer started to work on the case straight away, and very discreetly contacted a number of Benedictine monks at the Abbey and the witnesses. He compared the various versions and checked all the financial transactions. He found out that the monk, for years, had slyly disseminated a flurry of subtle negative comments about the Arch Abbott among his fellow monks, hinting at some strange favourable treatments and relationships he had, and that he, Blasius, was forced to accommodate. In his position of Chief Accountant, he had opened an account at the bank in Tuttlingen, depositing money there coming from the regular total income of the Abbey. To coerce his witnesses, he firstly engineered a mounting debt for the banker by lending him the money deposited in his bank – it was him in fact that had the vice of visiting prostitutes for sex and spending a fortune. Then he raised the vicious tenant's rent two-fold. Subsequently, he offered them both a way out: help him with a testimony against the Arch Abbot and get their debts written off, or pay back straight away, knowing all too well they couldn't, and would certainly lose their business if they did. For the prostitute, it was easy: he just paid her a large sum.

Schaeffer had to admit that Blasius had been cunning, as well as clever, in how he engineered the whole thing.

With his investigation complete, he was finally ready to confront that power-hungry monk. When he arrived in Beuron, Schaeffer thought that the Abbey looked more like a regal building than a religious house, with its white baroque façade and gorgeous architectural features. At first glance, it seemed the princely seat of a king. Blasius was expecting him. And he behaved like a monarch from the very moment Schaeffer stepped into his chamber. He had indeed the impressive, commanding presence of a ruler, but somehow, his spectral face and his long, dark mane gave the impression of a sinister actor trying to impersonate a part that wasn't completely his. Blasius had shown a good deal of arrogance and boldness, and appeared completely in charge at the beginning of their conversation. While Schaeffer outlined his findings, he kept slowly circling around him, like a shark, waiting to take a bite off his prey.

But by the end of the meeting the black-clad monk looked more and more defeated. Schaeffer had completely cornered him by taking apart his house of cards, and he knew that he hadn't any left to play. One by one, the lawyer had uncovered and dismantled all the lies of his three witnesses, who had quickly overturned their previous depositions. As well as documenting clear flaws in his brilliant plan, he was able to prove that the whole story was entirely Karl's diabolical machination in order to fulfil his voracious ambitions. He had rigged his accounts, coerced people into making false statements by blackmailing them, and would surely face fraud charges. But more than anything else, he would be officially labelled as dishonest by his congregation, with serious implications when it came to understanding that he broke his vows. Expulsion was certain.

Schaeffer, looking at an increasingly uneasy Blasius, calmly said to him, 'You have only one choice, Father Blasius: confess. Confess to your brothers, but primarily confess to the Primate and thus restore the Arch Abbott to his rightful post. Ask for his pardon. Consider what I told you with great attention. Because the alternative is to go to a public trial, and you certainly do not want that, do you?'

Schaeffer purposely did not make any reference to repentance. He did not think an individual that had done the things that Karl Blasius had was capable of such a noble, genuine gesture. During his research, he formed the personal opinion that this monk's soul was as black as his habit.

Blasius knew he had lost. He was fast to weigh up his options. In going to court, the Order had as much to lose as he did, and would provoke not only a telluric effect in the monastic community, but also among the faithful. So, perhaps, he still had a small bargaining chip to play.

He was ordered back to Rome. Here, in front of the Primate of the Order, Fidelis Von Stotzingen; the Arch Abbott, Petrus De Borg; a commission of Benedictine fellow monks; and under the watchful eye of Friedrich Schaeffer, Karl Blasius was obliged to depose that he had invented all the charges and to swear that he was prepared to make amends. His judges immediately deprived him of his prior-ship. Blasius wasn't allowed to go back to Beuron, where De Borg was reinstated.

'These are terrible, almost unforgivable actions, Brother Blasius,' the Primate said to him gravely, before he was told his fate, 'but I have the firm belief that, with the grace of God, the place we are sending you to will be the strongest inspiration for your repentance. You have obviously been exposed to great temptations by your mundane desires, and I can only see that the Devil has been successfully at work with you. The Devil only blandished you to false ambitions so you will go to the desert to atone for your sins and learn, like our Lord Jesus did before starting his ministry, to resist and reject Satan's seductions. The proximity to the places where He lived and preached will only reinforce your resolve and do you good.'

Blasius appeared shaken. But he was startled, perhaps more than Schaeffer was, that the Primate didn't expel him from the Order.

That was a victory in itself. He would be able to pursue a career again.

His judging panel exited the room, and Blasius was left with Schaeffer, who was still putting his documents back in his briefcase.

Blasius gave a corrosive, as well as victorious glance at Schaeffer. Then, he venomously hissed at him: 'You'll be damned! I acted for a greater good, to get rid of an old fool and lead one of the greatest centres of study in Christianity to heights it has never reached before, and that he could never guide it to!'

With what Schaeffer would remember later as a sign of mounting irrationality, Blasius' voice assumed a deep growling tone, as that of an animal ready to kill.

'God will make you pay for that. I will witness your death, and I will pray for it with all the fibres of my being. You ruined me, you destroyed God's design! I will never forget!'

Schaeffer wasn't normally frightened by threats, but in the days that followed, the crazy, vicious look he had read in the monk's eyes made him realise that Blasius, consumed by his insane ambition, might have lost his mind or, even worse, be mad. And it was never good to leave behind that sort of enemy. Only a totally deranged person or a true criminal would proffer those threats after what, in his view, was an acquittal. Absolution, in religious terms, had proved to offer a different outcome clearly, and Schaeffer wasn't sure at all that it was the right level of punishment for Blasius.

The highest ranks of the Black Monks Order had a different view.

A totally disgraced Karl Blasius was sent to a permanent exile in a Benedictine Abbey on Mount Zion in Palestine, never to return.

Rome, 1942

'Thank you, Adelio, that'll be all for today,' Karl Blasius told him.

The young monk stood up from his desk, put the fragile, old manuscripts he had meticulously examined that afternoon into a wooden box, smiled timidly at the Chief Archivist, and left the private section of the library of the Pontifical Biblical Institute, the prestigious institution run by the Society of Jesus since its foundation by the Pope in 1909.

Blasius closed his eyes and enjoyed for a minute the sound of silence granted by the thick walls of that ancient building in Piazza della Pilotta in Rome. He had loved his new home from the first moment he had stepped into this cathedral of Jesuitical knowledge.

He was back. Not just in any place. And he couldn't have found a more perfect nest.

He glanced to the other side of the small rectangular square, from where the façade of the Gregorian University, to which the Biblicum – as the Pontifical Biblical Institute was also known – was affiliated, stared back at him.

In a way, Blasius' personal journey that saw him travelling around, from place to place, before reaching his final destination, was strangely mirrored by that of the institution housed there. Called the Roman College at the time of its foundation, the university was initially located in Piazza dell'Aracoeli, at the bottom of the Capitoline Hill. After a few years, it moved to Via Del Gesù, in a bigger facility to house a growing number of students. The school became so popular that Pope Gregory XIII commissioned the refurbishment of a much larger building in Via del Corso, and from that moment it became known as the Gregorian University, in his honour. Soon, even this and the next generous new site dimensions proved no longer suitable, so it was Via del Seminario first, and finally, it found its new home in Piazza della Pilotta, where it still is today. The university even suffered a temporary wipe-out, when it followed the suppression of the Jesuitical Society, only to be reinstated years and years later, reborn from its own ashes like the mythological phoenix.

Blasius thought they both showed the same kind of resilience. And that building stood there, looking back to remind him every day.

Even if the black-clad monk wanted to, he would probably never forget the incredible chain of events that had brought him to Rome.

Blasius was convinced he was finished when that damned lawyer, Friedrich Schaeffer, had uncovered his scheming and made him confess in front of the Primate of the Benedictine Order. What a slur he had to suffer; what an indignity that moment was!

Had they expelled him from the clergy that day, he would probably have felt it as a lesser punishment over time. Instead, he was condemned to exile, a vicious form of penitence, and an example to all others who dared to think of following in his path, confined to eternal expiation in Palestine. He still vividly remembered the striking difference in the landscape compared to Germany, with its arid hills and dusty roads, and hardly any spots of green in sight, where large flocks of sheep roamed freely, guarded by a few shepherds with their donkeys. He thought he had travelled back to the time of the Crusades. Even more so when he got to Jerusalem, after a very uncomfortable journey in the back of an open truck with Arab and Jewish migrants – there was no welcome committee for him when he disembarked at the port in Haifa.

He had to walk through the narrow roads of that ancient city, one of the oldest in the world, as the Babylonians, the Persians, the Romans, and the Ottomans had done before him. It felt quite claustrophobic at times, as some of the alleys were really narrow, and one felt almost swallowed by the towering stone walls of the maze. If the labyrinth he had had to navigate wasn't enough to test his sense of direction, another distraction came from the smells, heightened by the heat, coming from the spices and other goods abundantly displayed in multiple varieties outside shops. And then voices, languages, faces, clothes of many fashions and geographical provenance were all jumbling together, creating an unintelligible cacophony of sounds and visuals. When he finally reached and got inside the Benedictine Abbey of the Dormition – called so

98

as the Virgin Mary fell asleep there – just outside the walls of the Old City, on Mount Zion, he felt as if the doors of paradise had opened; such was the sense of peace and calm inside, a shelter for the body, the soul and the mind. But, strangely enough, there was a sense of vague familiarity to it as well, and it wasn't a far-fetched perception, as he discovered soon. The monastery had been built by the German architect Theodor Sandel at the end of the nineteenth century. Therefore, its Romanesque style didn't feel as alien as the rest of the city.

If Fidelis Von Stotzingen had called for the desert as an ideal place for Blasius' cleansing, he would never have imagined that the desert would prove to be a place for a very different sort of redemption, and not of the kind the Primate had in mind.

If Blasius ever needed proof that the ways of the Lord are infinite, he found it in the Holy Land.

During a very hot day, after crossing the nearly empty square on the Temple Mount, Blasius decided to take a break and shelter from the scorching sun in the Dome of the Rock, one of the most sacred Islamic shrines, that stands in front of the Al Aqsa Mosque in Old Jerusalem. Inside, he was welcomed by a cool and empty space, with an enormous rock featuring at its centre. If the external décor was impressive, with its exquisite variety of blue and golden tiles, internally it was equally mesmerising. Blasius was stupefied by the intricate marble work and the inscriptions in Arabic around its circular shape. With his eyes focusing on the ceiling of the building, he didn't notice the figure who had discreetly materialised at his side.

The man read aloud one of the Arabic inscriptions of the inner octagonal arcade: '*When He decreeth a thing, He saith unto it only: Be! and it is.* A beautiful verse, isn't it? It tells all about the infinite power of Allah.'

99

The monk turned to have a good look at him. He had dark skin, a well-curated short beard, which was slightly grey. He was wearing a black jubba, a kind of Palestinian jacket, and a white Taqiya, the typical rounded Arab skullcap, except his had more of a triangular shape, with a slightly taller and larger top.

He asked: 'I hope I didn't spoil it for you. Do your read Arabic?'

'No, just Hebrew, Latin and Greek, but I have started to learn it. It's quite difficult for a Westerner,' Blasius replied. 'Thank you for your translation. I have always been enthralled by this magnificent building.' He had wanted to see with his own eyes what, at one point in history, was called the Templum Domini, thought to be the site of the original Temple of Solomon. 'It always intrigued me that the Knights Templars depicted it on the back of their official seal. They modelled their round churches across Europe on its structure when they had to leave the Holy Land. I guess they never wanted to forget it, perhaps in the hope to recapture it at some point.'

'Ah, the Crusaders! The infidels who turned it into their main headquarters in Jerusalem. In the end, the Muslims reconquered what was rightfully theirs and threw them out.'

'Now it's under British rule though,' Blasius said in a tone of contempt.

An annoyed look flashed across the Arab's face, but he immediately wiped it away, regaining his composure.

'Perhaps not for long. Soon it will be back in Palestinian hands,' he said, with quiet determination. Then he asked: 'You don't seem enthusiastic about the British. Nor am I. From your accent and your black habit, I gather you might be a German Benedictine from the abbey on Mount Zion, am I right? I am a great admirer of your Fuehrer, Adolf Hitler. I am Mohammed Amin al-Husseini, Grand Mufti of Jerusalem. We have more than one enemy in common. And we can help each other. Please come and see me at my home near Herod's Gate, we'll talk again.' In saying that, he told him his address and then left, making his way towards the exit.

At the time, Blasius would never have imagined that salvation would come in the form of a Muslim Arab nationalist. It was his fortuitous association with the Grand Mufti that had brought him to the attention of Reinhard Heydrich, the man with the iron heart as Hitler had described him. The fearsome Nazi commander of the SD, the secret intelligence agency of the SS, was keen to infiltrate the group that unleashed the Arab revolt against the British Mandate and the Jews in Palestine in 1936, as Blasius came to know later, a riot partly subsidised by the Fascist Government of Italy. Heydrich, eager to find a 'solution' for the Jews – of which he would become the main architect – as well as deploying a network of agents in the region, highly valued Blasius' ability to be the eyes and ears of the SD in that British dominated Middle Eastern territory. And Heydrich had rewarded Blasius for forging the Nazi link with the Arab nationalists with a one-way ticket back to the centre of Christendom. His good services were needed again for a much higher game now, which was being played in and around the Vatican, and the SD commander found in the Benedictine the perfect candidate. Blasius was not only reinstated in a senior position, but Heydrich made sure he got a place in a highly regarded, powerful Jesuitical institution, which not only granted him access, but also status, at the highest level in the Holy City, and across the top echelons of the clergy.

And from here, who knows what I can ascend to if I play my cards well, he thought, that late afternoon, alone in his study. His ambition had been unleashed again since he'd arrived in Rome, and this time he didn't intend to make the same mistakes as the past. He would plan carefully and serve whatever Himmler wanted on a silver plate. And he wanted that spy.

Perhaps, I will be able to kill two birds with one stone, he pondered, cunningly, if I can manage to drag Schaeffer down in the process. I would rather enjoy seeing him fall far more catastrophically than I did, with no hope of a comeback.

That idea gave him the foretaste of how sweet victory could be.

But how?

He put his chin in his hands and looked down at the stone-paved square, reflecting the last rays of light of the day.

CHAPTER 7

As soon as General Rommel had departed Rome, flying back to his base in Africa, Schaeffer was summoned by Albert Kesselring, the highest representative of the Third Reich in Italy.

The Wehrmacht Commander-in-Chief South, responsible for all of German military operations in the Mediterranean, had his headquarters at Villa Avorio, in Grottaferrata, a small town on the Alban Hills just a few miles south-east of Rome. Like Goering, he had preferred a more secluded place and chose a classic palatial mansion, away from the hustle and bustle of the Eternal City, sheltered from curious eyes and easy to be defended.

Schaeffer arrived with his newly appointed attendant, Captain Wolf.

'Wait here, Captain,' Schaeffer ordered Wolf. 'I won't be long.'

He entered the hall of the grand house and was shown into Kesselring's office straight away. The Field Marshall was on the phone when he entered, but made a gesture to come in, quickly dismissing his interlocutor and hanging up.

'Rommel has full confidence in you, Lieutenant Colonel Schaeffer. He said it to me again just this morning,' said the Field Marshall, after both officers exchanged salutes. 'You will have the men and equipment you requested.'

He sounded rather curt and didn't seem inclined to spend too much time in conversation with Schaeffer.

'Here's a personal order signed off. Hand it over to Sargent Jodl. He will sort everything out for you.'

'Many thanks, Field Marshall. I appreciate how fast you organised putting together resources for me. I intend to be fully operational in the next forty-eight hours,' responded Schaeffer.

He knew that Kesselring wasn't a fan of Rommel, or of him, but was sure that Hitler had issued a stark order, otherwise he wouldn't have obtained everything he had asked for so quickly.

Kesselring observed Schaeffer and remained silent for a few moments. He seemed reluctant to let him go straight away. After a minute, he asked, 'Tell me, Schaeffer, how did you come to choose Palazzo Roveri as your residence here in Rome? I have to confess I had never heard of it before and didn't even know where it was until Rommel notified me that you resolutely manifested your intention to base your headquarters there, while in the capital.'

'In a way I am glad that hotel isn't a major establishment or as well known as others in town, as this is the whole point: to hide in plain sight. Officially, as we all know, I am here to offer support to Fascist Major Marino Severi, but in fact I will be the commander of the whole operation. Feeding false intelligence to the enemy while we prepare a major ship convoy will allow us to work in the shadows, while, whoever is spying on us, looks the other way. Choosing a quiet place that isn't an obvious choice for a German officer, as Albergo Flora would be for instance, is a strategic, logistical and rather necessary move.'

Kesselring half smiled, but Schaeffer saw that it was a bit forced and that his gaze remained cold. He couldn't wait to take leave, but couldn't do it until the Field Marshall dismissed him. He didn't want to stay in the Field Marshall's company and the Field Marshall didn't want to be in his company either, from reading his body language.

'A clever diversion which hopefully will pay off. Report on progress first thing every Monday, Lieutenant Colonel.' Kesselring finally said, 'You can go now.'

'Of course, I will, Field Marshall. Heil Hitler!'

Clicking his heels, Schaeffer walked out.

He jumped into the driving seat of his car.

'I'll drive, Wolf.'

He entered the forward gear and pressed the accelerator pedal, and making the engine grumble, he turned around to head back to Rome, to Palazzo Roveri.

They passed the open-air vegetable market in a square close by, while it was in full swing. It was already mid-morning and a small crowd of people, mostly women and children, were flocking around the multi-coloured stalls to get the fresh produce coming from the farms around the city.

'Let's buy some of those cherries. I haven't had any for ages. I cannot even remember when I ate my last one,' said Schaeffer, who felt suddenly famished. He parked up and walked towards a smaller cart pulled by a donkey that had just stopped at the edge of the square. The owner, a young woman in her mid-twenties with a pair of shoes that had known better days, saw the two German officers coming in her direction, and appeared scared by their sudden presence there.

Schaeffer could see she was uncomfortable, and to demonstrate his good intentions, he pulled some Italian lire, the local money, from his pocket, showing he wanted to purchase some of her cherries. She was quick to understand, and was fast to grab a generous bunch, which she put in a small basket and said, 'Please keep it as well; it's easier to carry. I won't charge you for it.'

She wanted to get rid of them as fast as possible and offering a gift seemed like a good idea to send them on their way quickly.

'Thank you, they look rather delicious, but please here's some extra money. It's only fair,' said Schaeffer, trying to have a short conversation.

It had been months since he had spoken to a woman, and it was a refreshing change to hear a feminine, gentler voice. Clearly, though, the girl wasn't keen. She shoved the money into one of the pockets of her apron and turned the other way.

'She is frightened, it seems, or she doesn't like me,' the Afrika Korps officer joked while walking back to the car.

'Romans don't particularly like any of us German soldiers, Lieutenant Colonel, I'm afraid. They fear us, even more than they fear the Fascists,' commented Captain Wolf, who had been in town long enough to learn that was the case.

They drove down the road, towards what would become their new base. Schaeffer recognised the building straight away, and not only because it was quite magnificent from the outside, compared to its neighbouring buildings. He had admired it in the pictures that Count Nuvoli of the Divisione Ariete, the Fascist tank division stationed in North Africa, had shown him while they were in Tripoli together. Count Augusto Nuvoli shared with him many pictures, not only of the building, but also of his fiancée Cordelia Olivieri, talking about her at length.

Schaeffer had been bewitched by her image since the first moment he saw her: she was the most beautiful woman he had ever seen. He had been carrying one of her pictures since then, and in fact the photograph of the woman he had in his pocket was of her.

He felt anxious to see her all of a sudden.

With Captain Wolf in tow, he entered the reception of Palazzo Roveri. The interior was quite welcoming for a palace of the early Renaissance. The walls were lined with an antique turquoise silk wallpaper, while the ceiling still retained its original fresco, representing a sky dotted with ethereal white clouds with four winged baby angels at each corner. They all seemed to look towards the centre, from which a long chain, wrapped up in velvet fabric, supported a sumptuous Murano glass chandelier, with at least forty arms that illuminated the room as if the sun was shining in it. The reception desk, an ancient and richly carved refectory-style table, had been placed on an oriental rug whose blue, red and golden tones complimented the colour of the walls. A telephone and a bell were sitting on its polished surface, beside a Caltagirone ceramic vase of freshly cut roses, whose pungent scent pervaded the place. It looked enchanting; the owner certainly had great taste.

Schaeffer rang the bell and they heard the sound of fast steps on the marble floor. He recognised her immediately and felt his heartbeat slightly accelerating.

Unlike in many of the photographs where her hair was loose on her shoulders, today Cordelia had it styled neatly behind her neck in a beehive bun. She was wearing a sapphire-blue silk dress that wrapped around her voluptuous figure, showing off her tiny waist and long legs. Light make-up accentuated her eyes and full lips.

Both Schaeffer and Wolf were taken aback by her stunning appearance and just stood there, staring.

Cordelia was equally startled at seeing the two German officers. Even in that already warm morning, a shiver ran down her spine.

They have found me; they have found out who I am, she feared for an instant. They're here to arrest me.

Everyone, for different reasons, remained silent.

Breaking that awkward moment, Schaeffer said, 'Good Morning, Miss Olivieri, I am Friedrich Schaeffer, Lieutenant Colonel of the Afrika Korps, a division of the Wehrmacht.'

Looking at him, a sense of *déjà vu* came upon her, although Cordelia was sure she had never met him or heard his name before.

With the firmest voice she was able to produce, she said, 'Good Morning, Colonel, welcome to my hotel. What can I do for you?'

'We would be delighted to be your guests, Madame. In fact, we are here to hire the entire hotel,' said Schaeffer.

Cordelia's heart sank, but she managed to hold her nerve.

'All rooms in the hotel? I cannot do that, I'm afraid. It's impossible at the moment … I mean … I have a few guests here already. Besides, as we mainly cater for the clergy, we are quite close to the Vatican you see, we've got a few arrivals this week already. Perhaps I can suggest an alternative accommodation for you, gentlemen?'

'I understand, Madame. This is not a request, I'm afraid, and in fact you will get a letter from the Fascist command that will commandeer this entire building for military purposes. I wanted to come here first to communicate it to you personally and explain that we will pay you adequately and also refund you for your losses.'

Schaeffer handed Cordelia the document and noticed her face turning to stone.

In that instant, he felt sorry for her. He could just about imagine the feeling of shock in seeing her establishment taken over by foreign soldiers, uninvited and so unexpected.

Cordelia felt helpless, but she knew she wasn't in any position to refuse. They would do it anyway.

'Well, I see … There's nothing I can say then. May I please ask you to let me inform my guests. I will make sure all rooms are clear by the end of the morning. Let me call the hotel maid so we can start to notify them immediately.' In saying that, Cordelia summoned Flaminia.

'I am truly grateful, Miss Olivieri, and I promise we will try to avoid any disruption to your daily life as much as possible.'

Then, addressing his attendant, he imparted him with a command: 'Captain Wolf, please make an assessment of all the rooms in the building, so that when the rest of our officers arrive, you can start allocating them straight away for the set up.'

'Jawohl, Lieutenant Colonel!'

Meanwhile, a young girl in her early twenties wearing a black dress with a freshly ironed white apron and low-heel black leather shoes arrived. She was brandishing a feather duster and if she was surprised at the sight of the two German officers, she did not show it at all.

Looking rather bothered to have been distracted from what she was doing, with an unusual and annoying high-pitched voice, she asked, 'Did you need me, Miss Olivieri?'

'Flaminia, could you go to the first floor and notify our guests that they will need to leave their rooms, and that we are finding them alternative accommodation. Captain Wolf can come with you while he takes a look around the hotel. Thank you.'

The maid looked at Wolf and grinned mischievously. When she spoke again, her attitude had changed completely. 'Of course, Miss Olivieri,' she said, in a tone that left no doubt about her character. 'Please come with me, Captain. It will be a real pleasure.' She left wiggling, followed by Wolf.

All of a sudden, Cordelia realised that Schaeffer had called her by her surname.

Twice.

And she hadn't had the time to introduce herself. How could he …

but before she asked the question, he provided the explanation she was after.

'Your fiancé, Augusto Nuvoli, talked to me so much about this place, and indeed yourself. I am glad to say that it has surpassed all my expectations. You have decorated it magnificently,' the German officer said, looking around in admiration.

Cordelia was struck by his revelation.

Oh, my God ... he knew Augusto then! That explains it, she thought, surprised.

Schaeffer added, 'I am so sorry for your loss – my condolences. It must have been a tragedy to hear of his death, Miss Olivieri. He always spoke so highly of you.'

'Thank you, Colonel Schaeffer.'

'We were stationed together in Tripoli for a while. His Ariete tank division supported the Afrika Korps troops during the assault on Gazala. He was killed by a shell, the day before we conquered the town. He fought and died valorously.'

For some reason, for the first time since she'd received the cable from the War Ministry, Cordelia experienced true sadness. It was as if, finally, the news had dawned on her.

She had never really loved Augusto; she had known this for some time, but that notion fully crystallised when she had read the message that was delivered to her, already weeks ago. It felt like she had been notified that a distant relative had lost his life, rather than her fiancé.

In a way, albeit unconsciously, she had felt a sort of relief that she would not have to go ahead with a marriage to a man who would probably have continued to conduct his old bohemian life and enjoy racing cars as he always did as a bachelor. Augusto was not one for settling down in a quieter family type of existence. She and Augusto had got together for the wrong reasons, or perhaps for the right reasons at a point in time, but certainly it was not a relationship that would have lasted, or at least this is what Cordelia kept reflecting on while he was posted overseas.

Her emotional detachment from him had started back then, probably even earlier.

Nevertheless, they had a sort of mutual affection for each other, and Cordelia thought how scared he must have been, there, in the desert, an alien place away from home, under enemy fire. He was too young to die.

It was strange, but an unexplained sense of guilt came upon her, as if, had she truly loved him, perhaps it wouldn't have happened. It was irrational and absurd, like the stupid war. Her eyes filled with tears.

'Oh no, Miss Olivieri, apologies if I have upset you. I didn't want to trigger bad memories,' Schaeffer said contrite.

Great, he thought, first I requisition her property and then I remind her of the death of her fiancé. Well done, you're off to a good start, Friedrich.

Embarrassed, he didn't know what to say so he just stood there. He felt an impulse to hug that beautiful woman.

'Don't worry, Colonel, I will be fine in a moment,' Cordelia said in a broken voice, wiping her eyes with the back of the hand.

What the hell are you doing? This is not the moment to lose your nerve, Cordelia, pull yourself together, she mentally reproached herself.

'Would you like to join me for a drink at the bar, in the lounge? I feel I need one, even at this hour of the day.'

'With pleasure, Madame.'

They were about to head next door when a group of Fascists entered the hotel.

Marino Severi, accompanied by Lucifer and four other Blackshirts, in their dark outfits and leather boots, stepped into the reception.

As soon as Severi realised that the German Afrika Korps commander had preceded him, he extended his arm in the Roman salute and said, 'Major Marino Severi at your service! I would have been here earlier had I known you had plans to come today. I was notified only an hour ago.'

Severi sounded a bit annoyed to see Schaeffer there so unexpectedly and so soon.

So, that's my nemesis, the Fascist thought, the dishonour of having been stripped of his command still very raw, renewed by seeing who had taken over from him. Inside, his battered ego was struggling to accept this new command. He felt angry with his direct superior for signing his demotion, with Mussolini, who had given in to the Germans, and with that damned spy, whoever he was. All were guilty of causing a stop, as temporary as it might be, to his shining career. And now, even with his sudden appearance, this bloody German had beaten him in his duty, making him look inadequate and late in front of his men. Lucifer, who was just a couple of steps away from Severi, saw his boss's frustration clearly depicted on his face.

'Good morning, Major Severi. My men still haven't arrived, so you can carry on inspecting the hotel as I'm sure you've planned to do. By the way, my attendant Captain Wolf is here and he's gone upstairs.'

Is he a mind reader? What does he know about what I planned to do, which orders I have? Severi thought, even more cross.

'I thought I'd pay a visit to my comrade Augusto Nuvoli's fiancée, Miss Cordelia Olivieri, to personally inform her, before you arrived with your order of requisition of her premises.'

And a gentleman too, Severi noticed ironically. He hated him passionately already.

Lucifer, who kept watching the two of them speaking, guessed: so, here's why he has elected this place as his bolt-hole. This German was pals with that Italian guy.

This complicated things even further, knowing of Father Colombo's plan to get Cordelia out of the country. Lucifer reckoned that her movements would be under a magnifying lens from now on. No way could she quietly leave the hotel with both the Germans and the Fascists coming and going. But perhaps the very fact that the Germans had chosen this place ... Lucifer had a mad idea all of a sudden. He was thinking fast. His mental machinations were interrupted by Severi, who brought him into play.

'... and my attendant, Guido Rovo, will assist you.'

Lucifer, who had only seen Cordelia from afar, met her gaze for the first time and handed her the order from the command.

'Did we interrupt anything, Lieutenant Colonel?' Severi asked, having noticed that the two of them had been in conversation on his arrival.

'We were about to go into the lounge next door for a drink, but now that you're all here, perhaps I can offer you something as well, Major?'

'Thank you, Miss Olivieri, but we have our orders. Besides, with the German soldiers on their way here, we are better to get on with it,' Severi replied.

Having a drink with the German officer was the last thing he wanted at that moment.

'We'll leave you to your duty, Major,' Schaeffer was quick to add, glad to be left in her company alone.

They stepped into the grand room, leaving Severi, Lucifer and their men behind.

Cordelia went to the bar trolley, just beside a massive marble fireplace, an Art Deco piece that had belonged to her father, and poured two small glasses of vermouth.

While she handed the drink to him, Schaeffer's eyes were drawn to the large oil portrait of a priest, painted in profile and wearing a red dress and generous hat, hanging on the wall behind one of the velvet-covered sofas adorning the room.

'He's Cardinal Antongiulio Roveri,' she said, following his gaze. 'He descended from a wealthy Roman family, who built this palace in fact, at the end of the fifteenth century. He had a taste for pomp and was keen to show off his riches. Most of the furniture in this room, and in the hotel, is still of the period. When he passed away, he left the building to a dissolute nephew, who gambled it away. My great-grandfather bought it from one of his creditors, making it his home.'

'And now it's a hotel. How did that happen?' asked Schaeffer, genuinely intrigued by the transition from private dwelling to public establishment.

'My grandfather never liked living here; for him it was too big, cold and damp. So he bought a smaller home in the countryside. My father, who was gifted it for his wedding, lived here while my mother was alive. After her death, though, he refused to stay – too many memories, I guess, and we moved to my grandfather's home, which also had the space to house all his sports cars. He loved cars, you see. Like Augusto.'

She drank her vermouth in one go and felt slightly more relaxed. Now the memory of a picture Augusto had sent from Africa in one of his letters resurfaced: he and another two officers were photographed beside one of the sports cars he had shipped to Tripoli years before the start of the war. She was pretty sure that one of the men was Schaeffer.

Cordelia continued. 'My father, in turn, gave it to me when I got engaged to Augusto, but soon after he died as I had just started restoring it. With no job and no income of my own, I decided to turn the palace into a hotel. I moved back to Rome and into the dépendance at the end of the garden, from which it was easier to run it.'

'Augusto told me of your passion for this building and how much work you put in it and in the business – you did a splendid job. It is absolutely charming.'

As you are, Schaeffer thought.

Cordelia found herself strangely at ease with him now and, curious, she asked, 'How did you and Augusto meet?'

'He was one of the main liaison officers with the Afrika Korps on behalf of the Italian Army. We got along very well immediately. He had incredible *savoir faire,* tact and a great sense of humour. Plus, he knew Tripoli well, so I got a private tour of all the cafés, bars and clubs. I saw him racing in one of the last competitions allowed. I enjoyed our time while it lasted. He was a real ambassador, with a lust for life.'

Cordelia was about to say something when they heard the sound of roaring engines coming to a stop in front of the main gate. She looked out of the window and saw that the German soldiers had arrived. There were at least fifty of them.

Downstairs in the kitchen, Alma, the cook, had also heard the noise of the trucks and, soon after, men clattering over the stone front yard. Worried, she ran upstairs and found Cordelia in the lounge, in the company of a German officer.

'Pardon me for interrupting, Miss Olivieri, but there are lots of soldiers just outside. What's going on?' she asked, always addressing her formally in public, while still panting. She looked at Schaeffer interrogatively.

'Alma, this is Colonel Schaeffer of the Wehrmacht. He and his men are going to be our guests, the only guests we will have for a while.'

She saw her old nanny turn paler.

'I was about to come down and tell you of the new arrangement, of which I've just been notified myself.'

'You have to excuse me, Miss Olivieri,' Schaeffer announced, 'but I need to organise my men now. Perhaps we can continue our conversation later? I would very much like that.'

'I am going nowhere, Colonel. I will be in my office at the back of reception if you need me.'

'Splendid.'

He took her hand and kissed it, before taking leave. Her skin was warm and soft. He hated himself for having to let it go, longing already for their next encounter.

Flaminia crossed paths with Schaeffer on the way into the grand room and gave him the same lascivious look she had favoured Wolf with.

'You will get into serious trouble with these ones, Flaminia,' warned Alma, who knew the girl's inclination to flirt a bit too ostentatiously with men. 'I've told you many times that you're playing with fire, and if you don't control yourself, you're going to regret it.'

'Oh, stop it, Alma. Don't be silly. These are our allies, and very powerful allies too. I am just kind and friendly, that's all. Besides, I am young and I want to enjoy myself,' she said, and hinting at the cook's old age, she added with a sneering grin, 'unlike others. What's wrong with that?'

'When you are out of here, you can do what you want, Flaminia,' intervened Cordelia brusquely, 'but while you are in service, you will conduct yourself professionally and respectfully, with everyone, including your colleagues. Thanks, you can go now.'

It was not the first time that Cordelia had had to rebuke the maid, and she was annoyed to have to do it more and more often. Flaminia was becoming bolder in provoking Alma, and she didn't like it. She particularly hated to see that the young waitress enjoyed the effect her words had and how other people suffered from her intentionally vicious comments.

There's definitely something wrong with this girl. I will have to let her go one of these days, she reckoned.

But knowing that her family really needed the money, she kept postponing that decision, despite her conviction that the maid was developing more and more of a dodgy and insufferable character.

Flaminia was livid.

I can't flirt yet the grand dame can play the charming coquette, she thought. Well, not anymore. I am as attractive and beautiful as you can be without nice clothes on. And perhaps I will be able to buy those fabulous dresses that only she can afford now, if I play my cards right.

Cordelia spent the rest of the day organising different hotels for the forced departure of her guests. She sent out Flaminia to buy additional food supplies as requested by Colonel Schaeffer. He had elected to have his office in the library, on the first floor, just beside the master suite that he took as his own night accommodation. The rest of the soldiers occupied all the other rooms. Four of them were permanently stationed in the reception, both inside and outside the main door, while others patrolled the fence around the garden at the back of the building.

Captain Wolf told Cordelia that from now on, only the hotel staff would be able to access the premises; these were strict orders of Colonel Schaeffer.

'You and your employees are free to come and go as you please, of course,' he said to her, 'but this won't apply to anyone else. Deliveries will need to be left outside. My men will carry them inside from now on.'

'And I suppose that since I am not allowed to host anyone while you are here, that means also a restriction on my friends, Captain Wolf?'

The officer responded affirmatively.

So in reality she wasn't completely free. For the first time Cordelia would become *de facto* a guest under surveillance in her own home.

But not a prisoner, not just yet.

Not ever, if she could help it.

CHAPTER 8

Rome, June 1942

Cordelia was abruptly awakened by the rhythmic sound of multiple boots hitting the ground.

Darkness still wrapped everything outside. She looked at the clock on the cupboard beside her bed, trying to work out what time it might be: half past three in the morning. In the absence of the city day's cacophony, the noise of those heavy steps reverberated even more loudly, as if the volume had been pumped up by an invisible hand.

There must be dozens of them, she thought. And they're coming this way.

The wind picked up; the window slammed open.

Thunder roared, followed by a sudden downpour of torrential rain.

Lightning illuminated the sky.

She almost froze in fear.

The imperious clamour of men marching with deafening insistence was growing by the minute and sounded like an ominous countdown to her arrest.

Although she still couldn't see them, she knew they were not far away.

She panicked; she wasn't ready.

She had been postponing her escape too long and now it was too late. She should have asked for Father Colombo's help much sooner; she would be gone by now.

Stupid, stupid, damn stupid!

She needed to run away. Fast.

She tried to get out of bed and get dressed, but for some reason her limbs refused to spring into action. What was wrong with her? She needed to go, now!

Heavy sweat started to cover her forehead, while she shivered with angst.

As much as she tried, she couldn't move – she couldn't damn move!

Terror had frozen her ability to shift into motion.

As if they had a life of their own, both hands closed into a fist, with her finger squeezing more and more until her nails stabbed her palms so hard that they started to bleed. She looked at them in despair, dread and horror. She wanted to cry, but only a deep growl came out of her throat.

Knocking powerfully, the Blackshirts were here at her door.

She screamed with all the air in her lungs.

And in that moment, Cordelia jolted awake, still sweating, her fists still firmly closed.

Somebody was really knocking at her door, but it wasn't the Fascists. It was Alma, and when the old nanny heard her scream, she worriedly asked, 'Is everything all right, Cordelia, are you okay?'

A nightmare. It had been only a nightmare.

'Yes, Alma, I had a bad dream. I'll be up in a minute. Please could you leave my breakfast on the kitchen table. I won't be long.'

She sat on the edge of the bed, her heart still beating fast, her limbs still shaking.

It was not the first time she had had a bad dream of that sort. They had started after her engagement to Augusto. And they all related to men of the regime coming to arrest her and take her away. Augusto, jokingly, had told her of how his cousin, Anna Maria, had asked him to look into her ancestry, just to make sure he 'complied' with the necessity of marrying an Aryan.

'You know how nasty she can be. She's just jealous, that's all, my dear!' he had said to her, trying to defuse the strange anxiety he could see painted all over her face.

But Cordelia was worried. She was frightened that this wasn't just the boutade of a snobbish member of the high society trying to wind her up. That fear of being hunted like an animal in her dreams stemmed from that perfidious, one-time comment, she was sure about that.

Since the Racial Laws had been implemented, Jews had become pariah in their own country, with all sorts of restrictions and impositions. What would happen to her if someone found out her mother was a Jew? It was something she had never thought about. She tried to convince herself that it would be a hard thing to do, since her mother wasn't born in Italy. Nevertheless, her marriage had been registered here, so it would just be a matter of time should anyone decide to trigger a search and dig out that document buried in a small chapel of a remote Alpine town in the north of Italy. Looking back, Cordelia almost blamed herself rather than Anna Maria, for putting that sword of Damocles over her head. She didn't even know why she had agreed to the engagement with Augusto. He had pursued her just because she had played hard to get, although he didn't know that her tepid attitude stemmed from the lack of a real interest and feelings for him. She knew that he had a passion for conquering women, as many as he could. Augusto couldn't stop himself from resisting the impulse. He liked winning, and winning over a girl felt just like taking on another challenge to beat all the others to the finishing line.

He was about to leave for Libya with his regiment, so that would have been the perfect moment to break up with him. She did care for that joyful, daring man, whose passion for car racing – which was his real and only true love – reminded her so much of her father, but not enough to marry him. And it was probably just for the affection she felt that she couldn't find it in her heart to break his, just on the brink of his departure for North Africa.

'Will you wait for me, my dear? I do love you; you know that. You are the most beautiful, fascinating member of the female population I know!' he had said to her when she saw him off to the port, on the day of his embarkation.

'And after all, Tripoli is a second home for me. I've been there many times and raced there twice in a row. I have so many acquaintances in town that I surely will not feel so lonely.'

Cordelia was convinced of that.

'Here, have this, for good fortune,' she said to him, handing over an old talisman that once belonged to her mother.

'What a funny shape. It looks like a small hand with an eye on top. Thank you, my dear, but I won't need it. You keep it.'

He kissed her goodbye. That was the last time she saw Augusto.

Once he had gone, Cordelia put aside what Anna Maria had suggested to him, almost in denial. But since then, her anxiety levels had seemed to grow, and witnessing how Lea's life had been impacted became a crucial cause. It was one thing to see the theory applied to a faceless mass, but experiencing it through the eyes of somebody so close, the effects of what was in fact social segregation, brought it home in a way Cordelia hadn't thought possible.

Finally, she decided to seek the opinion from her father's most trustworthy friend, Father Colombo.

When the friar heard of her concerns, Cordelia was surprised that he hadn't tried to reassure her. She had hopes that he would be the voice of reason in a moment when she wasn't able to think clearly, her mind clouded by irrational thoughts, aggravated by her nightmares. He had always been a man of great logic and calm, able to take a step back and look at things in perspective. He had remained unusually silent, while she explained her fears.

'Father Colombo, I am unsure of what to do. My disquiet is taking its toll, as I believe I am in danger. But am I?'

'Perhaps you want to consider leaving the country, Cordelia,' he said, looking serious. 'It might not be safe for you to continue to live in Rome, at least for the time being. Think about it, and then come and see me – we'll discuss again. Do not mention it to anyone, not even to Alma.'

This last warning scared her, as he would not say anything of the sort if it wasn't important to keep it quiet or, rather, a secret.

Cordelia left, more nervous than when she'd arrived. And she attributed to her nerves the sensation that, since that day, she felt as if someone was following her every now and then. Unknown to her, Father Colombo had asked Lucifer to help.

Cordelia didn't take long to make the decision that she would leave the city. Being discovered had become an unbearable obsession. She went back to the Vatican to ask for Father Colombo's help. Her old friend told her he would help with the documents and the organisation of her trip through a safe channel. A quiet getaway, he said, so that she would go unnoticed.

'Chin up, my child, don't fret. You are going to be saved.'

By Lucifer and him, and with the help of God, he thought.

Now though, Cordelia's situation had radically deteriorated with the arrival of Colonel Schaeffer and his men. Had all the devils of the Universe coalesced against her? It seemed that with this German contingent parachuting right into the middle of her life, a few of them had decided to be a bit too close for comfort.

She had to find a way to inform Father Colombo.

Her escape would need to be sooner than expected.

Unlike in her dream, she would be prepared.

Lucifer's message had left Lord D'Arcy in dismay. The minuscule roll inside a candle had been delivered earlier, while the Ambassador was drinking his first cup of tea of the day, turning its sweetness into a bitter surprise. Deciphered straight away, Rufus Bridge, his secretary, had brought it into his office.

They were now sitting in front of each other, both startled and made sullen by the news.

Bridge spoke first.

'It's a bloody disgrace, Sir. We have been outfoxed yet again by Rommel! That devil seems always to find a new, ingenious way to outflank us,' he said with irony mixed with anger.

'This is a big blow,' the British Ambassador admitted. 'A dangerous blow. Our chances to cut down his supply line once and for all are significantly lower now, given that our pilots will no longer be pre-informed of the routes of the shipments. It puts our own resources under enormous pressure, since they will have to go onto more missions on the Mediterranean, in the hope of catching the convoys. And risk getting caught up in deadly dogfights.'

'At least we know what he's up to. It has always been a desperate race to stop the Afrika Korps getting the oil and the troops they need to push forward, and all of a sudden we've been denied access to the acceleration throttle.'

'Quite crucial, isn't it, Bridge? We have to stop their oil to avoid Rommel getting his hands on our oil. If that formidable bastard manages to reach the oil fields of the Middle East, it will be the end.'

On a wonderful Roman summer day, the Allies' prospects of rebuffing the Third Reich under the African sun couldn't have looked any darker.

D'Arcy rose from his chair and started to pace up and down nervously on the beautiful oriental rug of his study, trying to formulate what to do next.

'Shouldn't we inform London, Sir?' his secretary asked.

Immersed in his phlegmatic and meditative state, his boss did not answer.

In an effort to trigger a response, Bridge made another remark.

'And what do we do about Lucifer? His mission has been involuntarily aborted; he's in much more danger now if he continues to keep his post. More so now that Himmler has joined this game.'

'And could be dealing a fatal blow to our agent. He has been playing his cards well, old Peter, but you're right. He has to leave, or find a secure place to hide until he does.'

D'Arcy came back and sat at his desk again. He took a cigar from a silver box that his wife had given him as a present for Christmas and lit it. During the last festivities, they had listened to the Christmas Day radio programme broadcast by the BBC, during which King George VI delivered his speech to the nation.

Will I see another Christmas like this or will it be Hitler broadcasting from London? He wondered.

'Take one, Rufus,' he said, forgetting that his secretary only smoked cigarettes.

'Do you mind if I keep you company and smoke one of mine, Sir?' In saying that, Bridge pulled out a packet of Players.

A few swirls of smoke rose towards the ceiling. The Ambassador was still deep in thought and his secretary was still waiting to hear what instructions he had for him.

He muttered something, but Bridge didn't quite catch what he said, as the cigar had impeded him articulating his words properly.

'Pardon me, Sir, what did you just say?'

'Sorry, Rufus,' he said, taking the cigar out of his mouth and resting it in the ashtray.

'Lucifer mentioned that Colonel Schaeffer has taken residence at Palazzo Roveri, hasn't he?'

'Yes, he did. And that the German commander is giving access only to his men and no one else,' replied Bridge.

'And to the hotel staff, Lucifer confirmed. Palazzo Roveri is run by Father Colombo's friend, Cordelia Olivieri. What a bizarre coincidence, almost grotesque in a way …' he affirmed.

'Correct, Sir. And an unfortunate coincidence too: she's in much more danger, being in such proximity to the Germans. As you remember, Father Colombo asked for our help to provide travel documents and a safe passage a while ago. A plan is under way. You know her mother was Jewish. Especially now that Himmler is sniffing around, we must inform the Franciscan straight away. We may need to speed up her departure as well.'

'Naturally, Rufus. Let's not waste another minute. Please send a message to Father Colombo to come here as soon as possible, will you? But let's not inform London just yet, understood?'

'Of course, Sir. I will do as you ask,' Bridge said.

Flying out of his office, he immediately went to prepare a note that was delivered some thirty minutes later to the desk of the Franciscan friar.

CHAPTER 9

Brother Filippo found the envelope slipped under the main entrance door. It was addressed to Father Colombo, but it wasn't stamped nor did it mention who the sender was. He picked it up and took it to the study on the first floor. Father Colombo was out; he would read it later. Having returned back from his errands, he had to carry out some work in the garden, where he had started harvesting some medical herbs for exsiccation, and he totally forgot about the letter.

It was late afternoon when Father Colombo returned. He had been organising the classification of ancient manuscripts at the Vatican library all day, and was longing for a cup of carcadé, an aromatic red tea obtained by the infusion of the dried petals of the Hibiscus Sabdariffa plant. As many Italians, he had switched to it from tea, which had become hard to find after the League of Nations imposed sanctions on Italy for its invasion of Ethiopia in 1935.

Not finding Brother Filippo, he went to the kitchen to prepare the hot drink himself, and sat down, enjoying its aroma while waiting for it to fully brew. He had just added a slice of a fresh Sicilian orange to his drink, when his assistant came in from the garden, carrying a huge bunch of lemon balm.

'Oh, hello, Father Colombo,' he saluted him. 'I had such a productive day today. I harvested most of the herb beds towards the end of the garden, and left some to dry in the sunroom, but I will use this lot fresh – it's wonderful in a salad, you know? I will save some to make a cold sore lip balm. Here's how I will do that,' he went on to explain.

Father Colombo knew Brother Filippo could go on and on talking about herbs and their remedies and was happy to listen to the soothing tone of his assistant, when for the whole day he had done most of the talking. Filippo had almost the same calming effect on him as his tisanes.

'You make it sound really easy, Filippo, but now, if you will excuse me, I still have a bit of work to do before dinner.'

'I almost forgot, Father Colombo: a letter has arrived for you. But it was delivered by hand. I found it on the mat in the hall, and there's no sender. I've placed it on your desk.'

That detail slightly worried Father Colombo. It was highly unusual for him to receive mail in that form, so he went upstairs and found the envelope.

It looked anonymous.

He grabbed his paperknife and opened it.

It read: 'Your kind presence is required at your earliest convenience.'

No signature. No indication of where he had to go.

But he knew who it was coming from. And he knew it must be urgent.

He turned around, went downstairs again and rushed out of the door, shouting to a startled Brother Filippo, 'I am going to see a friend. I won't be long.'

Walking as fast as he could without attracting any attention, the Franciscan's mind was in turmoil. Although unsure, he could probably figure out why he had been summoned. It was related to what

Lucifer told him in his last 'confession'. They almost certainly wanted him to leave the country, and who wouldn't under the circumstances the agent found himself in now. Out there, so many more Germans had been crawling around town lately. Not ideal to brush shoulders with them, if you were a spy.

The Ambassador will probably talk to me about helping him make his escape, he guessed, accelerating his steps. Unless there is something else … but what?

His mental assumptions stopped momentarily as he turned to a secondary entrance of the British Embassy building, protected from curious eyes by being located in a narrow side street. Recognised by the guard, he slipped in through the gate leading to the back garden, climbed the steps and entered from the French doors leading straight to the Ambassador's office.

Lord D'Arcy was at his desk. He seemed to be waiting for him.

'My dear friend, thank you for getting here so expeditiously,' he said to the friar. 'I wouldn't have asked you to come and meet me in person at such short notice, but it's important.'

'Naturally, I imagined as much,' Father Colombo commented. 'It is to do with the last message Lucifer sent you, isn't it? He told me about a German commander taking over from Marino Severi, which means he can't get any intelligence from now on. You must have arrived at the same conclusion as me: he needs to make his way out, as soon as possible. I can help to move him to a safe place, even if temporary, if necessary, and I guess it has come to this point.'

Father Colombo had been crucial in this sort of operation. Back in January, it was the turn of a young professor of the University La Sapienza, a Jew, but not an Italian national, who had not only lost his job because of his religion, he was also declared a political prisoner, soon to be interned in a camp. Father Colombo, using a fake transport of furniture, helped him travel to Florence, hidden in a trunk with a double bottom. There, he was given a new passport, with which he crossed into Switzerland. He sent him a postcard from Geneva a month and a half later, as confirmation he had made it. A month earlier, in December, just a few days before Christmas, a journalist, author of a number of articles that were declared 'unpalatable' because of the fierce criticism expressed towards a member of the regime, was arrested, beaten and thrown in prison, from which he managed to escape. Father Colombo, who knew the man well, sheltered him in the Certosa di Trisulti, near Frosinone, a small monastery of enclosed monastics of the Carthusian Order, strictly eremitical and with almost no contact with the outside world. The saddest case was that of a middle-aged Jewish lady, who, due to the incessant physical vexations inflicted on her son by a neighbour, went to the police to report it. Despite the complaint, nothing was done and the neighbour continued. One day, while trying to stop that evil man, she pushed him so hard that he fell, breaking his neck. It was a tragic accident, but both mother and son, panicking and convinced the authorities would blame them, fearing a murder charge and, likely, a death sentence, ran away and hid in an abandoned building site, where they lived for days before being rescued. Father Colombo moved them during the early hours of a dark winter morning to the house of Costantino and Laura Bulgari, themselves disgusted by the discrimination and abuse of the Jews. The friar was sure nobody would look for them in the famous jeweller's home. Later, with the clothes and new identity documents that he provided them with to disguise themselves as two peasants returning to their farm after the fruit market day in Piazza Priscilla, they made their way towards the port of Ostia. Here, his faithful mariner friend Nino Conti embarked them on his boat, destination Genoa, from where they boarded a ship for South America.

'I am worried, probably more than you, about Lucifer,' Lord D'Arcy said, 'and I am even more concerned about the fact that now we will no longer have access to the intelligence he provided. He was a crucial informer of all the routes and the magnitude of the shipments to Tripoli.'

The Ambassador continued. 'Father Colombo, this is not the only reason why I asked you to see me. You see, as of yesterday, the new German commander has taken permanent residence at Palazzo Roveri, seizing *de facto* the hotel.'

Father Colombo was stunned by the revelation, feeling as if a massive blow to his stomach had just left him completely breathless.

'Nobody can enter or exit that building but his own Wehrmacht soldiers, whose contingent is stationed there as well. Nobody except for the hotel staff, and that includes Cordelia.'

'We need to get her out of there. This is of the utmost urgency. I need to bring forward the arrangements for her to leave,' Father Colombo said.

The Franciscan, ever so grateful that the Ambassador had agreed to help Cordelia even though hers was not an immediate life or death case, as many others, was already thinking of the practicalities of a new plan.

'Father Colombo, with Lucifer no longer able to get the information we need, Cordelia can help us. She is now in a unique position to do so. Our agent told us that, outside a small circle of high-ranking officers, nobody knows that the Italians have passed the reins of the Libya supply chain to the Germans. We think that's the reason why there is not a big contingent of them at Palazzo Roveri. It would attract attention to this highly sensitive, and crucial operation of theirs. We will supply her with a small camera. We want Cordelia to photograph those plans. All she has to do is to pass the microfilm to us.'

'That's out of the question, Ambassador!' Father Colombo almost shouted. 'Cordelia is not a spy. She will get caught without a shred of doubt, and her fate will be sealed. She will be imprisoned, interrogated and, as she doesn't know anything, most likely tortured. And we all know what the Gestapo is capable of.'

'I thought long and hard, but given the fact that Cordelia is currently the only one we can trust and that has access, I'm left with no alternative. Besides, this is not just about Cordelia, my friend. It's about the destiny of thousands of Allied soldiers. If we don't manage to stop Rommel, he will definitely turn the tide in his own favour in North Africa. A catastrophe for the war and a bloodbath for our troops.'

'This is sending a lamb to a sacrificial altar, Lord D'Arcy. You know it is. I am startled you even think it's possible for a young woman like Cordelia to perform such a risky task, as if it was the easiest thing to do in the world. I can only imagine how terrified she is now at the prospect of having to face those Germans every day. Her nerves won't bear it, not for long anyway.'

There was a hint of desperation in Father Colombo's voice. He thought of Cordelia and the state of distress she must be in, how desperate she must be to see this happening to her when the day of her departure was in sight.

'Father Colombo, she is our best option, our only option, given the time frame we have. There's no way an agent can get in. Lucifer told us the place is swarming with German soldiers and is very well guarded. Besides, we don't want them to know we have their plans, so that our aircrafts can sink this crucial cargo shipment.'

The British man continued: 'I don't want to sound ruthless, Father, but Cordelia needs to help us. She has to. I know it is hard to hear it, especially because it's regarding somebody close to your heart. Please can you contact her – you will need to instruct her. I didn't want to resort to this, but she will have to play Lucifer's game, just for a little while.'

So this was the real objective of the British, to bring in Cordelia and ask her to help steal the plans of the Germans. He also knew that there was no room for discussion.

'Her documents are almost ready. Your secretary, Rufus Bridge, told me just a few days ago.'

'They will be here for her once we get the microfilm. Her documents and safe passage are guaranteed, but we must get those plans.'

There was a slightly veiled menace in his tone and words.

'I know how merciless it sounds, Father. But I know that you need no further explanation about how vital it is to get those routes,' the Ambassador said.

'That's a big gamble, Lord D'Arcy. And I hope, for both your and Cordelia's sake, that it will pay off.'

The Franciscan was out early the next morning to reach Palazzo Roveri and talk to his protégée. He wanted to reassure her that he was aware of her situation, and that he was already taking steps to get her out of it. Walking along the Via Lungotevere, Father Colombo cringed knowing what she was facing at present. Living under the same roof as the Germans was certainly nerve-wracking at best, and now what she was asked to do for the British seemed to be an impossible task.

But was it? He knew Cordelia had displayed a sense of independence since a young age, a sign of a strong-minded person, and she had risen to the challenge when, upon her father's death, she decided to sell the family business and set up her own from scratch. Not many women of her age would display such an entrepreneurial spirit. Most would settle for a secure, quiet married life instead.

He had to tell her about the conversation with Lord D'Arcy.

He turned into Via Giulia and in approaching the gate of Palazzo Roveri, he saw a German sentinel.

'I am here to see the hotel director, Miss Cordelia Olivieri. I am her spiritual advisor,' Father Colombo said, answering the soldier's question about why he was there.

'I'm afraid nobody can enter these premises. They are being commandeered for the exclusive use of Lieutenant Colonel Schaeffer of the Afrika Korps.'

The same sense of impotence that the friar had experienced in front of the British Ambassador came upon him again.

'Father, we can't allow anyone standing here,' the sentinel said, with the intention of sending the friar on his way.

At that point, the Franciscan heard a voice behind him saying, 'Soldier, is there a problem?'

A black-clad cleric, accompanied by a Gestapo officer, had just arrived at his side.

Father Colombo had never seen him before; he had a commanding presence and a piercing gaze, almost more menacing than his sinister companion. He recognised his habit; he belonged to the Benedictine Order.

'Heil Hitler!' the sentinel said, immediately snapping to the attention position. 'This religious man wanted to get in and I stopped him as per my orders.'

'Of course, of course …' the Benedictine said, and addressing Father Colombo asked, 'May I be of assistance, Father?'

'Colombo, my name is Pietro Colombo,' the Franciscan responded, 'and yes, I was telling this soldier that I would be grateful if I could see Cordelia Olivieri, the lady who runs this hotel. She is one of my parishioners and it's quite some time since I saw her. I wanted to check how she was getting on during these difficult times.'

'I see ... well, let's find out if you can be escorted by myself and this officer as an exception today. I am Karl Blasius, and this is Major Krause of the Gestapo.'

'Thank you, Father Blasius, God bless you.'

Obviously, this monk is in a very privileged or powerful position – or both – to exercise this sort of influence, Father Colombo thought, and I wonder why. I'd better be careful while I am in his company.

The German sentinel, though, didn't move aside.

'I have strict orders by our commander Lieutenant Colonel Schaeffer. No one can pass this gate.'

Father Colombo noticed Blasius' irritation.

'I can't seem to be able to convince this good soldier, Father Colombo. I hope it wasn't urgent. May I pass on Miss Cordelia a message on your behalf?'

'No, nothing urgent. I will see her at another time, thank you Father Blasius.'

'If I may ask, which monastery are you from?'

'I am a librarian of the Vatican library. I don't live in a monastery at the moment, but inside Vatican City.'

'What a coincidence, I am to visit it soon for some manuscripts I am working on. I am the Chief Archivist of the Biblicum. I hope to meet you there. I'd be keen to have a chat with you.'

'Well, Father Blasius, I don't want to keep you any longer.'

Father Colombo wasn't at all interested in continuing that conversation, and in saying that, he left the two men.

Palazzo Roveri had become a fortress, he thought, annoyed and worried. How would he reach Cordelia? He needed to find a way to give her a message.

In the meantime, Blasius and his Gestapo companion were allowed to proceed across the cobbled courtyard and to the reception.

They found Cordelia at the main desk as she was hanging up the phone.

She was startled by seeing that odd couple, although she couldn't decide which one of them was looking more threatening, the glacial Gestapo officer or the dark-haired stringy monk.

'Good morning to you all,' she said, 'welcome.'

'Miss Olivieri, I suppose? Father Blasius and Major Krause,' the Benedictine said. 'Lieutenant Colonel Schaeffer is expecting us.'

'Let me call Flaminia, our hotel maid. She will escort you to his office.'

She rang the bell to summon Flaminia, and while they were waiting, Blasius asked Cordelia: 'I've been told that your establishment has been mainly catering for guests of the religious orders, is that right? It must be a dramatic change for you, given that now the hotel has been taken over by the army.'

'All men are the same in front of God,' she said, 'and we, at Palazzo Roveri, in our charitable spirit, are happy to welcome anyone.'

'Very commendable and diplomatic, Miss Olivieri. As long as they are paying, I suppose.'

The slightly insidious nature of the comment didn't escape Cordelia's attention, and she was glad that Flaminia had just appeared so she could dodge the implied question.

'Ah, here you are Flaminia! Could you see these two gentlemen up to Colonel Schaeffer's office, please?'

They left with an ever-simpering Flaminia. Cordelia was about to go back to her office, when she saw Alma waving at her from the kitchen door, signalling to come over.

She quickly glided through the corridor and slipped in, preceded by the cook. With the door closed behind them, Alma told her that just a few moments before, she had heard Father Colombo's voice through an open window, but couldn't quite hear what he said.

'And I couldn't make out who the people he was chatting to were, as I did not recognise their voices. When I looked out of the window, he was gone; the other two were walking in.'

'He must have been refused entry by the sentinel, Alma. Somehow he must have heard of the Germans to decide to come here. One of those two men you just saw arriving, a monk with a black habit, had a strangely inquisitive tone, which I did not like. I must warn Father Colombo to stay away – it's just too risky at the moment. In the meantime, let's behave absolutely normally.'

Meanwhile, Flaminia was being sounded out by Blasius, who was trying to find in Schaeffer's organisation an Achilles heel to exploit. He was intrigued by Schaeffer's choice of location. Given the fact that the Gestapo had sent him to keep an eye on a possible channel where information could get into the Vatican, he was convinced there was something dodgy going on there. Wasn't it odd that Schaeffer had elected a place which, until a few hours ago, was full of priests? Suspicious by nature, Blasius wanted to find out more about it.

'Here we are, if you need anything else …' Flaminia said, after showing them up to the first floor where Schaeffer had his office.

'As a matter of fact, I do,' Blasius said, seizing the opportunity.

He took her to one side.

'I am sure that a clever girl like you could be of good use to me. Perhaps you can tell me a bit more about Cordelia Olivieri and what's happening here, going forward.'

'Seriously? And why would I do that?'

We are negotiating already, little slut … the black-clad monk thought.

Blasius believed that loyalty was an overrated quality.

'God always pays back the good deeds of the faithful.'

'I can do with a bit of extra money, if that's what you're referring to,' she said with a smug and malicious smile, quick to spot the opportunity.

'Ah, yes. Indeed. Come and see me at the Biblicum, in Piazza Pilotta. Once a week. You will receive your reward.'

That was easy, Blasius gloated.

Easier than I thought.

Marino Severi had been sitting enraged in his office, since coming back from his unexpected encounter with Afrika Korps Lieutenant Colonel Friedrich Schaeffer at Palazzo Roveri.

He didn't want to see anyone, speak to anyone, hear from anyone.

Not even Lucifer had managed to extract a word from him since their arrival at the command.

Severi asked his attendant to shut the door and told him that he wouldn't receive a soul for the rest of the week. That was unusual for somebody who, until a few days ago, was the perfect embodiment of Mr Swagger at the Fascist command, always parading around like a peacock. All came to an end because of a damned spy and a damned German, he thought.

But in reality, their only sins were to have shown his ineptitude to see what was under his very nose. That's why he was hiding, livid. He feared that his comrades would see him as a loser.

Severi couldn't stand the thought of people gossiping and laughing behind his back, or worse, pitying him. He knew he had made enemies among his own fellow Blackshirts. He didn't mind having enemies, as long as he was in a position of power, able to crush them if any attempt to undermine him was made. In fact, he rather enjoyed it. It gave him a sensation of superiority. Severi had that type of arrogance that sprung from having been a mediocre individual all his life. A manifestation of the necessity to take vengeance for not being a better person, with better morals, better looks, better intelligence. It was as if his own shortcomings were always somebody else's fault. Severi was a specimen that liked to take out his frustrations on others, in an attempt to feel better.

Now he had been frustrated. Enormously.

In his ambitions as well as his public image.

He needed to find a way out and up again, he thought, and quickly.

One way would be to arrest the spy of course; the sooner he managed that, the sooner he'd take back his old job.

But where to start?

Severi needed to find him before anyone else. He began to picture himself receiving the praise of the Duce ...

A hard knock on the door interrupted his fantasy.

It was Lucifer.

'Guido, I said I want to see no one for the rest of the day. No one!' he shouted with spiteful anger.

Ignoring him, Lucifer entered his boss's office and walking up to his desk, said, almost in a whisper, 'Major, I think you want to make an exception.'

'Really, I want to make an exception, you say ...' he responded derisively '... and why should I? Who is the visitor, the Pope?' he said with rolling eyes.

'Not quite. It's a Benedictine monk ...'

Immediately interrupting, Severi said sardonically, 'A bloody monk! Today is full of surprises, isn't it? Do I look like I need to confess, perhaps? Or need a blessing? Are you out of your mind? The last thing is for my comrades to think that I summoned a monk, for what, my funeral? Get him out of here!'

'Major, he is not just any monk. He is German and a strict

collaborator of the Gestapo. He looks a bit demonic to me.' Lucifer told him his name.

Severi stared at Lucifer, widening his eyes.

What would he want from me, he thought? I'd better find out.

'Ah … then it's a special case. I will receive him. Please let him in, Guido,' Severi said with calm nonchalance.

Lucifer always marvelled at how quickly the Fascist Major could change his mood.

He went out to fetch the cleric.

Blasius walked into the office of the Fascist Major. Next to him, Severi looked even chubbier and shorter, and the two of them together reminded Lucifer of a modern version of Don Quixote and Sancho Panza in the famous Cervantes novel.

His attendant was right, Severi thought. The priest looked like a wolf in sheep's clothing. How odd!

'You can go now, Guido, thank you. And close the door behind you, will you?'

The last thing he wanted was for his attendant to know the monk's intentions for now.

He might fill him in later, and only on the basis of what he needed to know.

Lucifer nodded and, reluctantly, left them.

Damn, he thought. Now I will have to wait to know what's going on.

Lucifer reckoned that things were definitely getting hotter around there – a bit too much for his taste. And he didn't want to get burned, or worse, if he could help it.

'I guess your attendant has given you my credentials, Major Severi.'

'Of course, of course, Father Blasius, but please have a seat. What can I do for you?'

'What can I do for you, rather, Major.'

'Well, Father, I believe you haven't come here to administer any sacrament,' Severi said half-mockingly, but he quickly realised that the German monk wasn't amused by his sense of humour.

Germans, what a sad race, people too damned serious for his liking. They just fed on potatoes and sauerkraut. How could you possibly be a happy person if you ate just that? This one even had to give up another type of appetite, he thought.

Severi already felt superior. He smiled at the thought and continued. 'So, perhaps you want to enlighten me.'

'I have come to see you exactly for that reason, Major: wouldn't you be glad to be in the spotlight, triumphant like a victorious Caesar over your enemy?'

Hmmm … this monk has some cards up his sleeve, but he wants to see mine first; I'm not going to do it, my friend, not just yet, a suspicious Severi ruminated.

'And what might that enemy be?' he asked.

He is either dumb or wants to play dumb, Blasius thought. Let's see which one it is.

He produced a quiet laugh, but was quick to regain his composure.

'Lieutenant Colonel Friedrich Schaeffer, for one. I am told that he insisted on shutting you out completely, pointing out to both the German and Fascist command what, in his opinion, are your major failures. How unkind that was. The fact is he wanted your command. And now that both our armies are close to the capture of Cairo, he's going to benefit from all the work you've done and become the hero of the day.'

Blasius saw a hint of interest substituting that blasé attitude Severi had displayed since the moment he walked in.

'And of course, let's not forget that Allied secret agent, who got hold of the shipping routes. If you catch him, you can be reinstated back in your post. After all, what excuse could there be not to. And that's the best victory you can claim, with two prizes at once. Perhaps you can lay a trap. Is it plausible to think that the spy would want to try to get his information at Schaeffer's expense this time? Are you sure that the people at Palazzo Roveri could not be corrupted? Imagine if one of them turns out to be an informant for the enemy.'

Severi was listening and thinking on his feet. The monk had a point; he might just have suggested to him how to get resurrected, so to speak. There was no doubt the Benedictine had a dislike for Schaeffer. And that was probably why he was here. Severi really didn't care, as long as he could be of use to him.

'I see. You are incredibly well informed, Father Blasius, and seem to have figured it out already. So, how do you propose we go about it in practical terms?'

'You and I will keep in close contact. I want to be informed of everything you can find out about Cordelia Olivieri and her staff. I also saw a Franciscan friar there, who seems to be a regular visitor. As a matter of fact, I have been told that the hotel is a favourite of the Vatican crowd. There's a strong suspicion that some of them might be helping the enemy. I tell you this as the Gestapo has asked me to keep an eye on my fellow clerics. I see no reason why I couldn't share this intelligence with you, to help you speed up your investigation.'

Severi's fantasies of triumph began again.

'You are truly a godsend, Father Blasius,' he said to him. 'I will issue an order to look into Miss Olivieri and her employees straight away, and I've got just the right man for the job.'

CHAPTER 10

Rome, July 1942

Father Colombo had acted quickly in delivering Cordelia a message to come and see him at his home in Vatican City. Instead of sending her a written note that, as innocent as it might appear to be, could be intercepted and, coming from him, arouse suspicion, he opted to send Brother Filippo to the vegetable and fish market at Campo dei Fiori. He recalled Alma telling him that she visited it regularly for her kitchen supplies, as the 'vignarole', the women coming from the countryside with their fresh crops, had the best produce available. It happened twice a week in a square in the old centre of Rome, under the watchful eye of Giordano Bruno, the philosopher whose statue had been placed in the exact spot where he was burned alive for heresy at the beginning of the fifteenth century.

It didn't take long for Brother Filippo to find her. When he saw Alma standing beside a stall, leaning over a bunch of artichokes left in a bucket of water near the Fontana della Terrina, he quietly approached her and whispered in her ear that Father Colombo wanted to see Cordelia, and to tell her to make sure she wasn't followed.

Alma, who had just about finished her shopping, nodded and rushed back to the hotel to give her the message.

And now Cordelia was here, in his private study, and Father Colombo was as glad and sad as he could possibly be.

He had decided to give her the good news first, illustrating for the first time the plan for her escape.

Explaining the plan in detail was something he needed to do anyway, but now he was also to tell her it would not be possible to go ahead with it just yet, and, more importantly, why.

There was something she needed to do: a most perilous mission.

Father Colombo took a sip from the tisane that Brother Filippo had prepared for them, and slowly put his cup back on the table.

'Cordelia, the other reason why I summoned you today is quite significant. Of course, I wanted to see you were safe and well, given the arrival of your new German guests, which is in part why I came by Palazzo Roveri the other day.'

Father Colombo's face darkened; he had a troubled look, Cordelia noticed, thinking that he must have been dismayed when he saw how things had become even more complicated for her by the presence of Schaeffer and his men.

In an effort to reassure her old friend, Cordelia told him: 'Believe me, Father, I am fine at the moment. I haven't had any trouble from them so far. And I try to keep out of their way as much as possible. The only reason Palazzo Roveri was chosen is because apparently the German commander, Lieutenant Colonel Schaeffer, and Augusto knew each other, and he spoke warmly about my hotel to him. Nobody suspects anything and there's no reason why they should ...' but while she was finishing her sentence, Cordelia saw that Father Colombo looked even more troubled. She could not possibly know what he had on his mind.

He felt elated to have been able to secure her getaway, but also disheartened about what he had to say to her now, almost regretting the help that he was granted by the British. He felt guilty in a way, as that help came at a price, and he couldn't do anything about it. He hoped it wouldn't prove fatal.

'There's something else important I have to discuss with you,' Father Colombo said to her, after a moment of hesitation. 'There's somebody you need to help before you leave.'

'You mean Alma? I have made arrangements as you suggested, for her to go and stay with one of my father's trusted friends, who has a farm in the countryside. I will send her a ticket to join me as soon as I am settled in America. I don't want to be alone; she's all I have left.'

'No, it's not Alma. I know full well you've made arrangements for her already.'

'If not Alma, who is it then?'

'It's the British. They want you to photograph the supply route plans that are going to General Erwin Rommel in North Africa that Schaeffer is secretly preparing, and deliver the microfilm to me, so that I can give it to them in turn.'

The news took Cordelia by surprise. And, as she was trying to digest the full extent of those words, she experienced a slight sense of vertigo mixed with fear, the same she had felt as a child, when her father had taken her to the top of the Leaning Tower of Pisa many years ago.

Now she understood why Father Colombo had appeared to be so uneasy a few moments before. This was a huge deal to ask of anyone and he must have felt overwhelmed under the pressure.

'So, it is the people who are helping me that have asked you that, is it, Father?'

'Yes, you are their last resort. They have no other choice at the moment. They will give you your documents once you deliver the photographs,' the Franciscan said.

Cordelia couldn't remain seated any longer and nervously stood up.

She thought of her friend Lea and her family, of many others like them, of what life would look like if Hitler and Mussolini's regimes were to win the war. They had taken everything away from her, including the possibility to live in her own country for fear of being persecuted, obliged to leave all she had ever possessed behind.

Cordelia felt really angry.

She could do something to help bring them down.

'I suppose I do not have a choice either, Father,' she stated. Then, resolutely, she said, 'I will do it. I think I know how to.'

It was Father Colombo's turn to be surprised now, taken aback by her bravery.

'Are you sure?'

'I am, Father. I believe I can do it. I feel I have to pay the British back for what they are doing for me.'

'Very well, Cordelia. Here's what we are going to do…'

But he couldn't finish his sentence as a breathless Brother Filippo opened the door saying: 'Father Colombo, apologies for the interruption, but downstairs there's a Benedictine monk asking to see you. From what you described, it might be that German, Father Blasius, who you met at Palazzo Roveri!'

Addressing Cordelia, the Franciscan said, 'Cordelia, stay here. Do not move. Close and lock the door once I am gone. Wait until I return and don't make a sound.'

Followed by Brother Filippo, he left his study to go downstairs.

Could Blasius have managed to see Cordelia entering the house? She said she was pretty sure she hadn't been followed, having changed roads and directions quite frequently. Nevertheless, it was a possibility. That wasn't good.

Blasius was there in the hall, his scrutinising gaze directed at Father Colombo, while he was descending the last steps of the stone staircase.

'Father Colombo, I am glad I found you still at home,' he said with a cold smile. 'I have just been to the Vatican library and they told me you would be out all day today. I was keen to discuss these manuscripts with you. You may remember I mentioned them in our first encounter at Palazzo Roveri.'

Thank God, he's not here for Cordelia. Father Colombo sighed with relief.

'Oh yes, I remember, Father Blasius, welcome to my home. I'm afraid I will not have much time today. Why don't you come back tomorrow? I will be at the library and we can have a look at them. There are further sources to consult, codes and books that I do not have here in my house.'

'Naturally, how silly of me,' he said, craning his neck to get a better view of what was behind Father Colombo.

'You have a wonderful garden. I can see it through that glass door. Would you mind if we wander out. I am passionate about plants,' Blasius replied, ignoring Father Colombo's subtle implication that he had been invited to leave.

Annoyed, the Franciscan, who didn't want to antagonise him as forcefully as he desired, agreed to his request and they made their way outside.

'It's a beautiful orchard that my assistant, Brother Filippo, is in charge of. He is an expert herbalist.'

'How marvellous – what sort of herbs do you cultivate here? I can recognise a couple. This one is an aloe vera – we had so many of them in our garden on Mount Zion, in Palestine. I was in a monastery down there, before being recalled back to Rome, to the Biblicum. As a matter of fact, I'd like to discuss with you about helping me on another front, Father Colombo.'

So, he's not here for Cordelia or the manuscript only, the Franciscan thought.

'I see, and what would that be?'

'Well, I have been concerned for some time, as I hear that some of our brothers and sisters could be inclined to listen to the voices of dissent. And that some are actually helping unscrupulous opponents of the Axis to act against it. Although they might be meaning well, this is sending them down such a dangerous path, but more importantly, putting the Pope and the Vatican in a very bad light. Some may come to think that the Holy Father is turning a blind eye.'

Blasius rubbed the tip of his aquiline nose, like a hound that had sniffed a scent and wanted to firmly track it.

'These are serious allegations, Father Blasius.'

'And the Third Reich is even more serious about it. If something like this transpires to be true ... well, I don't need to say anything more, do I? We need to avoid this happening, at all costs, Father Colombo, for their own sake and to preserve the neutral position of the Vatican.'

Father Colombo noticed for the first time how his long, thin white fingers kept interlacing while Blasius was speaking, like the tentacles of an octopus.

'I understand your concerns.'

'And I am sure you and I can collaborate to keep these straying souls on the straight and narrow. If you hear anything, I would be grateful if you could share it with me. I shall go now. Apologies for intruding this way today. I leave you to your duties, Father Colombo.'

The German monk cut the conversation short.

Although he couldn't get anything from the Franciscan today, he had planted the seed, as he had planned to do.

Brother Filippo accompanied him to the door.

'It has been a brief yet interesting conversation, Father Blasius. Please keep me updated on your progress as well,' said Father Colombo.

As soon as the door closed behind him, his assistant said, 'I am not sure Father Blasius means well.'

'Nor am I, nor am I …' Father Colombo replied, convinced that the real reason why he came by was to ask him to become an informer and spy on his fellow friars, monks, priests and nuns. And he was sure that the Gestapo would be the primary recipient of that intelligence.

It was a fortunate coincidence that Cordelia didn't stumble into him today. From now on, given what had just happened and knowing what Blasius was up to, she shouldn't come here anymore.

He was fast to return upstairs. Cordelia unlocked the door, hearing it was Father Colombo.

'My dear, do you remember the Benedictine monk that came to Palazzo Roveri the other day? Well, it was him downstairs, just now. I am fairly sure that he did not see you, but from now on, we will have to be much more cautious. I will not meet you in person anymore unless it's absolutely necessary. Once we finish talking today, Brother Filippo will accompany you through a private passage at the bottom of the orchard: there's a cluster of small alleys that lead straight to Porta Sant'Anna. Once there, you can easily slip out of Vatican City and mingle with the crowd.'

Cordelia left an hour later with her scarf to cover her.

Hidden in a handkerchief, pushed down at the bottom of one of the pockets of her skirt, there was a Minox micro-camera.

Cordelia re-entered the garden of Palazzo Roveri from the same side door she had exited from earlier that day. She approached and slowly opened the iron gate and had a quick peek inside. From what she could see, no one was around. She slipped in and stood still for a moment, hidden by the huge jasmine that climbed the wall beside the portal. There were just a few bees buzzing around its scented white flowers and a colourful dragonfly resting on a leaf that seemed to observe her with its huge iridescent eyes. Apart from that it was completely quiet.

Trying to walk as noiselessly as possible, she stepped on the small stretch of gravel and reached the lawn, gently moving towards her home. She reached inside her bag, searching for the front door key but couldn't find it. She almost panicked and then she remembered she hadn't locked it up, as usual. Pushing the door open, she saw that the room had been tended to by Flaminia.

I need to tell her not to do it anymore, she thought, and I need to remember to lock it from now on.

As soon as she was inside, she had a scan around. She had been thinking all the way back from the Vatican where to hide the micro-camera, which was burning like hell in her pocket. It was small, approximately no more than eight centimetres by three, and light as a feather, so it could fit in many places. The base of the silver candelabra on the mantelpiece could be unscrewed; the stem was hollow inside: it was perfect. Taking the camera out of her pocket, she placed it there.

With that little object now in a secure hiding place, Cordelia felt lightened, eased of a burden that, if found by the Germans … She was quick to brush off such a possibility. Thinking the worst could only do her more harm than good, so she refused to give in to her nerves.

She needed to keep a cool head and remain as calm and lucid as possible.

After freshening up, she changed into a light-green skirt and matching sleeveless top, then went back to her office at the hotel.

She was halfway across the reception when she saw Schaeffer coming in from the main entrance door. He was carrying a bunch of fresh flowers.

'Hello, Miss Olivieri, a florist insisted on giving me these wonderful roses as I keep buying her fruit at the market nearby. I suppose it is her way of saying thank you. They belong more in your office than my room.'

'They are marvellous, thank you, Colonel Schaeffer,' Cordelia said. She pondered for a moment, then added, 'Are you sure you didn't buy them? These days people don't give away things for free, especially if they have to feed their children, whatever gratitude they want to express.'

Caught out, Schaeffer looked a bit embarrassed.

'I admit it. Yes, I bought them for you. It's a small way to say that I am thankful for your hospitality. I understand that the imposition might feel like an unwanted burden.'

'The war has put us all in a position we wouldn't have necessarily chosen, Colonel. I appreciate your gesture,' she said, smiling.

Cordelia was secretly very pleased. She hadn't been given flowers by a man for some time now, and it had been really kind of him to do that.

'I would be so delighted to continue the conversation we started the other day. Would you do me the honour of having dinner with me? I haven't enjoyed a conversation with a woman for ages, let alone going on a date. It seems such a long time ago that I had a normal life. You know, I was a lawyer,' he said.

Cordelia noticed a sort of regret mixed with sadness while he was talking. His manners were very charming and gentle and he made her feel quite special the way he looked at her. As much as she didn't like it, she was strangely fascinated by him.

'You don't have to if you don't feel comfortable,' Schaeffer added, hoping she would not refuse.

Perhaps she could find out more about how well guarded the library was, Cordelia thought, and maybe more. Besides, he seemed genuinely missing a bit of female company and it had been a while since she had had a meal with an attractive man.

I might even enjoy it, she thought.

'I am comfortable, Colonel, and I'd be delighted to. The evenings are quite cool, so we can have dinner on the terrace if you like.'

'Sounds marvellous, I am truly pleased.'

'I'll go to instruct Alma to set everything up for tomorrow evening then. See you later, Colonel.'

With the roses in her arms, she headed to the kitchen. Flaminia was there.

'You have a new admirer, Miss Olivieri,' the maid said to her. She had obviously observed the previous scene and her hint was aimed at triggering a reaction.

'Sometimes people are just kind, Flaminia. You don't have to read anything more into it.'

'Well, the Colonel seemed quite enthralled with you.'

Cordelia didn't respond to the passive provocation, deciding to ignore her insidious comments.

'Take the flowers, please, and put them in a vase on the reception desk. Do you know where Alma is?'

'She just popped down to the larder.'

'Could you please tell her to come to the dépendance when she comes back?'

Then she left.

She didn't want to say anything within Flaminia's hearing range. That maid was too nosey and liked to gossip too much.

What she had to say to Alma was not simply about the cooking.

PART II

A DIABOLICAL GAMBLE BEGINS

'If the sinkings continue at the present rate, all that Italy would have left within six months in the way of a mercantile marine would be our fishing fleet'.

Benito Mussolini

CHAPTER 11

'What do we know about Cordelia Olivieri? Do we have anything on file, Guido?' Severi asked.

Lucifer had just entered his office after being summoned in by his boss. He looked first at Severi, then at Blasius. The question had left him briefly astonished.

'Are you asleep, Guido? Did you hear what I just said?'

The monk was rhythmically drumming his long, gangly fingers on the wooden desk, while his intense gaze was fixed on him, as if he was waiting for Lucifer to confess, I am guilty.

Realising he had frozen for a moment, Lucifer quickly recovered.

'Apologies, Major Severi, I was just trying to recall our records. No, I don't believe we have. I can check. May I ask why we are looking into the owner of Palazzo Roveri?'

In a theatrical gesture, Severi lifted both arms in the air and let them drop down again at his sides, then he snapped sarcastically.

'Here you go! You see, we know something about her, and I didn't know that. How come you have this information about the proprietor of the hotel and I don't?'

Lucifer tried to think fast, and said, as convincingly as he could, 'I am sure she mentioned it when we went there to meet Colonel Schaeffer.'

'Really? I don't remember hearing her saying that,' Severi commented, with a hint of suspicion, almost insinuating that Lucifer might not be telling the truth.

The Major's eyes narrowed, trying to read Lucifer's face for a sign of uncertainty. He never really trusted anyone in his life. But then he abandoned his target and addressed the monk.

'Anyway, Father Blasius, the hotel is hers, apparently. It's not much but it's a start. And Guido here, will find out everything there is to know about Miss Olivieri and who works for her, won't you Guido?' Severi said, walking towards his attendant and amicably patting him on his shoulder.

Although appreciating his change of mood, Lucifer considered for a moment that he might have made a blunder. He would have to be much more careful going forward. He was pretty sure he'd be much more closely watched now.

'Sure, I will start working on it immediately, Major. I seem to understand it is urgent, correct?'

'The sooner, the better,' he responded curtly.

'Excellent, excellent, Major Severi.' Blasius seemed pleased, and, turning to Lucifer, he confirmed: 'and yes, it is urgent. I want to make sure that all involved in Colonel Schaeffer's operation, even if just as a passive host, have their lives passed through a fine sieve. Please be absolutely certain that no stone remains unturned. I want to know everything, down to the smallest detail.'

'I understand. Rest assured I will be painstakingly meticulous, Father,' Lucifer said, although his mind had descended into a state of turmoil.

Everything was happening very quickly, like in a vortex: one moment it was calm, the next you were thrown up in the air without even knowing it. This was an escalation he couldn't have predicted at all. If, with the death of her fiancé, Augusto, no one in his family would pursue the investigation on Cordelia's origins that had been lodged with the Ministry of Race any further, now the Benedictine had potentially resurrected it again.

Lucifer blamed himself for not having been able to bury it once and for all, when he could. He would finish this business though. He would pay a visit to his old mistress.

'I have to say that I am puzzled by her first name, Cordelia. Quite unusual for an Italian girl ... I wonder if there's a story behind this choice. As far as I remember, it's a character from King Lear, a Shakespearian tragedy.'

Lucifer felt a sudden shiver going down his spine.

He knew the answer as he, himself, had been curious about that once. When he had asked Father Colombo, the Franciscan explained to him that, since her mother was an English actress who had interpreted and loved that character in Shakespeare's historical play, she had named her daughter after her.

'That's an interesting question ... Don't worry, Guido is very good, Father Blasius. I have full confidence that if there is something to find on her account, he will dig it out without any doubt.'

'What can I say, Major. I am impressed by your efficient response. I look forward to our fruitful collaboration,' said Blasius, gloating. 'I will be at the Biblicum. Come and see me with a full report. I trust it will take priority over everything else.'

Blasius sounded more like he was imparting an order rather than giving an invitation.

'Now, if you will excuse me, gentlemen, I have some important work to do too.' And in saying that, the Benedictine rose and, as swiftly as he had arrived, he was gone.

Severi looked spooked by the encounter.

'What a personage, that Father Blasius. His devilish look gives me the creeps. I wouldn't want him as an enemy for sure,' Severi commented to Lucifer. Even he had sensed there was a dark side to the German monk, an almost poisonous aura seemed to surround him. But in pure Severi's twisted style, he would look to exploit that.

'In this case, the enemy of my enemy is my friend,' he said.

For the first time in days, his boss had a smile on his face. That was never a good sign. He clearly had something in mind and Lucifer knew it.

'What a peculiar request, Major. I wonder what the real reason behind it is. Did he explain that to you?'

Severi walked to the window, waiting a moment before giving a cryptic response.

'Let's say that it's going to be a *quid pro quo* situation, Guido. We give him something; he gives us something.'

'And what does he give us, Major?'

'My command back. He will help us capture the spy who put me in this disgraceful situation! I lost my command because of him. And I want it back. So the sooner we catch him, the sooner I can send that Afrika Korps Colonel to hell. And in the meantime, if we find any other reason why his whole operation should come back here to the Fascist command, even better. It will be a step in the right direction, as even that German could prove to be prone to making mistakes.'

So they are onto us, both me and Cordelia, Lucifer thought. They were on the same ship, and they'd better leave with it.

'I want you to follow Cordelia Olivieri. See where she goes, who she sees, what she does. Put a couple of other men to watch her staff. And pay a visit to the Ministry of Race; after all, the monk has raised an interesting issue regarding her name. Let's see if there's anything there.'

Thank God he asked me instead of others. And why wouldn't he? I can buy some time still, but not for much longer, Lucifer thought. I wonder how I could delay it without raising any suspicions…

He snapped to attention. 'Aye, Major,' he said, and set out to follow his orders.

To keep up appearances, Lucifer went first to the file room as if to conduct a search.

He had to think of a plan of action that would satisfy Severi while avoiding supplying vital information that could endanger him and Cordelia. After what would be considered a reasonable amount of time to have gone through the existing paperwork, he went downstairs and headed for the barracks. There were a few Blackshirts present at that time of the day. The others were out on patrol.

'Comrade Neri,' Lucifer shouted to one of them, 'go and find comrade Varone and comrade Bardi and ask them to report to my office.'

He had chosen two *squadristi* that he knew were not very bright nor particularly inclined to do any work and would rather hang around in a café or a bar and watch the world go by. He would allocate them to monitor the Palazzo Roveri staff.

The two men arrived in his office some thirty minutes later. Lucifer instructed both and dispatched them to start the surveillance immediately.

'And remember, you will report everything only to me, is that clear? And I will take care of Cordelia Olivieri myself,' he told them.

While Lucifer was dealing with her newly arranged supervision, Cordelia headed back to the dépendance, having agreed to dine with

Schaeffer. Through the window, Cordelia saw Alma trotting in her direction across the garden.

'Flaminia told me you wanted to see me? What's the matter?' she asked anxiously as soon as she was inside.

It was unusual for Cordelia to summon her over there, and Alma was nervous it might be something serious.

'Apologies you had to come here, but I categorically didn't want Flaminia to be able to listen to what I need to talk to you about, Alma. Let's sit down please.' Gently taking her arm, Cordelia guided her towards the armchair next to the fireplace.

She had dreaded that moment, but knew it was going to come sooner or later.

They sat opposite each other.

'Alma, I want to leave Rome, or, rather, I need to. I have been thinking about if for a while, and I cannot risk anyone finding out that my mother was English and a Jew too. With the current Racial Laws, I fear I would be banned from keeping Palazzo Roveri open. Possibly, the regime would consider me an enemy and jail me, given my mother's nationality. Father Colombo thought it'd be safer for me to go to another country, instead of waiting for it to happen. The time has come. He has organised my escape.'

Alma was startled but the worried look instantly disappeared, drowned by the tears that filled her eyes.

'Oh, Alma, please do not cry,' Cordelia said. 'I have made arrangements for you to come and join me where I am going. I don't want to lose you – you're all I have got left of my family.'

Her nanny took out her handkerchief to wipe her wet cheeks. It was hard on her; it was a lot to take in, in just a few moments. Cordelia felt a sense of remorse for having had to tell her the sad news, unable to somehow soften it in any way.

'I knew it was going to happen. I sensed it. I feared it. I don't blame you. With Augusto dead there's nothing holding you here anymore. And I am sure these Germans were the last straw,' Alma said.

'I have organised a temporary dwelling for you to go to, a safe haven where you can stay while I settle into my new place. Travelling with me is too risky. If I get caught, I don't want you to end up in the same boat as me. Then I will send you a ticket to come over. I don't want you to remain here in Italy too long after I leave as it might be dangerous – they might consider you an accomplice.'

Cordelia explained that Alma would go to a farm outside Rome, and that Father Colombo would take care of her documents of travel.

Despite that brief show of confidence, Alma saw that Cordelia was shaken at the prospect. But she also noticed the same sense of resolution in her eyes that her father had had before a project, or a race.

Except, her life and her future were at stake here.

'What will happen to Palazzo Roveri? You have put so much work into this hotel. It's just sad that you have to abandon your proudest achievement.'

'Palazzo Roveri will continue to live on without me, Alma. I have already prepared and signed all the paperwork to hand it to the Church. Father Colombo has arranged that as well. I will receive the money in a bank of the country where I am going. I will not be completely destitute.'

'So, it's all organised, and when are you set to leave?'

'Very soon. With a mercantile ship from the port of Anzio. I don't have much time left. Nor do you. I want you to get prepared, but quietly, without anyone suspecting anything. Especially Flaminia. She seems besotted by our new German guests, and I don't trust her malicious gossiping habits.'

'I know perfectly well what you mean. She's always been envious of you, Cordelia, you know that. Just today she mentioned you got quite friendly with Colonel Schaeffer earlier, by the way, a rumour she won't hesitate to spread further afield.'

So, dear Flaminia was spying on her. She knew she did that, but never really minded it much. Now it was becoming a serious nuisance.

'She saw him giving me a bunch of flowers earlier today. And obviously made her own distorted assumptions.'

'He gave you a bunch of flowers? What for?'

'I guess he is just a gentleman. He seems to regret that he had to commandeer the hotel. It was his way of saying sorry.'

'Well, Flaminia also said that he definitely looks at you with a lot of interest, and for once, I think she's right, so be careful.'

Reluctantly, Cordelia said, 'There's something else about Schaeffer that I need to talk to you about. He invited me to have dinner with him.'

'Seriously? I hope you said no – did you?'

'I said yes. How could I say no, Alma? I have no intention of upsetting him and, at this point I want to keep on friendly terms with him. As I said before, he seems innocuous. It's just a dinner, nothing else.'

'Just a dinner! And nothing else for you, certainly. But how about him? I am not sure he can be the gentleman you believe he is.'

'I am certain I can handle it, Alma. I'm old enough,' said Cordelia, preferring to cut the discussion short.

'Now remember, officially, I have asked you here to discuss the dinner arrangements, understood? I am sure Flaminia will be quite inquisitive about your trip to the dépendance today and I am equally sure she's already cudgelling her brain with her twisted hypothesis. Anyhow, in the end, she's going to find out about the dinner, so be pretty open about it, as if it was almost normal.'

'Very well, what would you like me to prepare then? I need to write down a menu, just in case Flaminia asks, and that meddling girl will, believe me.'

'Yes, well, let me think ... How about a fresh tomato salad with basil and olive oil, for a start? They are gorgeously sweet and tasty. See if you can also find some prosciutto di Parma, to go with ripe melon slices and fig halves. That can be followed by a plate of bucatini all'Amatriciana, a few saltimbocca alla Romana and, to finish, your delicious cherry cake. And please, make sure there's plenty of Montefiascone and Frascati wine. That'll be enough, I think.'

Cordelia knew that if Schaeffer ate and drank a lot, sleep might come more easily to him. And she needed him to be as inebriated as she could get him, but she strictly avoided saying that to Alma. It would have raised questions she not only couldn't answer, but wouldn't, for her old nanny's peace of mind.

'That's quite a generous selection. Isn't it a bit too much? Well, if it's good for you, it's good for me too. I will have to go out and buy all this stuff.'

Cordelia was silently grateful that the nanny did not ask her to explain further the reason for so much food.

'Alma, you'd better go now. I don't know what I would do without you. You've been better than a mother to me. Rest assured that I have thought of everything and with Father Colombo's help, all will go according to plan, for us both. Now, hurry back.'

Closing the door behind Alma, Cordelia turned the key to lock it, and looked out of the window to watch her nanny returning to the hotel.

That day, Cordelia remained in the dépendance, and cooked herself a light dinner, after which she listened to the radio for a bit, until day turned into darkness. They were playing 'La barca dei sogni' – the boat of dreams – a big hit of 1942, sung by Caterinetta Lescano, with the accompaniment of the orchestra Cetra directed by the maestro Barzizza.

Cordelia had been haunted by nightmares as of late. She hoped that when on board the ship taking her away, she would be able to dream good dreams again.

In the interim, though, she had to look to another more important matter.

As soon as the sun went down, she drew the curtains of all the windows, and left just a small side lamp on.

Instead of going to her bedroom to put on her nightdress, she chose a very practical pair of cotton trousers, an old comfortable shirt and a pair of shoes with rubber soles. She tied her hair in a tight ponytail.

She was ready.

She went back to the living room and walked up to the fireplace. Made of travertine, it dated back to the Medieval period. It was quite imposing; a person of normal height could stand inside it.

She waited a moment, listening for any sound coming from outside. All was quiet.

She moved one of the heavy wrought-iron andirons to one side, squatting down to be in a better position to reach the larger stone on the bottom right corner of the surround.

She ran her finger along the edge of the cold surface. It was there – it had to be there.

She found the tip of a strip of leather.

She pulled it out a bit, enough to grab it with both hands. Then she pulled it again, very gently, but steadily.

There was a thud, a muffled sound of stone against stone.

Cordelia saw that the back of the firebox had moved slightly and heaved a sigh of relief.

Thank God, it could still be unlocked!

The stone that had moved was mounted on a vertical plinth and could rotate on itself, thus opening a tunnel: it was a passage that led to the palace. Cordelia's builders had found it by chance when working on the restoration of Palazzo Roveri a few years before. A young and zealous apprentice, keen to clean up the fireplace to its smallest detail, finding the same strip that Cordelia had pulled earlier, had tried to remove it, and instead had opened the back of the fireplace. He followed the passage up to Palazzo Roveri and later told Cordelia, asking her if she wanted it sealed. As its presence did not bother her, and it would be a big job anyway, she decided to leave it as it was.

She never thought it would be of any service.

Until now.

With her feet firmly pressed on the ground, she leaned against the stone and pushed it, to test how easily it could be manoeuvred: it was heavy, but it didn't present any resistance, turning all the way, at ninety degrees.

Once fully open, a whiff of cold air came from the passage, bringing a musty smell of damp and decay into the room. It was the same stale air of death she had smelled only once before, when, during a school trip, the teacher had taken the class to visit the catacombs of Priscilla, on the Salaria way in Rome. It was a network of underground tunnels that ancient Christians dug to practice their rites and hide from the religious persecution of the Roman Empire, started by the ferocious emperor Nero in 64 AD, just after the Great Fire of Rome.

It was completely dark on the other side.

A torch. She needed the torch that was in the cupboard beside the door.

She went to fetch it, checked that the batteries were working and switched it on.

A shaft of light came out of it, illuminating what was just pitch black before.

Cautiously, Cordelia slid in.

Just as on the other side, she found a similar strip of leather that could be pulled to close that stone door, but since she was afraid of being trapped inside, she put a log of wood at its foot to block it from completely shutting up.

After a couple of tests to check that it would work, Cordelia decided to close it completely behind her.

I will just explore it tonight, she thought. I need to make sure that I see exactly where this passage ends up, and that I can retrace my steps back quickly and efficiently.

Her watch read almost midnight. She started to walk ahead, guardedly. The tunnel was quite narrow, and, after a short stretch, bent to the left. After a sharp curve, the torchlight revealed that there was a flight of steps going down, possibly underground, since the secret corridor had to be running under a section of the garden in order to reach the palace on the other side. Some of the steps were in poor condition, and Cordelia almost lost her balance before getting to the bottom, scratching the palm of her hand on one of the side walls in an effort to keep upright and avoid falling.

The subterranean atmosphere was more humid, with a few rivulets of water exuding from the earth walls ending up on the floor. She stopped after a moment. Down there the air was more rarefied and the smell of mould that filled her nostrils was stronger, more pungent. The ceiling was very low in this section of the tunnel, and looking up, she noticed that an enormous black spider had woven an intricate web; his multiple lucent eyes seemed to observe her, intently and immobile from its centre, as she ducked to walk under it.

It was colder as well, and she didn't know if it was the lower temperature, or the cavernous feel of the place itself, or perhaps the sight of that giant eight-legged arachnid, but sudden chills went up her spine.

Shivering, Cordelia kept going forward. About ten metres ahead, part of the wall had collapsed together with the ceiling, leaving a smaller section in the passage to go through. Struggling past it, she ended up in front of another set of steps. This time though, they were arranged in a spiral staircase.

Although at the time of its discovery, Cordelia had decided not to go down into the tunnel, she recalled that the young builder had told her it continued up to a higher level than the palace ground floor, behind the library and another room as well.

She started to go up and kept going until, by her calculation, she had to have reached at least the first floor of Palazzo Roveri. Which meant that she was beyond the soldiers that guarded the access, as they were stationed at the bottom of the main staircase in the central lobby.

After climbing all those steps, she got to a landing.

Up there, it was definitely less humid and the air she breathed felt drier.

Cordelia found herself having to choose between two options: to go to the right, or to the left after the landing, as the passage divided both ways at the top of the staircase.

It must have run along the external wall of the palace. With no point of reference, she decided to turn right first to find out where it led, walking very softly although she could hear no noise coming from the other side.

Initially, the light of the torch illuminated a section of the wall that had a slight recess.

This could be an entrance, she thought.

Of the same dark brown colour as the walls, it felt warmer to the touch when she placed her hand on it. It was a wooden panel, with a small window, some twenty inches from the top, that could be opened by pulling the minuscule knob at its centre.

She did that, finding a peephole just behind. She looked through it: it was total blackness in the other room. Cordelia had to know which room it was. So, she placed the torch at the level of the peephole letting the light shine through. It was the library! From her position, she could see the volumes arranged on the opposite shelves, plus the corner of the main desk on which a shaft of paper had been left. She switched off the torch immediately and closed the small window.

Her attention now focused on the wooden panel. She had to find a way to open it. There was no handle, apparently. But inspecting the recess more closely, she saw a metal lever hidden on the left. It was a bit rusty, but, at first glance, not damaged.

She placed the torch on the ground, pointing it up at the lever, and took hold of it with both hands.

Nothing, not an inch of movement.

She tried again, applying more pressure: it came down a little, then a little more, while at the same time the panel unlatched, rotating on itself, in the same fashion as the entrance from her dépendance. Then the lever got stuck and the panel stopped moving.

Unlike the stone in the fireplace, the mechanism must have jammed, as the panel wouldn't open more than three inches. Not enough for Cordelia to slide through and reach the other side.

With a renewed effort, she pulled the lever hard once more to try widening the gap.

Although she managed to progress its movement a little more, the lever got stuck again.

Cordelia tried another six or seven times, pulling as hard as she could, but got no further.

Dejected, she gave up and closed the panel, calling it a night. Not a complete disaster, but not a full success.

I need some sort of contraption to exercise a higher pressure, she thought.

At that point, there was nothing left to do but go back to the dépendance. Cordelia reckoned that the other corridor would probably lead to a bedroom, and it was not worth exploring it, for fear of awakening the occupant. She had found the library and this was where Schaeffer had his office, hence all the plans had to be kept there.

Down the spiral staircase, then tunnel, steps up, round the curve and she was again in front of the rotating stone at the back of the fireplace; she pulled the leather strip and, very easily, it swung open letting her slip out. She turned and pushed the stone to close it.

How much time had gone by? She looked at her watch and it was almost a quarter to one. Not too bad.

After placing the wrought-iron andiron back inside the fireplace, she was surprised by the stench of her clothes. The smell of mould was all over them, so she took them off; they would have to be washed.

Looking at herself in the mirror, she noticed that some traces of cobweb were still left on her hair and face, while her hands were dirty from touching the earth walls. She went to the bathroom to clean up, then went into the kitchen, reaching for a bottle of alcohol to disinfect the scratch on the palm of her hand.

It was time to go to sleep. Lying down on her bed, she wondered where to find a suitable object that could help to easily manoeuvre that lever, forcing it to go all the way, and, more importantly, how to smuggle it into her dépendance without being seen or questioned.

Aronne Ravà was the right man to find a solution to that problem.

CHAPTER 12

The alley had always been quite dark. The light had been taken away centuries ago, when the growing population of the Jews of Rome, barred by a Papal edict from living outside the walled quarter of the Ghetto, had no choice but to build vertically to alleviate an endemic over-crammed condition. This meant that the already narrow streets had essentially been deprived of any exposure to the sun, and the alley was no exception. Besides that, its proximity to the Tiber river made it unpleasantly damp and cold.

The forge of Aronne Ravà was located in that alley, not far from the Via Portico D'Ottavia, in the heart of the Ghetto of Rome. His family had relocated from the Venice Ghetto, regarded as the oldest in the world, to Rome over a hundred and fifty years ago now, and as they were used to the humidity of the *Serenissima*, as Venice is also known, they didn't mind the dankness as much as others, adapting quite well.

Today the blocked sun was a blessing, not only because it protected the alley from its intense heat, but also because the shade projected by the buildings was providing convenient cover from the prying eye.

Aronne Ravà was an old acquaintance of Cordelia's. He had done work for her father, and she had employed him when Palazzo Roveri needed to replace many of the hinges of its tens of windows and shutters during the restoration phase. He had also made the two wrought-iron andirons for her dépendance, modelling them on the bigger ones held in the fireplace of the main lounge, original pieces from the Middle Age era of the palace.

Cordelia had left Palazzo Roveri under the watchful eye of the German sentinel, while crossing the internal courtyard of the hotel to reach the ornate exit. That young soldier seemed intrigued by the bicycle she had brought with her, which she had fetched earlier from the shed at the end of the garden. So, pre-empting any question, with a big smile on her face, she addressed him with, 'Lovely weather for a ride, isn't it?' As she reached the exit, her hand was about to push down the handle, when she heard the sentinel's running steps resounding on the cobbled square, as he shouted, 'Wait! Wait, Miss!'

Stunned, she broke stride, with her heart in her throat, remaining pretty much immobile as he arrived beside her.

'Let me help you.' He opened the gate for her, to let her out.

'How kind of you, many thanks,' she said, trying to regain her composure, smiling nervously at him, truly grateful not only for his gesture, but also because he did not stop her.

It was indeed a very bright day outside. After removing a strand of hair from her face to put her hat on, she got on her bike and rode on.

She tried not to rush. Even pedalling slowly, it took her no more than fifteen minutes to get to the Via dei Funari, only to turn, after a few yards, into Via di Sant'Ambrogio and then lose herself in the maze of narrow streets of the Ghetto. Every now and then she looked behind her, but did not notice anyone.

The front entrance of the forge, a rusty green metal door, was unusually shut, and it looked as if the shop was closed. Cordelia pushed it, but it was locked. She tried the side entrance: this one was unlocked, so she entered, bringing the bicycle in as well and closing the door behind her.

Aronne Ravà was hard at work. He was dressed in a dark leather apron that covered him from his neck to his knees, from whose two side pockets a number of instruments of various sizes peeped out. Upon her arrival, he turned towards a huge anvil to put down the piece of metal he was holding with his gloved hands, still bright red from having been in a fire burning at over one thousand degrees Celsius. The place had a strong smell that was a mix of sweat, acrid coal smoke, a bit of sulphur, but mostly industrial fumes produced by the burning of products and metals together. The closer to the furnace you went, the thicker the stench was. Not to mention the ferocious heat it produced.

Aronne Ravà took off his protective helmet.

'Hello, Mr Ravà, I thought your shop was closed since the main gate was shut.'

'Hello, Miss Olivieri. These days I rather avoid keeping it open as I used to do,' he explained. 'Once I didn't mind who stepped in, and it was good for business to showcase my work to the public when they passed by. But now times have changed. Not everyone means well when they come in. And I prefer to keep my laboratory sheltered from certain people's eyes, especially those who mean trouble. I have already suffered some damage, and the police do not seem to care to stop what some of these hot heads do when they willingly decide to stray into the Ghetto. Nothing too serious, just youngsters who probably simply want to prove themselves to their mates, especially when they see somebody like me. I had to

174

discourage them the hard way, so to speak. Nevertheless, what they don't see, they're not tempted to damage. It's better not to attract their unwanted attention.'

At almost six foot six, he was a giant of a man, with large muscular shoulders, a neck like an ox and a totally bald skull, which gave him a rather menacing appearance. He looked more like a wrestler, or even an executioner, possibly an ogre-like figure to a child, instead of a blacksmith. Even though he was in his late fifties, he could still have taken care of two young men at a time, in a fight, which he probably had. She rejoiced, as she was pretty sure he had taught those young men a good lesson. Nevertheless, she was saddened to hear of his vexations: like many others, even Aronne Ravà had been harassed because he was a Jew. Not even his massive physical presence was threatening enough to avoid it.

She was reminded of what might happen to her if she stayed here. At the same time, her resolve to help Father Colombo's Allied cause grew stronger; this absurd, grotesque, evil tragedy has to stop, she thought, and I can do something about it. But how extreme could one possibly become to fight another extreme? The secret to that was to stop it before it got to the point of no return, on both sides. But it was too late now; it required other more radical solutions.

'What brings you to my lair, Miss Olivieri? I didn't think it was very convenient for an Aryan to visit the Ghetto as of late – it could ruin your reputation!' he said. But it was evident that Aronne didn't enjoy his own joke very much, as it left a bitter taste in his mouth.

'Believe me, Mr Ravà, my reputation is the last thing I am worried about at the moment. I am here as I need a favour, and I am willing to pay extra for the rush. I came to this side of town as I trust you will keep the fact that you saw me, and what I ask you for, to yourself.'

If Cordelia had gone to another blacksmith, he might have been inquisitive about why she wanted something of that kind so urgently, let alone be able to meet her deadline, even if extra cash was on offer. But most crucially, as she had to hide it, her request would spark an interest that would surely end up in the man alerting the authorities.

'I need a sort of solid iron bar, almost like a crowbar, with two handles on both sides. It needs to be placed across a lever, which is currently stuck. I need something to apply pressure and pull it down.'

'I am not going to ask you anything, or tell anyone, don't you worry,' he reassured her.

'Can you make it now?'

'It will take a bit of time. Can you spare one hour? It should be ready by then.'

'One hour will be a dream. Ah, and one more thing, I need to hide it in my bicycle. If I take the seat off, there should be enough space to insert it down there.'

'Got it, so it's better if it is made of steel. It's stronger even if thinner and it will fit better into your hiding place.'

'Aronne Ravà, you are my salvation!' And she meant it in more ways than one.

She watched the blacksmith while he was working with alacrity, making the piece of kit she had asked him for.

Despite his huge body size, Aronne moved back and forth from the forge with the lightness of a dancer. He handled and bent the metal with pliers and a hammer, whose rigidity was tamed by the heat of the fire, with the precision of a watchmaker. In less than forty-five minutes the bar was ready.

'It's not the most beautiful object I have ever created,' he stated with a grin, 'but it's going to do just the job.'

He plunged it into a bucket of cold water, from which an acute hissing sound, accompanied by a cloud of hot vapour came out.

Cordelia admired it as if it was Queen Margherita of Savoia's magnificent diamond tiara rather than the humble piece that it was. In fact, it was much more precious to her than any jewel of the crown.

Fetching the bicycle, Cordelia took its seat off and Aronne lowered the bar into the tube, then placed the saddle back on top of it.

She paid him and went back into the dark alley, retracing the same route to go back to Palazzo Roveri.

She hadn't noticed her when she went out earlier, nor when she returned from the Ghetto.

Flaminia had managed to follow Cordelia that day.

She was eager to report what she had observed to Father Blasius as soon as possible, and, as Judas, get her thirty pieces of silver.

On the other side of town, Lucifer was heading for the bakery of Cosimo Farina, to leave a message that would trigger a meeting with Father Colombo. He reckoned it would be the last one with the Franciscan, as his intention was to disappear as soon as possible. With Marino Severi and that German monk, Blasius, both demanding information on Cordelia Olivieri, he would not be able to keep up the fake show of her surveillance for much longer. They were not stupid and it was just a matter of days before he was found out. Besides, his boss was now teaming up with the Gestapo, and they were after the spy who had leaked their plans to the Allies. There was nothing left to do, other than turning into a sitting target. And wouldn't it be ironic to be freed from one prison at home, just to end up in another abroad, with torture benefits? He had no intention of being a guest of a jail ever again in his life, following his unwise juvenile experience.

This time, Lucifer did not have the luxury of choosing a perfect moment of the day, when Cosimo's shop was likely to be quiet. Thankfully, though, inside there were just a couple of customers, a middle-aged lady, who was finishing putting all her shopping in a white canvas bag, and a crippled old man, leaning on a wooden crutch.

Lucifer patiently waited for them to be served. The shop would be empty after they left, even if just for a few moments, which was all he needed. The lady paid and went out, but the old man, after he got his pound of flour and a bread roll, decided to sit on a bench inside the bakery to rest, before heading back home.

'You don't mind, do you, Cosimo?' he said to the baker.

He was a kind man and always asked his permission. One of Cosimo's oldest customers, he had difficulty walking, so he used to stay for a few minutes to take the weight off his badly damaged leg, alleviating it for a little while.

Talking, or even whispering, was impossible. Lucifer had to think of an alternative to communicate the day and time for Cosimo to pass on the message to Father Colombo. The place, as per their secret protocol, had been agreed during their last encounter back in the Church of St. Francis, days ago.

'May I have a bread loaf and a slice of that fresh pizza, please?' he asked the baker, while placing his hand inside his pocket, but leaving two fingers visibly out.

Cosimo saw that sign and nodded, while preparing his order.

'It's one lira and twelve centesimi,' he told Lucifer, who took a few coins out of his pocket and placed it on the counter. He put the right amount on one side and added a five centesimi coin on the other. Cosimo nodded again, acknowledging the final part of the message, then sweeping the money away from the surface.

Lucifer took the goods and winked at him before exiting the bakery, although Cosimo couldn't imagine it was his only way to say goodbye. Lucifer would miss Mr Farina, as he would miss magnificent Rome, the Eternal City, with its ancient decadent monuments and streets full of smells, and colourful shops and restaurants. And the food, the entertainment and the people, who had such a *joie de vivre*, even if, in all honesty, some of them he was happy to leave behind.

In all those months, he had played a good hand, but even the most skilled gambler knows that there is a time when the game has to stop, or there is a risk of losing it all in one go.

Brother Filippo rushed to alert Father Colombo as soon as he picked up the message at Cosimo Farina's bakery. It was the second time in a few days; hence, he thought it had to be urgent, so he hurried back to the Vatican, forgetting the rest of his errands for the day.

'I will lose all my hair with the stress if it continues to go on like that,' he said to the old Franciscan when he returned home. Father Colombo was grateful for the haste, enthusiasm and zeal Brother Filippo had demonstrated in his secret missions.

The gardens of Villa Borghese were no more than a thirty-minute walk from the walls of Vatican City. Father Colombo headed for the entrance at Piazza del Popolo, crossing the Tiber on the Regina Margherita Bridge and passing one of the two majestic fountains in the huge square, the Fontana di Nettuno, on the south-west side, as it was the more direct route to his final destination, the Esculapio Temple.

The location Lucifer had chosen for the meeting was a small Ancient Roman style temple with ionic columns dedicated to the Greek God of medicine, which had been built during the late eighteenth century on an artificial island of one of the lakes, the biggest in that Roman garden.

One had to cross a narrow wooden bridge to get there, but since the temple was immersed in vegetation, it provided a level of privacy from the rest of the visitors. Moreover, Lucifer could see any pursuer approaching on foot from a distance and lose him in the plethora of small paths running across the park in many directions.

The gardens had been very popular with international tourists in the past, but now, with the war, the stream had dried up. Still, at that time of the day, many Romans enjoyed its shaded and cool spaces and were out in good numbers. Lots of children were playing and shouting on the grassy grounds, while their mothers or nannies kept an eye on them.

Lucifer, looking at a group of little boys while passing by, tried to remember what it was like to play all day, without a care in the world, and to fall into a peaceful sleep, exhausted, but completely content and looking forward to doing it again the next day.

The war and his job had taken a toll on his ability to relax, and he often woke up covered in sweat, not even remembering the bad dream that caused it, or because his sleep was so light that he had been awakened by a siren, or by the sound of a car engine, whose noise reverberated even louder during the night.

Lucifer had disguised himself a bit, wearing a pair of fake reading glasses, a striped cotton beret, and carrying with him a sketchbook in one hand, and a coloured pencil case in the other. The idea was to look like an amateur artist, many of which regularly dotted the place, since the gardens provided much inspiration.

He got there first, entering the park from the Porta Pinciana in the south-east. Having arrived at the lake, he crossed the bridge linking the artificial island to the Viale del Lago walking path, leading to the Temple from the back. He then went round it on its right side, and positioned himself near an oblique stone jar, part of a fountain which had a pressurised jet of water continuously gushing out and splashing with a vigorous sound into the water of the lake. Even if somebody else had decided to visit the monument, the noise of the spurts would make it pretty much impossible to capture a whispered and short conversation.

Which was what Lucifer intended to have today.

With his sketchbook open, he took out a pencil and started to study the monument as if he wanted to choose the right angle to draw it.

Lucifer saw Father Colombo slowly walking towards him and gave him an imperceptible nod of the head, signalling he was alone.

The Franciscan went to stand near him, as if interested in what the artist was doing.

They exchanged a few words, and Father Colombo heard of the peculiar interest that Blasius had in Cordelia, who was now the subject of an investigation instigated by his boss, Marino Severi.

'I am keeping them at bay for now, but the clock is ticking faster every hour of the day. Yesterday, I bought a train ticket to go north, dressed as you see me today, so hopefully in that busy Stazione Termini office, the clerk won't remember me. If the Fascist militia went looking, they would be on the hunt for a Blackshirt, if it comes to that. And I am afraid it will, after I've been gone a day or so. But that would be advantage enough. By then I'll be crossing the Alps into Switzerland.'

'So I won't see you again, after today,' Father Colombo said to him, a note of regret in his voice. 'Thanks for the information and the help with Cordelia. I will pray you get safely home, Lucifer.'

Father Colombo never knew his real name, only his coded one, and thought it would be the only devil he would ever say a prayer for.

The friar put his hand on the British agent's forearm for a brief moment, a gesture of farewell.

'God be with you, Son.'

'And with you, Father. Now go in peace.'

As soon as Father Colombo had departed, a young mother and her child crossed the wooden bridge in the opposite direction. The small boy ran towards Lucifer and asked him what he was doing there.

'I am trying to draw this building, but I am not very good at it. Would you like to try?'

The young boy smiled and said yes, while grabbing the pencil case and paper book Lucifer offered to him.

'You can keep it all. I won't need it anymore.'

CHAPTER 13

Schaeffer heard, in the distance, a church bell striking eight o'clock.

The sky, inexorably but slowly, was turning to a deeper shade of blue, which made it possible to distinguish the first and more brilliant stars, while a half moon looking like a massive, curved silver blade was preparing to illuminate the night once the sun had completely set.

The Afrika Korps officer was deep in thought, while leaning on the marble parapet of the terrace, just above the walled garden at the back of the hotel.

A huge linden tree, whose light green branches stretched up to almost touch the balustrade, was in full bloom, and its pale yellow, star-shaped flowers exhaled a most intoxicating and intense scent of honey and lemon, which enveloped its surroundings, a fragrance that attracted lots of bees, still buzzing around it, despite the impending darkness. The combination of that sweet perfume and that gentle, monotonous sound was hypnotic and soothing.

Schaeffer started to relax for the first time in days and turned to face the façade of the palace.

The dinner table had been elegantly set for two, and, on an exquisitely embroidered white linen cloth, a pair of fine, almost translucent, bone china plates, and wine goblets made of an elaborate cut crystal glass were facing each other. Silver cutlery for the starter, main course and dessert completed the skillful arrangement. As there were no lights outside, an eight-arm candelabra had been placed at the centre of the table, so that candles could be lit as the evening turned into night.

Schaeffer thought it was a marvellous display.

When was the last time he had dined at a table like that? It must have been in late 1938, he reckoned, when he was dating Reni Hausmann, a journalist who used to report on court hearings in Berlin. She was not as attractive as other girls he had flirtations with, but surely compensated her lack of physical beauty with a great sense of humour and an ability to please him sexually. She possessed an uninhibited appetite that he had never encountered in a woman before. Actually, now that he thought of it, it was her who had proposed to go out to dinner the first time they met, ending up in his flat just a few hours later for the first of the many heated love sessions that always followed their evening meals.

Schaeffer strongly doubted it would be the case tonight with Cordelia, although the thought of it excited him. He had fantasised of having a romantic encounter with her before, since Augusto had started to talk about his fiancée back in Tripoli, showing the many photographs he had carried with him when he was posted to Libya. Schaeffer was almost instantly smitten with her. Although she had remained just an image for a long time, he simply couldn't get her out of his head.

She was the most beautiful woman he had ever seen, so different from the others he had met back in Berlin. Her features were more pronounced, with those dark and thick eyebrows framing her green eyes, and her lips looked almost too big for that delicate face, surrounded by a rebellious golden-brown mane with blond highlights.

He imagined what it would be like to pass his fingers through her long, soft hair, and then move his hand down to massage the nape of her neck.

He sipped the cold white wine, closing his eyes to further enjoy its refreshing notes and prolong, uninterrupted, this imaginary sensation. He realised he had started to have an erection.

He downed the rest of the wine and poured himself another glass, before returning to gaze at the garden below.

Someone in the immediate neighbourhood had put music on, for he could hear the distant notes of a trio singing a languid tune, accompanied by an orchestra.

He heard the light noise of high heels on the marble floor behind his back.

Cordelia had arrived to join him on the terrace. She was stunning and more beautiful than ever, he thought. Although she wasn't wearing a formal evening outfit, her short chiffon dress looked quite smart, and was gracing her figure perfectly. It was made up of a black top that surmounted an impalpable cream skirt that seemed to float ethereally around her legs while she walked. The rounded neckline was low enough to allow a glimpse of her cleavage. Her hair, loosely tied at the back with a silk bow, left her neck and shoulders almost bare.

'Good evening, Miss Olivieri, you look very elegant tonight, and, if you allow me to say it, absolutely ravishing,' he said, politely kissing her hand.

'Good evening, Colonel Schaeffer. Thank you, you're overly generous with your compliments, but very kind,' said Cordelia, slightly embarrassed by his evident appreciation.

Always on time for her appointments, that evening she was late, as she couldn't decide what to wear and had changed outfit a number of times.

Initially Cordelia thought she didn't really care how she would look for Schaeffer and had chosen an ordinary dress. But then she realised she did in fact care.

She wanted to feel desirable again, and went for a simple, yet elegant tailor-made model by Zoe Fontana, a young designer who had relocated from Paris. It might be the last time I wear it before I leave, she thought.

'May I pour you a drink? I've already taken the liberty of having one while waiting.'

'I apologise. I hope you haven't been here too long.'

'Oh please, don't,' he said, handing her the glass. 'You're fashionably late. And in any case, it's been a while since I had some time to unwind, all by myself.'

'Cin cin, then,' she said, 'or shall I say, prosit, Colonel.'

'Please, call me Friedrich. May I call you Cordelia? Even if just for tonight. It will make me feel normal again, and help me forget the war for a few hours, to hear that somebody doesn't address me by my military rank. And also help me forget that we are almost complete strangers.'

Raising their glasses, they both had a sip.

A waiter arrived discreetly pushing a trolley with their plates all covered by a silver cloche, which he positioned beside the table, gliding away immediately to leave them alone again.

'But I am not a complete stranger to you, Friedrich. Augusto must have talked about me, among other women I suppose.'

'Among other women?' Schaeffer said.

'I had noticed his eyes started to wander around once we got engaged.

Soon I understood that this was the real Augusto, and that I had just been a prize he wanted to conquer, before directing his attention to the next one. It was his nature, you see, a nature I couldn't change: he loved the thrill of the challenge and the taste of triumph, women, car races, it was the same for him. Did you know that before the war started, he made the podium a number of times at the Mellaha racetrack of the Tagiura oasis in Libya? He used it as an excuse and stayed down there for months on end. A number of friends reported that he had a local girl set up in a flat in the coastal city of Misurata. I wrote him a few letters, asking for clarification, but then I ceased. I was ready to call off our wedding, and if that wasn't a good enough reason, at the same time I came to realise that I did not love him anymore, really. I loved his humour, his enthusiasm for life, his contagious effervescence, but not him. When he was notified he was going to be posted to the North Africa front, I did not have the guts to break up with him before he left. Sorry, I don't know why I am telling you this. You must think I'm a horrible person to talk like that about my dead fiancé.'

She didn't know why. It had been on her mind for too long, she convinced herself, and now that she had told somebody, she felt better, like a weight had left her shoulders once and for all. The Afrika Korps officer, for some reason, felt the right person to tell. And, strangely, she wanted him to know.

Schaeffer knew that Count Nuvoli was a regular visitor of some of the brothels in Tripoli while they were stationed there together but did not suspect that he had been unfaithful in any other manner to Cordelia, or romantically attached to another woman. In a way he was equally as surprised as he was pleased to hear that she hadn't been in love with him for some time before he passed away. It made him feel less guilty being here with her, betraying, even if just in memory, a deceased friend.

He moved closer to her, and briefly touched her forearm with his hand, feeling an immediate impulse to comfort her. Her skin was soft and silky and left a scent of jasmine on his fingers.

As Schaeffer did this, Cordelia saw an almost palpable warmth radiating from his eyes, an instant understanding of what she had gone through, for which she was grateful.

'You seem to be saddened for me, Friedrich.'

'My uncle always told me that, as a lawyer, I was getting too emotionally involved in my cases, and I shouldn't have.'

'So, have I become a case of yours?'

'As I told you when we first met, Augusto always spoke about you, telling me lots of things about your personal life, like the loss of your mother in a tragic accident when you were still an infant. I've known you before I've known you, if you understand what I mean. Also, through the many pictures he showed me. He was a good judge of character. In person you are exactly as he described you.'

Flattered, she replied, 'A lawyer, you said? I just cannot picture you as such. The war seems to have swept away any sense of justice. Certainly, for those poor people who have been overrun by the tanks and seen their families and possessions crushed.'

'Nor can I at the moment. I wonder if I can go back to being that person again, after the war. It is as destructive for its perpetrators as much as it is for its victims. It changes you: it changes you forever. The truth is nobody wins, really.'

'So, how can you go on doing what you do, if it feels that horrific, or wrong, or both.'

'I am a soldier. I follow orders. It's my duty to serve my country.'

'Perhaps we should forget there's a war for tonight, should we, Friedrich?'

And with a gentle nudge, she guided him to the table and he

helped her to sit down on her chair. They continued their conversation and he clearly appreciated the menu, because he ate everything in abundance. And he drank, copiously.

Cordelia found herself enjoying his company, much more than she could have ever anticipated. She loved the way he talked about his job and his life back in Berlin, the way he quietly laughed. His voice was low and gentle. She found herself enjoying the way he looked at her. It was genuine, honest. And he was incredibly attractive tonight.

The music in the distance was still playing. The sky had turned to a deep indigo, dotted by brilliant celestial bodies, the air still warm, despite the hour approaching almost eleven o'clock. Time had flown.

They finished their dinner. He stood up, and extending his hand in search of hers, with an enticing smile he asked, 'May I have this dance?'

She placed her hand in his. He put his arm around her waist, gently pulling her towards his body. His thighs were pressing on hers as they started to sway to the music, and she felt the rough touch of his bearded jaw against her cheek. He smelled of fresh tobacco, an aroma she found herself abandoning to, after a while, her olfactory sense seduced by his masculine scent.

He was a skilled dancer, and moved lightly, in perfect sync with her, graciously smiling when she met his gaze.

Schaeffer bent his face towards the side of hers.

She felt the warmth of his breath on her neck.

They turned and he squeezed his arm around her a little more, bringing her nearer. Her breasts were now gently pressing against his buttoned jacket. His heart rate increased with the closer physical contact. He realised his member was hardening again.

Suddenly he felt an irresistible desire to kiss her.

Cordelia almost lost her balance, bumping into him when he unexpectedly stopped the dance. Confused, she looked up.

'Friedrich …'

His expression had become very serious. Schaeffer took her face with both hands, very tenderly, and pressed his lips against hers.

He found she was parting them without any resistance, allowing his tongue to slip in her mouth.

She was responding with equal desire. Only then he understood how desperate he had been to do that.

For a moment they passionately explored each other.

Cordelia was surprised by how much she was enjoying the sensation of being penetrated by his tongue, feeling his mouth thirsty for more and more. He embraced her tighter, placing his right hand on the back of her shoulders and letting it slowly run down towards her bottom.

She felt her excitement growing as her body, after months of abstinence, naturally responded to his ardent touch.

Could she fall for a man like that? Taken aback by this very thought, startled by her own easy surrender, she abruptly stepped back, breaking that embrace and the spell under which she had momentarily fallen.

He didn't stop her, letting her go immediately. They were both shocked by what had just happened.

Schaeffer broke the embarrassed silence.

'I am so sorry, Cordelia. I don't know what got into me. You are so beautiful. Please forgive me. I have taken unfair advantage and I shouldn't have, I shouldn't,' he said, apologetically.

For a moment, still shaken and unsure of what to do or say, she remained quiet.

'We both drank a bit too much, I guess, and the splendid evening with the music did the rest,' she said. 'And perhaps we are both a bit lonely. There's nothing wrong in what you did, only, it's just bad timing.'

'Yes, it must be that. And I'm even more sorry that it is. If only you and I had met under different circumstances.'

Cordelia saw how disheartened he was, sensing that, to him, there was much more to it than simply having had their kiss interrupted.

'I think I should leave now, Friedrich. It has been a wonderful evening, and I don't have any regrets.'

'Please, let me accompany you to your dépendance; that's the least I can do. I promise I won't attempt to kiss you again.'

And she believed him.

They walked side by side down the marble staircase leading to the garden and then across it to reach her dwelling on the other side. She noticed he was a tiny bit wobbly on his legs. He had definitely drunk too much.

'Good night, Cordelia. Sleep well,' he said, and turning on his heels, he left.

She responded, 'You too, Friedrich,' hoping that he really would.

It was not time to go to sleep just yet for Cordelia.

She went inside the dépendance, locking the door behind her. As she had left the window open, she heard the sound of his steps resounding farther and farther on the gravel path, until all was silent. After closing all the curtains, she went to the kitchen to make herself a strong pot of coffee. Although she tried to avoid eating and drinking too much, she felt the effect of the alcohol. Nothing that a good cup of espresso couldn't cure though.

While waiting for the water to boil, she went to her bedroom to get rid of her dress, and she slipped into a comfortable outfit. A quick trip to the bathroom cleansed her face of the make-up she had carefully applied before dinner. The fresh water shook her from her impending torpor. It wasn't enough though.

The clock struck eleven thirty.

The coffee was ready. She drank a full cup, allowing the stimulating caffeine of the beverage to take effect. It kicked in very quickly, and she was perfectly awake again in no time. She then switched off the light of the kitchen and the living room, leaving just a small table lamp on.

Cordelia went to the fireplace, grabbed the silver candelabra and unscrewed the bottom base. The minuscule Minox micro-camera slipped into her hand. She opened it to check the film was positioned correctly, closed it up again and clicked it a couple of times: it worked. She stored it in one of the zipped pockets of her trousers.

Removing the heavy wrought-iron andiron as she had the first time to reach the leather strip easier, she squatted down, grabbed it with both hands and pulled it, opening the back stone of the fireplace. The sound of the rotating mechanism felt so loud that when she went back to the cupboard to fetch her torch, she had a quick glimpse through the gap of the curtains, just to check if anyone had been alerted.

I am too far from the palace, and these walls are too thick for anybody to hear anything, she thought, in an attempt to reassure herself. Nobody came to enquire.

Thrusting open the secret passage made the stale air invade the room again. A smell of old mould took hold of the back of her throat, filling her nostrils. Suddenly and unwillingly, a thought materialised, comparing its stark difference to the fragrance emanating from Schaeffer's chest. She asked herself if Cardinal Roveri's mistress had such thoughts before setting out to meet him for a secret sexual encounter via that same way. Brusquely, she made herself erase those thoughts from her mind. She did not have time for that now. She had a job to do.

Ducking to slip through the opening and once she reached the other side, she closed the stone door, switched on the torch and found the steel bar that Aronne Ravà had prepared for her, and that she had hidden there as soon as she came back from his forge, together with an old can of engine lubricant she had retrieved from the garage earlier that day. Carrying all the equipment she needed, lightly and quickly she pressed ahead inside that ancient and claustrophobic man-made bowel that had been dug into the earth beneath her feet centuries before.

Down the first set of steps, the huge black spider she saw the first time was still there, immobile, awaiting its prey at the centre of its web. Along the tunnel, mid-way through she noticed that the section with the collapsed side had suffered further damage, leaving a smaller gap, but still she was able to squeeze past it, even though the humid soil stained her clothes. She was at the bottom of the spiral staircase now. She started to climb it, when she heard a high-pitched squeak, followed by a scurrying noise.

The hair on the back of her neck stood up and she froze as a small mouse ran in the opposite direction at very high speed. Her heart skipped a beat at the sight, so she stopped just for a minute to take a breather. With a hand on the wall, she continued to go up in circling turns, and arrived at the landing. Turning right, she forced herself to proceed more circumspectly, trying to minimise the noise her feet produced on the floor.

The recessed panel had the lever on its side still in the position she had left it in. But before attempting to pull it down to open the door, she slid the small window concealing the peephole behind it that allowed her to see through to the other side.

It was totally black.

Good.

Cordelia could turn her attention to the lever. First, she greased its bottom hinges with the lubricant to loosen its movement. Next she placed the bar made by Aronne in a perpendicular position to the lever itself. With her hands placed on each side, she started to move it towards her, steadily and without hurry. The lever got stuck again in the same position it had the previous time. Cordelia silently swore, then, gritting her teeth, she dragged it down harder with as much force as she could exercise. This time it gave in and went all the way down in one go.

The wooden panel, rotating on its vertical axis, opened completely. She wiped the sweat from her forehead with the back of her hand, placed the bar on the floor and, with her torch on, entered into the library.

There was no danger that people could see the light beams emanating from the torch. The room had a thick wooden door and all the window shutters had been closed tightly. She aimed at working as fast as she could. She did not want to spend a minute more than was necessary in there.

She went around a red velvet sofa that had its back to the panel, glad to have chosen a thick Persian rug, with its welcome muffling effect. It covered the floor up to the writing desk, which was full of files. Placing the torch on one side, she decided to risk switching on the large brass reading lamp, which allowed her to use both hands for the Minox.

Flipping through the pages, she started to read one, then another. Information on ships and what they were carrying: tinned food, weapons, petrol, troops, ammunition, medicines. She took photographs of all those lists. Methodically, she went through all the documents that were on the desk.

The operation took her a good few minutes. Her heart was beating madly and her breathing was increasing under the urgency of bringing her task to an end. Eventually, she had to stop, as her hands were shaking.

Father Colombo had mentioned that it was crucial to find the itinerary of the convoy.

Nothing about that in those papers though, just what they were transporting.

There was another pile on a cupboard, just behind the desk.

Again, nothing there.

She returned to the desk and started to look inside the drawers. In the bottom one, stored there, she found a small leather case. Carefully, she picked it up and placed it on the top of the desk; it had a latch with a keyhole, which fortunately wasn't locked.

She opened it.

The top of the first page of the document read: 'Operation Seafarer' with a red swastika and 'Top Secret' stamped across it. The plan with all the routes, the dates of the sailing of the vessels, and the ports of departure were all listed in the following pages. They were leaving from different harbours, then gathering at a certain point of the Mediterranean for their final leg to Tripoli. Clever. The odds of finding them was far lower, and RAF bomber squadrons would need to split, becoming more vulnerable. Only when the ships were to converge, would they become a perfect target to concentrate on.

Cordelia was ecstatic!

Diligently, she took out one page at a time, rushing to take pictures of the whole file as fast as possible. Her heart was beating faster and faster now that she was almost finished.

Click, click, click.

Last page.

One more click.

Done!

She looked at her watch: a quarter to one.

She hastily reassembled together, in chronological order, all the pages. She closed the file, placed it back in the leather case, and put it in the drawer where she had found it.

She was about to switch off the table lamp, when, to her horror, the telephone on the opposite corner of the desk began to ring.

When he had reached the top of the marble staircase leading back to the main lounge of the hotel, Schaeffer stopped and turned to look back in the direction of the dépendance, where he had just left Cordelia.

He had been completely mesmerised by her beauty that night. But it was not just the fascination with her physical appearance that had struck a note. The more he was in her presence, the more infatuated he had become with her warm and charming personality. To the point of succumbing to his impulse to embrace her and kiss her. The realisation that she was not just a fantasy, a fixation caused by his loneliness in the desert, made him ponder if he was starting to have real feelings. Or if he had had real feelings all along. Perhaps they were real. But was it possible to fall in love with somebody just through images and stories heard, before even meeting that person? And then realise that such a sentiment was actually genuine?

His attendant, Captain Wolf, appeared in the frame of the door and walked towards him, his salute interrupted his thoughts. 'Seig Heil, Lieutenant Colonel! I hope you had a nice evening.'

'I did, Captain. The best evening I have had in years.'

'I saw her briefly when she crossed the hall to get to the terrace earlier. She's a magnificent creature, Miss Olivieri.'

'She is a splendid woman, and very graceful. Good company too, Captain.'

Wolf saw how fervent Schaeffer's eyes were when he said that. That was the look of a man who was in love, he thought.

'You seem truly fascinated with her, Sir. All of the soldiers are, to be honest, from what I hear. And who could blame them? Perhaps she will have dinner with you again.'

Was it so evident? He wondered if others could see more than he had even allowed to admit to himself, until then.

'I hope so, Captain, I really do. Would you care for a cognac, Wolf? I am really pleased with the ground we have managed to cover so far. We can allow ourselves a small celebration.'

'With pleasure, Sir.'

Having walked back inside the building together, they went into the lounge where there was a drinks trolley. Schaeffer poured two glasses, handing over one to his attendant.

'Prosit, Wolf,' he said, downing it in one go. Wolf did the same.

'Are you married, Wolf?'

'No, Sir, I love women too much, all of them.'

'So did I. Oh, don't get me wrong, I thought it was great fun for a while, and, I guess, good experience. One must find out what one really likes or dislikes. But now ... I don't know, maybe it's the war. Maybe I've got to an age when I need more than just a warm body to wait in a bed for me. I'd like somebody to talk to, to share my hopes, my dreams. Maybe have a family, children.'

'Rome is a very romantic city, Sir. It makes people sentimental.'

'Maybe. I wish it was just that, Wolf. For now though I'd better go to bed. It's late. We still have a lot of work to do tomorrow.'

'Good night, Lieutenant Colonel.'

Schaeffer left him down in the lobby and went up to his bedroom on the first floor, the same as the library.

It was well past eleven thirty when he looked at his watch.

Cordelia was right, he had drunk too much that night, and felt quite inebriated. He took off the jacket of his uniform, and sat on the soft bed to unbutton his shirt. It still smelled of her perfume. When he rose to take off his trousers, his head started to spin a bit, but he managed to get completely undressed without losing his balance.

He felt quite hot. So, naked and slightly staggering, he went to the luscious marble-tiled bathroom and let the water of the shower run until it reached a tepid temperature. He stepped under the jet, and with both hands he leaned on the wall while enjoying its cooling and invigorating effect. He stayed there, immobile, for a good twenty minutes as he gradually started to feel better.

When he turned the water off, his head had stopped spinning. That was an improvement. He stepped out of the shower, grabbed a generous linen towel and wrapped it around his hips.

The bedroom was still quite warm, so he slammed the huge window open to let the fresher night breeze in. The light of the moon hit his body, making the droplets on his hairy chest shine. The cooler air woke him further. From there he had an interrupted view of the garden with the dépendance at its end. He wondered if Cordelia was already asleep.

Did she wear a nightgown or did she sleep naked in her bed? The thought of her sensual, totally naked body aroused him with rapacious vehemence. He imagined her in a supine position, her soft white breasts spreading across her chest, her delicate rosy nipples, her long legs languidly parted to reveal her …

Oh, stop it! Stop it, Friedrich! Nothing good will come of it. I am just torturing myself, he thought, trying to get rid of those open-eyed reveries.

He went to sit on the bed but kept brooding. A mounting desire for her, a physical need to possess her body was becoming stronger and stronger, like a potent tide that was overwhelming his senses with its irresistible waves.

He lay down and tried to relax.

Those mental images just wouldn't disappear. He felt even more excited now than after the dinner, when he had held her in his arms and kissed her.

Just a few days more and then he would have to leave. Back to North Africa, to the front. That thought came with the realisation that he might never see her again, talk to her again. He might never know what making love to her would be like. Cordelia would be confined to a picture only, exiled in his fantasies, relegated solely to his imagination, as she had been at first.

An irrational urgency took hold of him.

What time was it? As soon as he had formulated that thought, the church bell struck half past twelve.

He got out of bed and went back to the window to see if there was still a light on in the dépendance. He noticed a tenuous gleam coming from behind a curtain.

Perhaps she was still awake.

Possessed, he furiously dressed again.

He wanted to go and tell her that he loved her and implore her to make love to him.

He hurried downstairs and exited the back door, walking with great determination towards the dépendance.

He wanted her, badly.

He got almost to Cordelia's door, when he heard the footsteps of somebody pounding on the gravel behind him. He stopped, turning to see who it was.

Breathing heavily from the run, a soldier said, 'Sir, it's the General,

Sir! The sentinel upstairs has sent me to tell you that General Rommel is on the phone looking for you!'

One ring, then another, then another one – the telephone had begun to ring with unrelenting regularity.

Cordelia stopped dead.

Panicking, she switched the reading lamp off, but that was a mistake.

Now she couldn't see exactly where on the desk she had put the Minox camera. Not daring to switch the light back on, she desperately tapped on its surface. It didn't take long to find it.

She grabbed it and with her heart racing, she rushed back to the passage, just a few yards away behind the sofa. But groping in the dark, she stumbled and ruinously fell. The thick rug deadened the sound of her body hitting the ground, thankfully.

Because of the impact, the hand that was holding the Minox lost its grip.

The small camera flew up in the air, only to fall down and then slide under the sofa. Cordelia heard the swishing sound coming to a stop and knew it wasn't far, but couldn't see where it had landed. She flattened herself to the floor frantically trying to find it.

Meanwhile, she heard somebody on the other side of the door, trying to open it but having difficulty unlocking it, tinkering with the key in a frenzy.

There was no time left; she needed to make her way out. She was quickly on her knees and crawling towards the secret panel, slipping through just when she heard a third successful attempt to open the door.

The light was still off when it slammed open.

Simultaneously, she hurried to push the panel closed, by reversing the lever to its original position with all the force she could manage, helped by Aronne's steel bar. It went all the way without jamming and shut with a muffled thud.

Immediately, the light in the library was switched on. She could see above her head, the horizontal beam coming from the peephole that was still open. The noise of boots dashing on the floor. The telephone had stopped ringing. Somebody had picked up the receiver. From her hideout, she dared to take a look to see who had come in. A burly looking soldier was answering the call.

Cordelia closed the small window softly while he was still talking. Her heart rate had slowed down but now she began shaking. The fear of being caught, blocked by the adrenaline rush of the past minute, now took hold of her body without mercy. She forced herself to move and with a gingerly jog, she went all the way back to the dépendance, to safety. As soon as the back stone of the fireplace closed behind her, her legs gave in and she slowly slid down with her back against the wall, and sat on the floor, deflated as a lifeless doll.

When the phone started to ring, the guard outside the library was deeply asleep on a wooden chair that had been placed just outside the door, his half-open mouth making a quiet snoring sound. The Wehrmacht soldier had been up and down all day and, exhausted, despite the large dose of coffee, he had felt the heaviness of his eyelids more and more. I will close my eyes just for a minute, for a minute only, he said to himself.

That had been approximately thirty-five minutes ago. So he didn't hear Cordelia coming into the library and moving around.

He jolted awake at the loud sound of the telephone that incessantly rang on the other side of the door he was staking out. He sprang into action and picked up his Maschinenkarabiner rifle that had slipped on the ground.

He was now desperate to go into the room to answer the call and he searched for the key to open the library door as fast as possible. It was one of two he kept in the side pocket of his jacket. But his eyesight was still obfuscated by the abrupt awakening and he picked the wrong one. He tried to put it in the lock but it wouldn't go in. Panicking, he tried to push it once again, only to realise it was not the right one. Damn, he thought, immediately switching keys: this one went in smoothly and he turned it, slamming the door open.

He switched on the sumptuous chandelier on the ceiling in the centre of the room, its twenty-four lightbulbs inundating it with their bright light. Covering the space from the door to the desk where the telephone was, took less than three seconds.

'Hallo? Sieg Heil, Mein General! Yes, right away, Sir!' he said, snapping to attention as if the caller was right there in the room.

Erwin Rommel was at the other end of the line, demanding to speak to Lieutenant Colonel Schaeffer immediately. He would hold until he came to the phone, he said to the soldier.

He put the receiver on the desk without hanging up and ran through the corridor towards Schaeffer's bedroom.

'Lieutenant Colonel,' he said, while knocking on his door.

No answer.

He knocked with more vigour. Then, knowing that the danger of not waking him up was far greater than the risk of incurring his rage, he dared to enter.

The room was empty.

Seeing the window open, the soldier peered out and, in the light of a shining moon, he saw Schaeffer down in the garden.

He rushed back and from the top of the staircase he shouted to the guard below, 'Corporal Becker! Go and tell immediately, Lieutenant Colonel Schaeffer, that General Rommel is on the phone. He wants to speak to him now! I just saw from up here that he is in the garden! Find him, fast!'

Becker was quick to react and set out after his commanding officer to deliver the urgent request. He reached the terrace at the back, speedily travelled down the stairs and dashed towards him.

He got to Schaeffer and breathless he shouted, 'Sir! It's the General, Sir! General Rommel is on the phone looking for you!'

That peremptory demand had the effect of breaking the spell under which Schaeffer had been, his military duty kicking in and shaking him up. He gave a last sad look at the door of the dépendance, then turned around and went back with the guard.

CHAPTER 14

The small hamlet of Castel Madama lies at the top of a hill, about thirty kilometres west of Rome. In 1942, almost all of the land around it belonged to small farmers, who cultivated mainly olives trees, wine grapes and raised sheep. Despite being quite close to the capital, the village had always been quiet due to its geographical position up in the Tiburtine mountains, a set of high hills arranged around a valley. There was no traffic going through, so life there went on peacefully, despite the war, dictated only by the slow rhythm of the agricultural season. Apart from the field labourers and a few shepherds, there was no sign of the Fascist regime, and the only time its inhabitants had seen a Blackshirt was when a local boy had decided to join them and was seen in uniform leaving his parents' home to reach the train station just at the foot of the village for his barrack in Rome.

Alma was on her way to that small town. Cordelia's old nanny wanted to quietly transfer a few of her essential belongings to Tenuta Belfiore, the farm of the Belfiore family on the outskirts of Castel Madama, the safe place that she would move to once Cordelia left the country. She needed to get organised, Cordelia had told her.

Alma didn't possess many personal things, since she had lived for many years with the Olivieri family, only taking on a tiny flat when a grown-up Cordelia moved back to Rome from Castel Gandolfo, after her father's death; Cordelia had taken her on as a cook at Palazzo Roveri. She made a trip to Castel Madama to take her clothes and a precious tablecloth she had almost finished embroidering, and that she had planned to give to Cordelia as a marriage gift, all packed in a small suitcase. She was travelling light.

Early in the morning, Alma had made a quick trip to Palazzo Roveri for a last word with Cordelia telling her, as agreed, that she would take the day off to go to Tenuta Belfiore and that she would not be back until the following day. Yes, she had left Flaminia in charge. The maid had been supplied with clear instructions and a schedule to follow, so hopefully all would go smoothly until her return.

'Be careful,' Cordelia urged, giving her a hug and a kiss goodbye. Alma noticed she was looking a bit lethargic, a sign she had lacked some sleep. Perhaps she'd had trouble relaxing after she went to bed, because of the forced presence of the Germans. They had been behaving so far; nevertheless, they were uninvited, powerful and potentially dangerous guests.

Alma set out for Stazione Termini. The main train station in the capital centre was busy as always, with people coming and going. Alma went to the office where a clerk was serving two people queuing up in front of her. Since she had a good ten minutes spare before her *accelerato* train would leave – a slow train stopping at all the stations from Rome up to Castel Madama – she bought a return ticket in good time and went on the platform to board the third-class carriage. She was the first in the compartment and decided to sit on the wooden bench next to the window, after placing her suitcase and bag directly above her, on the overhead rack. Soon after, a young woman with two small children joined her, together with an older lady accompanied by her niece, a nun and a mature gentleman.

The train departed on time, its line running beside the Tiburtina way, and after an uneventful journey that lasted approximately forty-five minutes, it reached the station of Castel Madama, where the last of her companions, the mature gentleman, alighted with her.

With her suitcase, she exited the station and turned into a country road. When she reached the farm, she couldn't help but gaze at the spectacular panorama. The farm was facing the valley on the west, with an almost uninterrupted view of the plain where Rome could be seen in the distance, framed by rolling hills abundant in luscious greenery.

No doubt this was why Ancient Roman families had elected to build their country retreats up there, ruins of which were still dotting the countryside, with the famous Emperor Hadrian's villa a few kilometres down the road. Those vantage points were enchanting and very relaxing; even at that time, people probably wanted to escape far from the madding crowd of the Eternal City.

Celestina Belfiore, a lady in her late forties with a mass of white hair, lively brown eyes and the shoulders of somebody who was used to physical work, waved at Alma from the barnyard just beside the main house. Together with her husband, Mario, she ran the farm and welcomed her with a big grin.

'Good morning, Alma, welcome! We were expecting you. Cordelia told us you would come! You're just in time for lunch. I am really glad! Let me take you to your room first, so you can put down all your things and then join us for a meal,' she said cheerfully, taking her arm and guiding her inside.

When Alma saw the room, she instantly loved it, with its beautiful view of the olive grove that she found calm and relaxing.

'I have prepared a frittata with zucchini fresh from the garden. Mario brought up a piece of pecorino romano cheese and a bottle of our red wine from the cellar. He's in the kitchen and the table is already set.'

Mario was a man as placid as his village, who made the most delicious cheeses and wine. They were a lovely couple that had been supplying Cordelia's family with their produce for years and were completely trustworthy and very reserved. 'I will love it here, Celestina,' Alma said, once they had finished eating. 'It's so tranquil, you can't hear a fly. And rest assured that for the whole time I spend here, I will be a working guest. Of course, I will miss Cordelia a lot.'

'It's almost time, isn't it?' Celestina asked, and saw Alma's eyes suddenly reddening.

Cordelia had informed them that she had to go away for a while, and that Alma needed a safe place to stay in her absence.

'It's going to be soon, that's all I can say. I am not sure of the exact date myself just yet.'

'Mario, why don't you go and fetch that small package I put in the stash – this is something that will cheer you up, Alma.'

Her taciturn husband rose from the table and, compliant with his wife's wish, went to retrieve a paper bag full of rice.

'Here you go, Alma. Rice from Vercelli for you. I know you love a good risotto, and I thought you and Cordelia would enjoy a plate of it before going, even if only for a period of time, your separate ways.'

Alma was almost on the brink of crying when she saw the bag of rice. With the rationing it had become incredibly hard to find rice, impossible really, in Rome. Vercelli, in Piedmont, the area where most of the Italian rice was produced, was far away in the north-west of Italy and hardly any of it reached the capital anymore.

'You have been mad to risk being arrested for buying goods on the black market, Celestina! It must have cost you a fortune. Thank you from the bottom of my heart. It will be an absolute luxury to cook and enjoy it again. I will give it the justice it deserves! And a great farewell for Cordelia for sure. She will be so pleased. It's a favourite of hers.'

Alma put the rice in her bag, closed it and took her leave to go to the station and make her way back to Rome.

The *accelerato* slow train on its return stopped at all stations as it had before: Tivoli, Lunghezza, Tor Sapienza, Serenissima. But once it reached Roma Prenestina, the station just before Stazione Termini where Alma had to get off, a small group of *squadristi,* the Fascist militia, boarded the train. They were all wearing their black uniforms, knee-high leather boots and the fez, the typical Blackshirts cylindrical hat with a big tassel coming down on one side. Alma watched them passing in single file in front of her compartment through the narrow corridor of the third class and disappear further down. Her fellow passengers stopped chit-chatting and went quiet at their sight, even the little boy beside her, who had run riot until a minute before. As there was not a compartment completely free for all of the men, the group split and two of them, who looked like the higher-ranking officers, doubled back and went to sit in front of Alma. They nodded in greeting. Alma nervously gave an artificial smile and lowered her gaze to the ground, as if they wouldn't be there if she didn't look at them.

The train guard gave a final whistle, a signal to the last passengers that they had to hurry if they wanted to board the train which was ready to leave. The locomotive was set in motion a moment later, and the train started chugging along towards its final destination.

Plic … plic … plic … plic …

From the corner of her eye, Alma saw the boy sitting beside her pointing his finger at the hat of the Fascist officer.

She looked up in horror.

From her bag, placed in the overhead rack just above his head, rice grains had started to slowly drip down, inexorably, one at a time bouncing on his black fez.

'What the hell …'

As soon as the Fascist officer realised what was happening, in a mix of confusion and surprise, he jumped up from his seat and half turned to face the rack above his head. Seeing where the rice grains were coming from, he violently reached for the bag and opened it, finding the packet of rice that Celestina had gifted to Alma earlier that day.

'Whose bag is this? Answer me, right now! Or I will arrest you all!' he shouted, enraged.

All of them understood that his order was not to be disobeyed.

The trembling hand of one of the passengers pointed to a petrified Alma, who clammed up with fear.

'Is it yours?' the Blackshirt asked disdainfully, addressing Alma directly now with his rapacious gaze.

Still unable to proffer a single word, seeing all eyes were on her, she nodded in assent.

'Give me your identification papers! You are under arrest!' the officer roared, seizing the document she was handing over. Then he and his comrade hastily grabbed a distraught Alma, forcing her to stand up and walk towards the exit, just when the train was gradually slowing down to enter Stazione Termini.

The arrest caused commotion at the station, and a few people assembled nearer to the scene, to see better what was going on.

'There's nothing to look at, move on!' the Fascist officers said to the small crowd, while continuing to drag Alma between them. Her legs felt weak and unwilling to cooperate all of a sudden, so she had to be almost carried all the way out.

They took her to the nearest command, where she was thrown in jail, awaiting interrogation.

Fascist comrade Varone had been following Alma that morning as per Lucifer's instructions, but he had lost her at the Termini Station. He decided to wait for her there, in the hope of catching her upon her return. When he saw that she had been arrested, he rushed back to the barracks to report what had happened to his boss.

'They have her in Via Armerino, Sir,' he told Lucifer.

'Have who, exactly?' came a voice from the doorway.

Obstructed by comrade Varone's body, Lucifer hadn't seen that, while he was listening to his report, somebody had popped his head through his office door asking that question.

He craned his neck to see who it was: Marino Severi.

'It's Alma, Sir,' Varone answered, 'the cook of the Palazzo Roveri hotel.'

Lucifer saw Severi curving the corners of his mouth upwards in a cunning grin, while his eyes narrowed, like the cat that has spotted a mouse.

He wickedly said, 'Well, well, what did she do to get arrested, I wonder…'

'I'll go there to find out straight away, Major.' Lucifer was quick to reply to the indirect question, dismissing Varone in the meantime.

'We'll do better than that: ask the officer in charge to bring her here. I want to see personally to her interrogation,' Severi said. His imperious tone didn't leave any room for discussion.

The only thing Lucifer could say was: 'Aye, Sir! I will give them a call now then, Sir.'

Not even an hour later, Alma was driven to Severi's Fascist command by her former captors. She had timidly asked where they were taking her, but nobody bothered to answer. Instead of putting her in a room on the ground floor, which was normally used for ordinary cases, she was taken one level underground. Hurried and yanked down a steep, dark staircase, with her hands cuffed behind her back, unable to hold on to the handrail and to see where she was putting her feet, she almost fell as they reached the bottom. The two Blackshirts unceremoniously continued to push her ahead, until they reached the end of the corridor. While walking along it, Alma heard a scream of pain coming from behind one of the metallic doors they passed by. Breathless from the forced and fast walk, completely disconcerted and frightened, she was then left alone to wait, locked up down there, with nowhere to sit. The room was empty, smelling of a mix of mould and sweat and it had no windows, its floor and walls painted leaden grey. Alma began to weep silently.

One hour, possibly two went by. She didn't really know. Then she heard a key turning in the lock. The door slammed open. Marino Severi, followed by Lucifer and another towering, muscular and beastly-looking officer, the latter carrying two sturdy metal chairs as if they were as light as feathers, came in. The giant put them down, one in front of the other.

'Hello, Alma,' Severi said. 'Sit down.'

She was tired with the tension and with having to stand for all that time, and was grateful for the order, although she was sure he didn't mean it as a favour. Her cuffs were not removed, so she couldn't lean on the back in a more relaxed position.

He sat in front of her, while Lucifer and the giant stood behind him, one at each side.

'You are under arrest for buying rice on the black market. You know this is a crime, don't you?'

With a feeble whisper, she answered his rhetorical question.

'Yes, I do.'

'Who asked you to do that?'

'Nobody asked me to do that,' she said.

'Oh, Alma, Alma …' Severi said ruefully, as if he was sad that she had found herself in that position.

'If you don't cooperate, your already very serious situation will worsen for you. It was Cordelia Olivieri that asked you to go and buy it for her, wasn't it? Did she send you to her black-market friends? Be honest. After all, you are just a simple employee carrying out the demands of your employer. You don't want to be the scapegoat here, while somebody else gets away with it, trust me.'

Alma shook her head and in a desperate tone reiterated, 'Nobody asked me anything.'

Out of the blue, Severi slapped her hard with the back of his hand and yelled, 'You will tell me the truth, do you hear me? Cordelia has asked you to buy goods on the black market, and it's not the first time, is it? What other illegal activities is she up to? Who is she in contact with?'

Alma was bleeding copiously from her mouth, the violent impact with Severi's hand had broken her upper lip.

Lucifer clearly saw what Severi was trying to achieve. He wanted to find a way to incriminate Cordelia, and Alma's arrest had provided the perfect opportunity. Lucifer knew that his cruel methods of interrogation made people confess to things that were not necessarily true, in the hope that torture stopped.

Severi didn't wait for Alma's answer and slapped her again and again.

She started to cry, warm tears mixed with blood rolling down her cheeks and wetting her shirt. Her bladder gave in and she peed involuntarily, feeling ashamed and even more vulnerable, distraught and helpless.

With a switch of tactic and a low and gentle tone that seemed to completely deny the violence he had just been capable of, he tried to defeat her resistance once more and said, 'Alma, Alma … look what is happening to you, my dear – that's not fair, is it. If you confess right here and right now, you'll be free to go. I know you're not a crook. She is. Why do you want to pay for her crimes?'

Alma looked at him and with all the force she could gather she growled, 'Go to hell, filthy bastard!'

Stunned by the reaction of the woman's new-found courage, Severi turned red, widened his eyes, jumped up from his seat and hissed at her: 'Very well, old fool, you don't know what troubles you are in for, and this lovely comrade of mine here will show you what I mean.' Addressing the giant, he said, 'She's all yours now. Spend the night well.'

The Fascist Major left, closing the door behind him, followed by a powerless Lucifer.

CHAPTER 15

On the day that Alma was arrested and detained by Marino Severi, Karl Blasius was sitting in his study at the Pontifical Biblical Institute.

And he was livid.

So far, the reports that the Fascist Major had sent him were nothing short of worthless. His men had been running around town following Cordelia Olivieri and her staff without bringing him a shred of useful information that would serve to undermine Schaeffer. They were either incompetent, or stupid, or both. On the other side, a signalling unit of the Gestapo radio bureau service regularly circling around the Vatican had intercepted the final sequence of a secret message and deciphered it. It read … *alternative in place. Our man at the Fascist command is in critical danger. He will abort his mission shortly, over.*

The message raised more questions than answers. The missing bit must have contained a vital clue, without which the content was partly to be conjectured.

What was this alternative?

Did it mean the enemy would be able to get the intelligence from another informer?

Was the spy no longer able to gather information as he did before in his position?

Was it because he felt his hunters were dangerously onto him that he was about to abort his mission?

Who was he? And which Fascist command, of the many in Rome?

Damn. He felt his window of opportunity was closing. If he did not succeed in helping to identify the spy, then Himmler would lose confidence in his ability to be a trustworthy, capable and valuable asset, with the consequence of seeing his power diminish, let alone being able to progress further and be sent back to Berlin to become a prominent spiritual advisor to the Fuehrer …

Put together with the highest-ranking Nazis, Blasius' megalo-maniacal visions could comfortably rival theirs, without a shred of a doubt.

But then a visit from that little slut, Flaminia, the hotel maid, had rekindled his feeble hopes. And also raised some worrying question marks.

She had been there earlier, her appearance as plain and dull as ever. Taking advantage of Alma's absence, she had sneaked out from Palazzo Roveri, unseen.

'Hello, Father Blasius,' she said with her annoying tone and a grin as false as Judas.

Blasius knew that she was there only for the money and didn't bother to play the part of the magnanimous priest as he normally would, with a chosen audience.

He looked at her coldly, but avoided displaying the antipathy that the sad creature provoked in him.

'So, you're finally here. I was wondering if you would ever show up with something interesting to tell me, Flaminia,' he said with a blunt nonchalance, as he hardly expected her to be of any service, really.

'Oh, Father, I think you should think a bit higher of me, as I reckon you would find what I came here to tell you interesting indeed, intriguing I dare say. It certainly was rather surprising for me, when I saw what I saw, but I'll reserve my judgement and leave to you the pleasure of assessing its value,' Flaminia quietly boasted.

She paused and noticed that she had got the monk's full attention now.

'Let's find that out, shall we? What did you see then?'

Flaminia went on to narrate her observations of Schaeffer's behaviour, which clearly denoted, in her view, his growing fascination with Cordelia. She mentioned the flowers he had bought for her, and the dinner invitation, which she was quite sure, albeit not being a direct witness unfortunately, had resulted in a romantic *tête-à-tête*. He had surely fallen under her spell and was it not inconvenient for a man in his position?

Blasius observed how she skillfully dropped her own deductions and perfidious questions amongst the facts, in a creeping effort to corroborate them, a method obviously aimed at influencing the opinion of her listener by bending truths enough to trigger the desired reaction. A professional backstabber, for sure.

'… and then, Cordelia, one morning, took her bicycle and headed straight to the Ghetto. Isn't it weird, or even unwise to go there, when those people have practically been proclaimed enemies of the regime? To do what, I ask myself?'

To Blasius that news felt like a bombshell. He leaned forward and asked her in rapid succession: 'Does she have friends there? Who did she go to visit? Any distant relations perhaps?'

The simple thought that Cordelia was somehow linked to the Jews was incredibly stimulating for Blasius, so much so that he almost jumped up with excitement. It opened a whole range of opportunities.

Not even he could have thought of a more fortunate circumstance. That certainly needed further investigation, but also begged a nagging question: why had none of Severi's men managed to find that out? Supposedly, they had set up a constant surveillance on her, so how come nothing had ever been reported of that magnitude? He parked those questions for a moment, promising himself a quick revisit and follow-up action.

He now wanted to focus on Flaminia, to whom the Benedictine's surge of interest had not gone unnoticed. She had to make sure to cash in on that later, she thought.

'Cordelia had a friend there, for many years, a girl named Lea Segre. Her father was a spice trader I believe. As far as I know the business is closed. I don't know where they are, but I know they left for somewhere else, as Alma, the cook, mentioned that Lea had died shortly after their departure. I am not sure if Cordelia has any relations or other friends in the Jewish community, but I suppose she must have, otherwise she wouldn't travel there. Unless it is for other motives …'
Again, she dropped a hint at the end, left there lingering in the air.

'Those are very serious facts, Flaminia. Thank you for reporting them. I will make sure your information is conveyed to the relevant officials. Do not mention it to anyone else. I wouldn't want you to become the target of a retaliation from your employer, so I will be your exclusive confidant in this whole affair, understood?'

'Father Blasius, you can trust me – cross my heart.' She mimicked the sign across her chest and continued with a fawning tone. 'You can rest assured that the information I will pass on to you is going to be as valuable as what I just gave you today.'

Then she began quietly singing the first lines of the song *Se potessi avere mille lire al mese* – If I could have a thousand lire a month – a popular melody by Gilberto Mazzi that was also turned into a successful film. Although Blasius wasn't a frequent visitor of movie theatres or an expert in Italian music, he got the gist of what Flaminia was trying to tell him, and the level of reward she was expecting. A cunning and subtle way to make a suggestion, he had to admit.

The black-clad monk clasped his hands and leaned back on his chair.

The maid stopped humming her song, looking forward to the payback for her service with the ferocious expression of a hungry predator waiting to be fed. The freckles that covered her face reminded him of the drops of blood of an animal that had already started to devour its victim. Metaphorically speaking, that devious girl had, in fact.

'Time to get your good work rewarded, Flaminia,' he said.

Blasius half turned and then pulled open the central drawer of a cupboard behind him to reach for a purse. He extracted a few coins, which made a jingling sound when he let them drop in pairs onto the wooden surface of his desk.

The maid was quick to sweep them away and hide the money in her pocket. She gave him a little bow as a sign of gratitude, and with a triumphant smile, left. It was nowhere near a thousand lire, but she was satisfied enough. For the time being at least. She'd ask for a rise the next time.

This was money well spent, Blasius congratulated himself, more pleased than he let Flaminia see. He poured a small glass of Malvasia delle Lipari, a rather sweet and aromatic fortified wine with a hint of orange, from the Aeolian islands, just off the coast of Sicily. Today's successful find tasted as sweet as his drink, and he allowed himself to enjoy it a bit longer by sipping it very slowly.

Now that he thought of it, if Cordelia was found to be of Jewish descent, Schaeffer would suffer irreversible damage. He would almost certainly not only be removed from his current mission, but be put under immediate investigation as a precautionary measure. Himmler would demand that nobody with an association with a Jew could be anywhere near the centre of operations. His military career would surely come to a stark halt: who would trust a Wehrmacht officer that had voluntarily elected to stay with a Jew? Schaeffer would look like a fool at best. There was a good chance he might be demoted or even be summoned in front of a court martial and completely stripped of his rank. That goddamn lawyer would have a taste of what it was like to be on the receiving end of a trial.

Blasius gloated at the image of a humiliated, completely annihilated Schaeffer, imagining his ashamed look, on his knees, begging for forgiveness. And unlike the Benedictine, the Afrika Korps Colonel would not have the option of an appeal. He could not come back, not from that sort of fall from grace. Not even Rommel could protect him from such a scandal. And if Schaeffer was buried once and for all, by contrast, Blasius would be catapulted into the stratosphere, covered in glory, of God and of the Gestapo.

Blasius stopped his delirious train of thoughts, realising his mind had raced ahead too much. First he needed to make sure that things would go exactly as he imagined.

And he would oblige Marino Severi to do that.

Cordelia wasn't worried when Alma did not show up in the evening, never suspecting in a million years that she had been arrested and was being tortured by a sadistic towering giant.

She remained for most of the day in her office at the back of the reception, partly because she was tired from the previous late night, but also because she preferred to avoid Schaeffer. She felt sorry for him and did not want him to feel embarrassed.

But was it just that?

She couldn't help admitting that she'd had a most pleasurable time with him. She perceived that deep down, under that Afrika Korps uniform, there was a kind and intelligent human being. And like no other man before, he had been able to put her at such ease, and so quickly. She felt almost as if they had known each other for years by the end of the dinner. It felt easy and natural to accept a dance with him. And when he kissed her, she had been happy he did.

Unconsciously, she had expected him to kiss her. And it was not for the simple flattery of the gesture. Cordelia really enjoyed the sensation she'd felt by being passionately embraced by a man again. A very handsome, fascinating man, with a charming personality and a real sense of humour. The more she thought of him, the more attractive she found him in many aspects.

The truth was that she did not trust herself in meeting his gaze again. She was afraid of her own impulses. And that certainly didn't help, as this was the moment to keep a cool head. Although she tried to distract herself from the thought of him, every now and then she found herself straying from her resolve.

The two of them managed to miss each other until later in the evening, when their paths crossed and their eyes met. He seemed on the brink of saying something, as he hesitated on his way across the hallway, but then his attendant Wolf joined him and they began to talk. Cordelia left them behind and retreated to her dépendance.

She had to recover the Minox, which she had clumsily managed to lose, shivering at the thought of having to go back to the library, the memory of being almost caught vivid in her mind.

That night, after the usual operation of opening the secret passage, she let herself be swallowed up again by the underground tunnel, then up the spiral staircase to reach the landing. On the tips of her toes, in order to walk quietly and faster, she got to the wooden panel leading to the library. Before even attempting to open the peephole, she put her ear against it to hear for any human presence on the other side.

Silence.

She delicately slid the small window to see if someone might be there.

Total darkness.

It was going well.

After successfully repeating the exercise of gently forcing down the uncooperative lever that activated the rotating mechanism opening the panel, she slid out the other side and ducked down behind the sofa, the place closer to where she had heard the Minox making that swishing sound when it fell on the floor.

She switched on her torch, directing its beam under that piece of furniture. There it was, lying idle and shining brightly from the impact of the light. Stretching her arm under the sofa, she recovered it easily.

Then she stood up, ready to return to the secret passage.

A sudden noise outside the door.

Cordelia swallowed nervously, holding her breath and standing absolutely still.

The muffled voice of somebody speaking.

Then the hushed sound of steps getting farther and farther away.

It was quiet again. A simple change of the guard probably, she thought.

She started to breathe normally again.

Time to leave.

On this occasion she secured the micro-camera in one of the zipped pockets of her trousers. With feline moves, she approached the exit gap, closing the panel once she was through to the other side.

As soon as she was back in her room, Cordelia reached for the silver candelabra on the fireplace mantel, unscrewed the base and hid the Minox, slipping it into the cavity of its column.

Although it had been a smooth ride, Cordelia still felt quite shaken, and for a while she sat in her armchair, curled up, feeling the tension abandoning her ever so slowly.

Then, calm again, she went to bed.

She dreamed of Schaeffer that night.

It was the following morning when they came to arrest her.

Cordelia was coming back from the Campo dei Fiori vegetable market with two heavy bags full of produce, when a Fascist militia truck appeared out of nowhere, its brakes squealing, and it jerked to a stop. Two Blackshirts jumped out.

'Cordelia Olivieri, you are to come with us immediately!' Without any further explanation, they grabbed her and took her away, forcing her to clamber into the back of the vehicle, obliging her to drop the bags: tomatoes, zucchini, onions, fruit, all ruinously rolled out and were left abandoned on the road.

They drove to the Fascist command of Marino Severi. Cordelia was confused and terrified. A thousand thoughts went through her mind, but none of them were providing any logic for the reason she had been arrested.

Marino Severi had ordered her capture early that day. Despite the effort of literally beating Alma into submission, the giant Blackshirt ogre Severi had left her with did not manage to succeed in making her admit Cordelia was guilty of buying goods on the black market. Perhaps that old witch needed a stronger type of coercion, which wouldn't necessarily include physical torture. Severi had thought of giving Alma a vigorous nudge.

Cordelia was driven down into the basement of the barracks, where Alma had been confined since the previous night.

As her nanny before her, she was pushed along the dark corridor, and into an even darker room, with a single lightbulb giving a tenuous light from the centre of the ceiling. Severi had joined her after a few minutes, and was now standing in front of her, feet apart, arms slightly bent, hands closed in fists resting on his hips, as Mussolini was often seen posing during public gatherings.

'So, we see each other again, Miss Olivieri,' he said triumphant, as if he had welcomed her to a pleasant function rather than to an interrogation room.

He had always enjoyed the moment when his victims were left clueless about the motive of their arrest, observing the mounting fear in their eyes, their muscles tensing, the droplets of sweat appearing on their foreheads, their legs trembling involuntarily. It gave him extreme pleasure to know he was in full control, the absolute master of their destiny.

But, more than anything else, he enjoyed the certainty he could do whatever he wanted with their bodies, and Severi was looking forward to being able to exercise that particular privilege on Cordelia Olivieri.

He stood back for a moment, his eyes lecherously scrutinising her figure from top to toe. That room below ground was colder than outside, with the result of giving people goosebumps, and Cordelia was no exception, with the addition that her nipples also hardened, a vision that gratified Severi even more.

The dirty way he was looking at her made her cringe.

'Why am I here, Major? I protest!' she replied.

'You are here for questioning on a very serious account. You have asked your cook, Alma, to buy forbidden goods. It is an offence to source food on the black market. Do you know that? Sorry, that was a rhetorical question, of course,' he yelled, at which point Cordelia took a step back, scared by his sudden change of tone, startled by what he had just revealed.

'What … Alma? What does Alma have to do with this?'

He jumped straight in, trying to twist her words: 'Very well, I see you are admitting your guilt. It was you that instigated her to purchase the rice.'

'The rice … what rice? Where is Alma? Where is she?' Cordelia asked, truly alarmed now, realising what the accusation might be. She felt as if she had been thrown in a Maelstrom, spinning around in that gigantic water vortex, powerless.

'Do not play with me, Miss Olivieri,' he threatened her. 'Do not take me for a fool or you'll regret it.'

'I do not know what you are talking about – this is all a mistake. It is a ridiculous accusation!'

With a swift movement, Severi circled around her, grabbed her right arm and bent it behind her back, forcing her body against a wall. Cordelia banged her cheek on its cold surface, screaming in pain.

'Confess your crime,' he hissed at her, while pressing his thighs against hers.

She felt his nauseating heavy breath, smelling of cigarettes and rotten teeth, blowing warm into her ear.

'I cannot confess what I did not commit!' Cordelia said in a mix of desperation and defiance.

Severi let her go, and hysterically demanded again and again, 'Confess, for God's sake, confess, confess, confess!' while taking her by the shoulders and starting to shake her. Then he mercilessly slapped her, twice.

Cordelia was incredulous. It made no sense at all, like one of those terrible nightmares. Why did he want her to say she was guilty? Was it true that Alma had bought rice on the black market? Where was she? What had happened to her? What would happen to Cordelia herself? All these questions deliriously crowded her mind.

'Perhaps seeing what we've done to your precious cook will help you to soften your position.'

She stared at him in despair. He opened the metal door of the interrogation room and moved her to the next, where Alma was. Her poor old nanny was lying on the floor, her face a collection of bruises, a rivulet of blood that had trickled down from the side of her swollen lips was dried up. A subdued lament was coming out of her mouth. As soon as Cordelia saw her, she kneeled and hugged her.

'Alma, my dear Alma, sacred mother of God, what have they done to you?' She started to sob quietly.

In her semi-conscious state and recognising it was Cordelia, Alma managed to whisper, 'I am sorry … I am sorry, child …'

Cordelia stood up and wiped away her tears. The shock of seeing Alma in that state caused a massive adrenaline rush and, with all the strength she could muster, she shouted back at Severi: 'You bloody delinquent! You've treated her as if she was a thief! You are the criminals, all of you! Who do you think you are, kidnapping people going about their business, beating and torturing them? You are sadistic, cruel, horrible despots, that's what you are!'

For reasons she didn't completely understand, she was now convinced he was trying to set her up. Well, she would not allow him to succeed, no matter what.

Severi was outraged. What a piece of work, he thought.

She might be a hard nut to crack. But he was determined to crack her, and he knew how to break her.

'Shut up, bitch! Do you think Alma is in a bad state? Wait and see how far I can go, and let me tell you, it'll be a long way,' he snarled.

He called for the giant Blackshirt ogre that was just outside the door and asked him to bring in some castor oil.

This was one of the preferred methods of intimidation of the Blackshirts during the Fascist regime, and a large use had been made with its opponents, who were usually tied up and forced to drink a large quantity of the oil, with the unpleasant consequence of severe diarrhoea. For that reason it was also called the subversive purge and the torture had indisputable effects.

Cordelia, who knew of this violent method of persuasion, watched in horror as the Blackshirt grabbed Alma's mouth and opened it up for Severi to pour the oil in.

'Let's see if a bit of this will convince you.'

CHAPTER 16

'You are required immediately in your office, Sir!'

Severi turned around, furious at having been interrupted during his interrogation. Lucifer, who had just slammed the door open, was standing in the middle of its frame.

'A German officer requires to see you, and it is urgent,' he said to the Fascist Major.

'Can this wait?' Severi barked back, glaring at him. He was keen to continue with Alma and to keep Cordelia under pressure. A few moments more and he was pretty sure he would have induced her to say she was guilty to save Alma. Giving her a break now might irreversibly spoil it and he would need to start all over again.

'I don't think so, Major. He said he wants to see you straight away, and his tone left no doubt that he really meant it.'

'Fucking Germans! Let's see what the hell he wants that is so damn urgent,' Severi said.

Followed by Lucifer and the giant ogre, Severi exited the room, banged the metal door shut and locked it, leaving the two women alone inside.

Cordelia heard the steps of the three booted men becoming fainter and finally disappearing, and, with it, the immediate danger of their physical abuse.

She kneeled to help Alma get up and sit on the only chair, where she would be a bit more comfortable. Alma was heavy and unstable on her legs, but with some effort Cordelia managed to get her there.

'Here you go, Alma – that's better, isn't it? Let me see your poor face …'

Cordelia delicately touched the bruise that had formed on one of her cheeks. Alma groaned at the touch. In the faint glimmer provided by the light bulb, she looked ashen and afflicted.

'I'm so sorry, Alma. As soon as we are home, we'll put some ice on it. You will be back to normal in no time. Are you able to tell me this story about the rice?'

'I … wanted … to surprise you … with your favourite dish … It was supposed to be a farewell present … before you left … But I … I did not buy it on the black market … Celestina gave it to me,' Alma managed to answer, her speech slurred by a swollen tongue.

So it was true. Nevertheless, Cordelia remained astounded that Severi was so adamant she was to blame. Thankfully, his attendant had temporarily stopped him in his attempt to give Alma the castor oil; nevertheless, she shivered at the prospect of him coming back to continue what he had started. What would they do to the two of them if Cordelia did not admit she was the one who asked Alma to commit a criminal offence? She knew that it was just a matter of time before one of them made a confession to save the other. Cordelia felt lost, for Alma, for herself, impotent and vulnerable. They were trapped with no way out or the ability to ask for help.

An hour went by, and still no sign of their torturers.

Was it a way to weaken their victims' will to resist?

By then, Cordelia had taken the decision that she would tell Severi it was her fault, but only if he let Alma go. Then, at least, she would have the chance to defend herself in front of a judge, and say that she had been forced to confess, proclaiming her innocence.

Noise of boots coming down the stairs and walking along the corridor again.

Sound of the key in the door lock, turning.

'You two, stand up! Come with us!'

There were four militia men this time. The Blackshirts grabbed the two women and dragged them out of the interrogation room, leading them down the corridor and up the stairs.

A Fascist truck was waiting with the engine on in the courtyard of the barracks. They pushed them into the back, two men either side of them.

'Where are you taking us? Where is Major Severi. I want to speak to him. We are innocent!' Cordelia told them aghast, noticing that Alma had a glazed look, unable to react, clearly still in shock.

'You are not allowed to ask any questions! Shut up and be quiet!' one of the men shouted back at her.

There was no point in challenging them further, she thought. They were only following orders as somebody else was calling the shots. Afraid to provoke a more violent response, angry yet dismayed, Cordelia remained silent for the whole journey. Sitting on a metal bench, in semi-darkness, it was impossible to see where they were going. The back of the truck had no windows and there was a green tarp that had been pulled down after they boarded the truck, sealing the back end.

It took no more than half an hour to get to their destination. When the vehicle stopped, she heard the muffled voice of the driver asking for a gate to be opened, and almost immediately they were let through, only to stop again shortly after.

The engine of the truck switched off.

Booted steps at the side.

Then the green tarp went up.

Almost blinded by the sudden light, Cordelia squinted, and did not immediately realise where they were until the four Blackshirts helped her and Alma get off the truck.

To her surprise, they had taken them back to Palazzo Roveri.

A small squad of German soldiers headed by Captain Wolf was there in the cobbled courtyard.

The Wehrmacht officer said, 'Thank you, comrades! We'll take over from here.'

The Blackshirts saluted their German allies, mounted their vehicle and drove off, while the gates of the hotel closed behind them.

Cordelia was startled and this time she saw the surprise in Alma's eyes too, as she was coming out of the emotional torpor caused by her ordeal.

'Miss Olivieri, you are free now,' Captain Wolf told her, 'and Alma too.' And in saying so, he gave orders to one of his men to help her old nanny, still limping. They were escorted into the hotel lobby.

'Thank you, Captain,' Cordelia said. 'I will take care of Alma from here.' But she did not dare to ask the burning question: why is this happening?

'As you wish, Miss Olivieri,' he said. Then he went, followed by the rest of the German soldiers.

Still shocked by the unexpected twist of fate, Cordelia accompanied Alma to the kitchen to medicate her bruises and clean up her face. She gave her some aspirin, the only painkiller she could find to help her through the pain, then prepared her a strong cup of coffee and asked if she felt able to have something to eat. The old nanny shook her head, her stomach still in a knot from the rough treatment endured at the hand of Marino Severi.

'Maybe later – apart from a drink, I can't swallow anything else. I will go home now. I need to lie down and have a good rest, if you don't mind me leaving you, Cordelia. I am really tired.'

'Of course not. I will do the same. See you tomorrow, Alma.'

She watched her slowly get up and leave by the kitchen side door, with a timid smile on her face.

Cordelia sat there for a little while longer, finishing the cup of coffee she had poured herself as well. While sipping it, she started to mull over the reasons why, until a few hours ago, the world seemed to have come down on her head and yet now she was back home, as if nothing had ever happened.

So, Marino Severi had released them without saying a word: why?

It was certainly not attributable to his own will, she reckoned. His attitude throughout the whole time she and Alma had been in his power was nothing short of cruel, mean and aggressive, determined to obtain what he wanted. It was certainly not the attitude of someone who, all of a sudden, would change his mind and release them.

Something or, rather, somebody else must have intervened, and with a power bigger than his. She suspected that if that person hadn't got involved, both herself and Alma would have been subjected to further violence only to end up in jail in any case.

Cordelia was exhausted. The awful experience had drained her energy, and for an instant she remembered the disgusting stench of Severi's breath, as if it was still filling her nostrils. She felt the need to have a hot bath and wash it all away, so she headed to the dépendance.

She got rid of her clothes, went straight to the bathroom, and turned on the hot tap to fill up the bathtub. After a while, the sound of the babbling water began to have a calming effect.

She stepped in, immersing her body, allowing the warmth to soothe her muscles, while her mind gradually relaxed, trying to come to terms with those terrible earlier events.

After her bath, Cordelia must have drifted off to sleep, as she found herself still wrapped up in her bathrobe, curled up on the sofa in the living room. A quick glimpse outside the window told her it was already late evening, as she could already see a few stars appearing against a darker shade of blue sky. On the fire mantel, the silver candelabra with the Minox safely inside stared back at her. She shivered at the thought of how close she had been to jeopardising it all.

She felt much better now, safe, back home.

A soft knock at the door. Then another. A male voice calling.

She was tempted not to respond.

But the knocking continued.

'Miss Olivieri, are you there? Are you okay?'

'Yes, yes,' she hurried to answer. 'Just a moment.'

Still a bit wobbly on her legs, she cautiously half opened the door, and had a peek through, leaving it slightly ajar.

It was Captain Wolf.

'Sorry, Captain, I am not presentable at the moment. Would you mind coming back a little bit later, so that I can get dressed?' she said.

'I see,' he said.

To Wolf, she looked like she had just woken up, and looking down he noticed her bare foot through the gap.

'I am just here to tell you that Colonel Schaeffer is keen to see you are all right. He is in the lounge if you are well enough to join him there. He asked me to invite you for a drink. Personally, it might be a good idea to have one, after what I imagine you've been through today.'

'Perhaps you are right. Thank you, Captain. Please tell the Colonel I will be there in a few moments. I wanted to see him too, anyway.'

Cordelia combed her hair and got dressed. She left the dépendance to cross the garden. She found Schaeffer in the lounge, standing in front of the Cardinal Roveri portrait.

When he heard her steps, he turned to reach out to her. She looked quite pale and tense, despite attempting a timid smile.

'Cordelia, I am so pleased to see you are safe and sound,' he said, with a genuinely pleased expression. 'I was worried for you. I hoped you would come although I also expected you wouldn't.'

Cordelia saw that he had prepared two glasses. She stepped closer, stared at him in the eyes and said, 'I wouldn't be here at all, if it wasn't for you, Colonel. Because it was you, wasn't it? You ordered that horrible Marino Severi to free Alma and me. I cannot think of anyone else that could have done it, that had the power to exercise such pressure. I was about to come and see you to thank you from the bottom of my heart, for me and for Alma. I've been so afraid …'

She couldn't finish her sentence, as she felt a growing lump in her throat.

He looked at her and saw her mounting emotion. He desperately wanted to embrace her, to console her, but restrained himself.

'I am a lawyer, still with a strong belief that everyone deserves a fair trial. You have been subjected to summary judgment to say the least, which has nothing to do with the application of the principles of justice.'

He hesitated and then said, 'But the truth is I couldn't bear the thought of you being mistreated, Cordelia, of your beautiful face being harmed, of your body being subjected to any violence. I know men like Severi are able to inflict irreversible damage to people, and not only of the physical type, which is bad enough. They are disgusting and sadistic individuals, taking advantage of the system, of their status and rank to subject their fellow human being to their sick, degenerate will, and I couldn't accept anything bad happening to you.'

His tone was low, soft and comforting.

Cordelia was moved and felt confused at the same time by the acknowledgement that he had clearly gone beyond his duty to save her and Alma.

She was incredibly grateful he had.

Her eyes filled with tears, which started to roll down her cheeks.

She began to shiver uncontrollably, her mind re-living with instant and visceral revulsion those terrifying moments. It had all happened so fast that despite being safe now, somehow part of her still felt trapped in that terrible, vertiginously dangerous vortex of events. Things could have gone in a totally different direction if it hadn't been for Schaeffer's intervention.

Her legs felt weak.

She faltered.

Seeing that Cordelia was about to lose her balance, Schaeffer was quick to take her by the arm, fearing she could fall.

'You are having deferred shock, Cordelia,' he whispered to her, suave and persuasive. 'Don't worry. I've got you, my darling. It is absolutely normal. It will go away, I promise; in no time you will forget it all.'

His kind-hearted, sympathetic reassurance made her feel protected, cared for, and impulsively she caressed his face, his unshaved cheek feeling rough under her fingers.

His skin was warm, and he smelled of a sweet tobacco scent, like the other night.

He moved closer, his lips slightly touching her forehead, his nostrils invaded by the perfume of fresh soap in her hair.

She looked up, her eyes meeting his.

Schaeffer took her face very tenderly between his hands, as he had done after their dinner on the terrace, and bent down to kiss her, but for fear of being rejected again, he stopped halfway.

'Why did you stop?' she asked, almost in reproach.

'I don't want to upset you more than you already are. Sorry, once more I have been carried away. You are extraordinarily beautiful.'

He sighed, equally exasperated by his own weakness and frustrated at not being able to satisfy his own desire.

'Please don't,' she said, guiding his face down again towards hers.

Obedient, he bent over, while her chin lifted.

Her lips were warm and moist.

His tongue slipped easily between them, the tip exploring every corner of the inside of her mouth.

In return, she welcomed him in, avidly responding to his passionate kiss.

A sensation of heat began to mount inside her body, feeling his excitement growing as well.

This time she had no intention of taking a step back and breaking their embrace.

Then Schaeffer lifted Cordelia up, and holding her in his arms, he took her to the bedroom on the first floor.

The shutters were not completely closed and the window had been left open in his room, allowing the glowing moon to enlighten the otherwise dark inside.

He could see her almost as clearly as during the day.

His hand unzipped the back of her dress.

She let it drop on the floor.

Her heart was racing while she remained immobile.

He knelt before her and took the waistband of her lacy panties between his fingers, gently lowering them down at her feet.

She reached behind her back to untie her bra. She was completely naked now. Schaeffer allowed himself to admire for a moment that supple white body of hers, as he had imagined in his daydreams many times before, in the heat of his tent in the African desert.

'You are extraordinarily beautiful,' he repeated.

Cordelia moved towards him and started to unbutton his trousers, lowering its zipper, her desire to see him undressed too becoming more urgent.

He quickly discarded his jacket and shirt, revealing a wide hairy chest.

His muscular, athletic body was incredibly seductive without clothes. She caressed it with her hands, then moved them around his neck. Schaeffer kissed her again with more energy than before, while gently pushing her back on the bed.

For a minute, he looked at her generous and round breasts, then lowered his face and closed his mouth on one, then the other, gently sucking her nipples, while caressing her heart-shaped bottom.

'Aahh …' she moaned with pleasure, deeply enjoying his touch.

He lifted his head and looked at her, smiling with satisfaction, letting his finger lasciviously glide from the cleft between her breasts, down across her flat abdomen and over the small triangle of fluffy dark hair at the bottom.

Cordelia saw his member had hardened, while he started to massage her there.

She was very soft inside.

His hands were warm and had an expert touch.

Penetrating her deeper, he found a particularly sensitive spot not even she knew she had.

She felt her excitement grow, her hips beginning to sway now, faster and faster. He stopped just when she was about to come, and at that point he got on top of her.

Cordelia parted her legs and lifted her hips to facilitate him getting inside.

He began gently rocking back and forth.

She saw a savage, mounting desire in his eyes – he was losing control.

Like an unstoppable tide, she let waves of pleasure invade her body.

They were moving in perfect unison now, more and more rapidly, until together they exploded in an intense orgasm that left them both exhausted.

Still breathing hard, he rolled on the side, supine on his back, covered in droplets of sweat.

'I love you, Cordelia,' he said. 'I think I have loved you for a long time. I desired you for a long time. Since I saw your pictures and heard stories about you, I just could not get you out of my mind. I think I have fallen in love with you since then.'

She turned and leaned on one elbow, startled and flattered.

His eyes were closed.

She reached out to him and ran her finger along the profile of his face.

He looked at her.

'I am grateful you made love to me.'

'You say it as if it was some sort of favour, of payback for saving me from the claws of that thug.'

'Well, if that did not happen, I wonder if you would have ever made love to me.'

'You are mistaken. I don't tend to make love to men who save me from the brink of an abyss. As a matter of fact, after dinner the other night, when you kissed me, I almost lost control of myself. You are a very attractive man, Colonel Schaeffer,' she said, running her hand through his hair.

And the most handsome man she had ever come across, she thought.

'If I confess that it was not only the drinking, and the music, and the sweet perfume in the air, then you would not mind what I did, would you?'

'I guess not. To tell you the truth, unconsciously, I hoped you would. I wanted you to like me. I dressed up so that you liked what you saw. I enjoyed having your eyes on me all night. You made me feel genuinely appreciated and desirable again. When I went back to my room, I kept thinking about you. I even dreamed of you.'

'That's infatuation, not love, though.'

'If it is, it is much stronger than what I ever felt for Augusto, or anyone else. And if you stay around long enough, I will definitely fall in love with you, Friedrich, I'm afraid. And you won't get rid of me that easily then.'

She was surprised to hear her own words, realising what she said was really how she felt. She could love this man. She curled up beside him, scared at the thought, sadly aware that the strange time they lived in would not allow her to make any commitment.

'I don't want to get rid of you, Cordelia. I love you, gorgeous, terribly sensual woman.'

His tone left her in no doubt that he was telling the truth.

And for the first time in years, she felt somebody really cared for her, that she would not be left alone again.

'You are a very capable lover, Friedrich – you have been wonderful,' she teased.

He laughed hard.

'Wonderful? Really? I was hoping for more, darling! Like: you have been the best lover ever of my life!'

It was her turn to laugh hard now. She was enjoying his company. She looked at him.

He had become serious again.

She saw in his eyes the same rapacious desire that had got hold of him before.

'Don't tell me that you want …' He didn't let her finish the sentence.

'Yes, darling, I do …' and he covered her mouth again with his.

His head moved down between her legs and with his tongue he began stimulating her clitoris first, then slipped it between her labia, letting it explore deep inside her, with crescent strokes.

She arched her back, letting out a cry of intense satisfaction.

When she couldn't resist any longer, he was quickly on top of Cordelia, and penetrated her with urgency, losing himself in her again, totally transported by the intensity of the act.

She came first, and then he did, and this time he made a low, guttural and blissful grunt while he was reaching climax.

After they had made love, they fell asleep, side by side.

CHAPTER 17

Marino Severi felt incredibly frustrated and was still fuming from having been forced to submit to the German's peremptory request to release Cordelia and Alma immediately. He'd tried to resist Schaeffer's demand at first. There had been a flurry of phone calls between him and his superior officers before he'd finally had to give in. In the end they had ordered him to obey, afraid to upset their more powerful ally when they most needed its support in the war effort. They had bigger fish to fry. The Fascist high command wouldn't risk jeopardising their relationship to protect one of their own for what appeared, in any case, too small an incident. And he was not important enough for them to care, anyway.

Severi had been defeated, and in front of his men yet again. The short man felt even smaller than he was, totally emasculated, in a double whammy that enraged him beyond belief. He closed his fists and banged them hard on his desk.

He reached for a cigarette from a packet of Nazionali inside one of the drawers, the second he had opened that day, and lit it, inhaling furiously from the filter.

He had lost the challenge with that fucking Afrika Korps Colonel.

The green packet featuring a sailing ship stared back at him, green as the envy he felt for the German, for his power, while his own, like the vessel, was drifting away.

He looked with hatred when one of the newly recruited Blackshirts stepped into his office. He had been assigned to the switchboard downstairs. The air in the room was unbreathable due to the smoke and the impalpable, yet toxic embittered atmosphere projected by the Fascist Major, whose reputation was well known.

'What now?' he barked harshly at the young officer who had stood to attention, before he could even proffer a single word.

'Aye Major, I came to see if you were here, Sir!'

'Where the hell do you think I would be, comrade, in Calcutta?' he asked him, using that typical Italian expression indicating a far-away place.

'You are not answering the telephone, Sir!'

'I don't want to answer the telephone! I reached my quota of calls for the week!' he shouted at him bitterly.

'Major, there's somebody sounding like a German who wants to speak to you, Sir! He told me to personally check if you were in your office. He says it's important.'

'Another German? Ah, that's great! I didn't have enough of them telling me what to do already, did I?'

The young man shifted nervously seeing that his superior officer was getting angry now and, unfortunately, he was in the firing line. He decided to make one last attempt and then he would beat a retreat.

'Shall I put him through, Sir? He is still on the line.'

Severi weighed the pros and the cons of not wanting to speak to the mysterious caller. If he didn't, he would certainly enjoy the same pleasure of slamming the door right in his face. But then the German could retaliate and go above his head to complain of his obstructionism.

That would create another pandemonium and further harm his position, and in the end he would be forced to swallow his pride and succumb once again. Which would be even more humiliating. He decided to avoid an ephemeral Phyrric victory, purely in service to his ego, and opted for a more cooperative attitude, which on paper was less costly for sure.

'Yes, yes, put the damn man through!' he roared to the poor switchboard operator, who was happy to disappear from his sight and run back to his post.

After a minute the phone rang.

Severi clenched his teeth in anger and then with the most neutral tone he could manage he answered: 'Hello? Major Marino Severi speaking.'

'My dear Major!' a voice at the other end said.

Severi thought he recognised it, but preferred to ask to avoid any doubt.

'Who's speaking please?'

'It is Karl Blasius. I am calling you from my study here at the Biblicum.'

It was that sinister, ghostly-looking, black-clad German monk.

He was not a friend of Schaeffer's either.

What the devil did he want? Add to his misery perhaps? Pity him? Or console him by providing advice? He was curious to investigate.

'What can I do for you, Father?'

'I have something to tell you that I am sure you will find of great interest, especially after your recent debacle,' he said sharply.

Bad news travelled fast.

That Benedictine monk was well informed, and promptly too, he had to admit.

'I am all ears, Father.'

'I would prefer to see you face to face, Major. I want to make sure the information stays completely confidential between you and me. Can you come here to the Biblicum, straight away?'

He was not at all in the slightest mood to face him, but then what did he have to lose? Maybe the monk was right – he might find what he had to say of some use.

Begrudgingly, he agreed.

'I will happily listen to you, Father. See you soon then.' He hung up the phone.

'I am going out. Hold the fort while I am away, will you, Guido?' he said to Lucifer, strolling in front of him towards the exit.

'Do you want me to come with you, Major?' he said.

He knew that even if he asked where he was going, he might decide not to answer.

'No, not this time. I'll be back in a couple of hours maximum,' Severi replied.

Then he stopped just before closing the door and asked Lucifer, 'By the way, do we have the response on Cordelia Olivieri from the Ministry of Race yet? You requested it a while ago. It's taking them some time.'

'I will check with them again, Major,' said Lucifer.

'I will leave it in your capable hands, but make sure you give them a robust nudge,' And he left.

Outside it was very hot. Rome had been sizzling throughout July. Severi rarely decided to walk, but given that the weather made women wear very light dresses, he would definitely enjoy looking at their sinuous bodies, with their legs bare and their cleavage in sight. He remembered Cordelia's hourglass figure, with her long legs and round breasts pressing against the fabric of her dress, his body against hers, down in the interrogation room. I will have you in my power again, he thought with renewed determination, and this time you will not be saved by anyone. I will show you what Marino Severi is truly capable of.

He decided that next time, at the end of the special treatment he had in mind, he would fuck her, and fuck her hard. He would show her who the master was. Yes, he definitely planned to have a lot of fun with that sensational bitch.

He felt aroused at the thought.

Tonight he would visit the whorehouse in Via delle Carrozze, he mulled.

Madame Yolanda knew his taste well and always managed to make him feel very satisfied. After all, the Duce encouraged the virility of Italian men, and Blackshirts were expected to perform better than the average citizen. For the Fascist militia, calling at such establishments was considered almost a necessity to constantly prove they were up to the job.

With that in mind, Severi felt better and began to stride with more energy.

The Fascist Major would be Blasius' second visitor that day. When Severi reached the Biblicum, the Benedictine had already received Flaminia again. And it was because of what she'd told him that he phoned Severi earlier.

Flaminia had demanded more money this time; that little slut was becoming greedy.

But it was the additional strange request she made that completely galvanised his attention.

'… and when Cordelia is arrested again, I want one more thing, Father. After all, if that happens, I reckon I will fully deserve an extra reward for my service. And it's a small thing really,' Flaminia had said.

'And what small thing would you want?' Blasius asked.

244

'A very nice jewel she has. I've always loved that necklace of hers with that gold and enamel pendant. She keeps it in a lovely velvet-lined silver trinket, on top of a chest in her bedroom. Once Alma caught me wearing it and she was really angry, shouting at me to put it back and not to touch it ever again, that it belonged to Cordelia's mother. It was the only precious thing she had left of her, and it had a very special meaning. It is very exotic – I've never seen anything like that. It's like a little hand, I would say, with an eye on top ...'

While listening almost distractedly to what he thought was the petty demand of a malicious servant that had long envied the possessions of her rich employer, that last detail had unexpectedly triggered something at the back of his mind. He frantically searched in his memory.

Flaminia noticed that Blasius had assumed an expression of stupefaction as if he was having some sort of vision.

The black-clad monk moved his transfixed gaze towards a shelf full of books. He rose from his desk and grabbed one, opened it and began to quickly leaf through its pages, back and forth. Then he stopped when he seemed to have found what he was looking for. He came back and put the open book in front of Flaminia, asking with urgent trepidation: 'Does it look like this? That pendant, does it look like this one?'

It was an image of an identical object.

'Yes, it does,' she said. It looks pretty much the same.'

For Blasius it was a true moment of jubilation. He felt elated, thinking that if the sensation he was experiencing in that moment was anywhere near one of the revelations described in the Sacred Scriptures, then he finally knew what a real epiphany must have felt like.

Flaminia had just confirmed that Cordelia owned the Hamsa.

He had seen many during his forced exile in the Holy Land. They were pretty common there. It was an amulet believed to protect from evil, and it symbolised an open hand with an eye whose power was to deflect its malignant forces. Although its origins could be traced back to Babylon, the ancient capital city of Mesopotamia, where it was associated with the goddess Ishtar and later with the Egyptian Tanit, it was in the Ten Commandments that it was definitely established as the Jews' potent symbol of guidance, blessing and protection. It was adopted by the chosen people to become one of their most traditional, sacred emblems. Blasius mentally recalled the Israelitic verse of the Deuteronomy, the fifth book of the Jewish Torah: '... *and the Lord heard our voice and saw our affliction, toil, and oppression. So the Lord brought us out of Egypt with a mighty hand*'.

Blasius had seen Hamsas, the hand of God, depicted outside many of the synagogues in Jerusalem and throughout Palestine. The Hamsa was a most religious and divine object for a Jew. If Cordelia's mother had one, she was almost definitely Jewish; Blasius was absolutely certain of that.

He had been in this state of exultation since that moment. That marvellous, incredible, unique moment of magical, incomparable discovery!

When he told Himmler what he had for him, it'd be the beginning of the end for Schaeffer. Blasius would see him implode in the most spectacular, ultimate way.

He wanted to be there to watch the spectacle.

To make sure that he had all his ducks in a row, he needed a final, official confirmation. What was that expression lawyers always used? Beyond any reasonable doubt. He would use the same weapon against him.

And that was a job for Marino Severi.

The short Fascist Major was here in front of him now.

'I am always amazed when I look at the square below,' Blasius said to him, while he was directing his gaze outside the window of his study.

Severi looked around him, finding that for a monk, the place was very richly decorated, full of elegant and probably quite expensive objects.

He returned his attention to his interlocutor.

'What's so special about it, Father Blasius; it's just another old Roman square and not even one of the biggest in town.'

'You are mistaken, I'm afraid, Major. Piazza della Pilotta has possibly been the cradle of football in Italy. Did you know that? Its name is derived from *pelota*, the Spanish word for ball. It was introduced by the Florentines, who had probably learned it from the Spaniards in fact, after the Sack of Rome back in 1571. It was a very different sport back then. Players did not use their feet to kick the ball; rather, they hit it with their fists. Then, at a certain point, somebody changed the rules obviously.'

'A life spent in Rome and I never heard this story,' Severi commented, observing him more closely, sure that the monk did not mention it by chance.

Blasius turned and looked at Severi straight in the eyes. He had changed his earlier benevolent tone when he spoke again.

'We are playing a game here, Major, and your team is currently on the losing side. Old rules don't apply anymore, as you have just found out. I am referring to your ability to make your own decision in your own backyard. That affects me as well, as we both lost an opportunity to damage Schaeffer. And with that your command of the supply operation to Libya seems farther and farther from being returned to you. You are still empty handed.'

Severi felt humiliated once again by this reminder of his failures. Blasius knew about Cordelia obviously.

He said with a growling voice: 'I had her. I had her and she would have confessed, and that would ...'

Blasius interrupted him.

'Oh, Major, that did not translate into reality though. Schaeffer is a highly regarded officer with an exceptionally strong backing, and unless there's something concrete and serious that we could find to weaken his position, then the game is over.'

Blasius did not have any intention of sharing with him that he was convinced that Cordelia was a Jew. Not yet at least. He wanted to avoid that imbecilic Major rushing into any action before getting solid proof. He would give him something, but just enough to get what he wanted. So he kept those cards close to his chest.

Severi lost his patience, as even Blasius seemed to be playing a game with him, and he'd had enough of being treated like a puppet.

'Let's cut to the chase, Father Blasius. You told me over the phone that you had something really interesting to tell me, and I hope it was not your little lesson in history. So, let's see if it has been worth my time coming down here to see you.'

'First, the reports of your comrades have been useless so far. And I have proof of that. Another source of mine told me things about Cordelia Olivieri that your men should have found out instead, if they were doing their job, that is.'

Great, didn't this damn priest love to belittle him? Severi thought.

But he was also thinking fast, and the same burning questions that Blasius had formulated in his mind, came to his as well: if what the monk said was true, why didn't his attendant perform as he should? He would be punished for this. He had made him look like a bloody incompetent as well.

'Like what?'

'For example, that she went to the Ghetto the other day and spent a few hours there.'

'She went to see some Jew? What for? Did your source tell you that?'

That news ignited the Fascist's interest.

'Unfortunately not, but the fact is that it does not really matter. What matters is that the hostess of the hotel where one of the most important German operations of the war is being managed from, is visiting declared enemies of the regime, of the Axis in fact!'

'Naturally, my thinking as well,' Severi said, angry with himself for not seeing the full implications immediately. Blasius noticed the same fawning tone Flaminia kept using with him. A sign that he was the one to agree with, and not the other way around.

'What for is an interesting question, though, and I don't want to dismiss it,' Blasius said. 'In fact, there's something more that corroborates the need to answer it. My source tells me that Miss Olivieri is trying to seduce Schaeffer, and he's falling for it. He seems to have eyes only for her. Flowers, a romantic dinner for two. And then, in the morning the other day she was seen coming out of his bedroom, when her dwelling is on the other side of the garden, in the dépendance. I leave to your imagination why she would ever have been there.'

'Fucking bitch …'

So that damn Afrika Korps Colonel was screwing her. That's why he wanted her back so badly. Bastard, he had beaten him to that as well, Severi thought, scorned.

'I wouldn't necessarily use that language, but she is definitely using her sexual abilities to induce him to let his guard down. And possibly to help the enemy spy steal his plans. This is extremely serious. But there's one more thing that would represent a categorical seal to our success: if it was proved she is actually a Jew, that would be the definitive stone on Schaeffer's grave, don't you think?'

'Yes, yes, you have a point … I asked my attendant earlier to check again at the Ministry of Race; the request for the necessary certificate has been made already, a while ago.'

'May I suggest, given what your men have obtained so far

in terms of results, that you go personally to find out. Just in case they fail again to deliver. If you want something done, do it yourself, Major.'

The German monk was right, Severi reluctantly thought.

Blasius wanted that information badly. He really did not care if Severi was getting his command back or not. He was after Schaeffer; he wanted to destroy him in a big way. Although the information that he had received from Flaminia was probably already enough for Himmler, he would wait for the report from the Ministry of Race which would finally validate his theory. It would be the cherry on the cake for him.

'Also, Major, you have certainly seen the report of the Gestapo. They told me they sent it to you. It's regarding their investigation of the spy; he's apparently still here at the Fascist command.'

'With my men, we have narrowed down who had access to the plans, but we still do not know who that man could be – all of them are above suspicion.'

'Keep digging – it must be somebody in your Fascist circle. The deciphered message they intercepted said as much. And although the plans are kept elsewhere at present, as I said, the spy might well have enlisted somebody to help him.'

'I will catch that devil. If it wasn't for him …'

'I think you'd better get on with it, Major. I won't steal anymore of your time. But bring me that report as soon as possible, please.'

And with those words, Severi was dismissed.

Lucifer headed for the Ministry of Race at around one o'clock. He had no intention of following the order of his boss to ask for an update on Cordelia's file, as of course he had never made the enquiry when he was given the assignment in the first place. He was going there to make sure that the existing request was destroyed. He had promised Father Colombo that he would do it before he disappeared. Perhaps that would be but a temporary measure, but by the time the whole process was started again, both he and Cordelia would be gone, well beyond reach over the Italian borders.

He hoped that at lunchtime, as usual, the secretary of the department, Maura Boni, his old squeeze there, was still around and alone. Her colleagues went back home to eat, while she preferred to bring in a packed lunch and have the time to smoke a couple of cigarettes with her coffee in total solitude. That depended on whether her husband, for whom they had had to interrupt their heated affair, had gone back to the front after his military licence.

Lucifer entered the austere building and clambered up the stairs. Her office was on the second floor. He knocked on the door, although it had been left slightly ajar.

'May I come in?'

A female voice answered, 'Yes.'

'Hello stranger,' Maura said when she saw him. 'Where have you been all this time? I began to think you were dead or had been thrown in jail or something.'

She was alone. Perfect.

'Hi Maura, you told me to stay away from you, remember? I begged you not to leave me when your husband came back from Libya – you know that.'

'Well, he's gone now, away for who knows how many months, the poor soul.'

'You look fabulous, my dear, by the way, even better than I remembered.'

And there was some truth there, Lucifer thought. Although she wasn't a stunning beauty, Maura was very pretty. Perhaps a bit too petite for his liking, but her well-proportioned body and cute face made her a tempting little catch.

At his compliments, she became coquettish, and the tip of her tongue darted out to lick her generous red lips, reminding him of a fox before a meal.

'May I have a little taste too?' Lucifer asked lasciviously.

Her cheeks reddened a bit.

'If you really insist ...'

Good, Lucifer thought. She is still attracted to me, and he bent over to kiss her. He embraced her more passionately and started to nibble her neck.

But his eyes were busy doing something else.

A rapid scan of the room revealed that nothing had been modified compared to his last visit. He would start to look in the same sheaf of papers first, hoping that Cordelia's request was still in the place he had put it.

'Oooh ... you still leave me quite breathless,' she said, breaking away from him.

'Not as much as I was when I saw you today. My excitement is growing by the minute.'

Maura stepped closer again, and she reached out to grope his crotch.

'Something else is growing too ...' she said in a tone of mischievous satisfaction, as she started to massage him there with more energy, a pretty direct indication that she did not seem to want to lose any time. It was going exactly as Lucifer had envisaged.

'Let me show you how big it is then,' he teased her, feeling his own excitement building up quite rapidly for that sexy little babe.

'Wait a minute. Let me lock the door first,' she whispered with a most mischievous smile and a libidinous look in her eyes.

He unbuttoned his trousers while she was lifting her skirt up above her hips. Lucifer stripped her of her knickers and then, placing both hands on her buttocks, he lifted her onto the desk behind, then penetrated her immediately. They reached an orgasm quickly, as it had always happened during their previous encounters. Maybe it was the position or maybe the fear of being caught in the act, quite literally. The rapid conclusion served his purpose in any case, as, right after, Maura unlocked the door to go to the bathroom just outside her office, to freshen up as usual.

He had been waiting for that moment. As soon as she was gone, he was quick to jump round the desk. He looked in the pile of documents he had eyed before, and starting from the bottom, he began to flick through as rapidly as he could. Halfway up, he found Cordelia's request. He pulled it out, folded the papers in four to hide them inside his shirt.

Mission accomplished this time. Phew!

Father Colombo would be delighted.

Lucifer returned to the front of the desk just as Maura returned.

'I hadn't realised how much I'd missed you. You will come and see me again regularly now, won't you?' she asked, in an almost pleading tone.

'My dear Maura, I wouldn't be able to keep away from your delicious self even if the Duce in person ordered it.'

Maura giggled, very pleased with the acknowledgement of her indisputable appeal.

'I'd better go now – see you soon,' he said, winking at her.

She blew him a kiss goodbye as he walked away.

Maura would never see Lucifer again.

CHAPTER 18

Schaeffer woke up shortly after five o'clock in the morning. The window of the bedroom was still open, and the first rays of light shone through the wooden horizontal slats of the semi-closed Persian shutters, hitting his eyelids. He heard a rooster crow in the distance.

He opened his eyes, then looked to his side.

Cordelia was deeply asleep, lying languidly on her back.

The regular cadence of her breathing made her chest slowly move up and down. His right forearm was still stretched on her abdomen, as if he wanted to make sure that she wouldn't leave him before he was awake. He carefully lifted it to avoid disturbing her sleep, but then couldn't resist the need to feel the silky texture of her skin. He reached out to her, caressing her thigh as gently as he could.

She moaned and in her semi-consciousness, mumbled something unintelligible, while turning her head towards his. Her light brown hair was scattered all over the linen fabric of the pillow, reminding him of an image of the mythological Medusa and her impressive mane. But unlike that creature, she was real. Schaeffer remembered when he had woken up, very excited, in his tent in the desert, after dreaming of making love to Cordelia. But he could never have imagined back then that his dream would come true.

She opened her eyes, a little at first, then completely, and saw him staring at her.

'Good morning, my love,' he said tenderly, continuing to stroke her hip and thigh.

Schaeffer thought she looked absolutely beautiful even though she had just woken up.

He bent down to give her a kiss.

'Friedrich … hi,' she said, when he lifted his lips from hers. His eyes were a darker shade of blue in the morning, she noticed. She combed his blond hair with her hand. If it wasn't for his strong masculine traits, he would probably look quite angelic.

'You are very handsome, even in the morning.'

'Funny, I was thinking the same thing of you a minute ago.'

She moved her leg across his body, resting it above his hip, with her knee slightly bent, her left foot stroking his hairy thigh in small circular movements.

'It's early – the sun has just about risen,' he said. 'I have a few more moments to spend with you.'

Cordelia would have liked to spend more than just a few moments with him. She enjoyed the contact with his lean and muscular body and the warmth it emanated.

'We can stay here in bed and sleep a little longer then,' she said, placing a hand on his chest.

'Sleep? I've got a better idea, darling.'

He kissed her again, more ardently now. He gently grabbed her by the hips and guided her on top of him. She easily sat astride, feeling his erection.

Then he was inside her again and moving his hands on her buttocks. She placed her hands on his as if she wanted him to maintain his tight grip.

'Oh, Friedrich … ooh … ooh …don't stop – please, don't stop…' she implored, feeling the pleasure rapidly growing inside her.

'I've no intention of stopping,' he answered, his breathing harder, his pelvic strokes more and more potent.

They rocked back and forth intensely until, in an explosion of delight, they reached a climax together. With a big sigh, she collapsed on him, feeling a deep sensation of solace still invading her body. He was equally satisfied, thinking he had never experienced such intense pleasure with a woman before.

'I will never let you go, Cordelia. I love you,' he said, kissing her neck and ears, and squeezing her in his arms.

She remained silent for a moment, then said, 'You will leave me, Friedrich. You will go away, back to your command in North Africa and I will be alone again.'

Schaeffer knew she was right and a deep sadness came over him.

He flipped her on her back and looked her straight in the eyes.

'Now that I have found you, I will come back for you, Cordelia. I promise – you have to believe me.'

'Don't make promises you can't keep, Friedrich. None of us can while we are at war.'

'This war will end.'

'In the meantime, it's taking away from me everyone I care for.'

'So you care for me, darling.'

Cordelia had to admit to herself that she did. There was not a more potent aphrodisiac than the love of a man, and she was starting to feel its powerful, reciprocating effect.

'I do, Friedrich. I really do, I'm afraid.'

'That's progress! Just a few hours ago you only liked me; now you care for me. Next, you'll love me,' he said jokingly, but seriously wishing for it.

Outside, birds were chirping louder and louder. The sky was brighter.

'I will love you, when you come back to me, Friedrich,' she whispered, but the moment the sentence came out of her mouth, she felt a pang of regret.

Because although she knew her feelings for him were true, it was also true that destiny would prevent that from happening.

Cordelia would not be here waiting for him.

She would be gone to some place on the other side of the world.

Alma was already in the kitchen when Cordelia arrived to have some breakfast.

'Good morning, Alma. How are you? You did not have to come so early today. You did not have to come at all, in fact,' she said to her old nanny, while she fiddled around preparing a pot of coffee.

'I am well and being alone in a flat wouldn't help to put that horrible experience behind me. Here, let me do that, child.'

Alma got hold of the pot, opened a can of freshly ground coffee and filled the filter of the coffee maker.

'You need to learn to do these things, otherwise what will you do when you get married?'

As soon as she proffered those words, though, Alma regretted it, not even sure why she had said that. Her fiancé was dead and Cordelia did not have other prospects, let alone the fact that she was about to leave the country for good.

'I see you are back to your old self, Alma. It's not even seven o'clock and you're already telling me off. I am happy to see that,' she mumbled with her mouth full, elated to know that Alma was beginning to leave her shocking experience behind.

'You seem famished today and you are glowing. I've never seen you like that so early in the morning.'

Is she seeing through me so easily? Cordelia thought, worryingly.

She preferred not to comment, feeling a bit embarrassed, afraid she would give away something.

Alma went to the door and closed it, so that they could have a quiet conversation.

'Why has Major Severi let us go, I wonder?' Alma asked, changing the subject.

'It was Colonel Schaeffer. He ordered our release. I asked him last night and he confirmed,' Cordelia said, providing a further explanation. 'He told me he did it because he is a lawyer, with a great sense of justice. What happened to us was not just, according to him.'

Alma listened quizzically, then looked at Cordelia and said, 'I am not sure I completely buy this. There's more to it than that, I am sure. Something tells me you know what that is, don't you?'

Cordelia, who had known Alma all her life, could not lie to her. Her old nanny always displayed a great sense of intuition and there was no point in hiding what she had already started sensing.

'He told me he couldn't see us being hurt,' she admitted.

'Us? He doesn't care about an old bag like me, Cordelia! He cares about you though. And he must care a lot to do something like that. Look at me. He cares for you – he likes you. He keeps looking at you with the eyes of a man who has a clear infatuation, and probably a little more than that. I am old, but I still have eyes.'

'Alma, there's no point in talking about it,' she replied sharply. 'What's important is that you and I are free, able to go wherever we want now.'

'Are you in love with this man, Cordelia?' Alma asked abruptly, not letting her off the hook just yet, 'Because if you are, you have chosen the wrong moment to fall in love with somebody, especially a German officer.'

'Oh, Alma! Don't you think that I don't know that!' she responded distraught. 'I am very attracted to him – I really like him. He is kind, clever, and very sweet. And I will never see him again after I leave. How do you think I feel about that?'

Alma felt deeply sorry for Cordelia. The girl hadn't been lucky in her affections, and she had been a primary witness to that.

'I don't want to tell you how to feel, Cordelia. You know that I've never judged you nor do I intend to start now. You are grown up and you are capable of knowing what is right for you. What I know is that the man for you is out there, and you will find him one day. But for now, I want you to think about your own safety first, and you are not safe here. Not even with him.'

'I know that when he's gone, the Marino Severis of this world will be after me. And you for that matter. I have one more thing to do, Alma, and then I will leave. And you will be right after me, understood?'

'I am ready. Don't you worry, Cordelia. In the meantime, please be careful.'

'I will,' she said, hugging and reassuring her old nanny. 'I will.'

'You'd better go now, Cordelia. I don't want Flaminia to suspect anything. I will bring your coffee to your room as soon as it's ready,' Alma said, unaware that the maid had already seen Cordelia slip out of Schaeffer's bedroom earlier and would report it to Blasius later that day.

Cordelia went out of the kitchen back door and straight to the dépendance. When she was almost at her door, she impulsively turned

259

to face the hotel façade. She looked up to where Schaeffer's bedroom window was.

It was still open.

He was bent on the sill, still half naked, looking at her.

He waved.

She smiled.

Cosimo Farina was having a busy day. A large quantity of flour had been delivered and he and his apprentices had been up since the crack of dawn to store all those large, heavy jute sacks. He was getting old, he reckoned, as his back ached so much more than last year under their weight. He sat down for a moment, thinking that after the war he would go and visit his brother Fabio in New York to see how they managed the business over there. In his last letter, Fabio had mentioned that they were using some sort of machinery to get things around the shop. Perhaps he would invest in it as well after seeing how it worked, who knows.

Cosimo had just left the laboratory at the back to go into the front shop, when he saw a stunning beauty coming in. She was a bit taller than the average girl, with very sinuous features, curvy but not vulgar, and an extremely pretty face. He wasn't young anymore, but he felt quite taken by her presence.

It was the first time that Cordelia had visited him. She was following Father Colombo's instructions. Her old Franciscan friend had explained to her in detail what she would need to do once she got the micro-film with the pictures of the convoy plans detailing their cargos and routes to Libya.

She had waited for the right moment to slip out of the hotel, undetected, and had walked up to the streetcar stop at the end of the road. When she arrived at Via della Dogana Vecchia, she got off and walked to Cosimo's bakery. She entered the shop, just as another customer was leaving.

'Hello, Miss, may I help you?' Cosimo asked.

'The Abbess of the Convent of St John the Baptist would like you to prepare her loaves of rye bread. It's a special order.'

The baker nodded. He understood she was here to deliver a secret message.

'When would you need it by?'

'How about this Friday?'

'That'd be perfect. It'll be prepared for you by then,' he said smiling.

'Thank you, goodbye, Mr Farina.'

'Good day, Miss.'

Later that day, the message was picked up by Brother Filippo. When Father Colombo received it, he was jubilant.

She had managed to succeed!

Clever girl.

One more step and this business will be concluded. He would get her documents from the British and Cordelia would be able to leave next Sunday.

'I want you back here with me, Lieutenant Colonel, and that's an order!'

Erwin Rommel had just got off the phone with Schaeffer.

Now a Field Marshall, he had received the promotion from Adolf Hitler after his extraordinary successes in Cyrenaica, a region of Libya. The Desert Fox was sitting in his office, in the city port of Tobruk. Conquering the town had been a strategic victory, as its geographical position, with its protected harbour, meant that his supply lines had been drastically cut and cargos coming in would be supporting the action of his troops in what he hoped would be the definitive push towards Cairo and the oil fields of the Middle East.

Ensuring the ships would get there intact was, therefore, absolutely vital for his future action. He looked at the map in front of him and, with a pencil, he circled the precise point he planned to attack: El Alamein.

Rommel was very pleased with the work that Schaeffer had done, and the operation he had set up was working splendidly well, according to the reports he kept receiving. Aerial attacks by the RAF had greatly diminished, which meant that he had been right in imposing that the command be taken over by one of his most trusted men. And a very capable officer Schaeffer was too, in the field. Which is why he had ordered him to come back to the battlefield.

He needed his best men to win the next battles, and the most important battle on the horizon now was winning Egypt. Rommel was also not feeling very well. The African desert had exerted its toll on him, and he'd had his fair share of ailments provoked by that unforgiving climate. In addition, he was also suffering from high blood pressure and in a letter, his wife, Lucia, had begged him to take a break and go home to recover, and see their fourteen-year-old son, Manfred. Having officers around that he could fully count on was of critical importance. And Schaeffer had proved invaluable on more than one occasion.

Schaeffer was extremely happy about the recognition of his work, and Rommel's appreciation felt particularly good. And he was proud that his efforts would help Germany to win the war. He loved his country.

If this operation proved successful in shortening the conflict, then many soldiers' lives would be saved, and people could go home, back to their families, to real homes, real beds, real jobs, and enjoy life instead of killing other human beings. No more stale rations to feed upon instead of having the possibility of a home-cooked meal or choosing to be served in an elegant restaurant, in the company of a splendid woman. He longed to return to that kind of life, to be able to practice law again, get married, have a family, children.

With Cordelia.

When I am back, I will ask her to marry me.

I am becoming sentimental, he thought, Wolf was right.

He wasn't really afraid to go back to North Africa.

He was afraid of not being able to see her again.

Having to leave her now was going to be as hard as it was necessary.

He would tell her tonight.

CHAPTER 19

Madame Yolanda had been true to her word when she told Marino Severi that this new girl would make him particularly happy.

As he had promised himself, Severi had decided to pay a visit to that bawdy madam's house, which was classified by law as a second category institution. There were three categories of brothels: in the third, the lowest, girls were not particularly young anymore, or attractive and only capable of basic, simple and dull performances; in the first category, the top one, you could find the crème de la crème, but with it came a high price tag and it was difficult to find girls wanting to do anything particularly rough. Severi found that second category brothels were much more to his taste, not only because they were cheaper and the girls were still young enough, but also, they were certainly much more creative than those of the third category, while at the same time willing to satisfy a certain set of fantasies.

Madame Yolanda, who had been in the business since she was thirteen years old, knew how to please men and her ability to read their sexual desires had been the driver of her career, bringing her to own one of the most sought-after brothels in town. She understood Severi well, and adulation was certainly his sweet spot.

'Good evening, Major, I missed you, as always. I was worried when I did not see you last week. All the girls were eager to have you back. They all say you are the best,' she said with the most fawning tone.

She continued: 'I have a new girl that has just been delivered from Trento, in the north, as a matter of fact. Tall, as you like them, blond and with a spectacularly sexy body. And a special ability; I have verified it myself. As you know, I never let my clients have bad experiences.'

'Let's see her then,' Severi said.

He didn't want to lose any time in chit chats today.

Madame Yolanda's lips curved upwards in a lupine smile, while her eyes narrowed, cold and calculating.

'It's a bit more expensive than the others, but I assure you, you'll be more than delighted with her service,' she said ruefully, but in a tone that did not leave any room for negotiation.

'How much more expensive?' Severi asked curtly.

He knew that haggling wouldn't work with Madame Yolanda, besides he wanted to conclude and engage in a different type of action.

'It's thirty-five lire for half an hour. But in this case, as it is your first time with her, I will give you scented soap, cologne and linen towels for just eighty centesimi,' she said, while making a swift nod at a young maid to bring those things upstairs.

Then she rang a bell.

From behind a set of heavy purple velvet curtains, with an almost regal stride, a slender Valkirian girl of no more than twenty stepped in.

She had very full lips coloured with a bright shade of red. She wore an intricate black lace garter, black silk stockings, black high-heel shoes and nothing else to cover her tender rosy breasts and almost bald intimate parts.

Madame Yolanda looked at her and, seeing Severi's libidinous gaze, she was secretly very pleased with herself to have reached maximum effect in her choice of appearance for the girl.

She took her by the hand, making her turn slowly round to let her client check the goods from every possible angle.

'As you see, she is gorgeous. I keep her under wraps for the best clients only at present. Just to maintain her freshness as long as possible.'

Compared to the girl, Madame Yolanda, at about forty-seven, seemed her grandmother. Under the heavy make-up, she was the picture of somebody who had lived too soon, too fast, her skin tired, her face a collection of wrinkles.

To further arouse Severi, she went close to the girl, lowered her face towards her breasts, closed her lips on her nipples and intentionally sucked both, very slowly, first one, then the other.

The girl softly moaned, slightly arching her back.

When Madame Yolanda finished, they were both hard and erect, wet and shiny. Looking at them, she smiled in approval.

Then she put her hand between her legs and began stimulating the girl's intimate parts, to further induce her arousal.

Severi found that small erotic spectacle very exciting, and his phallus hardened.

'She's all yours and ready for you now, Major,' she said, not waiting for an answer.

The blond girl led him into one of the heavily ornate rooms upstairs.

As soon as they had disappeared behind its white door, Madame Yolanda told the maid, 'Go check she's all right after he leaves. He's an animal.'

Severi left the brothel fully satisfied with the service and, more than anything else, his performance had been, in his opinion, quite out of the ordinary. He would request her again next time. Severi had taken what he wanted and given the girl what she deserved. She had been a real professional, even at that young age, he had to admit.

He always felt better when he could assert his power, especially this time, on a German-looking specimen.

A power that that Benedictine monk had reminded him he no longer had.

He decided that he'd follow his advice and go directly to see what was going on at the Ministry of Race. Over there, those lazy bureaucrats did not really understand who he was. Perhaps his attendant had not made it absolutely clear when he presented his request to check the birth origin of Cordelia Olivieri, that it was a demand from the great Marino Severi.

What if he had though? And they did not really care since he was no longer in charge of one of the most important military operations?

Severi thought it would be a good test to find out how high he still ranked.

After his sex session, early that afternoon, he was feeling quite optimistic.

I should go to Madame Yolanda more often, he thought. I feel recharged after being there. I will show them who they are dealing with.

When he arrived at the office at the Fascist command, Severi checked on his desk whether, in the meantime, a report from the Ministry of Race had been delivered, but he did not find anything. So he took one of the cars in the courtyard and drove there. Had he walked, he'd have been faster in reaching the ministerial building. In Rome not even the Duce had fully succeeded in making Romans abide by the rules of traffic, and it remained as chaotic as it had always been.

Finally, he managed to get there.

The doorman indicated the office he was after was on the second floor.

There was only a male employee working behind a wooden desk and huge piles of papers on different tables were dotted around the room.

No wonder things didn't get done quickly, he thought. The man, middle-aged, sickly looking, wore a pair of glasses with very thick lenses. He did not immediately recognise the man that had appeared at the door, and with the tone of somebody who had asked the same question a million times that day, said: 'May I help you?'

'I am Major Marino Severi. A while ago my attendant Guido Rovo made a request to check the records of Miss Cordelia Olivieri. This was an urgent matter and I don't understand why it still hasn't been followed up with the due attention!' he said, arrogantly.

'I … I am sorry, Major,' the employee said, feeling the imperiousness of somebody used to imparting orders.

Knowing all too well who Severi was, he added hurriedly, 'Let me have a look for you now. My secretary, Maura, might have processed the request herself already. In fact, I saw your attendant come here a couple of times recently, but we only crossed paths, as I was on my way out to lunch.'

The man was looking at Severi with a certain degree of concern, trying to remember if he had seen Cordelia Olivieri's file somewhere. No, he hadn't.

He went to the archive of the pending dossiers, which contained the existing paperwork created following up an initial request, and where the file stayed until all information had been received.

He looked under the letter *O*.

Nothing.

Perhaps Maura had made a mistake, he thought, and put it under the first name, but he could not find anything even under the letter *C*.

Maura was a bit messy at times, so he checked in the sheaf of papers on her desk.

No result there, either.

He started to sweat a bit, as, out of the corner of his eye, he saw that Severi was getting impatient. The latest reports had been shipped out earlier that day, so the only way to find out if Cordelia Olivieri's dossier was among them was to check the logbooks, which contained who had requested what, when and about whom, and if the file had been closed.

The clerk reached for a big leather file on the top of a shelf and opened it, thumbing through its pages with his index finger, scanning all with great attention.

'The last request under the name of your attendant, Guido Rovo, goes back to January this year, Major, but it was for a certain Alberto Birmano. Nothing after that, I'm certain. And nothing has been logged under the name of Cordelia Olivieri. I just cross-checked as well. We are very precise, I assure you,' the spectacled man said anxiously, already afraid of the reaction of that menacing Blackshirt.

Severi widened his eyes and grinded his teeth, his jaw becoming almost white with the pressure, but he contained his rage and said nothing in front of the little man.

'I want you to log a request today, and I expect an answer in the next twenty-four hours at most. Have I made myself clear? And one more thing: when you have it, you call me at my command straight away. I don't want to wait for the post to arrive,' he yelled.

'Of course, Major Severi. I am taking down your request as we speak and I assure you I will make the necessary investigation myself as a matter of urgency,' he said, scribbling all the details as fast as he could.

'Excellent. I will remember that. I will make a phone call myself from here to my office, to check that you don't claim your phone is

269

not working,' Severi said, not waiting for permission but grabbing the receiver of the telephone on the desk and asking the operator to be connected with his Fascist command.

'Hello there, the Ministry of Race here. I have Major Severi on the line. Can you put him through to the office of Guido Rovo, please?' the operator asked the command switchboard.

As Lucifer wasn't in the office at that moment, a comrade of his picked up his phone and said he wasn't there.

'Tell him to wait for me in the office and don't go anywhere until I arrive. Have I made myself clear?'

'Yes, Major!'

Severi hung up and left without even saluting. The poor employee was relieved to see him go.

He stormed out of the Ministry of Race and got back in the car.

He was absolutely fuming.

Guido had lied to him, that son of a bitch!

He felt betrayed, enraged that his attendant had not carried out his orders to get the proof he was after. Why had he disregarded his precise instructions? What reasons could his attendant have for not doing what he had been asked to do, more than once? Was he trying to stall his demand? There was only one way of knowing, and he wouldn't refrain from using a very heavy hand to get the truth out of that bastard.

You will not make fun of me, he thought.

Infuriated, Severi turned on the engine, pressed the clutch to the floor, forced it into first gear and accelerated, driving back to the barracks as fast as possible.

Lucifer was down in the barracks when Severi's call was answered. He was carrying out his last duties for the week, handing over a couple of jobs to a colleague. He had obtained a licence to go and see some distant cousins in the north of the country over the weekend, to avoid raising any suspicions, just in case he was seen leaving with a suitcase and in civilian clothes at the train station. He had no plans to come back, of course, and had bought his one-way train ticket to Varese, near the alpine border, from where, on foot, he planned to cross the border into Switzerland.

Time to see good old England again, he thought.

So it was only when he got back to his desk that he was given Severi's message. He thought nothing of it, at first, but then the comrade that had responded to the call on his behalf distractedly added, 'And by the way, the call arrived from the Ministry of Race, so he shouldn't be long.'

That information really alarmed Lucifer.

His mind began working feverishly.

If Severi had gone to the office, they would have told him there was no such request on Cordelia Olivieri. So Severi knew by now, and the fact that he had bothered to call from there and make sure Lucifer was going to wait for him was worrying. The Major would surely have questions for him and, unfortunately, Lucifer did not have any plausible answers. None that would satisfy his boss anyway. Knowing Severi, and reckoning what was probably going to happen to him, Lucifer said to his comrade: 'Sure. I'll just be down in the barracks in the meantime. I still have a couple of things to tell the guys.'

But instead, as soon as he was downstairs, he slipped out of the gate of the Fascist command and quickly disappeared into the crowd of the late afternoon. Even though he was wearing his uniform, he felt vulnerable. A Blackshirt would normally be the hunter rather than the hunted. So he tried to avoid the main roads, walking in the shade as much as possible, taking a bus, then a streetcar, then doubling up, just to check if anyone seemed to be looking for him already.

He decided not to go back to his flat. Too risky.

Even if Severi wasn't the cleverest of men, he was cunning; hence, it wouldn't take long to work out he had cleared off and then draw his conclusions. And his flat would be the first place they would go to look for him.

His train ticket would be found, he thought, so he could not even risk taking that route now, as it would be monitored for sure. He could not go to Cosimo Farina and ask for an urgent meeting with Father Colombo to seek help, since during their encounter at the Esculapio Temple with the Franciscan, they had agreed it was their last.

What to do then?

Lucifer turned into a very narrow side street and stopped for a minute. His heart rate had increased and he reckoned he was on the brink of panicking.

He needed to think; he needed to calm down.

First, he calculated he had to change his appearance as soon as possible. If an order to capture him was issued – and knowing Severi he reckoned it was imminent – they would look for a Blackshirt initially, so his current clothes would not protect him for long, rather the opposite.

He needed an effective disguise.

Something quite specific came to mind.

With only a couple of thousand lire in his pockets – he always carried money just in case of emergency – he headed for a clothes shop he recalled.

It was in front of the Basilica of San Lorenzo in Lucina, not far from where he was standing now. With renewed energy, he set off at a brisk walk.

He reached it in a few minutes. There it was, and still open.

The shopkeeper was startled when she saw him coming in, not because Lucifer was a Blackshirt really; she wasn't bothered by that, but because the customers she catered for belonged, usually, to one religious order or the other.

It was in fact a shop of sacred vestments.

'Good evening, Madam. I would like to buy a monk's habit.'

'Of which order, please?'

Lucifer realised he would have to choose one, and the first that came to mind was the same as Father Colombo.

'Franciscan. I am joining that order. I heard the sacred call of the Lord, I'm afraid.'

Peter Lord, in fact, he thought.

'Nothing to be afraid of, young man. Any time is good to convert to a higher vocation. You cannot choose. When the call comes, it must be followed, mustn't it?'

Lucifer knew that the lady couldn't be more right, but not in the way she thought she was.

'Indeed, I hope you have what I am after.'

'Yes, Sir, you have come to the right place. Hmm, let me see – you are a size fifty, I reckon? Perhaps it'll be a bit loose, but a perfect appearance is not going to be that important for you anymore.'

Lucifer secretly couldn't disagree more. Appearance was of paramount importance for him right now.

She handed over the brown habit; he paid and left.

With his package under his arm, he crossed the square and entered the basilica on the other side.

It was empty. Good.

He slipped into one of the confessionals and pulled the curtains. He quickly put the robe over the top of his Blackshirt uniform, tying the rope around his waist. He found a rosary on one of the church desks and put it around his neck. He grabbed a book of prayers and then pulled up the hood to conceal his face.

Dressed like a friar, he went out.

He would be safe on the streets for a little while.

At least until he met Father Colombo again.

He needed his help this time.

It was Friday.

He looked at his watch.

He knew where he would find him.

Unknown to the Franciscan, he would meet Lucifer once more.

The car arrived in the courtyard of the Fascist command at high speed and then jerked to a harsh stop. Marino Severi jumped out like a fury, clambered up the stairs incredibly fast, like he was running an Olympic one-hundred-metre race, or, rather, had a very burning matter to attend to.

First, he went straight into Lucifer's office.

Empty!

Like a tiger hunting his prey, he moved around the whole floor, looking in every room. His men watched him almost in a trance, trying to figure out what drove that behaviour.

No one interrupted his search. In that mood, they knew he would not react well to say the least.

In the end, unable to find Lucifer anywhere in the building, he burst out and shouted: 'Where the fuck is he?'

The comrade that had taken his call knew instantly who he was referring to.

'He is probably down in the barracks, Sir,' he said, nervously.

Severi gave him a piercing look.

'In the damn barracks? Go and find him and bring him here to me. Right now!' he roared.

His comrade did not wait even a second to spring into action. He was followed by another couple of Blackshirts, who preferred to be out of their boss's sight for the time being, wondering why Severi seemed to be so mad at Lucifer.

The Major went to his office and waited. Approximately half an hour later, the three came back saying they had turned the barracks upside down, but nobody had seen Lucifer in the last hour or so. They had also checked on all the other floors of the Fascist command, and there was no sign of him anywhere. He had vanished, apparently.

'Really?' Severi grunted, 'Like a ghost? Let me tell you this then, I will turn him into a ghost for sure, because when I get him, I'll kill him!'

Severi gave instructions to find him and he sent all his men out in Rome to look for him. 'You, you, you and you, follow me,' he then said, and with the four of them, he headed to Lucifer's flat, to see if he had been foolish enough to hide there.

Seeing those four Blackshirts running like devils up the stairs and in front of their flat, the old couple living on the floor right below Lucifer wondered what was happening. Despite their curiosity, however, they avoided enquiring and withdrew into the safety of their dwelling.

Having reached the front door of Lucifer's flat, not caring about the noise they made, Severi gave an order to knock it down, and, after a couple of powerful kicks to the lock, it flung open. They dispersed throughout the flat, entering all rooms, looking under the bed, on the terrace and behind the sofa.

No sign of Lucifer.

Severi stepped into the lounge and looked around.

A train ticket had been left on top of a cupboard. One way to

Varese. Bought at least ten days ago. Well before he had signed Lucifer's leave.

'Major,' said one of the young comrades he had asked along, 'look what I've found at the top of the bathroom water tank.'

He handed over a wooden box. Inside, a small book, ink, a pen and tiny pre-cut strings of white paper. Severi's face became incandescent, his upper lip curling up in anger. It was a kit to encode messages.

'Search everywhere!' he screamed.

In a frenzy, all the men began to open cupboards, sweeping out all of the contents. The sofa cushions flew up in the air; they moved furniture; turned the bed mattress upside down; looked in all the drawers. Concealed at the back of a drawer, one of the men found a micro-camera and he ran to show it to his commander.

Severi gaped.

He did not need any other proof.

He had been searching for a traitor, and instead he had found a spy.

And most probably the spy he was looking for.

The spy who had deprived him of his command, of his position, of his dignity and the respect of his men and superiors.

A ferocious indignation started to mount inside him. His seething resentment of months reached a boiling point.

Severi exploded in a spectacular way.

'I want him dead! I want that bloody son of a bitch hanged by the balls, impaled and castrated! I want him quartered, strangled, stabbed, shot and burned on the highest pyre!'

CHAPTER 20

Now that Cordelia was on the brink of delivering the micro-camera containing the film with the pictures of the Libya convoy route plans to Father Colombo, she felt relieved but also strangely deflated. It felt like the calm before the storm. It was like being in limbo, waiting to get through to the other side. On paper, it seemed quite an easy step. But once taken, there was no way to go back. Her documents with her false new identity would be released, and she would travel to the port of Anzio to board the Portuguese merchant ship.

Why am I not over the moon about that? I should be, she thought, anxious to disband that sudden sense of uneasiness.

Wanting to leave was one thing, and she had wanted it for quite some time now – it was the logical, sensible, safe thing to do.

Now that the crucial moment was fast approaching, having to do it felt quite different.

Maybe she was afraid to find out that her dream would not come true and she would crash hard on the rocks of her illusion.

Maybe the thought of it becoming reality made her more aware that she had to leave the few people and things she loved behind, perhaps unable to see them ever again.

It also meant she would not be able to see Schaeffer ever again.

All of a sudden, Cordelia felt a great sense of sadness. For her. For him. If only they had met in a different place, at a different time.

Why is it that every single person I love, sooner or later, I cannot be with? I must be cursed. She seemed unable to escape from that kind of persecution and her emotions were in turmoil. It was the first time she'd realised too that she had considered Schaeffer as her love. And that made her feel even more miserable.

Enough of this – it's not helping, Cordelia thought, determined to remain cool and practical. But in spite of her cerebral efforts, that disheartening feeling continued to dwell inside her.

A coffee, she thought. I need a good coffee.

From her office, just behind the reception desk, she reached the kitchen, where Alma served her a cup.

Flaminia appeared just a few moments after Cordelia had finished her hot drink. She had been out that morning, fetching a few groceries for Alma. The maid put the bag on the table, but took out a small package from it, saying: 'That's mine, though.'

Alma noticed it was a pair of silk stockings, and very expensive ones, judging by the name of the brand written on its wrapping paper.

'They look very nice, Flaminia,' she said to the maid, who responded with a satisfied smirk.

'Beautiful, aren't they? They will look great when I wear them,' Flaminia added.

'They also look expensive. I didn't think you could afford them,' Alma commented.

'Now I can,' she said arrogantly.

'What does, now you can, mean exactly?' asked Alma.

Flaminia, who certainly had no intention of revealing the source of her sudden fortune, replied, 'It means that sometimes I do some extra work here and there, and with the additional money I get, I give myself a little reward for a job well done.'

The last few words were actually the only true ones.

Father Blasius had told her she had done a good job. Unwilling to be quizzed further, the maid left the kitchen, saying: 'I'd better get on with my work, see you later.' She exited out the back door.

Cordelia assumed a serious tone and with a lower voice she said to her old nanny: 'You have to make your way to Tenuta Belfiore tomorrow, Alma. Once you leave this evening, go straight home and pack your last things. Then go to Stazione Termini first thing in the morning and take the train to Castel Madama. If somebody asks, I'll tell them I've given you a day off. Do not come back here anymore, for any reason.'

That evening, Cordelia was to take the secret Minox and the day after, with her new documents, she would be able to leave as well, as per the escape plan agreed with Father Colombo.

'So the time has finally come,' Alma said, sombre. 'Come here, child, let me hug you goodbye while I still can,' she said with a broken voice, putting her arms around Cordelia and squeezing her as she had when she was a little girl.

'Goodbye, Alma. It's not forever though, you know it's not,' Cordelia said, equally emotional, trying to convince herself that would be the case, more than Alma.

The old nanny's eyes were full of tears when she looked at her again. Cordelia took her handkerchief to wipe them away.

'Don't Alma, don't,' she said, 'or otherwise you'll start me off as well. We'll give ourselves away, won't we, if we do.'

'How foolish of me, sorry child,' Alma apologised. 'We have been preparing for this – I should know better. I'll do as you say, don't worry.'

'That's what I want to hear, Alma. I'll go straight to my dépendance now, so I might not see you before you leave, and it's better this way. All will be looking as normal as it has always been.'

'Take care of yourself, child. Promise me you'll write as soon as you reach your destination.'

'I will, Alma, I will.'

Cordelia turned around, fighting back her own tears now, and left Alma, not knowing if they would meet again.

Flaminia had been watching the scene from afar.

After she had left, she realised she'd left her precious purchase on the table of the kitchen and having come back to fetch it, she stopped and listened, hiding against the outside wall, daring to peep only a couple of times to see what was happening. Their voices were low and muffled, so she heard only chunks of their conversation, but what she gathered would be just about enough to have Father Blasius putting his hand in his pocket again.

Schaeffer had been putting it off all day.

It was not what he wanted to do, but there was no way he couldn't.

He had to tell her and that evening was the last possible chance.

The Afrika Korps Colonel was sitting on his bed, drying himself with a white cotton towel after a shower, brooding on the best choice of words.

Funny, he thought – all the eloquence I developed in years of law practice seems to be just useless at the moment.

He stood up and got dressed. He would go to Cordelia's dépendance now.

To say goodbye.

With a heavy heart, he crossed the garden and knocked.

Light steps behind the door.

'Hi, Cordelia, I'd like to talk to you for a moment,' he said, when she opened it.

She smiled, truly happy he had come to see her, but she detected an uneasy tone in his voice.

She stood aside to let him enter.

She went to sit on one of the blue velvet armchairs, inviting him to take his place in front of her, on the sofa. Even in this simple white dress, and with no make-up on, he thought she was more beautiful than ever.

'I have been thinking of you all day, Cordelia,' Schaeffer said, 'and there is no easy way to say it, but I have to tell you that I will be leaving tomorrow morning. It's sudden, but my job here is done, and I have received orders from my commander to rejoin him on the battlefield. I am so sorry to have to leave you. I would never do that if I had a choice.'

Cordelia remained absolutely still as he spoke, feeling a pang to her stomach, while slowly acknowledging the news. Already shaken from her emotional goodbye with Alma earlier, here he was, bidding farewell too.

Why do I feel so sad? Not even for Augusto did I feel so bad.

Trying to control her voice and look calm, she said: 'Friedrich, you were never supposed to stay anyway, so don't feel guilty for something you cannot decide, not at present at least. There are things we have to do in these unfortunate times, and they are well beyond our control. You take care of yourself. I am happy to have met you. I am … I am happy to …' but she couldn't go on.

Her emotions were getting the better of her and she felt her resolve to remain as detached as she possibly could vanish.

Schaeffer saw her evident distress. He got closer and took her hands in his. They were tense and trembling.

281

'Cordelia, I meant it the other night when I said I will come back for you. All the fibres in my being are determined to do that. I have fallen for you. I desperately love you, darling.'

Deep inside of her, she knew his feelings for her were real.

He seemed to be the type of man who didn't say what he said unless he meant it.

She knew he profoundly cared for her. And what was worse, she very much cared for him, too. And once again, she'd lose somebody she loved.

Cordelia felt an irresistible impulse to embrace him, wanting to hold on to him as long as she could.

'I don't want you to leave me, Friedrich. If only we could disappear to some secret, faraway place where there is no war. This terrible conflict is killing everything. Even if people still look alive, they are very much dead inside,' Cordelia said dismayed, her head against his wide chest. But almost immediately she regretted being selfish and thought how cruel it was of her to have said that, as it made it more difficult for him than it should have been.

'Friedrich, you have to forgive me. I am behaving like a spoilt, silly girl.'

'I will take you wherever you want, after the war,' he said, 'as long as you promise you'll wait for me, my love.'

She couldn't bring herself to respond. Cordelia did not want to lie to him saying she would; she couldn't make that promise. When he came back, she would not be here. She would be in a place where he might never be able to find her.

She pulled his face towards hers and kissed him with the passionate avidity of somebody who knew might never have the chance to do it ever again.

Time was running out.

'I don't want you to ever forget me,' she said, breaking off from him. Then she took a step back and with one single movement, she pulled her dress above her arms and let it drop on the floor. She wanted him to make love to her, for one last time.

He understood. She got closer, her hands searching to unbutton his fly and his shirt, while he fumbled to undo her bra and get rid of her knickers and his trousers at the same time. Putting both hands on her buttocks, he lifted her up. She clasped her legs around his waist, tightening her grip while he put his arm around her hips. They wanted each other urgently, and still standing, he placed her back against the wall and penetrated her. Furiously rocking back and forth, they reached an orgasm almost too quickly.

They looked in each other's eyes and without saying anything, still with her legs around his waist, he brought her to the bedroom, where they made love again and again. He took the time to explore every inch of her body, slowly, as if he needed to indelibly fix in his memory every single detail. She loved having him inside of her, his hands all over her body, feeling his weight on hers, feeling the tickling of his hairy chest on her breasts, the warmth of a man lying beside her. But more than everything, the incomparable feeling of belonging to the man she loved. And him belonging to her.

'I love you, Friedrich,' she whispered, when she was sure he had fallen asleep.

They remained together all night.

When he woke up, he saw Cordelia's eyelids were still closed and assumed she was asleep. He preferred not to wake her, knowing he would feel miserable to look at her lovely but sad face.

'You are beautiful, Cordelia. I love you, darling,' he said with an almost imperceptible voice, while softly kissing her shoulder.

He very carefully slipped out of bed, got dressed and left her.

She heard him leave the room and close the door behind him. At that point, Cordelia wept.

CHAPTER 21

When Cordelia finally decided to abandon the dépendance and go back to the hotel, she found it strangely empty without Schaeffer, even though Captain Wolf and his men were still around.

Now that the Afrika Korps Colonel had been summoned back by Rommel, Wolf had been given the responsibility of the operations until further notice.

The German officer drove Schaeffer to Ciampino Airport and during the journey he noticed that the Lieutenant Colonel had an unusually serious and melancholic expression since they left Palazzo Roveri. Wolf preferred to leave him to his thoughts, suspecting that the reason he was feeling that way was because of their fascinating, gorgeous hostess, Miss Olivieri. He had been right in thinking that Schaeffer was more than attracted to that beautiful young lady. The two men did not exchange a word until the moment they arrived next to the Junker which was going to fly him back to Libya.

The car stopped and both got out.

'Captain, keep an eye on her – that's an order,' Schaeffer said to the officer.

'Yes, Colonel, do not worry. Keeping an eye on her won't be difficult at all, I assure you. And if I may say so, Sir, that's the best order I have ever received.'

'Thank you, Captain.'

'Goodbye, Sir, have a good flight.'

With a wave, Schaeffer signalled to the pilot to kick the engine into life and then he clambered up the short steps of the aircraft, sealing the door behind him. Wolf waited until the Junker had taxied onto the runway, reached the necessary speed and finally took off. Then he drove back to Rome.

In the meantime, as Alma was absent, Cordelia was left in Flaminia's company, and after instructing the maid on the chores to carry out, she took refuge in her office, and spent the day thinking about Schaeffer and her future life.

She missed him terribly already, and it was not even twenty-four hours that he had been gone. But it was the thought of not being able to see him again that was incredibly difficult to accept.

Cordelia remained in a state of affliction all day. When she finally emerged in the late afternoon, she dispatched Flaminia home and headed back to her dwelling.

It was Friday and she had to prepare to go out.

This was the day she would meet Father Colombo to deliver the secret film.

He had instructed her to go to the church of Santa Chiara, not far from the Pantheon, where on Fridays the monk was due to hear confession. When she arrived, her old Franciscan friend would, therefore, already be waiting for her.

Cordelia would just need to reach the church, queue up with the other penitents and wait for her turn, and when it arrived, slip the micro-camera through the criss-crossed pattern of the latticed window of the confessional booth. Easy. Mission accomplished.

After that, Cordelia just had to return home and on Sunday, according to the escape plan, get her temporary disguise as a Clarissa nun, together with her travel documents containing her new identity, make her way down to Anzio, and board the Portuguese vessel, which would take her away from all this.

She looked at her watch. She had plenty of time to get there. She chose to wear a pair of low heel shoes and a dark grey cotton top and matching skirt, which had two zipped pockets. She reached for the silver candelabra and, unscrewing its base for the last time, she extracted the Minox, hidden in its column, only to place it in one of the pockets, which was zipped closed again. The skirt had a quite loose, pleated design, so the light protuberance of the small object was lost in the floating fabric, becoming almost invisible.

All of a sudden she was very nervous, the palm of her hands sweating.

Nothing will go wrong; nothing will go wrong; nothing will go wrong, she repeated to herself, in an effort to ease her anxiety.

She managed to calm down and then felt ready to go.

With a black lace veil on her arm, as all women were expected to wear when entering church, she left through the garden gate. It was already dusk. She turned right and started to briskly walk in the direction of the Quartiere Pigna, where the church of Santa Chiara was located.

At that time of the day, there were still a few people on the streets, and many were sitting outside their houses, chatting with their neighbours, watching the world go by. A few smiled at her as she passed by.

It was a lovely, warm end of the day, and yet Cordelia felt a chill going down her spine.

As soon as Flaminia left Palazzo Roveri after hearing those bits and pieces of conversation between Alma and Cordelia, she decided it was worth informing the Benedictine monk sooner rather than later. The maid took a diversion and headed for the Biblicum. And there, she told a very interested Father Blasius what she had heard, receiving again a few lire coins for her service.

'By the sound of it, I think Miss Olivieri might be on the brink of going somewhere, maybe far away. She must have got very scared by Marino Severi,' Flaminia cunningly commented.

Blasius, who didn't have any intention of entertaining a conversation with that unpleasant girl, nor revealing his thoughts to her, cut their talk short, paid her and said, 'Thank you again for your valuable information, Flaminia. Now go home and continue to report back to me as soon as you hear anything else.'

Without further delay, he hurried her out of the door.

Alone, the Benedictine began to speculate on the possible scenarios, especially in light of his certainty that Cordelia was in fact a full-fledged Jew.

Perhaps that little slut was right, and Cordelia had been really scared after being seized by Severi that night. Or instead, she had been afraid of her secret being found out, as once somebody was placed under arrest, their name was logged and further investigation would follow. She realised that with Severi being deprived of his prey, the Fascist Major would be determined to exact revenge, and would not take long to discover her racial origin. So, Blasius concluded, most probably she had been planning to flee and had inadvertently revealed her intentions while Flaminia, luckily, was eavesdropping. Her escape would not only rob Severi of his designed victim, but most importantly rob Blasius of the principal evidence he was planning to use against Schaeffer, besides the opportunity to further please Himmler with an unexpected gift to add to his 'Final Solution'.

What if she succeeded though?

'Absolutely not!' he yelled, pacing up and down his study like a ferocious animal ready to hunt its prey. 'You will not escape from me, you damn Jew! You are my trump card and I'll have you soon in my hands!'

Severi still hadn't produced official proof she was Jewish, and Blasius wanted that final confirmation before approaching Himmler. But now it would not take long. It was only a matter of hours, he reckoned. He had made sure to unleash the Fascist Major's wrath when he was last there, which in turn would get results, he was pretty sure.

In the meantime, as Severi's men had proved utterly ineffective, Blasius decided he would not bother asking them to follow Cordelia anymore. He would take the matter into his own hands and ensure that she would be put under adequate surveillance and avoid her slipping away under his nose.

There was only one person the Benedictine could completely trust to carry out this task of paramount importance. And as he had said to the Fascist Major, if you want something done, do it yourself.

He, Blasius, would watch Cordelia Olivieri.

Severi and his men got back to the Fascist command that Friday, after having literally trashed Lucifer's flat.

Nothing over there was in one piece anymore. They had recovered a coding kit and a micro-camera, besides discovering his one-way train ticket and two passports with different identities, one Italian by the name of Renzo Rossi and another, Pierre Armand, stamped on a French document.

Only a secret agent could be in possession of such things. The bastard had prepared to flee through the northern border of the country, and he had literally got away by a hair's breadth. Vanished into thin air.

Once again, he remembered a crucial phrase of the decrypted message the Gestapo had managed to intercept: '... *our man at the Fascist command is in critical danger. He will abort his mission shortly, over.*'

His attendant, Guido Rovo, was indeed a British spy and he had been operating under his very nose for all this time, without him suspecting it!

He couldn't get over the fact that one of his most trusted men had proved to be his most dangerous enemy, the one that had caused his demise, and possibly his ruin.

Unless he captured him and saved the day.

There was no half measure anymore. The Fascist Major was walking a very thin line: either Severi became a winner and arrested him, which would result in getting back his command with the glorious thanks of the regime and its powerful German ally, or turn into a definitive loser, by letting that fucking spy get away, which would make him look like a useless, pathetic fool.

He went to his office, his face a picture of pure rage, his brilliantined hair all over the place, his fists showing white knuckles because of the tightness of his fingers.

The telephone rang and, for a fraction of a second, Severi hoped it would be one of his men with good news about Lucifer.

'Hello? Hello, Major Severi? It's somebody from the Ministry of Race. Shall I put him through?' said the Fascist command switchboard operator.

If Lucifer hadn't managed to escape, that would have been probably the best news of the day, proving he could still exercise his weight in certain places.

Almost disappointed and in a deflated tone, Severi said, 'Yes, I was awaiting their call.'

A few crackles of the line later, the timid voice of a man at the other end of it said: 'Major Severi? Luigi speaking from the Ministry of Race. I personally followed up on your request of a back check on Cordelia Olivieri's lineage. It took a little while longer as her parents did not marry in Rome, but in a small village in the north of the country. I called the office of the mayor of that town, the Podestà, who was very cooperative. He immediately demanded a search in his archives for their marriage certificate. I will have it in the post shortly; he sent it with a priority courier. I also asked the Podestà to read it to me over the phone. I thought you would appreciate having the information straight away. I made a note. Shall I read it to you then, Sir?' he asked.

'Yes, damned, yes! Go ahead!' Severi replied impatiently.

'All right, Sir. Her father, Cesare Olivieri, was born in Rome, Catholic. Her mother, Elizabeth Levy, was born in London, Jewish.'

Severi sat bolt upright and thundered in astonishment, 'What? A Jew? Cordelia Olivieri's mother was a dirty Jew?' But he wasn't listening to the employee of the Ministry of Race anymore, hanging up the phone without even thanking him for having provided an utterly crucial piece of information.

Still astounded, Severi frenetically tried to bring order to the flurry of thoughts that all of a sudden crammed his brain, and the scenario they were quickly and confusedly depicting. It not only made sense, but the logical sequence of facts that began to appear in front of his eyes finally revealed a truth much bigger than he could have imagined.

All the pieces of the jigsaw were coming together and fitted in: Lucifer's clear intent to delay, possibly quash, the discovery about Cordelia's mother, his unusual failures to detect anything suspicious about her. More importantly, though, she was not only a Jew, but partly a descendant of a British citizen, which made her doubly an enemy of the state.

Perhaps they were working together, even, Severi cogitated, part of the same ring.

The Fascist Major grabbed the receiver of his phone and asked the switchboard operator to call the Biblicum, but after a few unanswered rings, he changed his mind and dropped the call. That damned German monk would inform the Gestapo straight away.

Instead, Severi wanted the glory all for himself and it would be he, the great Marino Severi, who would get Lucifer and Cordelia.

With that on his mind, he stormed out of his office and down into the barracks to unleash the hunt for both of them.

CHAPTER 22

'Forgive me Father, for I have sinned,' said the woman on the other side of the latticed grate of the confessional booth. She went on telling the confessor she had hit and badly scratched her neighbour when she had found her in the act of blatantly flirting with her husband in the kitchen of her own house.

'And do you want to know what she said when I asked what she was doing there? She pretended to have come round to have a little taste of the salami my husband brought back from his brother's farm! I am not stupid, Father, that bitch ... Mother of God, please forgive me for the bad language! As I said, that bitch was after another type of sausage, let me tell you!'

Father Colombo listened patiently to the rest of the story, and then assigned her with a penance. He heard the woman indistinctly grumble for the high number of *Ave Maria* he had given her to recite. After she moved away, the Franciscan bent forward and slightly parted the curtains that hid him from view to have a glimpse of how many people were left. He was anxious for Cordelia to arrive and scanned the interior of the church of Santa Chiara to see if perhaps she was there already.

No sign of her just yet.

He sat back again and waited for the next parishioner to kneel for confession.

Cordelia had walked briskly and was almost in sight of the church, of which she could already see part of the elegant Renaissance white façade.

Her heart was hammering inside and, instinctively, her hand touched the protuberance of the micro-camera in her pocket as she got nearer.

She was fast approaching the small square in front of the building from a completely empty Via della Rotonda, a short, narrow but straight street that ran towards it from the north side.

Cordelia was almost at the crossing of the street with the square, when she noticed a man dressed in a habit standing at the corner of another intersecting road.

The religious figure had his hood up, covering his head, and it was now slightly darker, so she could not see his face. Despite that, she was sure that he couldn't be Father Colombo, because her old friend was inside to administer absolutions to the parishioners. That man looked like he was waiting for somebody, and when he saw her, he stepped back into the recess of a huge gate that partly hid him. Much later she would recall that unconsciously she had found his move peculiar, but at the time Cordelia had something else on her mind and thought nothing of it.

So she crossed into the square, passed a few thigh-high travertine columns arranged in a semi-circle which protected the entrance of the church, went up its stone steps and pushed the elaborate wooden portal to enter. Inside, she arranged the black lace veil she had brought along on her head.

She relaxed a bit, lulled by the muffled sound of the people reciting their prayers of penitence after the confession.

The interior was glimmering with the light of the candles, the huge polished black and white marble floor reflecting their gentle luminosity. The familiar smell of incense added to the placid atmosphere of the place.

Stepping on those slabs to reach a bench to sit on, Cordelia felt like a pawn in a game of chess moving across its board, where many other pieces were positioned, waiting for their next turn.

Still outside, Blasius had followed her.

He had stopped at a safe distance, counting on the darkness of the street to avoid being spotted, helped by the colour of his habit, which had been in fact a lucky and very useful disguise in a city where priests, monks and nuns were a usual presence.

He did not want to scare her and, possibly, induce her to flee, so he had remained quite a few steps back from her.

The Benedictine wanted to see where she was going, and more importantly, who she was meeting at that time of the day. Himmler would be much more inclined to up his reward if he brought him more than one victim. Especially after having seen that Cordelia had exited Palazzo Roveri from a side gate and had looked behind her a few times during her journey up to here.

Blasius reckoned that hers was rather suspicious behaviour, the behaviour of somebody who had something to hide. He had been extremely careful to conceal himself just before she could see him, so he was sure his cover hadn't been blown when he saw her entering the church.

He waited for a while on the corner of the road as he did not want to immediately bump into her as he entered the building, but then, too curious, he couldn't wait any longer and impatiently moved to sneak in. For a moment, he was under the light of a streetlamp, which illuminated his face. The Benedictine was walking quickly towards the semi-circle of travertine columns in front of the entrance, when, emerging from a portal on the other side of the square, he detected a figure who sprinted towards him, only to stop right in front, blocking his way.

'What the hell do you think you're doing! You scared me to death, Brother!'

It was another monk, a Franciscan by the look of his habit, but Blasius could not see his face as he had the hood pulled over his head.

'I cannot let you go in, unfortunately,' said Lucifer.

The British spy had been roaming the streets of Rome dressed like that to avoid being captured by his ex-Blackshirts comrades. He had arrived at the church of Santa Chiara, waiting outside for the service to finish so he could ask Father Colombo for help. Lucifer knew that Father Colombo would be there on Fridays as he remembered the initial instructions on how to find him that his handler, Cecil De Clerc, had given him back in London.

He was now standing right in front of Blasius, his legs parted, feet firmly planted on the ground to prevent him from moving forward. As soon as Lucifer had seen Cordelia approaching, he noticed that she had been followed and, to his surprise, by none other than Father Blasius, the black-clad monk friend of the Gestapo.

The last thing Lucifer wanted was for the Benedictine to see Father Colombo meeting Cordelia. That would have sealed both their fates, with catastrophic consequences that would not only involve them and him, but also the many people that had worked at creating and running that British secret operation. In addition to the fact that, if Cordelia was there, it meant she had the micro-film, so it was of vital importance that she brought her mission to a safe conclusion.

Blasius hissed, 'Who are you?' and tried to step around him.

But Lucifer was determined not to let him pass, so he grabbed the monk by the shoulders and pushed him back. The provocation unleashed Blasius' ire and, outraged, he yelled again: 'Who are you! Get your hands off me right now!' Simultaneously, he reached for the fabric of the hood and violently pulled it down.

'You!' Blasius snarled, recognising Lucifer immediately.

The Benedictine did not know exactly why Severi's right-hand man was dressed in a Franciscan habit, but he certainly had not disguised himself for a futile reason, he thought. And clearly the Blackshirt was shadowing Cordelia, and yet his behaviour was more like that of somebody who was protecting her. Blasius' eyes narrowed as if he had been blinded by the sudden light of truth, as a St Paul on the road to Damascus.

'You!' he repeated to Lucifer, with a deeper growl, adding, 'Get out of my way!'

At that point, seeing that Blasius needed a stronger sort of invitation to back off, Lucifer punched him hard in the stomach. The Benedictine screamed in pain, stumbled and bent, but his hands held tight to his opponent, and he avoided falling.

With fury, Blasius charged him with his head down and Lucifer, who did not expect this swift attack, lost his balance and fell on the pavement, bringing Blasius down with him. With an athletic move, the monk managed to get himself upright, and while Lucifer was trying to do the same, Blasius hit him in the face with a robust fist.

The British spy felt the taste of blood in his mouth.

He swung at Blasius, who responded by punching him again. They started to wrestle, more powerfully now, and with a free hand, Lucifer tried frantically to reach the Beretta pistol he still carried, without success.

Blasius prepared to strike another blow. Lucifer saw it coming and, in an effort to prevent him, he clasped his arms tightly around the monk's upper body. Tangled in that embrace, they both lost their balance and went down onto the pavement again.

Blasius violently hit the back of his head against one of the travertine columns of the square, while Lucifer fell on him.

Stunned but still conscious, Blasius tried to push Lucifer away, who in the meantime had managed to extract his firearm.

A single gunshot exploded into the night.

Dizzy, Blasius felt the warmth of a sticky liquid; he looked down and saw blood on his hands.

He moved his gaze to his opponent, eyes wide open, an expression of sheer surprise on his pale face.

Lucifer backed away from him and tried to get on his knees to stand up.

But, all of a sudden, he felt very weak, his legs refusing to support him, as if slowly but inexorably his forces were abandoning him.

The bullet had gone through his chest, entering the top left of his heart.

Lucifer looked down at the tiny hole with a sense of stupor and incredulity, as the blood kept coming out in copious gushes.

Rien ne va plus, les jeux sont fait, he thought, realising the point of no return was fast approaching.

Lucifer died in less than a minute.

Blasius did not see it when he exhaled his last breath of life.

The Benedictine monk had fainted and, due to the strong blow to his head, he was unconscious.

The noise of the gunshot came as a shock to the worshippers gathered in the interior of the church, silencing them all at once, as if they had been muzzled by an invisible hand. Chaos ensued shortly after, with everyone screaming and trying to reach the exit, bodies cramming against the portal in an effort to get out.

Cordelia was caught up in the commotion and although she tried to resist, she was pushed by the panicking horde towards the door, dragged out by their desperation to escape.

On hearing the explosion, Father Colombo jumped out of the confessional booth and frantically looked for Cordelia, but he managed to see her only when she was already being driven out by the mob. He ran towards Cordelia. With difficulty, he pushed through the fleeing crowd, and when he finally got out, he saw from the top of the stairs the two bodies on the pavement. He sprinted down, kneeling beside them.

He recognised Lucifer immediately.

He was lying there by Blasius' side, lifeless, his eyes still open, looking up at the sky.

When Father Colombo reached out to touch them, Lucifer still felt warm.

'Oh, no, no, no … my poor, poor boy …' the Franciscan whispered, full of sorrow, taking Lucifer's head in his lap and caressing his hair like a loving father to a child. His voice was anguished and tears were rapidly filling his eyes. He gave him a silent blessing, recommending his soul to the Lord.

In the meantime, Cordelia had spotted Father Colombo, and moving in the opposite direction to the crowd, she fought against the tide to get next to him. She was totally flustered and still did not grasp completely the full meaning of what had happened, or why. She was scared and confused and, looking at the Franciscan in search of an answer, she saw tears rolling down his cheeks.

The sound of sirens in the distance galvanised their attention.

In a state of agitation, she said, 'Father Colombo, we have to get out of here. The Carabinieri are going to be here in a few moments!'

The Franciscan quickly regained his control and stood up.

'Listen, listen carefully, and do exactly what I tell you. We don't have much time,' he told Cordelia with urgent desperation.

'Do not return home, not now, nor ever again. Go to the hostel of Santa Marta. It is run by Franciscan nuns – they help prostitutes that want to change their lives. It's at the end of this road. They don't ask any questions from those knocking on their door. They will take you in. The Mother Superior is a good friend of mine – mention my name to her. She will help you to get out of Rome and take you to Castel Gandolfo by the end of tomorrow. Once there, head for the old cemetery, near the Villa of Domitian. I will meet you there and you will hand over the micro-camera then.'

Thinking fast, Father Colombo remembered the only place outside of Rome where it would be safe to make the exchange. And it was close to Anzio, the port where Cordelia would board the Portuguese merchant ship, which was due there the following Monday.

Castel Gandolfo, a small town on the lake Albano, some twenty kilometres south of Rome, was the place where the Pope had his summer residence – the Apostolic Palace, property of the Holy See. That building had extraterritorial status; hence, it possessed the same neutrality as the Vatican. They would be able to take refuge there should the need arise.

'I ... understand,' Cordelia answered distraught, 'but why don't you take the Minox now?'

'I am not leaving. I will wait for the authorities to arrive. If I left, it would look suspicious. It will not take them long to find out who was running the service. It's too risky to have the secret film on me; I might be taken in for questioning, even searched,' Father Colombo told her.

He grabbed Lucifer's Beretta and handed the gun to Cordelia.

'Take this. Now go!'

The sirens were much closer and they could already hear the noise of the car engines fast approaching.

Her mind in total turmoil, Cordelia took the gun and began to run.

Father Colombo had been right because when a police car arrived, shortly followed by another two, the Carabinieri, the military police, took him in for interrogation. Together with the dead body of Lucifer and a still unconscious Blasius, the Franciscan was rushed to the station.

The officer in command, the Maresciallo, heard that Father Colombo did not exactly know the dynamic of the incident, since he had been inside the church when the gun went off. He had rushed out only to discover those two people lying outside in front of the door.

Yes, he did know one of them, a Father Karl Blasius if he remembered correctly, a Benedictine monk.

No, he did not know the dead man, even though he wore a Franciscan habit.

And they believed him since, after lifting Lucifer's lacerated clothes to examine the cause of death, they not only found the wound belonging to the single gunshot that had killed him, but the Carabinieri also saw that the man was wearing a Blackshirt uniform underneath, which was definitely most bizarre. The Maresciallo called the Fascist command to inform them of their discovery. It was Marino Severi in person who stormed down to the station and identified the corpse of the deceased.

'So, this is one of yours then?' the officer asked Severi.

'Yes, a traitor we had been searching for, actually. He knew we were onto him and surely disguised himself as such to evade capture.'

Clever bastard, Severi thought. I hope you go to hell.

'Where did you find him?' he asked.

'In front of the Church of Santa Chiara, close to the Pantheon. He was already dead when we arrived, while the other, Father Karl Blasius, a monk, is still alive.'

What? Blasius was there? Why? Severi thought nervously.

'Where is he now?'

'He was unconscious and has been transported to the Santo Spirito hospital, near the Vatican. He was bleeding from the back of his head, but he could have just hit it on the pavement after he fell, as he was not injured otherwise. Another monk accompanied him in the ambulance, to make sure he was okay. He was heading that way anyway, he said.'

'What other monk are you talking about?'

'A witness we found at the scene of the crime. Father Pietro Colombo. He is a librarian at the Vatican, and lives there, he told us.'

Fuck! The Fascist Major thought.

What a fortuitous case to find a monk that lived in the Vatican next to the body of a British spy. Could his presence constitute the proof that what the Gestapo believed was true? That enemy spies were in fact helped by somebody inside the Holy City? That was too much of a coincidence for Severi. But as still many pieces of that puzzle were missing, he reckoned that the best course of action was to go and talk to Father Blasius. He would certainly help shed some light on that whole business.

For now, Severi was happy with the fact that, at least, Lucifer's run had come to an end, although it was unfortunate that he hadn't been caught alive to be interrogated.

Perhaps not all is lost, he thought with a glimmer of hope.

Father Colombo might have a number of very interesting questions to answer.

For that, though, he needed the Benedictine, the only one able to enter the Vatican and lure him out, where Severi would be able to arrest him.

CHAPTER 23

'Please open, open for the love of God!' Cordelia implored, knocking repeatedly on the battered wooden portal with a low voice full of urgency.

In a mad run, she had rushed to the hostel of Santa Marta, her heart still pounding like crazy, both from the effort and from the fear of the police arriving at the place where she had left Father Colombo just a few hundred yards behind her.

She was breathing heavily.

The few seconds that separated her from danger and a safe haven seemed interminable.

The noise of a key turning inside the lock.

Cordelia felt so grateful hearing that sound.

A young nun looked at her and smiled, moving aside to let her in. Cordelia heard the key turning again, shutting out the rest of the world behind her.

'Come this way – my name is Sister Sara,' the nun said, asking no questions, as Father Colombo had anticipated. Leading the way, the nun proceeded with light steps, closely followed by Cordelia.

The building was an old convent that had been converted into a shelter now, aimed at harbouring those women who no longer wanted to sell their bodies for sex. They walked along the open arcade of an internal cloister, at the centre of which there was an old well surrounded by a manicured garden divided into four sections by the paths leading to it. It was very quiet and Cordelia thought it must have felt equally calm and safe during the day, ideal for those who preferred a degree of separation from the hustle and bustle of the outside world.

When they reached the other end, Sister Sara entered a corridor, which had doors on each side.

Stopping in front of one of them, she said, 'We are full so unfortunately I cannot give you a room of your own for now. I hope you won't mind sharing with another girl.'

She gently knocked and opened it without waiting for an answer.

'Hello, Rosetta, this young lady will sleep in the other bed tonight,' the young nun said addressing the other occupant, and then to Cordelia: 'In the morning I will take you to the Mother Superior. Is that all right?'

'Of course, see you tomorrow. And thank you so much, Sister, I am totally in your debt,' Cordelia answered.

She was left alone with Rosetta, a very pretty brunette of no more than twenty years old. The room had two beds and one single table with a small lamp on it. It was simple, but clean, with fresh bedlinen and a bath towel at the end of the bed. Cordelia's nerves started to relax.

'You must have been expensive,' she said to Cordelia. 'First category, isn't it?'

What she meant was that a girl of Cordelia's beauty had certainly been working in a brothel of the highest level, where girls were paid vastly more than their colleagues in lower types of institutions.

'Not exactly.'

'Ah! You are like me then. I just made it to the second category. But I'm glad I took the step to leave that life. Men are perverts. Especially some of those high-ranking hierarchs who make you do things they would not dream of asking their wives.'

Cordelia thought that anyone who'd had that sort of experience must feel some level of rejection for the other sex. Rosetta continued to chat for a little while, telling her some funny stories, for which Cordelia was grateful as it was a good distraction.

'… and I had to take off all my clothes very slowly, but not the high-heel shoes – he liked them on. Then, while he was still fully dressed, he made me lie on the bed completely naked and licked me from head to toe. And that was it! How weird is that? I told you, men really are perverts,' Rosetta recounted.

Cordelia burst into laughter, which quickly became hysterical, and then she started to cry, her stress finally finding a way to vent.

'Oh dear! I reminded you of old times, didn't I? Sorry, I will leave you alone now. Please could you turn off the light when you are in bed?' After saying that, Rosetta gave her a smile and turned on her other side.

Cordelia undressed, folding her clothes around the gun, and placed the bundle under the bed, together with her bag. Initially, still on edge, she could not bring herself to close her eyes, but after a couple of hours, her tension started to ease and she fell asleep.

A soft knock at the door woke her up the following morning. Rosetta was snoring very softly and, mumbling something, she rolled over and continued to sleep. Cordelia quickly got out of bed to get dressed, glad the girl was not looking when she wrapped the gun in the black veil and placed it in her purse. She left the room and met Sister Sara coming down from the corridor. The young nun took her to the Mother Superior and introduced them, only to leave them to their conversation.

'Good morning, Cordelia,' the Mother Superior said. 'Welcome to our home.'

She had very lively eyes and a sweet expression that made Cordelia feel welcome.

'I am a friend of Father Colombo,' Cordelia told her, 'and I need to get out of Rome today. He mentioned you could help me. I need to go to Castel Gandolfo.'

'You must be one of his special cases, I reckon,' the older nun answered, 'and of course I am here to help, my dear child.'

It was not the first time that the Mother Superior had provided assistance to people Father Colombo had sent her way. He was a trusted old friend.

'We are taking the girls down to Torvaianica on the southern coast late morning, to enjoy its fresh and salty breeze, and bathe in the sea. You will be one of them. Just sit in the middle of the group, and you'll be fine,' the Mother Superior said.

She looked at Cordelia's grey, formal dress.

'We will need to find you something else to wear – this outfit is not suitable for somebody going to the seaside,' she added.

In the end Cordelia borrowed one of the girls' summer outfits, hiding the micro-camera inside her bra. And as the Mother Superior had promised, all the girls gathered in the courtyard and boarded the back of a small open truck, sitting on wooden benches running along its sides, while the Mother Superior and Sister Sara clambered into the cabin at the front. The truck was an old Fiat, and it took a couple of attempts to start it, but finally the engine kicked into life. Cordelia sat in the middle of the right row, next to Rosetta, who began to chat to everyone else from the moment they left the hostel of Santa Marta.

It was a warm, sunny day in the capital and a lot of Romans were out and about. It was so strange to see that the mayhem of the previous night seemed to have never happened: all was back to normal. Nevertheless, every time Cordelia noticed men in uniforms, she became rigid with fear, her head bending down to avoid attention. More than once, young men hollered out and waved at the girls as they passed by, making them laugh, while the men smiled back.

Cordelia envied their light-heartedness, despite having had such a difficult experience in life. They had turned a corner, while Cordelia was still desperately trying to reach it.

Instead of driving straight down the coast, the Mother Superior took the Appian Way, the same that Captain Wolf had driven along no more than twenty-four hours before to get Schaeffer to the airport of Ciampino. The nun had chosen that detour to bring Cordelia straight to Castel Gandolfo, drop her there and then head south-west towards the seaside town of Torvaianica. The truck was chugging along nicely; the road was clear and all had gone smoothly until then. They finally arrived at a crossroads where the truck stopped on the side of the road.

Sister Sara got out of the front cabin and reached the back.

'Here we are, Cordelia,' she told her, indicating she had to get off. 'Castel Gandolfo is just up that road.'

'Oh, are you not coming with us to the beach?' Rosetta enquired.

'Not today, I can't unfortunately – perhaps another time,' Cordelia said, waving goodbye to them all. She approached the Mother Superior, who was still in the driving seat.

'Dear child, it's better if we leave you here. A truck full of girls would be noticed in town and I don't believe it's advisable for you in the current circumstances.'

'Mother Superior, that's very wise. Thank you again so much for your help. I don't know what I would have done without it.'

'God bless you, goodbye and good luck!' the nun said, with a big smile of encouragement.

Cordelia watched them depart and then took the road in the opposite direction to get to the town.

While Cordelia was taking shelter at the hostel of Santa Marta, Marino Severi left the station of the Carabinieri military police and, acting on the information that their commander had given him, he went straight to the hospital of Santo Spirito where apparently Blasius had been taken to treat his head injury. Perhaps Father Colombo was still there; albeit, if Severi was right in thinking he had something to do with Lucifer and Cordelia, it would be hardly likely. The Franciscan friar would probably have taken advantage of motorised, fast transport to get as near to the Vatican as possible and shield behind its neutral walls.

And this was in fact what Father Colombo had done. As soon as he got to the hospital on the other side of the Tiber river, he quickly left the ambulance and, after talking briefly to the medics of the emergency room, he left Blasius in their capable hands and retreated back to the Vatican.

It did not take long for Blasius to regain consciousness and, after being treated for the blow received to the back of his head during the fall, he was placed in a bed for precautionary reasons.

'Take this,' a nurse said, handing him a painkiller and a glass of water to swallow it. 'If you aren't already now, you'll be in pain shortly.'

The Benedictine was suffering from the most horrendous headache when Severi managed to find him in one of the wards.

'Father Blasius,' Severi said, placing his hand on his forearm in order to wake him up. His eyes were closed and he seemed to be sleeping.

'Ooh, it's you, Major,' Blasius answered, his speech a bit slurred.

'Are you well enough to tell me what happened?'

Severi was not inclined to lose time in small talk and went straight to the point. Besides, he did not really care how Blasius felt.

The monk tried to get Severi into focus, his eyesight still slightly foggy. Slowly, he recognised his round face.

'I followed Cordelia Olivieri and I was attacked by your attendant, Guido Rovo, who was wearing a Franciscan habit. He blocked me, preventing me from seeing who Miss Olivieri was going to meet inside the Church of Santa Chiara. I want you to deal with him. I hope you have arrested the scoundrel already.'

'He is dead, unfortunately, so I can't interrogate him, which I wanted to do since we now know he was a British spy. We found all sorts of secret agent paraphernalia in his flat when we stormed it. As sure as hell, he was the informer of the Allied forces.'

Blasius was stunned by the revelation, and although he still felt fuzzy, a clear picture was quickly emerging in his mind.

'So if he was, then Cordelia Olivieri definitely has something to do with him, otherwise why would he attack me? And why was he there in the first place? Just to protect her or somebody else too? Who didn't he want me to see her meet?'

'I can probably tell you that with a degree of certainty now. It's your rescuer, Father Colombo, a Franciscan friar who was running a service at the church that evening. And it makes perfect sense, given what you told me about the Gestapo wiretapping. He is a librarian at the Vatican – that's what he declared to the military police earlier, anyway.'

'I know Father Colombo.'

'Do you? How?'

'I met him once, just outside Palazzo Roveri. He wanted to see Cordelia Olivieri but was stopped by the German guard at the gate and wasn't allowed in.'

'You never mentioned that to me before.'

'I never thought it was relevant.'

'Well, now we know it is, don't we, Father Blasius?' Severi said with bitter sarcasm.

He had been right again in suspecting that the Benedictine had not been revealing all his cards.

He added, 'And I also received confirmation from the Ministry of Race that Miss Olivieri is of Jewish descent by the way.'

Blasius couldn't be happier in hearing the official confirmation had finally arrived. Now he had all he needed for Himmler to demand Schaeffer's head and throw him in the depth of an abyss.

'And where is Cordelia Olivieri now?'

'Not at Palazzo Roveri. I've been there with my men to look for her.'

'Perhaps Father Colombo knows where she might be.'

'I see you've started thinking along the same line as me, Father Blasius. And you will be the one to find out. And if for any reason you can't, you'll lure him out of the Vatican so I can apply a bit of my special pressure, should he wish not to collaborate,' Severi stated.

Blasius was beginning to feel better and tried to get into a seated position. He touched the back of his skull and found the bandage that had been applied. His head wasn't spinning, a good sign the blow hadn't been all that bad. Even the headache seemed to start easing a little.

The monk thought Severi had figured it out correctly and decided that he was still an asset to help him get Cordelia Olivieri arrested and offer her in flesh and blood to Himmler. He was pretty sure the Gestapo Field Marshall would love that, very much.

Instead, for Severi, it was important to have her confess she was part of a spy ring, which meant his success would be much bigger than having found out who the spy was. And then he'd have the fun he had promised he'd have with that gorgeous bitch, before killing her.

'Very well, Major. I totally agree with you. I will visit him tomorrow, officially to thank him. We will get them both. I am perhaps more determined than you are,' Blasius hissed, gazing into the distance.

Severi looked at Blasius and saw the absolute evil in those pitch-black eyes of his when he proffered those last words.

That look frightened even him.

CHAPTER 24

Perhaps it was the effect of the blow to his head, or perhaps it was the visceral excitement of being so close to success, but in the morning, still at the Santo Spirito hospital, Blasius woke up feeling absolutely elated. Triumph was in sight, literally lying just a few steps away from where he was sitting now.

He went to the bathroom and looked at his image in the mirror. His long black hair had lost its usual composure and was back to being a bunch of chaotic curls. He noticed that a slight blue-coloured protuberance had appeared on his hook-shaped nose as a result of the violent fight of the previous night. Still tender to the touch.

Despite that, he felt ready. Ready to capture those who separated him from his final victory.

Blasius left the hospital and, on foot, headed straight for the Vatican. He marched along the road that led to St Peter's square, like a knight on the brink of conquering his coveted kingdom.

He felt he needed to stop and thank the Lord for being about to hand it to him.

He entered the Sistine Chapel, frescoed with one of Michelangelo's magnificent achievements, *Last Judgment*, and he once again marvelled at the sight of that opulent, grandiose and ingenious chaos of bodies crowding every inch of the decorated walls and vaulted ceiling. All the figures seemed to be fighting for the attention of Jesus, at the centre of the scene.

Blasius turned towards the northern wall to look at Pietro Perugino's, *Delivery of the Keys,* a fresco he had always been fascinated with. That fresco had a particular appeal for him; it never failed to trigger his imagination whenever he saw it. It represented Christ handing the keys of the kingdom of heaven to St Peter, who was kneeling in front of him, ready to receive that divine, powerful tool. Blasius tried to imagine what that man, of such humble origin, as the fisherman Simon Peter was before becoming an apostle, would have felt like when he achieved such power.

The Benedictine thought that they had a few things in common: both were not from a rich family, nor had had an easy life, but in the end they believed, and for that they would receive their prize. And it would be far bigger than they could ever imagine. He couldn't help but grin at the thought.

With that in mind, Blasius exited the chapel and headed straight for Father Colombo's house in Via del Pellegrino, inside the Vatican walls.

In the meantime, unaware of Blasius' intentions, the Franciscan was with Brother Filippo in his study, explaining what had happened, the plan he had in mind for Cordelia which would allow her to escape with the Portuguese merchant ship, as well as instructions on a specific job for him to do. Father Colombo had written a message to the British Ambassador earlier, communicating Lucifer's passing. His faithful assistant saw that he was distraught about the death of the British agent, and his face was tense, still bearing the signs of a night where sleep had been of no comfort. But he also saw his usual stoic determination to carry on the fight for what was right.

'I have to catch the first train to Castel Gandolfo this morning and meet Cordelia there. I am pretty sure she'll make it. She's been very brave and she is clever,' he said to Brother Filippo.

'What if the Carabinieri stop you again, Father?'

'I don't think they will – they have no reason to, since I answered all their questions last night. After all, even if they find other witnesses, which they might, everyone will testify that I was inside the church and did not see the incident when it happened. No, I don't think that anyone would be able to link me to Lucifer. Not even Father Blasius, as he never saw us together. Nor the militia of the Blackshirts, as far as I'm concerned.'

'I am happy to know that's the case; I can stop worrying then,' said Brother Filippo with a sigh of relief, 'but wouldn't they find it peculiar that you are leaving town?'

'Officially, I will be on a mission to make the necessary arrangements for the Pope to arrive at the Pontifical Palace for his summer vacation, so it'd be perfectly plausible for me to travel there. They wouldn't dare to cause any delay to that,' Father Colombo explained.

'I have a job for you, Brother Filippo. Stay here and do not go anywhere. You will wait for the British to contact you. I will telephone them from the Papal residence in Castel Gandolfo as soon as I have the micro-camera in my possession. At that point, they will bring you Cordelia's travel documents. Once you have them, go straight to Anzio and deliver them to Nino Conti, our fisherman friend, who will hide Cordelia until the ship arrives in port. Is that clear?'

'Yes, Father Colombo, all clear.'

'Excellent, you are an angel, Brother Filippo.'

'If only I had wings, though!' the old friar said to him.

'I'd better hurry now. The train leaves from Stazione Termini soon and I am still here!' Father Colombo said, seeing that he was already late and he would run the risk of missing the only train of the day.

'God be with you, Father!' Brother Filippo said, looking at him from the door as he bade farewell.

The Franciscan began to walk briskly the five kilometres that separated the Vatican from the train station.

Not even ten minutes had gone by before Brother Filippo heard somebody knocking at the door.

In his rush to get out of the house, Father Colombo had probably forgotten something, and he was back to fetch it, he thought.

He opened the door and to his surprise, it was a Benedictine monk.

Brother Filippo recognised him immediately: it was Father Blasius. What did he want?

'Good morning, Brother,' the black-clad monk said to him. 'May I come in?'

'Of course, please do,' Brother Filippo said, inviting him inside. 'How may I help you, Father Blasius?'

'Oh, so you remember me.'

How could I forget you, Brother Filippo thought, especially after what Father Colombo told me about your presence next to Lucifer's dead body.

He waited for him to continue.

'I need to talk to Father Colombo with some urgency. Is he here?' Blasius asked, his tone revealing his unwillingness to receive a negative reply.

Brother Filippo had to think fast for an excuse, trying to find a stratagem to delay him. He produced his most innocent smile as he was about to deliver his answer.

'He will be in a little while, Father Blasius. He had an important matter to attend to, but now it won't be long before his return. Would you like to make yourself comfortable while waiting?'

Perhaps it was the energetic walk, or perhaps the strength of the euphoria he had experienced, but because of that physical and emotional vortex, Father Blasius in that moment felt his legs weaker than expected, and the headache was fighting to resurface.

'Yes, that'd be a good idea actually. I need to sit – I feel a bit light-headed. I hit my head last night – it must be that,' he said. He followed Brother Filippo into a lounge next to the entrance. The room was not as Spartan as Father Colombo's study upstairs, as sometimes he received high prelates there and they liked their soft cushions, often citing their age, but more probably because they were used to their comfort. Blasius sat and let himself sink into one of the luxurious velvet armchairs, and rest for a moment.

Noticing that the Benedictine was touching the bandage at the back of his skull, Brother Filippo had a wicked idea.

'Let me prepare a herbal tea for you, Father Blasius. It's a tonic, a favourite of Father Colombo. It will invigorate you – you will see.'

'That'd be marvellous, Brother Filippo,' he said with a sense of gratitude, remembering that he was a knowledgeable herbalist and hoping the drink would help his momentary weakness.

Marvellous, maaarrrvellous, maaaaarrrrrvellous! Brother Filippo thought.

He glided away from the room and rushed into the kitchen to prepare his potion. Dancing around the cupboards, he picked a few fresh leaves here, a few others there and then he reached for a small glass jar at the top of the shelf, containing a finely ground, dark green herb powder. He put a pot of water on the stove, and when it came to the boil, he carefully moved it to the side and added all the ingredients for them to brew.

Finally, once the ideal concentration had been reached, he poured it into a large cup, added a spoon of acacia honey to adjust the taste and a fresh mint leaf for extra fragrance.

Brother Filippo looked at the gold-coloured potion and smelling its aroma, he thought: perfect, absolutely perfect!

He headed back to the lounge and offered it to his unwanted guest.

'Here it is. Drink it all, Father Blasius. You will feel a different person in a moment, I assure you.'

Brother Filippo looked at Blasius' long and bony fingers closing around the cup, and slowly but steadily the Benedictine drank it all.

A delicious sense of relaxation came upon him and he felt his eyelids becoming heavier and heavier.

Have a good sleep, Father Blasius, Brother Filippo said to him silently, hoping that God would forgive him for that bad deed.

The herbal tea he had prepared contained a strong sedative, whose effect would hopefully last as long as Father Colombo needed to get to Stazione Termini and catch his train to Castel Gandolfo, undisturbed.

The toll of a church bell. Muffled at first, then louder and louder.

Blasius was slowly emerging from his torpor. He heard the sound of steps getting closer and, still with his head leaning on the back of the armchair, he opened his eyes. Brother Filippo's good-natured expression appeared in front of his face.

'Hello, Father Blasius, are you feeling better now? After I left the lounge, you must've fallen asleep. Maybe you're still suffering from the post-traumatic effect of the blow to your head. I did not want to disturb you – a good rest works wonders even if short.'

Blasius was fully awake now and he was feeling decidedly better.

'How long did I sleep for? Has Father Colombo arrived back yet?'

'Oh, just some twenty or thirty minutes at most. No, he is not back yet I'm afraid,' Brother Filippo told him.

'Well, I can't wait any longer. Do you know where I could find him?'

'You may try the library. He is probably there, I reckon,' Brother Filippo lied.

At that point he preferred not to hold him any further, as he couldn't find any other plausible cause to, and it would have looked strange if he'd tried. He also thought that not only was the library in the opposite direction of where Father Colombo had gone, but with its twenty-six miles of shelving over three floors, it would take Father Blasius a while to search that vast building. By the time he realised the Franciscan was not there, Father Colombo's train would have left Rome.

'Thank you, and should he come back, please could you tell him I'd like to see him at the Biblicum, should I not be able to locate him today.'

Although the delay was not ideal, the Biblicum would be the exact place he had aimed for.

'I certainly will, goodbye, Father Blasius.'

The black-clad monk left. The fresher air outside helped him to wake further, and with renewed determination he resumed his chase.

Walking quickly along the Via del Pellegrino to reach the Vatican library whose entrance was through the belvedere courtyard, he was about to turn right onto the Via Sant'Anna, when at the corner he violently bumped into a young priest coming from the opposite direction, who was carrying some papers that went flying all over the pavement from the impact. The young priest had been walking up and down that street since the early morning, moving a pile of files from the library as requested by Cardinal Pini, who was getting ready to join the Pope in his summer retreat the following week.

Annoyed, the young priest snapped at Blasius.

'What is it with you monks, today!' he yelled in frustration. 'First Father Colombo, then you!'

319

The young priest knew the Franciscan well, as he had a prominent position at the library and saw him there often. Blasius, who was equally cross by the sudden clash, immediately asked: 'Father Colombo? When did you see him? Do you know where he was going?'

'It was about an hour ago. He was in a rush to get to Stazione Termini. He apologised as he was hurrying not to miss his train,' the young priest said, while trying to pick up all those sheets of paper that a light breeze was pushing far from reach.

Blasius exploded, his anger pouring out like the lava of a volcano in eruption.

'Damned you, liar! You will pay for this! Your little trick hasn't worked!' he shouted, referring to Brother Filippo, who certainly knew that the Franciscan was not at the library, but rather was heading for the train station. And as Father Colombo was hurrying there, it must have been urgent and certainly to do with Cordelia Olivieri, he assumed.

'But I will get you anyway, I swear to God I will!' he added, to the absolute astonishment of the young priest, who had never heard such aggressive language, especially coming from a monk of all people. Speechless, he looked at the outraged Benedictine, who had rapidly turned on his feet and run away, like a lunatic, leaving him there, without an apology or any offer to help.

Blasius had to get to the station in time to see where Father Colombo was going as the young priest was unable to tell him. He waved to a taxi and was fast to jump in.

'Stazione Termini, as fast as you can!'

Unfortunately, there was no time to go and tell Severi. It was essential for Blasius not to lose the opportunity to find the Franciscan, and with him, Cordelia Olivieri.

When he finally got to Stazione Termini, the train station was full of people. Blasius fought his way through the crowd, frenetically scanning the horizon in search of Father Colombo, who, with his towering height and distinctive white mane, he hoped would not be too difficult to spot. He tried the main concourse first, calculating that if he went there on foot, as he probably had done, he wouldn't have arrived long before him.

Nothing there.

He went to the ticket office, hoping for better luck.

God is on my side! Blasius thought triumphant, when he saw Father Colombo almost in front of the clerk who was handing out the tickets.

The Benedictine hid behind a column to avoid being spotted, waiting for the Franciscan to pay and leave. Then, jumping the queue to the irritation of the other passengers, he presented himself in front of the clerk and said, 'I need to buy a ticket, the same as the Franciscan friar you just served a moment ago bought.'

'A return to Castel Gandolfo then, but hurry, the only train of the day is about to depart.'

Blasius thanked the uniformed man, paid and headed to the platform, making sure to still keep at a certain distance from Father Colombo.

In a last attempt to make Severi aware of where he was going, the Benedictine tried to see if he could attract the attention of a couple of Blackshirts he had seen earlier, without success. They were too far away and he'd risk missing the train.

A blow of a whistle indicated the convoy was about to depart and, having seen that the Franciscan had boarded the train already, he clambered the three steps of one of the coaches behind his and went to sit in a compartment.

He could relax now – he knew where his prey was going to get off.

* * *

The journey from Stazione Termini in Rome to the smaller station of Castel Gandolfo took just under one hour. Since the time of Ancient Rome, the area's cooler, hilly climate had made it a favourite of the likes of Emperor Caligula and Nero, among others. The Papal Palace dominated the picturesque town on the banks of the beautiful Albano lake, which, with its high, thick walls and cupola, reflected in its waters and could be seen from afar.

The train began to slow down as it approached the single-track station, the locomotive chugging as the speed progressively dropped. Like Father Colombo, many of the passengers belonged to religious orders, and he was pleased to see that there was a small congregation of Clarisses nuns. In a brown jute sack, he had brought with him the Clarissa habit and sandals Cordelia had to wear as her disguise. That element of the plan, at least, had remained the same, and she would be able to blend into the crowd easily.

The convoy came to a stop and his fellow travellers started to trickle out onto the single platform of the station. The Franciscan got off and in the certainty of having evaded any type of surveillance, did not even bother to look for anyone following him. Hence, he didn't notice that Blasius, from his window, had watched him going down the stairs, waited for him to move a few yards away before alighting, and had begun to follow him.

Father Colombo walked up the winding road that led to the square in the centre of town, where a dramatic view of the lake below could be enjoyed from the belvedere nearby. He crossed the cobbled square and, with Blasius in tow, headed to the gardens of the Villa of Domitian, only to turn into an old cemetery nearby.

Once there, the Franciscan stopped next to the chapel and sat on a stone bench under a maritime pine tree, growing high just beside it. From there, he could see both entrances, the main one he'd entered from, and the other, a smaller one at the end of the cemetery.

If Cordelia isn't here already, it shouldn't be long before she arrives. And if she doesn't today, I'll come back tomorrow: she'll be here by then, Father Colombo thought, in the hope that his protégée, with the help of the Mother Superior of the hostel of Santa Marta, had managed to get out of the capital and find a passage to Castel Gandolfo.

There weren't many people around. It was almost one o'clock, the sun high in a cloudless blue sky. A man kneeled in front of a tomb, cleaning the engraved name of the deceased. There were two women, one arranging the flowers, the other gone to fetch some water for the vase and a nun accompanying an old lady with a flamboyant hat and a stick. In less than thirty minutes they had all gone and not a soul would probably visit the place for at least a couple of hours.

Except for Karl Blasius.

The Benedictine had found in a huge stone statue of the angel Gabriel, standing in the western corner of the cemetery, the perfect place to hide. Enveloped in the shadow projected by its big wings, his black habit was almost invisible due to the lack of light and the dark background of a wall covered in mould.

He kept watching Father Colombo, who had his back to the statue of the angel Gabriel. After all the visitors of the morning had left, the Franciscan continued to sit there, immobile. He was clearly waiting for somebody. There was no doubt about that.

From his position, Blasius was also sheltered from whoever came into the cemetery, and although he could not see the entrance, the gravelled path would alert him of anyone approaching as soon as he or she entered that graveyard.

Blasius saw Father Colombo turning his head and, soon after, the Benedictine heard the sound of light steps coming from behind him.

He retreated to the back of the statue, trying to make himself as small as he possibly could to avoid being seen.

A young woman with long light brown hair, wearing a colourful summer dress and a straw hat walked by, not even ten yards away from where he was hiding.

He recognised her straight away: it was Cordelia Olivieri.

She proceeded towards Father Colombo, who, on seeing her, stood up from his seat and hugged her. They exchanged a few words, but Blasius couldn't hear what they were saying. Father Colombo took her forearm and gently guided her inside the chapel.

Blasius came out from behind the statue and cautiously approached the entrance.

Although the main portal was closed, one of the side doors had been left open, but there was a purple curtain hanging in front of it, which blocked the view.

Blasius placed his ear against it and listened.

Voices, speaking very softly.

The Benedictine was desperate to know what they were saying, so he dared to part the curtain and saw them both with their backs to the entrance, near a huge free-standing brass candlestick. They did not see him when he slipped in, stopping behind a marble column of the central nave.

'Here it is, Father Colombo,' Cordelia was saying as she handed over the micro-camera to her old friend. 'Take it and give it to the British Ambassador. I took pictures of the German plans. I hope they make good use of them.'

'That's a huge achievement, Cordelia. I am so proud of you. You've been very brave,' Father Colombo praised her, while taking the Minox in his custody.

He handed her the jute sack.

'You will find a Clarissa nun's habit in this bag. Get inside one of the confessional booths and get changed. Then …'

He did not finish his sentence, interrupted by the sound of hands slowly clapping behind them.

In utter surprise, both the Franciscan and Cordelia turned and saw Father Blasius standing at the centre of the nave, the sinister gaze of his pitch-black eyes fixed on them, a malevolent smile depicted on his face.

'Well done, well done! I have to congratulate both of you. You had me fooled since the very beginning with your innocent attitude!' he said. 'You, Father Colombo, the magnanimous Franciscan friar that works for the Allied and helps Jewish enemies of the state. And you, Miss Olivieri, the good hotel hostess, a spy and a Jew yourself!'

'Father Blasius, what do you want from us?' a worried Father Colombo asked curtly, understanding that the Benedictine somehow, alone or with the help of somebody else, had worked out the truth.

The black-clad monk walked up to them and was now standing close.

'Give up. Give up your ridiculous plan whatever it is, and surrender. As soon as I am out of here, I am going to alert the authorities and they will be arriving soon. It's better if you collaborate rather than put up a fight. There's no point in trying to run – you will be caught.'

'Why are you doing this?' Cordelia asked angrily.

'Because you are both criminals acting against the Axis, my dear! And you haven't even tried to deny it – isn't that enough? Both Heinrich Himmler and Major Marino Severi will be very pleased that I have caught you in the act of passing secrets to the British.'

'You don't have to do this, Father Blasius,' said Father Colombo, as he tried to soften the determination of the monk.

It had the totally opposite effect.

Blasius erupted in a loud, sardonic laughter.

'Oh, but I do! I do indeed! Do you know what that means for me, Father Colombo? It means that I will be enormously praised for having single-handedly foiled a major plot against the Third Reich and Mussolini's regime. It means that I will be rewarded with the highest of all prizes: they will make me a spiritual advisor to the Fuehrer! The great Adolf Hitler! Can you possibly begin to imagine the importance and the power that such a role brings? I will become almost omnipotent! Omnipotent over men, as God himself!'

Father Colombo saw Blasius' face assume a delirious, almost dehumanised expression while he was speaking, accompanied by theatrical, erratic gestures, as if he was possessed by a dark, perverse and evil force.

His soul has been captured by the devil, the Franciscan thought.

But Blasius wasn't finished yet, as he continued his tirade now addressed to Cordelia.

'And you! A dirty Jew! You will be the trump card I will use to destroy your beloved Afrika Korps Lieutenant Colonel, Friedrich Schaeffer! Do you know what that lawyer has done to me? He tried to destroy me! He began all this in the first place! If it wasn't for him, I would not have been deprived of my position at the Abbey of Beuron!'

At that point, both Cordelia and Father Colombo were convinced Blasius was insane.

That last revelation was particularly mind blowing for Cordelia. She realised the sort of hatred the monk nurtured for Schaeffer and that she was just a token for him in a personal vendetta: a vendetta that would also help him to realise his mad ambitions.

'Give me that,' he said, snatching the Minox from Father Colombo's hands with a swift and sudden move, while firmly grabbing Cordelia's arm, to drag her away with him.

She tried to wriggle out and break away from his grip.

Father Colombo joined in to help her, as Blasius was clearly stronger and holding on. He let her go for a moment, and pushed the Franciscan in an effort to make him back off. But he failed as his opponent, although older, was also strong and fighting back.

Father Colombo had no intention of letting him get away with Cordelia and the micro-camera and fought to prevent him from getting out of the church.

Blasius pushed him again and, to finally stop the Franciscan once and for all, he took hold of the huge brass candlestick and lifted it to use it as a crowbar against him, shouting furiously, 'I will kill you. I will kill you!'

Cordelia, momentarily freed from him, pulled out the Beretta gun from her purse and, desperately aiming at the Benedictine to stop him from fatally hitting Father Colombo, she pulled the trigger and shot him twice.

The echo of the noise from the bullets reverberated loudly inside the chapel.

The Beretta fell to the floor as a shocked Cordelia let the gun slip from her hands.

Blasius, equally shocked, stood still for a moment, looking at her in sheer horror. Then he looked down at his chest, his habit quickly becoming wet from the blood copiously flowing from the two holes caused by the bullets.

He kneeled and then fell to the floor.

Karl Blasius was dead.

Everything was quiet again.

The thick walls of the chapel had managed to suppress the loud noise of the firearm. Only somebody in the close vicinity would have been able to hear something. But nobody was around and nobody heard.

As soon as Cordelia let the gun go, Father Colombo was quick to get up. He stepped towards Blasius and, squatting down, he touched the side of his neck to feel his pulse.

'In nomine Patris, et Filii et Spiritus Sancti,' he said, while making the sign of the cross.

'I killed him,' Cordelia said distraught. 'I had to. He was going to kill you.'

Father Colombo hugged her. She was shaking, traumatised.

'His soul was lost – evil got inside of him. He wasn't himself when he said what he said, when he did what he did. He probably hadn't been himself for a long time,' Father Colombo whispered, in an effort to explain to both of them why a monk like Blasius had turned into that mean, vengeful and corrupt creature.

They stayed like that for a moment and then Cordelia said: 'I need to change.' With the jute bag, she automatically headed towards the confessional booth and went in.

Father Colombo watched her, feeling an extreme sense of sorrow and guilt.

Please God, forgive us, forgive all of us, he silently implored in true desperation. Nobody should endure this: go through something as terrible as this.

He went back to Blasius' body and took back the Minox the dead monk was still holding in his left hand. He looked at his long, hollow face, of a deadly pallor now. He finally looked at peace, resting in an eternal sleep, free from the ferocious ambitions that had devoured his human life.

There was no point in trying to hide him – plus there was no time. Both he and Cordelia had to leave as quickly as possible.

She stepped out from the booth and was now fully dressed in the nun's habit, her hair hidden under the veil, a rosary tied around her waist, sandals on her feet. She handed back the jute bag, now containing the clothes she'd had when she arrived.

'Let's go back into town, Cordelia. A coach to Anzio will be leaving from the central square in about thirty minutes.'

She nodded and they walked out of the chapel, retracing their steps to the main gate of the cemetery. While coasting the southern side of the gardens of the Villa of Domitian, whose grounds extended between the cemetery and the central square of Castel Gandolfo, they saw an old woman slowly hobbling from the opposite direction, who nodded in salute. She carried a bunch of fresh roses and was clearly heading towards the graveyard. Cordelia and Father Colombo lengthened their stride as soon as their path had crossed.

Don't go inside the chapel. Don't go inside the chapel. Don't go inside the chapel, Cordelia prayed silently, while Father Colombo hoped that if she did, it would be as late as possible. He half turned briefly to have a glimpse behind him. The woman was still walking very slowly.

When they reached the square, all was calm and normal. A few customers were sitting at the table outside the only café in town, in the shade of a discoloured green awning. A group of priests in their long black habits and round hats were heading towards the Papal Palace main gate at the top of the square, guarded by two Lansquenets.

The coach stop was already crowded with a few people standing under the natural canopy created by an ancient wisteria, whose plush purple flowers scented the air around.

'Your travel documents will be delivered to Nino's house. And on Monday you will board the Portuguese vessel. When you reach Lisbon, send me a postcard so I know you've arrived safe and sound. And write to me from the Americas,' Father Colombo whispered to Cordelia.

'Thank you, Father Colombo. You saved my life and I will be ever so grateful to you for what you've done for me. I will never be able to repay you. I wish I could hug you and kiss you goodbye,' she said, trying to fight back her tears and knowing that in her disguise, it would not be the appropriate behaviour of a nun.

Father Colombo stood there with Cordelia for ten interminable minutes and then, right on time, the old grey coach arrived and passengers queued up to pay the ticket to the conductor.

'Goodbye, my child, God bless you,' the Franciscan said in a soft, broken voice, with reddened eyes.

'Goodbye, my good, faithful friend, I shall never forget you,' she whispered back, equally emotional.

Suddenly they heard the feeble screams of a female in the distance. Cordelia and Father Colombo knew she must be the woman whose path they had crossed in the cemetery. A few heads turned in that direction to understand the cause of the commotion.

Cordelia, about to get on the coach, was the last passenger to board. She clambered the steps up, but when she was at the top of the stairs, despite the imminent danger, she suddenly turned, rushed down and almost out of breath said desperately, 'If somebody, a man, comes back to Palazzo Roveri to look for me one day, can you please tell him ... oh, never mind, forget it. Goodbye, Father Colombo!'

The friar was a bit startled by the strange request, but assumed it was just the result of a sudden panic. He watched her taking a seat near the window. The conductor closed the door, engaged the first gear, the engine rumbled and the vehicle was set in motion.

The Franciscan followed it with his gaze until it disappeared at the first curve down the hill, and then headed towards the Papal Palace, taking shelter inside its powerful walls, as mayhem was about to erupt.

CHAPTER 25

As soon as Father Colombo crossed the gate of the Pontifical Palace guarded by the Swiss Lansquenets, he headed for the office of the administrator of the grounds.

He had a telephone.

The Franciscan asked to use it and dialled a number for Rome.

A voice at the other end answered.

'Hello, this is Father Pietro Colombo. There's a wonderful view from Castel Gandolfo today, and a perfect light to take pictures.'

'If you've got a camera, you can show me some of them later.'

'That's my intention. I am sure you will find them to your taste.'

Smiling, Lord D'Arcy put down the receiver.

Captain Wolf was on the phone to Lieutenant Colonel Friedrich Schaeffer.

'The command of the supply chain is to go back to the Italians, Sir. Major Marino Severi and his men have identified and killed the spy responsible for stealing the route plans, so there's no longer a risk of leaking intelligence from their side now.'

'That's good to know, Captain.'

'Severi was here earlier, Sir. He was looking for Miss Olivieri again. Before leaving my command, I thought you'd want to have a chat with him, face to face. So I asked him to join one of the vessels heading to Tobruk this week, to oversee that this shipping operation has gone smoothly. In front of his men, he couldn't refuse.'

'Well done, Captain Wolf. You are a clever man!'

The coach carrying Cordelia arrived in Anzio without any incident. There was a moment of confused panic on board when a military police car of the Carabinieri drove at high speed in the opposite direction when they were barely three miles into their journey out of the town of Castel Gandolfo.

After exiting the vehicle, she took the road that led to the house of Nino Conti, in the maze of small streets near the picturesque, colourful harbour. He lived alone and had just returned from tending to his boat when Cordelia arrived at his door.

Sheltered in the tiny fisherman's cottage, that night she didn't sleep, kept awake by the tension of being just a few hours away from finally making her escape and the fear of being arrested. As promised by Father Colombo, her travel documents, together with the passport with her new identity, were delivered by Brother Filippo.

By late morning of the following day, safely on board and already at sea, from the deck of the Portuguese merchant ship, Cordelia watched the coast of Italy gradually disappear from sight, the sound of the waves crashing against the bow of the boat sailing away across the warm waters of the Mediterranean.

She thought about all she had left behind.

Most of all, she thought about Friedrich Schaeffer, the man she loved.

EPILOGUE

After the conquest of Tobruk in the summer of 1942, Erwin Rommel pressed ahead to advance into Egypt, attacking the Allied forces in one of the most epic fights of the Second World War, the battle of El Alamein. But the massive supplies he was counting on, which had to arrive with huge shipments from Italy, suffered a number of catastrophic attacks by the Royal Air Force, ending up at the bottom of the Mediterranean Sea. As a result, the German Afrika Korps supported by the Italian Army, albeit fighting bravely, lacked the necessary fuel, trucks and ammunition, and were overwhelmed by the superior firepower of their enemy.

The battle was lost, and after that, so was the war in North Africa for Nazi Germany.

Many soldiers of the Axis forces were killed, and many fell to the hands of the Allies.

Lieutenant Colonel Friedrich Schaeffer was badly wounded near Mersa Matruh and later captured by the 4th British Armoured Brigade. He was transported to a hospital in Cairo, where he made a full recovery before being sent to a prisoner camp in the countryside of Southern England, where he stayed until the end of the war in 1945.

As soon as he could travel, he went back to Rome, looking for Cordelia at Palazzo Roveri.

But she was not there.

Besides, he discovered, the property of the hotel, his only link to her, had been passed on to the Vatican. Nobody seemed to know where Cordelia had gone or if she was still alive.

Italy had descended into civil war before the end of the world conflict, and it wasn't unlikely that she could have been killed either by the Fascists, the Germans, the Italian Partisans or even the Allied forces that later liberated the country from the Axis armies.

There was another possibility.

Captain Wolf had told him that she had disappeared right before Severi came to look for her. Schaeffer wondered if she had escaped somewhere safe and with this small hope, he wrote a letter with his address in England, and left it with the new director of Palazzo Roveri, just in case she ever came back.

Dejected and sad, Schaeffer left the Italian capital city.

For months, he waited in the hope of being contacted while he started to rebuild his life in London, practicing law again.

His newly acquired colleagues, seeing he was so depressed and lonely, tried to fix him up with this girl or the other, but although Schaeffer was desperately trying to forget Cordelia, none of them could remotely compare.

Darcy Jones, a senior lawyer at his practice, with a great sense of humour, a true lust for life, and for beautiful, sensual women, entered his office one day in the spring of 1947. He sat in front of him, picked a cigar from his pocket and before lighting it up, he announced:

'Friedrich, this time I reckon I've nailed it. I have found your woman. Now, you have to promise me you will not turn this one down. You have already turned down three of my lady friends in the last two weeks, and I had really thought that delicious Denise would win you over, with her fabulous juicy breasts, those hips, those legs and … Oh, but let's not digress! As I said, this girl is as fabulous as a gorgeous dream.'

'Darcy, I know you are doing what you believe is best, but I assure you that for the time being I prefer to be left alone.'

'Oh, don't be silly, Friedrich! Alone is bad, alone is sad, alone is not good for the soul and an absolute no-no for the body, especially for the body as far as I'm concerned. Listen to your old friend, Darcy. You are a clever, young, vigorous and, I have to admit, quite a handsome chap, and all the girls in the office, and out as far as I've observed, drool after you. They're all yours to take! I wish I had to work that hard to get laid.'

'I am not ready, not just yet. Perhaps I will one day. Soon, I hope.'

'Well, you'd better get bloody ready now. It's almost six o'clock – time for a drink. Besides, she is already here. I can't send her back, can I?' Darcy teased him with a rueful smile.

'Oh, Darcy! Don't tell me you've fixed me up again!' Schaeffer said, rising from his seat.

He went to the window and looked outside. The streets were busy and since the blackout was no longer necessary with the end of the war, large groups of people were preparing to crowd pubs and bars and enjoy life in that warm evening of early April 1947.

Darcy Jones stood up from his seat, went to the door and said, 'If you don't date this one, I will give up, I promise. She's the most beautiful woman I've ever met. Shall I bring her in?'

'Yes, do,' Schaeffer said with a big sigh.

After a moment, still with his back towards the door, he heard a female voice saying, 'Hello, Friedrich.'

He turned round.

Cordelia was standing in front of him.

As beautiful as ever.

Darcy Jones, who was next to her, looked at Schaeffer and seeing the look in his eyes, he said, 'Didn't I tell you that I had found your woman?'

ACKNOWLEDGEMENTS

I wrote most parts of this novel during the initial months of the Covid-19 pandemic back in 2020, for five days a week, and it took me a little over seven months to complete my initial manuscript. It is the most difficult thing I have ever done and, by far, the most rewarding. This book was inspired by the innumerable stories heard from both my grandfathers, Renzo Bernardi and Guido Loggia, who lived in Italy during World War II and experienced this terrible conflict first-hand. It is a historical period I am very passionate about and that I researched extensively for this work.

I have to thank my husband, Angelo Magnone, who for years insisted I had to write a book, and for supporting me throughout this process once I decided to put pen to paper. I also want to express my heartfelt gratitude to my publisher, Matthew Lynn, founder of Lume Books, and James Faktor, Publishing Director: a real pleasure to work with. Both of them were instrumental in making this happen and turning my dream into reality. The rest of the team at Lume Books are simply great too. My editor, Sharon Rutland, read the manuscript and made a number of invaluable, crucial suggestions, which I found enriching on so many levels. My sister, Désirée, and my friends, Victoria Squires-Toovey and Patricia O'Brien, together with my husband, also read the manuscript: having multiple pairs of eyes was a huge benefit. Their constructive comments and objectivity proved to be an incredible help.

Finally, I have to thank, from the bottom of my heart, my mother, Paola Bernardi, who read me bedtime stories, and for instilling in me the passion of reading and an enduring love for books.